GOOD GIRL COMPLEX

COMPLEX

Elle Kennedy

PIATKUS

PIATKUS

First published in the US in 2022 by St Martin's Griffin,
an imprint of St Martin's Publishing Group
First published in Great Britain in 2022 by Piatkus

1 3 5 7 9 10 8 6 4 2

A CIP catalogue record for this book
is available from the British Library.

ISBN 978-0-349-42883-3

Printed and bound in Great Britain by Clays Ltd, Elcograf S.p.A.

Papers used by Piatkus are from well-managed forests
and other responsible sources.

Piatkus
An imprint of
Little, Brown Book Group
Carmelite House
50 Victoria Embankment
London EC4Y 0DZ

An Hachette UK Company
www.hachette.co.uk

www.littlebrown.co.uk

GOOD GIRL COMPLEX

CHAPTER ONE

COOPER

I'm up to my eyeballs in Jägerbombs. Yesterday, I was married to the blender, pumping out piña coladas and strawberry daiquiris like sweatshop labor. Tonight, it's vodka Red Bulls and Fireballs. And don't forget the rosé. These dipshits and their rosé. They're all slammed against the bar, wall-to-wall pastel linen shirts and three-hundred-dollar haircuts, shouting drink orders at me. It's too hot for this shit.

In Avalon Bay, the seasons are marked by an endless cycle of exodus and invasion. The way the tides turn in a storm: Summer ends and the churn begins. Sunburned tourists pack up their mini-vans and sugar-slathered kids and head inland, back to suburbs and cubicles. Replaced by the surge of spray-tanned college brats—the clone armies returning to Garnet College. These are the trust-fund babies whose coastal palaces block out the ocean views for the rest of us scraping by on the change that falls from their pockets.

"Hey, bro, six shots of tequila!" some clone barks, slapping a credit card down on the sticky wet wood of the bar top like I should be impressed. Really, he's just another typical Garnet fuckhead who walked straight out of a Sperry catalog.

"Remind me why we do this," I say to Steph as I rack up a line of Jack and Cokes for her at the waitress stand.

She reaches into her bra and lifts each breast so they sit higher and fuller in her black *Joe's Beachfront Bar* tank top. "The tips, Coop."

Right. Nothing spends faster than somebody else's money. Rich kids spitting bills in a game of one-upmanship, all courtesy of Daddy's credit card.

Weekends on the boardwalk are like Mardi Gras. Tonight is the last Friday before the fall semester at Garnet begins, and that means three days of raging straight to Monday morning, the bars bursting at the seams. We're practically printing money. Not that I plan to do this forever. I moonlight here on the weekends to save up some extra dough so I can stop working for other people and start being my own boss. Once I've got enough saved, my ass is out from behind this bar for good.

"Watch out for yourself," I warn Steph as she places the drinks on her tray. "Holler if you need me to grab the bat."

It wouldn't be the first time I roughed someone up who couldn't take no for an answer.

Nights like this, there's a different energy. Humidity so thick you can slather the salty air on like sunscreen. Bodies on bodies, zero inhibitions, and tequila-infused testosterone full of bad intentions.

Fortunately, Steph's a tough girl. "I can manage." With a wink she takes the drinks, plasters a smile on her face, and spins around, long black ponytail swinging.

I don't know how she tolerates it, these dudes pawing all over her. Don't get me wrong, I get my fair share of female attention. Some get pretty bold, too friendly. But with chicks, you throw them a grin and a shot, they giggle to their friends and leave you alone. Not these guys, though. The crew team douchebags and Greek Row fuckboys. Steph is constantly getting grabbed and groped and having all manner of vulgarities slithered into her ear over the screech of the blaring music. To her credit, she hardly ever punches any of them.

It's a constant grind. Catering to the seasonal parasites, this invasive species that uses us locals up, sucks us dry, and leaves their garbage behind.

And yet, this town would hardly exist without them.

"Yo! Let me get those shots!" the clone barks again.

I nod, as if to say *Coming right up*, when what I really mean is *This is me ignoring you on purpose*. Instead, a whistle at the other end of the bar catches my attention.

Locals get served first. Without exception. Followed by regulars who tip well, people who are polite, hot women, little old ladies, and then the rest of these overfed jackasses. At the end of the bar, I put down a shot of bourbon for Heidi and pour another for myself. We toss 'em back and I give her a refill.

"What are you doing in here?" I ask, because no self-respecting local is on the boardwalk tonight. Too many clones kill the vibe.

"Dropping off Steph's keys. Had to run by her place." Heidi was the prettiest girl in the first grade, and not much has changed since. Even in ratty cutoff shorts and a plain blue crop top, she's undeniably the hottest woman in this bar. "You closing tonight?"

"Yeah, won't be outta here till three, probably."

"Wanna come by after?" Heidi pushes up on her toes to lean across the bar.

"Nah, I'm pulling a double tomorrow. Gotta get some sleep."

She pouts. Playfully at first, then more flippant when she realizes I'm not interested in hooking up tonight. We might've indulged in a string of hookups earlier this summer, but making that a regular thing with one of my best friends starts to resemble a relationship, and that's not where I'm trying to go. I keep hoping she'll realize that and stop asking.

"Hey. Hey!" The impatient towheaded dude at the other end of the bar tries flagging me. "I swear to God, man, I will toss you a hundred-dollar bill for a fucking shot."

"You better get back to work," Heidi says with a sarcastic smile, blowing me a kiss.

I take my sweet time walking over to him. He's straight off the clone conveyor belt: standard-issue preppy Ken doll with a side part and the best smile dental insurance can buy. Beside him are a couple of factory-made sidekicks whose idea of manual labor is probably having to wipe their own asses.

"Let's see it," I dare him.

The clone slaps down a Benjamin. So proud of himself. I pour a single shot of whiskey because I don't remember what he asked for and slide it to him. He releases the bill to take the glass. I snatch it up and pocket it.

"I ordered six shots," he says, smug.

"Put down another five hundred and I'll pour 'em."

I expect him to whine, throw a fit. Instead he laughs, shaking his finger at me. To him, this is some of that charming local color they come slumming it down here to find. Rich kids love getting rolled.

To my absolute amazement, this knucklehead flicks out five more bills from a wad of cash and lays them on the bar. "The best you got," he says.

The best this bar keeps in stock is some Johnnie Walker Blue and a tequila I can't pronounce. Neither is more than five hundred dollars retail for a bottle. So I act impressed and get up on a stool to pull the dusty bottle of tequila from the top shelf because, okay, I did remember what he asked for, and pour them their overpriced shots.

At that, Richie Rich is satisfied and wanders off to a table.

My fellow bartender Lenny gives me the side-eye. I know I shouldn't encourage this behavior. It only reinforces the idea that we're for sale, that they own this town. But screw it, I'm not about to be slinging drinks till I'm dead. I've got bigger plans.

"What time do you get off?" a female voice purrs from my left side.

I turn slowly, waiting for the punch line. Traditionally, that question is followed by one of two options:

"Because I want you to get *me* off."

Or, "Because I can't wait to get *you* off."

The follow-up is an easy way to determine whether you're ending up with a woman who's selfish in the sack or one who loves doling out BJs.

Neither is a particularly original pickup line, but nobody said the clones who swarm the Bay every year were original.

"Well?" the blonde presses, and I realize there's no cheesy line in store for me.

"Bar closes at two," I answer easily.

"Hang out with us after you get off," she urges. She and her friend both have shiny hair, perfect bodies, and skin glowing from a day spent in the sun. They're cute, but I'm not in the mood for what they're offering.

"Sorry. Can't," I answer. "But you should keep an eye out for someone who looks exactly like me. My twin brother is around here somewhere." I wave a hand toward the throng of bodies packing the place like sardines in a tin. "I'm sure he'd love to entertain you."

I say it mostly because I know it'll annoy Evan. Though on the other hand, maybe he'll thank me. He might despise the clones, but he doesn't seem to mind the rich princesses when they're naked. I swear the dude's trying to sleep his way through this town. He claims he's "bored." I let him believe that I believe him.

"Omigod, there's two of you?" Almost immediately, both girls become starry-eyed.

I grab a glass and shovel some ice cubes into it. "Yup. His name's Evan," I add helpfully. "If you find him, tell him Cooper sent you."

When they finally wander off, fruity cocktails in hand, I breathe a sigh of relief.

Bartending is such a crap gig.

I push a whiskey on the rocks toward the skinny dude who ordered it, take the cash he hands me. I run a hand through my hair and draw a breath before going to the next customer. For most of the night, the drunken masses manage to keep their shit together. Daryl, the doorman, kicks out anyone he suspects might projectile vomit, while Lenny and I smack away any idiots who get it into their heads to reach behind the bar.

I keep an eye on Steph and the other female servers as they work the crowd. Steph's got a table full of Garnet dudes salivating over her. She's smiling, but I know that look. When she tries to walk away, one of them grabs her around the waist.

My eyes narrow. It's the same guy I took for six bills.

I'm damn near over the bar when her eyes find mine. As if she knows what's about to happen, she shakes her head. Then she slyly disentwines herself from the handsy prick and comes back to the waitress stand.

"Want me to toss 'em?" I ask her.

"Nah. I can handle them."

"I know. But you don't have to. I pulled six hundred from those dumbasses. I'll split it with you. Let me get rid of them."

"It's all good. Just get me three Coronas and two Jäg—"

"Do not even say it." My whole body winces at the word. If I never have to smell that vile black shit ever again, it'll be too soon. "I gotta get some nose plugs."

"It's like you've got shellshock," she laughs, watching me suffer through these pours.

"I should be getting hazard pay." I finish up and push the drinks to her. "Seriously, though, if those guys can't keep their hands to themselves, I'm coming over there."

"I'm fine. But, man, I wish they'd just leave. I don't know who's worse tonight—Mr. Grabby Hands, or that senior on the patio who's crying about his daddy reneging on his promise to buy him a yacht for graduation."

I snicker.

Steph waltzes off with a sigh and a full tray of drinks.

For the better part of an hour, I don't look up. The room is so dense the faces blur into a smudge of flesh, and all I do is pour and slide credit cards until I'm in a trance, barely aware of my actions.

The next time I check on Steph, it's to see Richie Rich trying to persuade her to dance with him. She's like a boxer, bobbing and weaving to get away from the dude. I can't make out her exact words, but it's easy to guess—*I'm working, please let me get back to work, I can't dance with you, I'm working.*

She's trying to remain courteous, but her blazing eyes tell me she's fed up.

"Len," I call, nodding toward the unfolding scene. "Gimme a sec."

He nods back. We take care of our own.

I stride over, knowing I pose a menacing picture. I'm six two, haven't shaved in days, and my hair could use a trim. Hopefully I look menacing enough to deter these bros from doing something stupid.

"Everything okay here?" I inquire when I reach the group. My tone says I know it's not and he'd better stop or I'm going to toss him out on his ass.

"Fuck off, carnie," one of them cracks.

The insult rolls right off me. I'm used to it.

I raise a brow. "I'm not leaving unless my colleague tells me to go." I look pointedly at Richie Rich's hand, which is latched onto Steph's arm. "She didn't sign up to get groped by rich boys."

The guy has the sense to remove his hand. Steph uses the opportunity to clamber to my side.

"See? All good." He sneers at me. "No distressed damsels requiring rescue."

"Make sure to keep it that way." I punctuate the warning with a sneer of my own. "And keep your hands to yourself."

Steph and I are about to head off when a glass breaks.

No matter how loud a room, how full to the brim with sound-dampening bodies, a glass shatters on the floor and, in the immediate seconds after, you can hear a hummingbird's wings flutter two counties away.

Every head turns. One of Richie Rich's buddies, who'd dropped the glass, is blinking innocently when I meet his gaze.

"Oops," he says.

Laughter and applause crush the momentary silence. Then conversation bubbles up again, and the collective attention of the bar returns to its previously intoxicated amusements.

"Fuck's sake," Steph mutters under her breath. "Go back to the bar, Coop. I got this."

She marches off with an annoyed frown, while the douche crew dismisses us from their holy presence and proceeds to chat loudly and laugh amongst themselves.

"All good?" Lenny asks when I return.

"Not sure."

I glance back toward the group, frowning when I notice their leader is no longer with them. Where the hell did he go?

"No," I say slowly. "I don't think it's good. Give me another sec."

Once again, I leave Lenny to man the battle stations alone while I duck out from behind the bar to find Steph. I head toward the back, figuring she went for a broom to sweep up the glass.

That's when I hear, "Get *off* me!"

I throw myself around the corner, my jaw tightening when I spot Richie Rich's pastel polo. He has Steph cornered at the end of the short, narrow hall where the supply closet is located. When she tries to dip around him, he steps in her way, grabbing her wrist. His other hand slides downward and attempts to cup her ass.

Nah, screw this.

I charge forward and yank him by his collar. A second later, I lay his ass flat out on the sticky floor.

"Get out," I growl.

"Cooper." Steph grabs me, even as gratitude shines in her eyes. I know she appreciates the save.

I shake her off, because enough is enough. "Get up and leave," I tell the startled punk.

He's yelling out angry curses as he climbs to his feet.

Because the restrooms are right around the corner about ten feet away, it doesn't take long for his shouts of outrage to draw an audience. A group of screeching sorority sisters hurry over, followed by other curious bystanders.

Suddenly more voices fill the corridor.

"Pres! Bro, you alright?"

Two of his friends break through the crowd. They puff up their chests beside him, flanking their champion because if they get chased out of here in front of all these people, it's going to be a long year of drinking alone at home.

"The hell's your problem, man?" the groper spits out, glaring daggers at me.

"No problem anymore," I reply, crossing my arms. "Just taking out the trash."

"You smell that, Preston?" his buddy says to Richie Rich with a goading grin. "Something sure stinks in here."

"Was that a dumpster outside or your trailer?" the other mocks.

"Please, take two steps closer and say that again," I encourage them because, whatever, I'm bored and these dudes' faces are begging to get smashed.

I assess my chances. It's three on one, and they aren't scrawny—each of them around six feet tall, about my size. They could be half a water polo team sponsored by Brooks Brothers. But me, I actually work for a living, and these muscles aren't for show. So I like my odds.

"Coop, stop." Steph pushes me to the side to stand between us. "Forget it. I got this now. Go back to the bar."

"Yeah, *Coop*," Preston taunts. Then, to his buddies, "No piece of townie ass is worth this much trouble."

I look at Steph and shrug. Rich prick should have walked away when I gave him the chance.

While he's still laughing, so smug in his superiority, I reach out, grab a fistful of his Ralph Lauren and drive my fist straight into his face.

He staggers, falling into his friends, who push him at me. Bloody, he lunges like a creature in the third act of a horror film, swinging at me, smearing blood. We crash into the screaming sorority girls until we're against a wall. The old payphone that hasn't operated in fifteen years digs into my back, which gives Preston a chance to land a lucky punch to my jaw. Then I spin us around, pin him against the drywall. I'm about to smash his damn face in when Joe, the owner, along with Daryl and Lenny, hold me back and drag me away.

"You stupid townie trash," he gurgles at me. "You have any idea how dead you are?"

"Enough!" Joe shouts. The grizzled Vietnam vet with a gray hippie beard and ponytail points a fat finger at Preston. "Get on out of here. There's no fighting in my bar."

"I want this psycho fired," Preston orders.

"Kiss my ass."

"Coop, shut it," Joe says. He lets Lenny and Daryl release me. "I'm docking your pay for this."

"It wasn't Coop's fault," Steph tells our boss. "This guy was all over me. Then he followed me to the supply closet and trapped me in the hallway. Cooper was trying to kick him out."

"Do you know who my father is?" Squeezing his leaking nose

shut, Preston seethes. "His bank owns half the buildings on this filthy boardwalk. One word from me and your life gets real complicated."

Joe's lips tighten.

"Your employee put his hands on me," Preston continues angrily. "I don't know how you run this rathole, but if this happened anywhere else, the person who assaulted a customer would no longer be employed." The smirk on his face actually makes my fists tingle. I want to strangle him with my bare hands. "So either you handle this, or I pick up the phone and call my father to do it for you. I know it's late, but don't you worry, he'll be awake. He's a night owl." The smirk deepens. "That's how he made all his billions."

There's a long beat of silence.

Then Joe lets out a sigh, turning to me.

"You can't be serious," I say in amazement.

Joe and I go back a ways. My brother and I used to barback here in the summers during high school. We helped him rebuild after two hurricanes. I took his daughter to homecoming, for chrissake.

Looking resigned, he runs a hand over his beard.

"Joe. Seriously, man. You're gonna let one of them tell you how to run your bar?"

"I'm sorry," Joe finally says. He shakes his head. "I have to think about my business. My family. You went too far this time, Coop. Take what I owe you for the night out of the register. I'll have a check for you in the morning."

Satisfied with himself, Richie Rich sneers at me. "See, townie? That's how the real world works." He tosses a bloody wad of cash at Steph and spits out a thick clump of blood and mucus. "Here. Clean this place up, sweetheart."

"This isn't over," I warn Preston as he and his friends saunter away.

"It was over before it began," he calls snidely over his shoulder. "You're the only one who didn't know that."

Staring at Joe, I see the defeat in his eyes. He doesn't have the strength or desire to fight these battles anymore. That's how they get us. By inches. Breaking us down until we're too tired to hold on any longer. Then they pry our land, our businesses, our dignity from our dying hands.

"You know," I tell Joe, picking up the cash and smacking it in his hand. "Every time one of us gives in to one of them, we make it a little easier for them to screw us the next time."

Except . . . no. Fuck the "next time." These people are never getting a next time from me.

CHAPTER TWO

MACKENZIE

Since leaving my parents' house in Charleston this morning, I've had an itch in the back of my skull, and it only keeps growing more insistent, telling me to turn around. Take off. Run away. Join the proverbial circus and *rage, rage* against the dying of my gap year.

Now, as my taxi drives through the tunnel of bur oaks to Tally Hall on the Garnet College campus, a pure cold panic has set in.

This is really happening.

Beyond the green lawn and lines of cars, swarming freshmen and their parents cart boxes into the redbrick building stretching four stories into the clear blue sky. White trim frames the rows of windows and the roof, a distinct characteristic of one of the five original buildings on the historic campus.

"I'll be right back to grab those boxes," I tell my driver. I sling my duffel over my shoulder, and set my rolling suitcase on the ground. "Just want to make sure I'm in the right place."

"No prob. Take your time." He's unruffled, probably because my parents paid him a huge flat fee to play chauffeur for the day.

As I walk under the massive iron lantern that hangs from the beam above the front doors, I feel like a captured fugitive returning after a year on the lam. It was too good to last. How am I supposed to go back to homework and pop quizzes? My life dictated by TAs and syllabi when I've been my own boss for the last twelve months.

A mother stops me on the stairs to ask if I'm the dorm's resident advisor. Awesome. I feel ancient. A fresh wave of temptation to turn on my heels and split simmers in my gut, but I force myself to ignore it.

I slog up to the fourth floor where the rooms are a little bigger, a little nicer, for those parents willing to leverage the GDP of a small island nation. According to the email on my phone, I'm in room 402.

Inside, a small living room and kitchenette divide the two bedrooms on either side. The room on the left contains an empty bed with a matching wooden desk and dresser. To the right, through the wide-open door, a blonde in a pair of cutoffs and no shirt bounces and sways while putting clothes on hangers.

"Hello?" I say, trying to get her attention. I drop my bags on the floor. "Hi?"

Still she doesn't hear me. Tentative, I walk up and tap her on the shoulder. She jumps out of her sandals and slaps a hand over her mouth to muffle a yelp.

"Ooh, girl, you got me!" she says in a thick Southern accent. Breathing hard, she pulls the wireless earbuds from her ears and shoves them in her pocket. "'Bout peed my pants."

Her boobs are right there in all their bare glory, and she's making no effort to shield herself. I try to look her in the eyes but that proves awkward, so I divert my attention toward the windows.

"Sorry to barge in. I didn't expect . . ." *to find my roommate engaged in the first act of an amateur porno.*

She shrugs, smiling. "Don't sweat it."

"I can, uh, come back in a few minutes, if . . . ?"

"Naw, you're fine," she assures me.

I can't help but glance at her standing with her hands on her hips, pointing the high-beams at me. "Was there a nudist box on the housing form I checked by accident?"

She laughs, then finally reaches for a tank top. "I like to cleanse the energy of a place. A house ain't a home till you spent time in it naked, right?"

"The blinds are open," I point out.

"No tan lines," she answers with a wink. "I'm Bonnie May Beauchamp. Guess we're roomies."

"Mackenzie Cabot."

She smooshes me in a tight hug. Ordinarily I'd consider this a grievous assault on my personal boundaries. But, for some reason, I can't find it in me to be put off by this girl. Maybe she's a witch. Hypnotizing me with her witch tits. Still, I get a good vibe from her.

She has soft, round features and big, brown eyes. A bright white grin that's equally non-threatening to women and approachable to men. Everyone's little sister. But with boobs.

"Where's all your stuff?" she asks upon releasing me.

"My boyfriend's coming by later with most of it. I have a few things in the car downstairs. The driver's waiting on me."

"I'll help you bring it up."

There isn't much, only a couple boxes, but I appreciate the offer and the company. We grab the boxes and toss them in the room, then wander the halls for a bit, checking out the neighborhood.

"You from South Carolina?" Bonnie asks.

"Charleston. You?"

"I'm from Georgia. Daddy wanted me to go to Georgia State, but my momma went to Garnet, so they made a bet on the outcome of a football game and here I am."

Down on the third floor, there's a dude walking around with a backpack cooler of frosé who tries to offer us each a cup in exchange for our phone numbers. His arms, chest, and back are covered in scribbled black permanent marker, with most of the numbers missing a digit or two. Certainly all of them fake.

We pass on the offer and grin to ourselves, leaving him in our wake.

"Did you transfer from somewhere?" Bonnie says as we continue our way through the bazaar of micro communities. "I mean, don't take this the wrong way or nothin', but you don't look like a freshman."

I knew this would happen. I feel like the camp counselor. Two years older than my peers, on account of my gap year and the fact that I started kindergarten a year late, when my parents decided to extend a Mediterranean sailing trip rather than get me home in time for school.

"I took a gap year. Made a deal with my parents that I'd go to whatever school they chose if they let me work on my business first." Though if it were up to me, I'd have skipped this chapter of the coming-of-age story completely.

"You got your own business already?" Bonnie demands, wide-eyed. "I spent all summer watchin' *Vanderpump* reruns and partyin' at the lake."

"I built a website and an app," I admit. "I mean, it's nothing major. Not like I founded Tesla or anything."

"What kind of app?"

"It's a site where people post funny or embarrassing boyfriend stories. It started as a joke for some of my friends from high school, but then it sort of blew up. Last year, I launched another site for people to post about their girlfriends."

What began as me and a blog had ballooned in the past year to include hiring an ad manager, site moderators, and a marketing team. I have payroll and taxes and seven figures in my business checking account. And somewhere on top of all that, I'm supposed to worry about essays and midterms? A deal's a deal, and I'm as good as my word, but this whole college thing seems pointless.

"Oh my God, I know that site." Bonnie smacks my arm excitedly. Girl's got steel rods for fingers. "*BoyfriendFails*! Holy shit. My girls and I probably spent more time readin' those senior year than doin' our homework. What's the one? 'Bout the boyfriend who got food poisoning after a date and the girl's dad was drivin' them home and the guy got massive diarrhea in the backseat!"

She doubles over in absolute hysterics. I crack a smile because I remember that post well. It got over three hundred thousand clicks, thousands of comments, and double the ad revenue of any other post that month.

"Wow," she says, once she's regained her composure. "You really make money off those things?"

"Yeah, from hosting ads. They do pretty well." I shrug modestly.

"That's so cool." Bonnie pouts. "I'm jealous. I got no idea what I'm doin' here, Mac. Can I call you Mac or do you prefer Mackenzie? Mackenzie sounds *so* formal."

"Mac's fine," I assure her, trying not to laugh.

"After high school, college is a thing I'm supposed to do, y'know? 'Cept heck if I got any idea what I'm supposed to major in or what I'm gonna do when I grow up."

"People always say college is where you go to find yourself."

"I thought that was Panama City."

I snicker. I really like this girl.

About an hour later, my boyfriend shows up with the rest of my boxes. It's been weeks since we've seen each other. I had a stupid amount of work to do on the business before I could hand it over to my new full-time staff, so I couldn't take the time off to visit Preston.

This is the longest we've been apart since the summer his family went on vacation to Lake Como.

I had proposed the idea of getting an apartment together off campus, but Preston had roundly scoffed at that. Why slum it in subpar housing when he's got a pool, a personal chef, and a maid at home? I didn't have a good answer that didn't sound condescending. If independence from our parents isn't its own motivation to move in together, I don't know what to say.

Independence has been my sole motivation since high school. Living with my family was like sinking in a pit of quicksand—one that would've swallowed me whole if I hadn't yanked out my own hair to fashion a rope and pull myself out. I wasn't built to be kept. Maybe that's why, when the boyfriend I haven't seen in over a month enters the room with the first load of boxes, I'm not overwhelmed with loin-deep longing or that sudden rush of excitement after time spent apart.

Not that I didn't miss him or that I'm not happy he's here. It's just . . . I can remember crushes I had in middle school where the time between seeing them at lunch and sixth period felt like an eternity that tore at my little, pubescent heart. I've grown up, I suppose. Preston and I are comfortable. Steady. Practically an old married couple.

There's a lot to be said for steady.

"Hey, babe." A little sweaty from four flights of stairs, Pres wraps me in a tight hug and kisses me on the forehead. "Missed you. You look great."

"So do you." Attraction certainly isn't the problem; Preston's about as picture-perfect handsome as it gets. He's tall, with a slim but athletic build. Gorgeous blue eyes that seem impossibly bright when the sun catches them. A classic angular face that collects attention everywhere he goes. He's gotten a haircut since the last time I saw him, his blond hair a little long on top but cut close on the sides.

It's then that he turns his head slightly and I notice his face marked by bruises around his nose and right eye.

"What happened to you?" I ask in alarm.

"Oh, yeah." He touches his eye and shrugs. "Guys and I were playing basketball the other day and I took a ball to the face. No biggie."

"You sure? That looks like it hurt." It's nasty, honestly, like a burnt, runny egg on the side of his face.

"I'm good. Oh, before I forget. I got you this."

He reaches into the back pocket of his khakis and pulls out a plastic card. The words *BIG JAVA* are written across it.

I accept the gift card. "Oh, thanks, babe. Is this for the coffee place on campus?"

He nods earnestly. "Figured it was the most fitting 'welcome to college' gift for a coffee fiend like you. I loaded a couple grand on it, so you're all set."

At the kitchenette, an eavesdropping Bonnie gasps. "A couple *grand*?" she squawks.

Okay, two thousand dollars' worth of coffee is a bit extreme, but one of the things I love about Pres is how thoughtful he is. Driving three hours to my parents' house to pick up my stuff on his own, then all the way back to campus, and he does it with a smile. He doesn't complain or make me out to be a burden. He does it to be nice.

There's a lot to be said for nice.

I glance at my roommate. "Bonnie, this is my boyfriend, Preston. Pres, this is Bonnie."

"Nice to meet you," he says with a genuine smile. "I'm going to grab the rest of Mac's boxes, then how about I take you both out for lunch?"

"I'm in," Bonnie replies. "I'm starved."

"That'd be great," I tell him. "Thank you."

Once he's gone, Bonnie gives me a silly grin and a thumbs-up. "Nice job. How long you been together?"

"Four years." I follow her into the shared bathroom so we can fix our hair and get ready for lunch. "We went to the same prep school. I was a sophomore, he was a senior."

I've known Preston since we were kids, although we weren't exactly friends growing up, given the age difference. I'd see him around the country club when my parents dragged me out with them, at holiday gatherings, fundraisers, and whatnot. When I started school at Spencer Hill, he was nice enough to acknowledge me in the halls and say hi to me at parties—helping me gain some of the clout I needed to survive and thrive in the shark-infested waters of a prep school.

"You must be relieved to finally get to college with him. If that were me, I'da been outta my mind wonderin' what he was gettin' up to out here on his own."

"It's not that way with us," I say, brushing out my hair. "Preston's not the cheating type. He's big on family and the plan, you know?"

"Plan?"

It's never sounded weird until Bonnie looks at me in the mirror with a raised eyebrow.

"Well, our parents have been friends for years, so after we'd been dating a while, it was sort of understood that eventually we were going to graduate, get married, all that. You know, the plan."

She stares at me, her face crinkled. "And you're . . . okay with that plan?"

"Why wouldn't I be?"

That's damn near verbatim how my parents ended up together. And their parents. I know it sounds only a couple steps away from an old-world arranged marriage thing, and to be honest, I suspect Preston got talked into taking me out that first time. He was the upperclassman. I was the awkward sophomore who still hadn't mastered a flat iron. But whether or not it was initially suggested to Pres by his parents, neither of us felt like we were being forced to date. We genuinely enjoyed each other's company, and still do.

"If that was me, I'd be pretty bummed that my whole life was planned before I even started my first day of college. It's like gettin' the movie spoiled when I'm standin' in line for popcorn." Bonnie shrugs, dabbing on some lip gloss. "But, hey, long as you're happy, right?"

CHAPTER THREE

COOPER

Ever since we were dumb, barefoot kids racing each other up and down the dunes, churning up wake in front of million-dollar mansions, and running from the cops, we—the misfit, misspent youth of Avalon Bay—have had a tradition. The last Sunday of summer culminates in a bonfire blowout.

The one rule: locals only.

Tonight, my twin brother and I are hosting the shindig at our place. The two-story, low-country, cottage-style beach house has been in our family for three generations—and it shows. The rambling house is in disrepair and requires a ton of renos, but it makes up for its rough exterior with a hell of a lot of charm. Sort of like its inhabitants, I suppose. Although Evan is definitely the more charming of the two of us. I can be a moody fuck sometimes.

On the back deck, Heidi sidles up beside me, setting a flask on the wooden railing.

"We got liquor downstairs. Tons," I tell her.

"That's not the point of a flask."

She puts her back to the railing, leaning on her elbows. Heidi has this way about her. There's nothing in the world that can satisfy her, her interest so far beyond everyone and everything. When we were kids, it was one of the first things that drew me to her. Heidi's eyes were always looking farther. I wanted to see what she saw.

"Then what's the point?" I ask.

"Feeling a little naughty. A flask is a secret."

She looks over at me, a sly smile pulling at her lips. She's done up tonight, at least as much as one does out here in the Bay. Hair curled. Dark red lipstick. She's wearing my old Rancid T-shirt, which she'd cut into a tank top that now exposes a black lace bra. She put a lot of effort into her look, and yet it's lost on me.

"Not much in the spirit, huh?" she says when I don't take the bait.

I shrug. Because, yeah, I'm not in the mood for a party.

"We can get out of here." Heidi straightens, nods toward *away*. "Go take a drive. Like when we used to steal your mom's keys, remember? Winding up in Tennessee somewhere, spending the night sleeping in the bed of the truck."

"Getting chased out of a national park by a furious ranger at four a.m."

She laughs, nudging my arm. "I miss our adventures."

I take a swig of her flask. "Sorta loses the appeal when you have your own keys and drinking is legal."

"I promise you, there's still all sorts of trouble we can make."

That flirtatious spark in her eyes makes me sad. Because we used to have fun together, and now it feels strained. Awkward.

"Coop!" Down in the yard, my brother shouts at me. "It's a party, dude. Get down here."

Twin telepathy still works. I leave Heidi on the deck, head downstairs, and grab a beer on my way to the beach, where I meet Evan around the bonfire with some of our friends. I drink while they spend the next hour swapping the same stories we've been telling for ten years. Then our buddy Wyatt organizes a game of moonlight football and most of the crowd drifts toward it, leaving only a hand-ful of us by the fire. Evan's in the Adirondack chair next to mine, laughing at something our friend Alana just said, but I can't seem to enjoy myself tonight. There's a bug under my skin. Burrowing. Chewing out holes in my flesh and laying eggs of anger and resent-ment.

"Dude." Evan kicks my foot. "Snap out of it, man."

"I'm fine."

"Yeah," he says sarcastically, "I can tell." He grabs the empty bottle of beer I've been absently holding and tosses me a new one from the cooler. "You've been a moody little bitch for two days. I get you're pissed off, but it ain't cute anymore. Get drunk, smoke some weed. Heidi's here somewhere. Maybe she'll hook up with you again if you ask nicely."

I stifle a groan. There are no secrets in this group. When Heidi and I first slept together, we'd barely dug the crust out of our eyes the next morning before everyone else knew about it. Which is just more proof that it was a bad idea to go there. Hooking up with friends is only inviting trouble.

"Eat me, asshole." Heidi throws a handful of sand at him from across the fire pit. She flashes him the bird.

"Oops," he says, knowing full well she was sitting there. "My bad."

"You know, it's remarkable," Heidi says in that flat tone that is a glaring warning she's about to snip your balls off. "You two are identical twins, and yet I wouldn't touch your dick, Evan, even with Cooper's face."

"Burn," Alana shouts, laughing beside Heidi and Steph. The three of them have been the absolute torment of every boy in the Bay since we were in third grade. An unholy trinity of hotness and terror.

Evan makes a lewd gesture in response because comebacks are not really in his wheelhouse. Then he turns back to me. "I still say we wait till that clone leaves his house and we jump his ass. Word gets around, Coop. People start hearing you let that shit stand, and suddenly they're thinking anyone can mess with us."

"Cooper's lucky that prick didn't press charges," Steph points out. "But if you turn this into a war, he could change his mind."

She's right. There's no good reason why I haven't spent the last two days in a jail cell, other than that Preston guy was satisfied in humiliating me. While I'd never admit defeat, I'm still hot about getting fired. Evan's right—Hartleys can't let that shit stand. We have a reputation in this town. People smell weakness, they start getting ideas. Even when you have nothing, someone's always trying to take it.

"Who was he, anyway?" Heidi asks.

"Preston Kincaid," Steph supplies. "His family owns that massive estate down the coast where they ripped out those two-hundred-year-old oaks last month to put in a third tennis court."

"Ugh, I know that guy," Alana says, her bright red hair glowing in the firelight. "Maddy was running her dad's parasailing boat a few weeks ago, and she took him out on it with some chick. He was trying to talk some game to Maddy right in front of his date. Dude actually asked her out. When she made some excuse, right, because she's still trying to get a tip, he tries to persuade her into a threesome right there on the boat. Maddy said she damn near tossed him overboard."

Steph makes a face. "He's such a creep."

"There you go." Evan pops the cap on a fresh beer and takes a swig. "He's got it coming. We'd be doing a community service to bust him down a peg."

I eye my brother, curious.

"Revenge, dude. He took a pound of flesh from you. We take two from him."

Have to admit, I'm aching for payback. For two days, this chunk of seething anger has sat in my gut, burning. Bartending wasn't my sole source of income, but I needed that money. Everything I've been working toward got a lot farther away when that jackass got me fired.

I think it over. "Can't beat his face in or I'll wind up in jail. Can't take his job because, come on, who are we kidding, dude doesn't have one. He was born with a silver spoon up his ass. So what else is there?"

"Oh, this poor, dumb girl," Alana suddenly says, coming around to our side of the fire to show us her phone. "Just peeped his social media. He's got a girlfriend."

I narrow my eyes at the screen. Interesting. Kincaid posted a story earlier today about moving his girlfriend into her dorm at Garnet. The post includes heart emojis and all the performative, saccharine bullshit that are the telltale signs of a cheater overcompensating.

"Damn," Evan remarks, taking the phone. He flicks through photos of them on Kincaid's obnoxious yacht. "Chick's actually hot."

He's right. The picture Evan zooms in on shows a tall, dark-haired girl with green eyes and tanned skin. She's wearing a white cropped T-shirt that's falling off one shoulder, revealing the strap of a blue bathing suit beneath, and for some reason, that thin strip of fabric is hotter than any pornographic image I've ever seen. It's a tease. An invitation.

A terrible idea forms in the worst part of my mind.

"Take her," Evan says, because for all the ways we're completely different, we're exactly the same.

Alana's eyes light with mischief. "Do it."

"What, steal his girlfriend?" Heidi demands, incredulous. "She's not a toy. That's—"

"A great idea," Evan interjects. "Snipe that clone's girl, rub it in his face, then dump her rich ass."

"Gross, Evan." Heidi gets up and snatches Alana's phone from him as they continue to bicker. "She's a person, you know."

"No, she's a clone."

"You want her to dump Kincaid, right? So why can't we just catch him cheating on her, and send her the proof so she dumps him? Same end result," Heidi points out.

"Not the same," my brother argues.

"How is that not the same thing?"

"Because it isn't." Evan points the mouth of his bottle at Heidi. "It isn't enough for Kincaid to lose. He has to know who beat him. We have to make it hurt."

"Cooper doesn't have to trick her into falling in love with him," Alana tells her. "Seduce her enough that she dumps her boyfriend. A few dates, tops."

"Seduce her? You mean fuck her, then," Heidi says, revealing the real reason she hates this plan. "Again, gross."

Any other day, I might have agreed with her. But not tonight. Tonight, I'm angry and bitter and itching for blood. Besides, I'd be doing this chick a favor rescuing her from Kincaid. Sparing her a life of misery with a cheating bastard who'd only treat her nice enough to get 2.5 kids outta her before shifting all his attention to his mistresses.

I've encountered guys like Preston Kincaid my entire life. One of my earliest memories is of my five-year-old self down at the pier with my father and brother, confused why all those fancy-dressed people were speaking to Dad like he was a piece of dog shit mashed under their deck shoes. Hell, chances are Kincaid's girl is even worse than he is.

Steph brings up a potential snag. "But if he's already cheating on her, then how much does he really care about this girl? Maybe getting dumped won't faze him."

I glance at Evan. "She's got a point."

"I don't know . . ." A contemplative Alana reaches over Heidi's shoulder to look at the phone. "Scrolling through, I think they've been together for a few years. My money's on this one being end-game for him."

The longer the idea tumbles around in my head, the more I'm into it. Mostly for the look on Kincaid's face when he realizes I've won. But also because even if I didn't know she was Kincaid's girl-friend, I'd still try to date her.

"Let's make it interesting," Steph says. She shares a look with Alana, coming around to the possibilities of this idea. "You can't lie. You can't pretend to be all in love with her, or sleep with her unless she initiates it. Kissing is allowed. And you can't tell her to break up with him. It has to be her idea. Otherwise what's the point? We might as well go with Heidi's plan."

"Deal." It's almost unfair how easy this'll be.

"Omissions are lies." Heidi stands in a huff. "What makes you think one of them would step down from their cloud for you any-way?" She doesn't wait for an answer. Just storms toward the house.

"Ignore her," Alana says. "I love this plan."

Evan, meanwhile, gives me a hard look, then nods in the direction Heidi went. "You've got to do something about that."

Yeah, maybe I do. After a handful of hookups, Heidi and I re-verted back to platonic and were cool all summer. But then some-where the tide shifted and suddenly she's bent out of shape more often than not, and it's apparently all my fault.

"She's a big girl," I tell him.

Maybe Heidi's feeling a little territorial, but she'll get over it. We've been friends since first grade. She can't stay mad at me forever.

"Anyway. Final answer about the clone?" Evan eyes me expec-tantly.

I tip the beer bottle to my lips, taking a quick swig. Then I shrug and say, "I'm in."

CHAPTER FOUR

MACKENZIE

On Saturday night, our first week of freshman year behind us, Bonnie pulls me out on the town. *To get the lay of the land*, as she puts it.

So far, we're getting along great as roommates. Better than I expected, actually. I'm an only child and never lived anywhere but my parents' house, so I was a bit wary of the politics of sharing a space with a complete stranger. But Bonnie's easy to live with. She cleans up after herself, and makes me laugh with her endless supply of Southern sass. She's like the little sister I never knew I wanted.

For the past hour since we left campus, she's only reinforced my theory that she's some kind of sorceress. This girl possesses powers a mere mortal could only dream of. The moment we stepped up to the bar in this rowdy hole-in-the-wall place with panties hanging from the rafters and license plates on the wall, three guys practically bulldozed their way through the crowd to buy our drinks. All to get Bonnie to smile at them. Since then, I've watched her charm one guy after the other without even lifting a pinkie. She simply bats her eyelashes at men, gives them a little giggle, a hair twirl, and they're ready to harvest their own mothers for organs.

"You new in town?" One of our latest suitors, a jock-looking type wearing a too-tight T-shirt and too much body spray, shouts in my ear over the blaring music. Even as he chats me up, his eyes drift toward Bonnie as she talks animatedly. I can't imagine any of them can hear her, but it doesn't seem to matter.

"Yeah," I answer, my face glued to the glow of my phone screen as I text with Pres. He's at a friend's place tonight for a poker game.

While I pay the least possible attention to this dude, whose job is to entertain the "friend," his two buddies eat out of Bonnie's hand all the way to the dance floor. I occasionally nod and glance up from my phone as he valiantly attempts conversation that we both must know is useless against the band's set list blasting at full volume.

About forty minutes after the wingman has crept away, an arm catches mine. "I'm bored. Let's ditch these guys," Bonnie says in my ear.

"Yes." I nod emphatically. "Please."

She mimes some excuse to the two guys still clinging to her heels like ducklings, and then we pick up our drinks and take a circuitous route to the stairs. On the second floor, looking down at the live band on the stage, we find a table with a little more breathing room. It's quieter up here. Enough that we can carry on a conversation without shouting or resorting to rudimentary sign language.

"Not doing it for you?" I ask, referring to her latest victims.

"I can get those meatheads a dime a dozen at home. Can't throw a rock without hitting a college football player."

I grin over the rim of my glass. The fruity cocktail isn't exactly my jam, but it's what Bonnie asked her suitors to buy for us. "So what's your type, then?"

"Tattoos. Tall, dark, and damaged. The more emotionally un-available, the better." She beams. "If he's got a juvenile rap sheet and motorcycle, I'm open for business."

I almost choke on my tongue laughing. Fascinating. She doesn't seem like that kind of girl. "Maybe we ought to go find a bar with more Harleys outside. I'm not sure we're going to find what you're looking for in here."

From what I can tell, it's slim pickings. Mostly Garnet students, which skew toward country club types or frat bros, and a few beach rat townies in tank tops. None of whom approach Bonnie's leather-and-studs daydreams.

"Oh, I done my research," she says proudly. "Rumor has it, Avalon Bay's got exactly what I need. The Hartley Twins."

I raise an eyebrow. "Twins, huh?"

"Locals," she says, nodding. "But I'm not greedy. One'll do fine. Figure my odds are improved with a spare."

"And these Hartley twins tick all of your bad boy boxes?"

"Oh yeah. I heard about their exploits from some girls on campus." She licks her lips. "I wanna be one of those exploits tonight."

Humor bubbles in my throat. This girl. "You don't even know these guys. What if they're hideous?"

"They aren't. Their names wouldn't be comin' outta every girl's mouth if they were." She sighs happily. "Besides, that girl down the hall from us—Nina? Dina? Whatever her name is. She showed me a picture of 'em and don't you worry, Miss Mac, they are *fine*."

My laughter spills over. "Alright. Got it. I'll keep my eye out for a pair of bad boy clones."

"Thank you. Now, what about you?"

"Me?"

"Yes, you."

"I'm not in the market for a bad boy, no." My phone lights up again with a text from Preston telling me his next game is about to start.

Another thing I appreciate about Pres is routine, predictability. I prefer things that act within expected parameters. I'm a planner. An organizer. A boyfriend that's running all over town at all hours wouldn't fit in my life. Then again, I don't get the impression that Bonnie is in the market for a long-term investment. Maybe something more like a microtransaction.

"I'm just sayin'." Bonnie winks. "This is a circle of trust. I'd never snitch on a roomie if she wanted to entertain a little on the side."

"I appreciate it, but I'm good. Pres and I are loyal to each other." I wouldn't have done the whole long-distance thing if I wasn't confident we could be faithful. Now that we're both at Garnet, cheating would be even more pointless.

She looks at me a little cross-eyed then smiles in a way that's a bit patronizing, though I know she doesn't mean it. "So you're really the relationship type?"

"Yeah." I've only been with Preston, but even if it were someone else, monogamy is my thing. "I don't understand the point of cheating. If you want to be with other people, be single. Don't drag someone else along for the ride."

"Well, cheers to knowin' what we want and goin' after it." Bonnie raises her glass. We toast, then suck our cocktails dry. "Come on," she says, "let's get outta here. I got twins to hunt."

She's not joking. For the next two hours, I find myself trailing behind Bonnie as if I've got a dick-sniffing bloodhound on a leash. She drags me from one bar to the next in search of her elusive twins, leaving countless mesmerized victims in her wake. One poor loser after another throwing himself at her feet, slayed by her dimples. I've never had trouble attracting attention from guys, but standing next to Bonnie May Beauchamp, I might as well be a broken barstool. Good thing I have a boyfriend, or else I'd develop a complex.

As much as I want to help Bonnie in her crusade to locate and destroy her townie bad boy, the sidekick routine gets tedious as the night wears on. If she doesn't tire herself out soon, there's a chance I'll need to club her over the head.

"Last one," I warn as we cross the threshold of yet another boardwalk bar. This one's called the Rip Tide. "If your twins aren't here, you'll have to settle for any old bad boy."

"Last one," she promises. Then she bats her eyelashes and, like every guy we've encountered tonight, I find myself melting in her presence. It's impossible to stay annoyed with her.

She links her arm through mine and pulls me deeper into the Rip Tide. "C'mon, girl, let's do this. I got a good feeling about this one."

CHAPTER FIVE

COOPER

She's here.

Fate must be on board with the plan, because I'm out with some friends on Saturday night to see a buddy's band at the Rip Tide when I spot *her*. She's alone at a high-top table, placed directly in my path as if by some higher power.

Her face is unmistakable. And holy hell, she was good-looking in photos but a total knockout in person. The kind of girl who sticks out in a crowd. Stunning, with long dark hair and piercing eyes that shine under the lights from the stage. Even at a distance, she's got an effortless cool about her, an aura of confidence. In a white T-shirt knotted at her waist and a pair of jeans, she stands out for not trying too hard.

All that would be enough to capture my attention even if she didn't have a killer body. But she has that too—impossibly long legs, a full rack, a round bottom. She's the girl my daydreams daydream about.

"That her?" Alana leans in to follow my gaze to where Preston Kincaid's girlfriend is sitting. "She's better looking in person."

I know.

"Quick smoke while the next band sets up?" suggests our friend Tate. He rises from the table, dragging a hand through his messy blond hair.

"Nah, we're staying here," Alana answers for us.

He quirks a brow at me. "Coop?"

Once again, Alana is my mouthpiece. "Cooper is cutting back on the cancer sticks." She waves a hand. "You guys go on out."

Shrugging, Tate wanders off, tailed by Wyatt and Wyatt's girl-friend, Ren. The moment they're gone, Alana turns her gaze on me.

"Lemme hear it," she orders.

"Hear what?"

"Your game. Pitch some lines." She flips her hair and props her chin in her hands, giving me sarcastic doe eyes.

"Fuck off." I don't need a pickup coach.

"You need a plan," she insists. Thing about Alana, when she gets her claws into something, she tends to take over. "You can't just go over and drop your dick in her lap."

"Yes, thank you, I'm aware." I drain the last of my beer as I get up from the table.

Alana stops me, pulls the sleeves of my black Henley down and runs her hands through my hair.

"What's that for?" I grumble.

"Best foot forward," she says. "Just in case she's a prude. Tattoos scare off the prudes." Leaning back, she takes a final appraising glance before shooing me with her hand. "You're done. Go forth and conquer."

This is the problem with having girl friends.

Before I approach my mark's table, I take a quick scan of the room to make sure Kincaid isn't lurking somewhere. Not that I have any qualms about a rematch. Getting into a bar fight isn't part of the plan, though. This'll work best if I can swoop in there undetected until it's too late for him to intervene. Win her over before he even knows the enemy is inside the gates.

Satisfied that she's flying sans-boyfriend tonight, I walk up to her table. With her face glued to her phone, she doesn't notice me until I tap her on the arm.

"Hey," I say, bending my head toward her so she can hear me over the music from the loudspeaker. "You using this stool?"

"No." She doesn't lift her attention from the lit screen. "Go ahead." When I sit, her head jerks up. "Oh. Figured you'd just take the stool to another table. But okay."

"Settle a bet for me," I say, leaning in closer. She smells good, like vanilla and citrus. So good I almost forget why I'm here. That she doesn't pull away or throw a drink in my face is a good start.

"Uh . . . what sort of bet?" There's a flicker of hostility in her eyes before her expression softens. When she rakes her gaze over me, I know I've got her intrigued.

"What if I told you, an hour from now, you'd be leaving this bar with me."

"I'd say I admire your hustle, but you'd be better off aiming that arrow at another target."

"So we have a wager then." Holding her gaze, I offer my hand to shake on it. I find the best way to truly know someone is to push and see if they push back. Wind them up and let them go.

"I have a boyfriend," she says flatly, ignoring my hand. "You've already lost."

I meet her eyes. Insolently. "I didn't ask about your boyfriend."

For a moment she's taken aback. Of course she is, because no one talks to her that way. Certainly not her dumbass boyfriend. Chicks like her are used to parents doting on their every desire and servants waiting on them hand and foot. And as the notion of me settles into her mind, I see the moment she decides I'm more interesting than whatever was on her phone.

She puts it to sleep and pushes it away.

So fucking predictable. Every rich girl from a good family wonders what it's like to be with the guy from the wrong side of the gilded gates. It's the closest thing to a thrill they'll ever have.

"Is this a gag?" She looks around. "Did Bonnie put you up to this?"

"I don't know any Bonnie. I'm Cooper."

"Mackenzie," she replies with a furrowed brow, still spinning her wheels wondering what the catch is. "But I really do have a boyfriend."

"You keep saying that."

This time when I lean in, she doesn't back away. The gap between us falls to a few inches, the air between us growing thinner.

"In most of the civilized world," she says slowly, "that matters."

"And here I'm looking around, and I don't see this guy you're so concerned about."

Her face is incredulous, if a bit amused. She knows exactly how hot she is and is used to men chasing after her. Yet I sense her unease. I threw her off-kilter. Which tells me she's thinking about it. I've met countless girls like her, slept with a few of them, and right now, the farfetched fantasies and what-ifs are spiraling through her pretty head.

"I'm with my roommate tonight." There's still fight in her voice, the resolve to hold her ground, or at least appear to do so. This is a woman who's never played the easy target. "It's a girls' thing."

"Yeah, real wild night you're having," I drawl, gesturing at her glass of water. "Someone's got a good girl complex, huh?"

"I'm dying to find out how insulting me is going to win you this bet."

"Stick around and find out."

She holds up her water. "This is called being a good friend. I've already met my alcohol quota of two drinks."

"Whatever you say, princess."

She twirls the straw in her glass. "I'm trying to watch out for my roommate tonight."

"What if I thought you looked lonely?"

She cocks her head, eyes narrowing. I can see the gears working in her mind, analyzing me. "Why would I be lonely?"

"Let's cut the bullshit."

She nods with a smirk. "Yes, let's."

"You're an attractive woman alone in a crowded bar with your face glued to your phone because there's somewhere else you'd rather be. And wherever that place is, there's someone who's having fun without you. Yet you're sitting here wearing your boredom as a badge of loyalty, with some misguided notion that being miserable proves what a good person you are. So, yeah, I think you're lonely. I think you're so desperate for a good time you're secretly glad I walked over here. In the deepest, darkest part of your brain, you want me to give you a reason to misbehave."

Mackenzie doesn't answer. In the crackle of energy building in the tight space between us, I watch the indecision warring behind her eyes. She considers everything I just said, stabbing the straw into her glass of ice water.

If she's going to tell me to get lost, this is it. I've called her out and anything less than shutting me down is an admission that I'm at least a little right. But if she doesn't shut me down, then the path ahead of her is unmarked. There are no rules, and that's dangerous territory for someone whose whole world is mapped out for them from birth. Being rich means never having to think for yourself.

If she chooses to follow me, it only gets less predictable from here.

"Alright," she says finally. "I'll take that bet." I can tell she's still skeptical of my motivations, but she's intrigued. "But if you think this ends with getting me in bed, you might as well pay up now."

"Right. Wouldn't want to tempt you with a good time."

She rolls her eyes, failing to hide a smile.

"I mean, I could feel the bummer energy wafting off of you from way over there," I say, nodding toward the table where Alana and our friends are failing to pretend they aren't watching us. "Honestly, this is a mitigation protocol. If your attitude doesn't improve, we're gonna have to ask you to leave before your bummer spreads."

"Oh," she says, putting on an expression of mock seriousness, "if this is a medical emergency, then, by all means, please."

She's got banter, at least. I was afraid she'd be another stuck-up priss who couldn't string a thought together that wasn't about clothes or nail polish. I assumed going into this I'd have to contend with a typical clone attitude of bitchy entitlement, but this chick seems mostly normal, with none of that pompous pretension.

"So, what *did* drag you out tonight?" I ask. The more she can talk about herself, the more her walls will come down. Gives her the idea she's in control.

"My roommate is hunting a pair of twins," she informs me.

Oh really. "For sport or meat?"

"Bit of both." Her gaze travels the room, presumably searching the crowd for this elusive roommate. "She has a thing for socially unproductive boys who put their personality on their skin, and she's got it in her head that twins are good odds. Personally, I think a bout of herpes isn't worth the morning-after Instagram selfie, but what do I know?"

I struggle to keep a straight face. This is too perfect. I almost feel bad doing this to her, but then she did suggest I have herpes, so not that bad.

"You know these twins?" I paste on an innocent tone.

"No, but if they're so infamous their reputation on campus filtered all the way down to a freshman in the first week of school, their tales must be long and plentiful." Her face scrunches in disgust. If this wasn't so amusing, I might be offended. "Any guy that gets around that much is bound to fill up a petri dish with all manner of genital infestations."

"Obviously," I say solemnly. "Got a name for these twin patient zeros?"

"The Hartleys. They're local." Then her face lights up. "You don't know them, do you? I mean, Bonnie would be excited to pick up a clue on her quest, but if they're friends of yours or something . . ."

I almost can't stand the anticipation anymore.

"Nah, forget those guys." I'm fighting a grin. "Couple dirtbags, those two."

"Mac! I need another drink and then we— Oh." A short blonde walks up and stops short, staring straight through my skull. Her face turns a glowing pink as her big eyes dart to Mackenzie.

A few daunting seconds of mental gymnastics pass wordlessly between the girls before Mackenzie grabs my wrist and yanks one sleeve up my arm to reveal my tattoos.

"Oh fuck off," she says to me, glaring fire. "No. Nope. Not fair." She sits back and crosses her arms in defiance. "You knew I was talking about you and still let me go on like that?"

"I never pass up on free entertainment," I say, my grin springing free.

Her roommate slides onto the stool beside Mackenzie, watching us. It suddenly occurs to me that the roommate situation could be tricky. Either this girl derails my plans by calling dibs and scaring off Mackenzie before I've ever had a shot, or she's my ace in the hole. Get the roommate on my side and coast to the finish line. Luckily, I have a spare me to toss her way.

"You duped me." Emphatic, Mackenzie tells me, "An intentional attempt at deception. That's not allowed. In fact, this entire interaction is now moot. We didn't meet. I don't know you."

"Wow." I push back from the table, smothering a laugh. "You've given me a lot to think about. I'm gonna need another drink to soak that in. Another round?" This time I direct the question to the roommate, whose permanent look of awe has not waned.

"Yes, please," she says. When Mackenzie appears she might object, the roommate shoots her a look. "Thank you."

I head over to the bar and catch a glimpse of Alana, who gets up from our friends' table to follow me. She takes a circuitous route to pass slowly by Mackenzie and her roommate while I order three beers.

"Looks like it went well," Alana says when she finally slides in beside me. The current band's set ends and there's a brief lull before the canned music is pumped into the room as the next band sets up.

"She's cool," I answer, shrugging. "Kinda mouthy, but when has that ever stopped me?"

"Yeah, well, don't get attached." Alana orders a shot for herself.

"I just met the girl. Relax." Besides, attachment's never been my problem. Growing up the way I did, I learned a long time ago that everything is temporary. There's no use investing too much of myself. Easier that way. Clean. Saves everyone all sorts of grief.

"I heard them talking." Alana downs her shot and winces at the burn. "The blonde one was like, *He's yours if you want him*, but our girl was like, *Nah, go for it*. So . . ." She turns around to lean against the bar, looking over at the girls' table. "You've still got a lot of work to do there."

"Long story, but I might have to throw Evan at the blonde one."

"How ever will he manage," Alana says, rolling her eyes at me.

The roommate's hot, no doubt, but she's not really my type. Anyway, she's about half my size, and I hate throwing my back out bending down to kiss a girl.

The bartender comes back with our drinks and I gather them up, returning to the girls as Alana shouts something like *Go get 'em, tiger* at my back. I underestimated how obnoxious turning my sex life into a spectator sport would be.

At the table, I put the drinks down and take a seat. When Mackenzie pushes her water to the side to accept the beer, I know for certain she's along for the ride. If she was going to get spooked and bolt, it would have been before I got back.

"Cooper Hartley." I offer my hand to the roommate, who's studying me not at all discreetly.

She shakes my hand, her small fingers lingering. "Bonnie May Beauchamp," she says with a heavy Southern accent. "Don't suppose your brother is lurkin' around."

"No, he's probably getting into trouble somewhere." Actually, he's hustling rich kids out of their trust fund money at the pool tables a few doors down. It's practically his second job. "Can't take that kid anywhere."

"That's too bad." Bonnie gives a playful pout.

It's clear this Bonnie chick is a tiny bottle of fire. She's got all kinds of mischievous sexual energy bursting out of her.

"We were hoping you had the skinny on the after-party, right, Mac? Somewhere . . . cozier."

Mackenzie shoots a conflicted glance at her roommate. I bite back a grin. Now if she refuses, she's cockblocking her friend. *Tough spot, Mac.* This roommate and I are becoming fast friends. This'll be easier than I hoped.

"Cozy, huh?" I say.

Mackenzie glances back at me, realizing she never stood a chance at winning our little game. I'd feel bad if I were capable of giving a shit. This chick's hot, and not a total nightmare, but I haven't forgotten why I'm here. She's still only a means to an end.

"I know a place." It's too soon to try inviting them back to the house. That's coming on strong, and I know instinctively it's not the right strategy on this one. She needs the measured approach. Build a rapport. Become friends. I can be patient when I need to be; let her come to me. The mission is to break up her and Kincaid. For that to work, she has to be invested.

"That doesn't sound ominous at all." Mackenzie's got some bite to her now.

"I'll text my brother, see if he's interested in getting into some trouble with us instead of whatever he's up to. Yeah?"

"I'm game." Bonnie looks to Mackenzie with *Daddy, can I have a pony* eyes.

"I don't know." Torn, she consults her phone. "It's almost one in the morning. My boyfriend's probably home waiting for me to call him."

"He'll live," Bonnie insists. Her pleading tone grows more urgent. "Please?"

"Come on, princess. Live a little."

Mackenzie wrestles with her better judgment, and there's a split second when I begin to question myself. That perhaps I'd read her wrong, and she's not a bored rich girl who needs to let loose. That she's fully capable of getting up, walking off, and never looking at me twice.

"Fine," she relents. "An hour, tops."

Nah, still got it.

CHAPTER SIX

MACKENZIE

I don't quite know how we got here. I'm with Bonnie, Cooper, and his identical twin Evan, sitting around a glowing bonfire on the sand where the crashing waves and pulsing tide drown out the sounds of the boardwalk. The tiny sparks and embers flicker and float into the warm ocean air. Lights twinkle from behind the sand dunes and reflect off the water.

Clearly I've lost my mind. It's as though someone else hijacked my brain when I agreed to let this stranger drag us into the darkness. Now, as Bonnie cozies up to her bad boy, a growing sense of unease builds inside me. It's coming from the Cooper-sized space across the flames.

"You're so full of it," Bonnie accuses. She's cross-legged beside me, laughing yet skeptical.

"I shit you not." Evan puts his hands up in a show of innocence. "Coop's sitting with this damn goat in the back of the squad car, and it's scared, thrashing around. Kicks him in the forehead, and Coop starts gushing blood everywhere. So he's trying to calm the goat down but everything's all bloody and slippery back there. There's blood all over him and the goat, the windows. And I'm driving this stolen cop car, the sirens are blaring, lights are flashing and shit."

I laugh at his crazy description and animated hand gestures. Evan seems more playful than Cooper, who comes off as a bit intense. Their faces are identical, but it's easy to tell them apart. Evan's dark hair is cut shorter, his arms devoid of ink.

"And we can hear them on the radio," Cooper says, his way too attractive face a dance of light and shadow from the fire between us. "They're all, some damn fool kids stole a goat and a car. Set up a perimeter. Lock down the bridge. So we're thinking, crap, where are we taking this thing?"

I can't peel my gaze off his lips. His hands. Those muscular arms. I'm trying to trace the outlines of his tattoos as he gestures through the air. It's psychological torture. I'm strapped to a chair, my eyes held open, driven mad by images of his dark eyes and crooked smirk. And although Evan literally has the same face, for some reason I'm not responding to *him*. Not even remotely. Just Cooper.

"We're thirteen years old and set off a chase through town," Evan continues, "all because Steph saw this goat chained up in someone's yard and hopped the fence to liberate it just as the owner comes out with a shotgun. And Coop and I are thinking, aw man, she's about to get her crazy ass shot over this goat."

"We jump the fence after her, and I'm smashing the lock with a hammer—"

"You happened to have a hammer with you?" Even my voice sounds strange to me. I'm out of breath because my heart is pumping so fast, though I've been sitting the whole time. Perfectly still. Caught in his spell.

"Yeah." He looks at me like I'm weird for asking. "It's a cheap lock. You smack it good a couple times on the side, and the little parts inside break apart. So Evan grabs the goat and we're dodging buckshot, because the owner is drunk off his ass and can't aim for shit."

"But where'd the cop car come from?" Bonnie asks.

"We're running with this thing on a leash when a cop corners us, right?" Evan becomes animated, gesturing with a bottle of beer that he brought to the beach with him. "He draws his Taser but there's three of us and a goat, so he doesn't know who to aim at. He leaves the door open, so I'm like, screw it, hop in."

"Evan and I dive in," Cooper says. "Steph runs to distract the cop. Anyway, so the goat kicks the hell out of me, and I'm back there getting woozy, about to black out, when Evan says, bro, we gotta ditch this car and run."

"So what happened to the goat?" I demand, now sincerely invested in the fate of this poor animal, but acutely paranoid that everyone notices how out of sorts I am. How hard I'm staring.

"Evan pulls onto this fire road that cuts through the state park and somehow wrestles that thing out of the backseat and takes it into the forest. Leaves me passed out on the ground beside the car so when the cops get there and see me unconscious and covered in blood, looking dead as a doornail, they all start freaking out. They get me in an ambulance, and I wake up in the hospital. In all the confusion, I slip out of there and meet Evan at home like nothing ever happened."

"They never caught you?" Bonnie hoots with laughter.

"Hell no," Evan says. "Got away clean."

"So you left a goat by itself in the woods?" I stare at them, amused yet horrified.

"What the hell else were we supposed to do with it?" Cooper sputters.

"Not that! Oh my God. That poor goat. I'm going to have nightmares about the thing crying alone in the dark forest. Chased down by bobcats or something."

"See?" Evan smacks his brother's arm. "This is why we don't let chicks talk us into playing hero. They're never satisfied."

Still, I laugh despite myself. The image of those two tearing through town, barely able to see over the steering wheel, with a frightened goat kicking and bucking around, is too hilarious.

For a while longer, we trade silly stories. About the time Bonnie and her high school cheerleading squad turned a hotel grand staircase into a Slip 'N Slide at a competition in Florida. Or the time a friend and I met some guys when camping with her family and almost burned down the campground with fireworks.

And then, it finally arrives. The moment Bonnie has eagerly awaited all night.

Evan grabs the blanket he got from his car earlier and asks Bonnie if she wants to take a walk. Those two have been making eyes at each other since we came here. Before they walk off, she glances back at me to make sure I'm cool by myself, and I give her a nod.

Because as terrified as I am to be left alone with Cooper, it's exactly what I want.

"Well, my work here is done," I inform him, trying to act normal.

He pokes the fire with a stick to move the logs around. "Don't worry, she's safe with him. He talks like a delinquent, but Evan's not a creep or anything."

"I'm not worried." I get up and take Evan's spot in the sand beside Cooper. I shouldn't, but I'm a glutton for punishment. And I don't know if it's him or the intoxicating scent of burning driftwood, but I feel drunk despite only having one beer. "Honestly, neither of you are what I expected. In a good way."

Uh-oh. That sounded flirty, I realize. My cheeks heat up, and I hope he doesn't take the comment as a sign of interest.

"Yeah," he says, shaking his head. "I'm kinda still waiting on an apology for that herpes crack."

"I plead the fifth." I bite back a smirk, looking at him from the corner of my eye.

"So that's how it is, huh?" He arches an eyebrow, challenging me with mock bravado.

I shrug. "Don't know what you're talking about."

"Alright. I see. Remember that, Mac. When you had the chance to be the bigger person."

"Ohhh," I taunt. "So it's war now, huh? Sworn enemies to the death?"

"I don't start shit, I finish it." He makes a joking tough guy face and kicks some sand at my feet.

"Yeah, real mature."

"Now about that bet, princess."

That does me in. With that single mocking nickname, I blink and a terrible sinking awareness becomes undeniable.

Cooper's hot.

Insanely hot.

And it's not just his strong, angular face and deep, dark eyes that descend for ages. He also possesses a certain *I don't give a fuck* quality that gets right at the most susceptible parts of me. In the light of the fire, there's something almost ominous about him. A knife when the light glints off the blade. Yet he has a magnetism that's undeniable.

I can't remember the last time I felt such a visceral attraction to a guy. If ever.

I don't like it. Not only because I have a boyfriend, but because my pulse is racing and my cheeks are hot, and I hate feeling like I'm not in control of my own body.

"We never did set the stakes," he muses.

"What do you want, then?" Fair's fair. If nothing else, I'm a woman of my word.

"You wanna make out?"

I play it cool, but my pulse kicks into a new gear. "What else do you want?"

"I mean, I figured a blowjob was a nonstarter, but if we're negotiating. . . ."

Despite myself, I crack a smile. "You're shameless."

Somehow he manages to release the tension from the moment, erasing all awkwardness until I'm no longer hyperaware of myself.

"Alright," he says, a sexy grin tilting his lips. "You drive a hard bargain. I'll go down on you first."

"Yeah, I think we're at an impasse on this one."

"That right?" He watches me under heavy-lidded eyes. It's impossible not to feel he's undressing me in his mind. "Fine. But I'm keeping your marker. You're going to owe me one."

At some point I feel my phone buzz in my pocket. By then Cooper and I are knee-deep in an argument over the socioeconomic implications of pastries. I glance at my phone to make sure it isn't Bonnie asking for a rescue, but it's just Preston saying he's home from his poker game.

"No way," Cooper argues. "Pastries are rich people food. You never see someone making minimum wage popping into a bakery for a box of fucking croissants. We got donuts, cold Pop-Tarts, and maybe a biscuit out of a can or something, but none of that scone shit."

"A donut is absolutely a pastry. And a donut shop is a kind of bakery."

"Horseshit. There are five bakeries in this town, and three of them are only open in the summer. What does that tell you?"

"That the population swells during the tourist season, and the overflow shops open to support that demand. It says nothing about the demographics."

He scoffs, tossing a stick into the fire. "Now you're talking nonsense."

Though it sounds like we're fighting, the subtle turn at the corner of his mouth tells me it's all in good fun. Arguing is practically a pastime in my house, so I'm quite skilled at it. Not sure where Cooper learned to bicker so well, but he definitely keeps me on my toes. And neither of us take well to admitting defeat.

"You're not the most annoying clone I've ever met," he says a while later.

Bonnie and Evan still aren't back. The boardwalk behind us is now mostly quiet in the late hour, and yet I'm not tired. If anything, I feel more energized.

"Clone?" I echo with a wry look. That's a new one on me.

"What we call the rich folks. Because you're all the same." His eyes glint thoughtfully beneath the moonlight. "But maybe you're not exactly like the rest of them."

"Not sure if that's an insulting compliment or a complimentary insult." It's my turn to kick a little sand at him.

"No, I mean, you're not what I expected. You're chill. Real." He continues to study me, all the playfulness and pretense forgotten. On his face I see only sincerity. The real Cooper. "Not one of those stuck-up jackasses who has their head up their ass because they love the smell of their own shit so much."

There's something in his voice, and it's more than the surface annoyance with yuppie tourists and rich jerks. It sounds like real pain.

I give him an elbow jab to lighten the mood. "I get it. I've grown up with those people. You'd think it gets to a point where you hardly notice it, but nope. Still, they're not all bad."

"This boyfriend of yours? What's his story?"

"Preston," I supply. "He's from the area, actually—his family lives down the coast. He goes to Garnet, obviously. Business major."

"You don't say." Cooper dons a sarcastic look.

"He's not that bad. I don't think he's ever even played squash," I say for a laugh, but the joke doesn't land. "He's a good guy. Not the type who's a dick to the waiter or that kind of thing."

Cooper chuckles softly. "You don't think it's telling that your answer is basically, he's nice to the help?"

I sigh. I suppose I don't know how to talk to a guy I just met about my boyfriend. Especially when Cooper is clearly hostile to our entire upbringing.

"You know, this might shock you, but if you gave him a chance, you might actually get along. We're not all jackasses," I point out.

"Nah." Some light returns to his expression, and I take that as a good sign. "I'm pretty sure you're the one exception I've met, and I've lived in the Bay my whole life."

"Then I'm glad I could demonstrate some redeeming qualities of my people."

He smiles, shrugging. "We'll see."

"Oh, yeah? That sounds suspiciously like an invitation. But you wouldn't be caught dead making friends with"—I gasp for effect—"a clone, now would you?"

"Not a chance. Call it an experiment. You can be my test subject."

"And what hypothesis are we testing?"

"Whether a clone can be deprogrammed into a real person."

I can't help but laugh. I've been doing that a lot tonight. Cooper might have those brooding bad boy looks, but he's funnier than I expected. I like him.

"So are we really doing this?" I ask.

His tongue drags over his bottom lip in a positively lewd way. "Going down on each other? Hell yeah. Let's do it."

More laughter sputters out. "Being friends! I'm asking if we're going to be friends! Jeez, Hartley, you are way too focused on oral sex, anyone ever tell you that?"

"Firstly, have you looked in the mirror? Jeez—" He halts, looking over at me. "What's your last name?"

"Cabot," I say helpfully.

"Jeez, Cabot," he mimics. "How can I not think about oral sex when I'm sitting next to the hottest woman on the planet?"

A flush rises in my cheeks. Damn it. That rough honesty is wildly sexy.

Gulping, I force my body not to respond to his crudeness or the compliment. *You have a boyfriend, Mackenzie.* I spell it out for my brain. B-O-Y-F-R-I-E-N-D.

Is it bad that I've had to remind myself an alarming number of times tonight?

"Secondly," Cooper continues, "are you sure we're not gonna hook up?"

"Positive."

He rolls his eyes at me. "Fine, then thirdly—yes, I guess I'll settle for friendship."

"How kind of you."

"Right?"

"Oh God. I'm already reconsidering. I feel like you're going to be a high-maintenance friend."

"Bullshit," he argues. "I'll be the best friend you've ever had. I always go above and beyond what's expected of me. I mean, I've liberated goats for my friends. Can you say the same?"

I snicker. "Goats, plural? You mean it wasn't just the one?"

"Nah, it was only one goat. But one time, I did steal a goldfish for my friend Alana."

"Awesome. I'm friends with a thief." I poke him in the side. "I need to hear the goldfish story, please."

He winks. "Oh, it's a good one."

We talk for so long, the two of us around the dwindling fire, that I don't notice the black night turn to gray early morning until

Evan and Bonnie come strolling toward us looking rather pleased with themselves. By then I realize I have a dozen texts from Preston wondering what the hell happened to me. Oops.

"Take my number," Cooper says in a rough voice. "Text me when you get to campus so I know you made it back safe."

Despite the warning alarms in my head, I punch his number into my phone.

No big deal, I assure that disapproving side of me. It'll just be one text when I get home, then I'll delete the number. Because as fun as it was to joke about our impending friendship, I know it's not a good idea. If I've learned one thing from rom coms, it's that you are not allowed to be friends with someone you're attracted to. The attraction itself is harmless. We're human beings and life can last years. We're bound to feel physical attraction for someone other than our significant other. But anyone who places themselves directly in the path of temptation is only asking for trouble.

So when Bonnie and I stumble out of an Uber and climb up to our dorm, I'm fully prepared to purge Cooper Hartley from my phone. I send a solitary text: *Home safe!* Then I click on his number and hover my finger over the word *DELETE*.

Before I can press it, a message from him pops up.

Cooper: *That was fun. Let's do it again sometime?*

I bite my lip, staring at the invitation. The memory of his dark eyes gleaming in the firelight, of his broad shoulders and muscular arms, jumpstarts my tired brain and tickles that spot between my legs.

Delete him, a strict voice orders.

I click on the chat thread. Maybe a friendship with this guy is a terrible idea, but I can't help myself. I cave.

Me: *I'll bring donuts.*

CHAPTER SEVEN

MACKENZIE

Only two weeks into the semester and I'm already over it. It wouldn't be so bad if I could dig into some business and finance courses. Marketing and mass communications law. Even some basic web coding. Instead, I'm stuck in a lecture hall staring at an illustration of some hairy, naked pre-human ape-man that, frankly, varies little from the current iteration sitting three rows over.

Freshman gen-eds are bullshit. Even psychology or sociology could have had some application to my work, but those courses were full. So I got stuck in anthropology, which so far today has been ten minutes of swarthy protohuman slides and forty minutes of arguments over evolution. None of which benefits my bank account. My parents pushed college on me, but I was hoping I could at least be productive while I was here. Optimizing *BoyfriendFails* and its sister site, targeting keywords, looking at ad impressions. Instead, I'm taking notes because our professor is one of those *an A is perfection, so no one is getting an A in this class* assholes. And if I'm forced to entertain this exhaustive waste of time, I'm not going to walk around with a C average.

It isn't until I step outside into the blazing sunshine that I realize I can't feel my fingertips. The lecture hall was freezing. I head over to the student union for a coffee and sit on a hot concrete bench under a magnolia tree to thaw out. I'm supposed to meet Preston in thirty minutes, so I still have some time to kill.

I sip my coffee and scroll through some business emails, forcing myself not to dwell on the fact that I haven't heard from Cooper yet today.

And I say *yet*, because he's messaged me every day since Saturday night. So I know I'll hear from him at some point today, it's only a matter of when. The first time he texted, I'd hesitated to open the message, afraid a picture of his junk might pop up on the screen. Or maybe hopeful it would? I've never been one for dick pics, but—

But nothing! a sharp voice shouts in my head.

Right. There's no *but*. I don't want to see Cooper Hartley's penis. Period, end of sentence. I mean, why would I want to see the penis of the hot, tattooed bad boy I stayed up an entire night talking to? That's just ludicrous.

Welp, I'm not cold anymore. I'm burning up now.

I need a distraction. ASAP.

When my mom's number lights up the screen, I think about ignoring the call, because that's definitely not the distraction I'd hoped for. But past experience has taught me that ignoring her only encourages her to send increasingly demanding texts to answer her. Then calls to the FBI insisting I've been kidnapped for ransom.

"Hi, Mom," I answer, hoping she can't hear my lack of enthusiasm.

"Mackenzie, sweetheart, hello."

There's a long pause, during which I can't tell if she's distracted or waiting for me to say something. *You called me, Mom.*

"What's up?" I ask to get the ball rolling.

"I wanted to check in. You promised to call after you got settled, but we haven't heard from you."

Ugh. She always does this. Turns everything into a guilt trip. "I called the house last weekend, but Stacey said you were out, or busy or something."

I spend more time on the phone with my mother's personal assistant than I do with anyone in the family.

"Yes, well, I have a lot on my plate at the moment. The historical society is sponsoring a new exhibit at the State House, and we're already planning the fall gala fundraiser for the children's hospital. Still, persistence is everything, Mackenzie. You know that. You should have called again later that day."

Of course. My mother has a personal staff and still can't manage to return a call to her only child, but sure, that's my fault. Ah well. It's something I've learned to live with. Annabeth Cabot simply can't be wrong about anything. I inherited that trait, at least when it comes to pointless arguments about donuts or whatnot. Those, I must always win. But unlike my mom, I'm fully capable of admitting when I've made a mistake.

"How is school?" she inquires. "Do you like your professors? Are you finding your classes challenging?"

"School's great."

Lie.

"My professors are so engaging, and the course content is really interesting so far."

Lie. Lie.

"I love it here."

Lie.

But there's nothing to gain from telling her the truth. That half the professors seem to regard teaching freshmen as an act of spite, and the other half only show up to hand their TAs a thumb drive of PowerPoint slides. That my time would be better spent anywhere else, but especially on my thriving business. She doesn't want to hear it.

The truth is, my parents have never been interested in what I have to say unless it's something they've scripted themselves and forced me to read. In my father's case, the daughter script is typically recited during public events and accompanied by fake, beaming smiles aimed at his constituents.

"I want you to apply yourself, Mackenzie. A lady should be worldly and well educated."

For appearances is the unspoken part. Not for any practical purposes, but so the lady can carry on conversations at cocktail parties.

"Remember to enjoy yourself too. College is a seminal time in a young woman's life. This is where you meet the people who will form your network for years to come. It's important to build those relationships now."

As far as Mom is concerned, I'm supposed to follow in her footsteps. I'm to become a glorified housewife who sits on all the right charity boards and throws parties to support her husband's professional aspirations. I've stopped trying to argue the point with her, but that's not the life I want, and eventually, hopefully, I'll jump on another track and it'll be too late for them to stop me.

For now, I play along.

"I know, Mom."

"What about your roommate? What's her name?"

"Bonnie. She's from Georgia."

"What's her family name? What do they do?"

Because that's what it always boils down to. Are they *someone*?

"Beauchamp. They own car dealerships."

"Oh." Another long, disappointed pause. "I suppose they do well with that."

Meaning that if they can afford to put her in the same dorm room with me, they must not be dirt-poor.

I stifle a sigh. "I have to go, Mom. Got class in a few minutes," I lie.

"Alright. Talk soon, sweetheart."

I hang up and release the breath I was holding. Mom is a lot sometimes. She's been heaping expectations and projecting herself onto me for my entire life. Yes, we have our similarities—our looks, our tendency toward impatience, the work ethic she displays with her charities and I apply to my business and studies. But for as much as we're similar, we're still two different people with totally different priorities. It's a concept she hasn't grabbed onto yet, that she can't mold me in her image.

"Hey, gorgeous." Preston appears with a smile, looking fully healed from his basketball injury and bearing a small bouquet of pink snapdragons, which I suspect are missing from a flowerbed somewhere on campus.

"You're in a good mood," I tease as he pulls me from the bench and tugs me toward him.

Preston kisses me, wrapping me in his arms. "I like getting to see you more now that you're here."

His lips travel to my neck, where he plants a soft peck before playfully nipping my earlobe.

I try not to raise a brow, because normally he shuns all public displays. Most of the time, I'm lucky to get him to hold my hand. But he's never been an overly physical boyfriend, and that's something I've learned to accept about him. If anything, the lack of PDA is a plus, especially when we're around our families. I realized at a young age that masking my emotions and repressing my occasional wild streak were necessary survival tools in our world.

"You ready?" he asks.

"Lead the way."

It's a beautiful day, if a little warm, as Pres guides me on a tour across the campus. Our first stop, of course, is Kincaid Hall, which houses the business school. Preston's family is a legacy at Garnet, going back generations.

Pres laces his fingers through mine and leads us outside again. As we stroll down a tree-lined path toward the art school, I admire the passing scenery. The campus truly is beautiful. Redbrick buildings. A great clock tower over the library. Sprawling green lawns and giant, majestic oak trees. I might not be enthused about college life, but at least everything is pretty to look at.

"What do you think of school so far?"

With Preston, I can be honest, so I sigh. "I'm bored out of my mind."

He chuckles. "I was the same way as a freshman, remember? For the first couple years until you can start upper level courses, it's pretty tedious."

"At least you have a purpose." We walk past the theater department, where students are in the parking lot, painting what looks to be an old-timey street set. "You need a certain level of education to work for your dad's bank. There are expectations and requirements. But I already have my own business. I'm my own boss, and I don't need to get a degree to prove anything to anyone."

Smiling, Pres squeezes my hand. "That's what I love about you, babe. You don't wait for permission. You didn't want to wait to grow up to become a tycoon."

"See?" I say, beaming. "You get it."

"But look, if you really want to keep working on your little tech thing in college, then think of Garnet as your incubator. There's going to be lots of opportunities for you to grow your brand here."

Huh. I hadn't thought about it that way. Although I'm not in love with his phrasing—*my little tech thing?*—I realize he's right.

"You make a good point there, Mr. Kincaid." I stand on my tiptoes and kiss his clean-shaven cheek before ambling forward again.

Another reason Pres and I are well-suited to each other: We're both business-minded people. Neither of us is enchanted by an artist's idealism, or distracted by romantic notions of backpacking across Europe or hiking Machu Picchu. We're products of our upbringing, and our cold blood runs blue. Two formidable, future heads of empires.

There's a lot to be said for compatibility.

After we explore the art building and the small museum where student work is displayed, wander among the sculptures in the botanical gardens, and follow the footpath through the greenhouse and vegetable garden, Preston brings me around to his car.

"Come on, there's something else I want to show you." He opens the door for me, and I slide onto the sleek, leather passenger seat. He puts the top down on the silver Porsche convertible before we drive off.

It's a short ride around the back of the campus, past the sports complex and up a hill, before we eventually reach a tall, circular building with a dome. The astronomy department's telescope. Preston leads me to the side of the building, to a door that's been propped open with a small wooden block.

"Are we supposed to be here?" I ask as we creep inside a narrow hallway that wraps around the circumference of the building.

"I know a guy." Then Preston puts his index finger to his lips. "But no, not really."

We follow the hallway to a metal staircase. On the second floor, we enter a room with computers along the wall and a massive telescope in the center, pointed to the sky through a wide slit in the roof.

"Oh, cool," I say, walking toward the telescope.

Preston stops me. "That's not what we came to see."

Instead, he leads me to a door, then a ladder going up to the roof. We emerge onto a platform. From here, we can see the entire campus. Rolling green hills and white-topped buildings. Practically the whole town, all the way to the blue horizon of Avalon Bay. It's spectacular.

"This is incredible," I say, smiling at his thoughtfulness and ingenuity.

"It's not a VIP tour without a bird's-eye view." Preston stands behind me and wraps his arms around my waist. He kisses the side of my head as we appreciate the landscape together. "I'm really glad you're here," he says softly.

"Me too."

Admittedly, things were slightly strained between us the last couple of years, while he was at college and I was stuck in high school. Doing the long-distance thing, even when we could see each other on weekends, was stressful. It took a lot of the fun out of our relationship. Today, though, I'm remembering how it was when we first started dating. How enamored of him I'd been, feeling like I'd won a prize, being chosen by an upperclassman.

Still, as Pres holds me against him and nuzzles my neck, a thought nudges its way into the back of my mind.

A very traitorous thought.

Of Cooper's chiseled jaw and fathomless eyes. The way my pulse sped when he sat beside me and flashed that arrogant smile. I don't get palpations when Preston walks into a room. My skin doesn't tingle when he touches me. My thighs don't clench, and my mouth doesn't run dry.

Then again, those responses can be overrated. Too many hormones running rampant can cloud your judgment. I mean, look at the statistics—all those people who end up in a dysfunctional relationship because they base it on sex, not compatibility. Pres and I are right for each other. We get along well. We're on the same trajectory. Our parents already approve, and it keeps everyone happy. I could play the field with a dozen Coopers and get my heart broken by every one. Why do that to myself?

There's a lot to be said for knowing a good thing when you've got it.

"Thank you," I tell Pres, turning in his arms to kiss him. "Today was perfect."

But later that night, as I'm half watching Netflix in my room while doing my English Lit reading, a flutter of excitement races through me when Cooper's name pops up on my phone. Then I remind myself to calm the fuck down.

Cooper: *Want to grab dinner?*
Me: *I already ate.*
Cooper: *Me too.*
Me: *Then why'd you ask?*
Cooper: *To see what you'd say.*
Me: *So sneaky.*
Cooper: *What are you doing?*
Me: *Netflix and homework.*
Cooper: *Is that code for something?*
Me: *Busted.*
Cooper: *I can't even imagine what rich people porn is like.*

Those words on the screen make me squeeze my legs together and put terrible ideas in my head. Which I promptly shove in a box labeled *don't you dare*.

Me: *It's mostly eating scones off the pages of* The Wall Street Journal.
Cooper: *You people are fucked up.*

A cackle bursts out of me, and I slap my hand over my mouth before Bonnie hears me and comes rushing in to see what's so funny. She's a doll, that one, but she has no concept of boundaries.

Me: *What are you doing?*
Cooper: *Flirting with some chick I just met.*

I walked right into that one.

Me: *Still have a boyfriend.*
Cooper: *For now.*
Me: *Goodnight, townie.*
Cooper: *Night, princess.*

I know he's just pushing my buttons. Cooper's thing, I'm learning, is trying to get a rise out of me. I can't say I hate it, exactly. It's refreshing to have a friend who gets that part of my personality. And, okay, it's technically flirting, which is technically frowned upon, but it's all in good fun.

No matter how many hormonal reactions Cooper elicits in me, I'm not about to leave Pres for the first tattooed bad boy I meet at college.

CHAPTER EIGHT

MACKENZIE

The next afternoon, I decide to explore the town on my own since my schedule is free. Preston inspired me to try embracing my time at Garnet rather than looking at it like a prison sentence. With that thought in mind, I throw on a flowery summer dress and call a cab.

Avalon Bay is a paradoxical coastal town full of rugged fishermen and multimillionaires. On one side of Main Street are high-end boutiques selling handmade soaps. On the other, pawnshops and tattoo parlors. The boardwalk is quiet on a weekday afternoon. Most of the bars are sparsely populated with sweaty locals propped up on stools watching ESPN with their pals.

I walk farther than the last time I was here and reach a section still devastated by hurricane damage from a couple years ago. Several buildings are under construction. Nearby, a crew works on restoring a restaurant where scaffolding is erected around its exterior. Other businesses have been cordoned off with caution tape and plywood. It's apparent they haven't been touched since the storm tore off their roofs and flooded the interiors.

I stop when I come to a quaint late-Victorian-style hotel. It's white with green trim, and the entire back side of the building had been gutted by storm surge. The hotel's walls were ripped out, its innards exposed. Old furniture and wrinkled carpets still wait for the guests that aren't coming. The weathered sign out front reads *The Beacon Hotel* in gold script font and is broken in two places.

I wonder what happened to the owners that they never rebuilt. And how has no one swooped in to claim the property and restore it to its former glory? This is a prime location.

My phone buzzes a few times with incoming emails, so I stop at an ice cream shop and buy a vanilla cone. Then I settle on the bench out front, scrolling through my inbox one-handed.

The first email is an update from one of my site moderators. She informs me she had to block several users who'd been trolling every post on *GirlfriendFails*, leaving racist and sexist comments. I open the attached screenshots. My jaw drops at the level of vitriol I read in those comments.

I shoot off a quick email: *Good call blocking them.*

The next one is an SOS from the guy I hired to oversee *BoyfriendFails*. Apparently, a user is threatening legal action, claiming one of the posts on the site is libelous. I click on the post in question. The writer of it went out with a guy she calls "Ted," who didn't disclose he had a micropenis and blindsided her during their first intimate encounter.

I return to my email to skim the letter my admin, Alan, received from some DC law firm with a scary letterhead. I guess the user— butterflykisses44—picked an alias too close to her boyfriend's real name. Ted is actually Tad, who is suitably outraged, humiliated, and demanding *BoyfriendFails* not only take down the post, but pay him damages because of the emotional distress it's caused him.

Since the site is a platform and not a publisher, we can't be sued for the content of our users, but I tell Alan to forward the letter to my own lawyer just in case. Then I shut off my phone and slurp down the rest of my melting ice cream. Just another day in the life of Mackenzie Cabot, CEO.

If I'm being honest with myself, though, lately I've been itching for . . . something *more*. I love my apps, but nowadays there's nothing for me to do but say yes or no. Sign here, initial there. Read this email, approve this ad. The real excitement came at the beginning, when I was sitting with my friends and brainstorming features for the apps. Meeting with the developer and programmer and bringing my ideas to life. Creating the marketing campaign to attract users. The launch.

It was challenging and exciting. It was the most fun I'd ever had. *That's* the part I truly enjoyed, I realize now. The creation, not the maintenance. Not that I hate the sites and want to sell them. I don't. They're still mine. Part of my budding empire. But maybe it's time to brainstorm some new business ideas.

As the sun dips low in the sky, I walk onto the beach and sit on the sand, listening to the waves and watching the seagulls glide against the wind. Behind me, a construction crew is winding down for the day. The noise of drills and saws has ceased.

Mostly zoned out, I don't notice someone approaching me until he plops down beside me.

"What's up, princess?"

I jolt in surprise, staring at Cooper, who's in the process of taking off his shirt and work gloves.

He's as potent as the night at the bonfire, and I'm pinned by the sight of him. His hair and jeans are covered in sawdust and dirt. His muscular chest and abs are shiny with sweat. This is the first time I've seen so much of his ink, which runs up both arms and stretches toward his chest. I lick my lips then inwardly wince at myself. At the person I become when he's around. Lustful. Irrational. I take those thoughts and tamp them way down in a box labeled *stay the hell out*.

"Are you stalking me now?" I demand.

"You stroll by my jobsite in"—he gestures, looking me up and down—"some ridiculous ruffle dress thing and all this leg, like, 'Oh, don't mind me, boys, I *hate* attention.'"

"That is so exactly how I sound," I reply, rolling my eyes. "And what's wrong with my dress?" I smooth my hands over the hem of the floral print sundress.

"It's got flowers on it. You're not a flower person, Mac."

"Don't call me Mac."

"Why not?"

"Because it's a nickname reserved for friends."

"We are friends. Best friends." He flashes a crooked smile. "I see you didn't deny the not being a flower person part."

He's right. I'm not usually into girly prints and ruffly sundresses. My style runs toward white tees and worn jeans, or a tank and cutoff shorts when it's hot out. But every now and then, I like feeling cute. Sue me. Anyway, he's not allowed to be so presumptuous about my taste in clothing, so I argue just because.

"I happen to love flowers. Especially on clothes. The flashier, the better."

Cooper rolls his eyes as if he knows I'm lying through my teeth. "You know, you don't have to work this hard." He crosses his arms, pulling his knees close to his chest. "I'm pretty easy."

"I'm sorry, what? Who's working too hard? You've been blowing up my phone talking about scone porn."

"You're kinky," he says, shrugging. "I get it. It's not my thing, but whatever gets you off."

Ha. If he only knew. Preston and I have a perfectly fine sex life, but I'm not even sure we have enough spice to be vanilla. In the beginning, I thought maybe sex was supposed to be that way: functional, quick, a tad boring. I was sixteen when I lost my virginity to Pres, and more than a little naïve about that stuff. It was only when I spoke to girlfriends about my lackluster encounters that I realized sex is supposed to be—imagine this—*fun*.

When I'd very awkwardly broached the subject with Pres, he'd confessed that he hadn't wanted to scare me off by being "too passionate." I told him to feel free to step up his game, and our bedroom activities did get more fun after that. But if I'm being completely honest, it's been four years now and that passion he'd mentioned still hasn't made an appearance.

"I shudder to think what's rattling around in your spank bank," I say.

"If you're trying to get me in bed, you can just ask." Cooper nudges my arm with his elbow. He has this unflappable confidence about him. Arrogant yet charming. Completely self-assured but not overbearing. It's almost a shame he's wasting his natural talents on construction. He'd make a hell of a CEO if he had a mind for business.

"This half-assed reverse psychology routine isn't going to work on me," I inform him. Because I didn't make my first million by being easily manipulated. "I'm not going to be goaded into accidentally winding up in bed with some townie stranger because he dared me to."

Still, his playful smirk and roguish eyes are not lost on me. I'm not immune to broad shoulders and rock-hard abs. Moreover, he's a bit of a conundrum. Everything I learn about him makes me wonder if what he portrays—the tattoos, the attitude—is all clever camouflage. Hiding what, though? My brain loves puzzles.

"I wouldn't be caught dead sleeping around with some Garnet clone. I do have an image to protect."

"Right, of course. Wouldn't want anyone confusing you for a man of taste."

He bites back a smile, and in that fleeting look, I see all sorts of bad intentions. I see blurry nights and wild regrets. Heavy breathing. It's enough to make my pulse spike and my toes go numb.

This guy is dangerous.

"Coop!" someone calls from the jobsite. "You coming to the bar or what?"

He glances over his shoulder. "Go on without me."

Knowing laughter tickles our backs. I'm glad Cooper's co-workers can't see my face because I'm fairly certain I'm blushing.

"Why'd you have to do that?" I grumble.

"Do what? Tell them I'm not going to the bar?"

"Yeah. Now they're going to think you stayed behind to bang me on the beach or something."

He gives a deep chuckle. "I guarantee they weren't thinking that. But now *I* am. Would you like to bang here, or should we go under the pier?"

"Go to the bar with your little friends, *Coop*. You'll have a better shot of getting laid there than here."

"Nah. I'm good where I am." He lifts one hand and rakes it through his dark hair, and I can't help but stare at his flexing biceps.

"So you guys are fixing up that restaurant?" I force myself to stop gawking at his very sexy muscles. "It looks like a huge job."

"It is. And once we're done this one, we have about, oh, half a dozen more buildings to renovate." He waves that sculpted arm toward the boardwalk, highlighting the destruction left by the hurricane.

"Do you like working in construction?"

He nods slowly. "I do, yeah. Evan and I work for our uncle's company, so we don't have to deal with some jackass boss who tries to rip us off or does shoddy work to cut costs. Levi is a good man, fair. And I've always been good with my hands."

I gulp. There's no overt innuendo in his tone, but I'll be damned if my gaze doesn't shift to his hands. They're strong, big, with long fingers and callused palms. No dirt under his nails, even after a day of manual labor.

"What about you, princess?" He tips his head, curious.

"What about me?"

"This is the second time I've walked up to you and seen that look on your face."

"What look?" Apparently, I just repeat everything he says now. But the intensity in his eyes has triggered a rush of anxiety.

"The look that says you want more."

"I want more . . . And what more do I want?"

He continues to study me. "I don't know. Just *more*. It's like . . . a mixture of boredom, dissatisfaction, frustration, and yearning."

"That's a lot of shit packed into one look," I joke, but my heart is beating faster now, because he's pretty much summed it up. That's been my state of mind since I got to college. No, even longer—dare I say, my entire life.

"Am I wrong?" he asks roughly.

Our gazes lock. The urge to confide in him is so strong I have to bite the tip of my tongue to stop myself.

Suddenly, amidst the crashing waves and screeching seagulls, I hear a faint yelping.

"Did you hear that?" I look around for the source of the pained, desperate noise.

Cooper chuckles. "Stop trying to distract me."

"I'm not. Seriously, don't you hear it?"

"Hear what? I don't—"

"Shhh!" I order.

I listen, straining to discern another clue. It's getting darker, with the lights from the boardwalk overtaking the dwindling dusk. Another yelp rings out, this one louder.

I jump to my feet.

"It's nothing," Cooper says, but I ignore him and follow the sound toward the pier. He jogs after me, his voice frazzled as he assures me I'm imagining things.

"I'm not imagining it," I insist.

And then I see it, the source of the yelps. Beyond the pier, on the jetty, I make out a shape stranded on the rocks as the tide comes in.

Heart pounding, I whirl around to face Cooper. "It's a dog!"

CHAPTER NINE

COOPER

Before I can blink, Mackenzie tears her dress off.

As in, this chick is actually getting naked.

No, not naked, I realize when she doesn't remove her bra and underwear. My disappointment over the strip show ending prematurely is dimmed by the fact that she looks pretty goddamn good in a bra and underwear.

But as she runs into the rising tide and is quickly swallowed up to her neck, the rational part of my brain kicks in.

"Mac!" I shout after her. "Get back here, damn it!"

She's already swimming away.

Awesome. She's gonna drown trying to get that mangy stray back to shore.

Grumbling curses under my breath, I strip out of my jeans and shoes and chase after Mackenzie, who has reached the rocks and is now climbing up to the dog. I swim hard against the current, as the waves try to throw me against the pier's pylons or slam me into the rocks. Finally, I grab on to one of the boulders and haul myself out of the water.

"You're crazy, you know that?" I growl.

The shivering dog sits anxiously by Mac, who's attempting to comfort it. "We have to help her," she tells me.

Shit. This filthy, pathetic thing is just a puppy, but there's no way

Mackenzie is swimming with it back to shore. I had a hard time myself fighting off the current, and I probably weigh twice as much as Mac.

"Give her to me," I say with a sigh. When I reach for the dog, she hides behind Mac and almost falls in the water trying to back away from me. "Come on, damn it. It's me or nothing."

"It's okay, little one, he's not as scary as he looks," Mac coos to the mutt. Meanwhile I stand there glaring at them both.

The dog continues to hesitate, so finally Mac picks her up and deposits the unhappy wet bundle into my waiting hands. Almost instantly, the frightened animal is clawing and kicking to get away. This is going to be a goddamn nightmare.

Mackenzie pets the dog's soaked fur in a futile attempt to calm her. "You sure about this?" she asks me. "I can try—"

No chance. The waves would knock the dog right out of her grip and the damn thing would drown while I pulled Mac to shore. Not happening.

"Go," I order. "I'm right behind you."

With a nod, she dives and makes for the shore.

Standing on the rocks, I have a little pep talk with the pup. "I'm trying to help you, okay? Do not bite my face off. Let's get along for the next few minutes. Deal?"

The animal whines and whimpers, which I suppose is the best I'm getting.

As gently as I can, I climb down into the water and hold the dog like a football above the waves as I swim with one arm. The whole time, the damn thing is freaking out thinking I'm trying to kill her or something. She barks and scratches. Tries a few times to wriggle free. With every move she makes, a little more flesh is gouged from my body. As soon as we reach the sand, I let the dog go and it runs straight for Mac, all but diving into her arms. *You're welcome, traitor.*

"You okay?" Mac calls out.

"Yeah, fine."

Both of us are breathing heavy after fighting the waves. It's fully dark now, the only light coming from the boardwalk. Mackenzie isn't much more than a hazy shape in front of me.

My temper gets the best of me, spilling over as I stalk up to her. "What the *hell* was that?"

She plants one hand on her bare hip. Her other hand protectively holds the dog. "Seriously?" she exclaims. "You're mad that I wanted to save a helpless animal? She could have died!"

"*You* could have died! You feel that current, sweetheart? That shit could've sucked you right out to sea. At least once a year someone drowns down here because they're a reckless dumbass."

"I'm not your *sweetheart*," she grumbles. "And did you really just call me a dumbass?"

"Act like a dumbass, get called a dumbass." I angrily shake water out of my hair. Doesn't escape me that the dog is currently doing the same. We're both feral animals, I suppose.

Mackenzie tightens her hold on her new pet. "I will *not* apologize for having a heart. I can't believe you were prepared to let this poor puppy die. Oh my God. I'm friends with a puppy killer."

My jaw falls open.

Christ, this chick is turning into a handful. I've never worked this hard to win over a girl. And yet, despite being mauled half to death for her—and being accused of attempted dog murder—my anger dissolves into a wave of laughter. I double over, dripping sea-water onto the sand as I laugh my ass off.

"Why are you laughing?" she demands.

"You called me a puppy killer," I manage to croak between laughs. "You're insane."

After a second, she breaks out in giggles. The dog's gaze shifts uncertainly between us as we stand there laughing like a pair of idiots, soaking wet and half naked.

"Fine," she relents when her giggling fit finally subsides. "I may have been out of line. I know you were just worried for my safety. And thank you for swimming out there to help. I appreciate it."

"You're welcome." I hike up the waistband of my jeans. My wet boxers are plastered to my crotch, making it hard to zip up the jeans. "Come on, let's get our stuff and go back to my place. I need to get changed. You can dry off there and I can give you a ride home."

She doesn't say anything, staring at me.

"Yes," I sigh, "bring the dog."

The house is dark when we arrive. Neither Evan's motorcycle nor Jeep are in the drive, and the front door's locked when Mac and I step onto the wraparound porch. Thankfully, the place isn't a mess inside. With our friends frequently using our house as a party pad and way station between bars, it tends to get tossed around a lot. Evan and I, for our lack of other social graces, try to keep our home clean, though. We're not complete animals.

"You can use my shower," I tell Mac, pointing toward my ground-floor bedroom after I turn on lights and get myself a beer from the fridge. I deserve a drink after my heroic dog-saving efforts. "I'll find some clothes you can borrow."

"Thanks." She carries the dog with her, all cuddled and sleepy in her arms. I told her in the truck that if she wants to leave it here, I'll take it to the shelter in the morning. Though I'm starting to wonder if I'll be able to pry it away from her.

When Mac's in my en suite bathroom, I dig out a clean T-shirt and a pair of jeans Heidi left here ages ago. Or maybe they're Steph's. The girls are always leaving their stuff lying around after a party or a day at the beach, and I've stopped trying to return them.

I leave the clothes in a neat pile on the bed, then strip out of my wet clothes and throw on a T-shirt and a pair of sweatpants.

The steam rolling out from under the bathroom door is unbelievably tempting. I wonder how Mac would react if I stepped into the shower stall, eased up behind her, and reached both hands around to cup her tits.

A groan lodges in my throat. She'd probably saw my balls off with her fingernails, but it might be worth it, just to get to touch her.

"Hello, hello," my brother calls from the front door.

"In here," I answer as I head back to the kitchen.

Evan drops his keys on the splintered wood island. He grabs a beer and stands against the fridge. "What's that smell?"

"Mackenzie and I rescued a stray puppy from the jetty." Poor thing did kind of stink. Guess I do too now. Awesome.

"She's here?" A wicked grin spreads across his face as he looks around.

"Shower."

"Well, that was easy. I'm almost disappointed I didn't get more time to enjoy it."

"Not what you're thinking," I grunt out. "The dog was stuck out on the rocks and we had to get in the water to save it. Told Mackenzie she could come here to clean up, and then I'd take her home."

"Take her home? Dude. This is your chance. Close the deal." He shakes his head impatiently. "You helped her rescue a puppy, for chrissake. She is primed."

"Don't be a dick." Something about the way he says that strikes a nerve with me. This scheme isn't exactly ethical, but we don't have to be sleazy about it.

"What?" Evan can't pretend to hide his glee at how well this plan is working. "I'm just saying."

"Well . . ." I take a swig of my beer. "Keep it to yourself."

"Hey," comes Mac's hesitant voice.

She walks in, and the sight of her—in my shirt, dark wet hair combed back—brings all sorts of sinful thoughts to my head. She didn't put on the jeans, so her legs are bare and tanned and endlessly long.

Fuck.

I want them wrapped around my waist.

"Evan," she greets my brother, nodding at him as if she knows, somehow, he is up to no good. Unsurprisingly, she's still carrying the sleeping puppy.

"Welp." Evan gives her a parting smile as he grabs his beer and pushes off from the fridge. "I'm beat. You kids have fun."

My brother has no appreciation for subtlety.

"Was it something I said?" she asks dryly.

"Nah. He thinks we're gonna hook up." When I lift my arm to run a hand through my damp hair, her eyes grow wide with alarm. My brow furrows. "What?"

"Cooper. You're hurt."

I look down, almost forgetting that her precious little pup damn near filleted me alive not an hour ago. Both my arms are covered in red scratches, and there's a particularly nasty-looking cut on my collarbone.

"Eh. I'm fine," I assure her. I'm no stranger to cuts and scrapes, and these ones are definitely not the worst I've experienced.

"No, you're not. We need to clean those."

With that, she marches me to the bathroom and, despite my protestations, forces my ass down on the closed lid of the toilet. The puppy is promptly deposited in my claw-foot bathtub, where she curls up and sleeps while Mackenzie rifles through my cabinets for the first aid kit.

"I can do this myself," I tell her as she sets out a bottle of alcohol and cotton swabs.

"Are you going to be difficult?" She eyes me with a raised brow. The earnest conviction on her face is cute, in a stubborn *shut up and take your medicine* sort of way.

"Fine."

"Good. Now take off your shirt."

A grin tugs on my lips. "This was your plan all along? To get me naked?"

"Yes, Cooper. I broke into an animal shelter, stole a puppy, placed it in a perilous situation, swam out to rescue it myself—so as to not raise your suspicions that it was I, in fact, who trapped the dog on the jetty—then telepathically ordered the dog to scratch you up. All so I could see your perfect pecs." She finishes with a snort.

"Extreme actions," I agree. "But I get it. My pecs *are* perfect. They're transcendent."

"So's your ego."

I make a slow, deliberate show of removing my shirt. Despite her mocking, my bare chest elicits a response. Her breath hitches, and then she averts her gaze, pretending to focus on opening the rubbing alcohol.

I hide a smile and sit back as she begins to clean the wounds on my arm.

"Is it just the two of you here?" she asks curiously.

"Yeah. Evan and I grew up in this house. My great-grandparents built it after they got married. Grandparents lived here after them and so on."

"It's beautiful."

It was. Now it's falling apart. Roof needs replacing. Foundation is cracking from beach erosion. The siding has seen one too many storms, and the floors are worn and warped. Nothing I couldn't fix if only I had the time and money, but isn't that always the story? Whole damn town full of *if only*s. And just like that, I remember why I'm sitting here letting some clone's girlfriend run her hands all over my bare chest.

"There," she says, touching my arm. "All better."

"Thanks." My voice sounds a bit gravelly.

"No problem." Hers sounds slightly hoarse.

I find myself momentarily caught in her bright green eyes. Taunted by the flashes of her almost-naked body as the hem of my shirt rises on her thighs. Her warm palm against my skin. The thrumming in her neck that tells me she's not indifferent to me either.

I could do it. Take her by the hips, coax her into straddling me. Shove my hand through her hair and pull her mouth to mine in a blistering kiss. I'm not supposed to sleep with her unless she initiates, but if the chemistry sizzling between us is any indication, I suspect she won't stop with a kiss. It'll be a kiss that leads to the bed that leads to getting balls deep inside her. She'll dump Kincaid faster than you can say *game over*. I win. Mission accomplished.

But where's the fun in that?

"Now," I say, "about your friend."

Mackenzie blinks, as if snapping out of the same lust stupor I'd fallen into.

We draw a warm bubble bath for the puppy and put her in. She's a completely different animal all of a sudden. The drowned rat becomes a small golden retriever, splashing around and playing with a bottle of shampoo that falls into the tub. Poor thing is all skin and bones, lost or abandoned by its mother, and she didn't have a collar when we found her. The shelter will have to figure out if she's chipped or not.

After we scrub the dog clean and dry her off, I set out a bowl of water in the kitchen and feed her some cut up turkey franks. Not ideal, but it's the best we have under the circumstances. While the pup eats, I leave the door open and step out to the back deck. The temperature's cooled off, and the ocean breeze is blowing in off the water. Out on the horizon, a tiny blip of a boat's bow lights flickers as it travels.

"You know . . ." Mac comes beside me.

I'm acutely aware of her, every nerve attuned in her direction. This chick barely glances at me and I'm half hard. It's very annoying.

"I shouldn't be here," she finishes.

"And why's that?"

"I think you know why." Her voice is soft, measured. She's testing me as much as herself.

"You don't seem like the kind of girl who does anything she doesn't want to." I turn to meet her eyes. In my limited experience, Mackenzie is stubborn. Not the type to get pushed around. I'm under no illusion that she's here because I'm so damn clever.

"You'd be surprised," she says ruefully.

"Tell me."

She appraises me. Doubtful. Questioning how sincere my interest is.

I raise a brow. "We're friends, aren't we?"

"I'd like to think so," she says, wary.

"Then talk to me. Let me get to know you."

She continues to study me. Christ. When she stares into me like this, I feel her picking me apart, working things out. I've never felt so exposed in front of another person before. For some reason, it doesn't bother me as much as it probably should.

"I thought freedom was being self-sufficient," she finally confesses. "I'm finding out that isn't exactly true. I know this probably sounds stupid coming from me, but I feel trapped. By expectations and promises. Trying to make everyone else happy. I wish I could be selfish for once. Do what I want, when I want, how I want."

"So why don't you?"

"It's not that easy."

"Sure it is." Rich people are always going on about how money is such a burden. That's only because they don't know how to use it. They get so caught up in their bullshit, they forget they don't actually need their dumb friends and stupid country clubs. "Forget 'em.

Someone's making you miserable? Something is holding you back? Forget 'em and move on."

Her teeth dig into her bottom lip. "I can't."

"Then you don't want it bad enough."

"That's not fair."

"Of course not. What's ever been fair? People spend their whole lives complaining about things they're unwilling to change. At a certain point, either pluck up the courage or shut up."

Laughter sputters out of her. "Are you telling me to shut up?"

"No, I'm telling you there are plenty of ways that life and circumstances beyond our control conspire to keep us down. The least we can do is get out of our own way."

"What about you?" She turns on me, pointing the question back in my face. "What do you want right now that you can't have?"

"To kiss you."

She narrows her eyes.

I should regret saying that, but I don't. I mean, what's stopping me from kissing her, from telling her I want to? Gotta pull the trigger on this thing at some point, right? I've clearly got her on the hook. If I don't commit to this plan now, why am I wasting my time?

So I watch her, trying to discern her reaction through the stone-cold façade of indifference. This chick is implacable. But for a split second, I glimpse the flicker of heat in her gaze as she considers it. Gaming it out. One action begetting another, a cascade effect of consequences.

She licks her lips.

I lean closer. Just a little. Tempting myself. The need to touch her is almost unbearable.

"But then I'd screw up a perfectly good friendship," I say, because I've lost all control of my goddamn mouth. "So I behave myself. It's still a choice."

What the hell am I doing? I don't know what spooked me, but

suddenly I'm giving her an out when I'm supposed to be reeling her *in*.

Mac turns back toward the water, resting her arms on the railing. "I admire your honesty."

Frustration rises inside me as I look at her profile from the corner of my eye. This woman is gorgeous, she's wearing my shirt and nothing else, and instead of pulling her into my arms and kissing her senseless, I just friend-zoned myself.

For the first time since we hatched this plan, I'm starting to wonder if I'm in over my head.

CHAPTER TEN

MACKENZIE

I wake up in the morning to a text from Cooper. Only I guess Evan must have taken the photo, because it shows Cooper asleep in bed with the puppy snuggled on his chest, her face buried under his chin. It's fucking adorable. Last night, I thought those two were doomed, but it seems they worked out their differences.

I hope he and Evan decide to keep her. I know the right thing to do is to take the dog to the shelter—I certainly can't keep her—but my heart is breaking a little at the thought of never seeing her again.

I text a reply to Cooper, and by the time I get out of my second class for the day, I still haven't received a response. He's probably working. I tell myself it's just concern for the dog that causes the pang of disappointment. But who am I kidding? I can't ignore what happened on his deck last night. The sexual tension nearly spilling over, his rough admission that he wants to kiss me. If he hadn't pulled back I might have caved in a moment of blind weakness.

I have underestimated Cooper's allure. That's my fault—I know better than to be seduced by handsome, half-naked guys who race in to help rescue animals in distress. I just have to be more cautious going forward and keep reminding myself that we're friends. That's it. No use getting it twisted.

When my phone buzzes, I eagerly yank it out of my pocket, only to find a message from Preston. Not Cooper.

I banish the second wave of disappointment to the very back of my mind and use my thumbprint to open my lock screen.

Preston: *Waiting for you in the parking lot.*

Right. We're having lunch off campus today. I'm glad he reminded me, because I was about five minutes away from scarfing down a chicken fiesta wrap from the sandwich shop near the business school.

I slide into Preston's convertible, and we talk about our classes as he drives us to Avalon Bay. Pres finds some street parking near the boardwalk. My pulse quickens, and I force myself not to look in the direction of the restaurant that Cooper and his uncle are restoring.

I last about 3.5 seconds before I cave. But the jobsite is empty. I guess they're on their lunch break. Or maybe the crew is on another job today.

Once again, I pretend I'm not disappointed.

"You didn't tell me what you ended up doing yesterday." Pres holds my hand as we head toward the sports bar, where we're meeting some of his friends. "Did you come into town or no?"

"Oh, yeah, I did. I explored the boardwalk and walked down the pier, then watched the sunset on the beach. It was really nice."

I make an on-the-spot executive decision to omit the entire puppy encounter. Not that Pres is the jealous type, but I don't want it to turn into a whole discussion, especially when I've only just arrived at Garnet and we're doing so well. There'll be an opportunity to tell him about my friendship with Cooper. At some point. When the time's right.

"How did your poker game go? You didn't text me either, now that I think about it." But I'm also not the jealous type. Having done the whole long-distance thing, Pres and I are used to the occasional forgotten text or unanswered call. If we got worked up every time one of us didn't respond until morning, we'd have broken up a long time ago. That's trust.

"How was the poker game?" echoes Benji Stanton, who overhears my question as Pres and I approach the group. He snickers loudly. "You better watch out for your man. This kid is shit at cards and doesn't know when to quit."

"So . . . not good?" I ask, shooting a teasing smile at Pres.

"Not good at all," Benji confirms. He's a business major like Pres. They met when they shared a few classes last year.

Benji's parents own property in Hilton Head, and his father runs a hedge fund. All of Preston's friends hail from similar backgrounds. As in disgustingly rich. Finance, real estate, politics—their parents are all members of the billionaires' club. So far, everyone's been friendly and welcoming to me. I was nervous at first that they might look at me sideways because I'm a freshman, but I only get positive vibes from Preston's Garnet friends.

"Don't listen to him, babe." Pres kisses the top of my head. "I'm playing the long game."

A few minutes later, we're climbing up the stairs. Sharkey's Sports Bar has two floors, the upper one consisting of tables overlooking the ocean, the lower level offering game tables, a plethora of TVs, and the bar. As a server seats our group at a long high-top near the railing, the guys continue to rag on Preston for being terrible at cards.

"Lock up your good jewelry, Mac," Seb Marlow advises me. He's from Florida, where his family is a major defense contractor for the government. It's all very serious and secret. *I'd have to kill you*, and all that. Or that's the line he uses at parties, at least. "He was this close to throwing down his Rolex to buy back into the game."

Stifling a laugh, I question Pres. "Please tell me he's joking."

He shrugs, because the money means nothing to him, and he's got more watches than he knows what to do with. "How about you try me at pool?" he scoffs at his friends. "That's a real gentleman's game."

Benji looks at Seb and smirks. "Double or nothing?"

Never one to back down from a challenge, Preston is all too eager. "You're on."

The guys push back from the table as Preston gives me a parting kiss on the cheek.

"One game," he says. "Back in a flash."

"Don't lose your car," I warn. "I need a ride back to campus."

"Don't worry," Benji calls over his shoulder. "I got you."

Pres just rolls his eyes before sauntering after his buddies. Another thing I appreciate about him is that he's a good sport. I've never seen him get bent out of shape over a stupid game, even when his wallet is a little light at the end of the night. Granted, it's easy to get over losing when there's a seemingly endless supply of someone else's money to play with.

"Now that the boys are gone . . ." Melissa, Benji's girlfriend, pushes the collection of water glasses aside to lean in toward me and Seb's girlfriend Chrissy.

I don't know anything about Melissa other than she sails, and I know even less about Chrissy. I wish I had more in common with these girls other than the size of our parents' bank accounts.

Truth be told, I don't have too many female friends. And these past few weeks have confirmed that I still suck at building connections with my female peers. I love Bonnie to bits, but she feels more like a younger sister than a friend. I had girlfriends in high school, but nobody I'd consider a ride-or-die type of friend. The only one who comes closest to being my "best friend" is my old camp friend Sara, who I raised hell with every summer until I turned eighteen. We still text periodically, but she lives in Oregon and it's been a couple years since I've seen her.

My social group now consists of my roommate, my boyfriend, and my boyfriend's friends, who waste no time bending their heads together to gossip.

"So what did you find out about that Snapchat girl?" Melissa demands.

Chrissy takes a deep breath like she's about to dive to the bottom of a pool for a pair of Jimmy Choos. "It was some sophomore chick who's at Garnet on scholarship. I found her roommate's best friend on Instagram and DMed her. She said her friend told her that her roommate said they met at a boat party and made out."

"So they only kissed?" Melissa asks, as though she's disappointed in the answer.

Chrissy shrugs. "Supposedly someone at the boat party walked in on someone getting a BJ. Maybe it was Seb, maybe not. Doesn't really matter."

If I'd known my mother in college, I imagine she'd have been a lot like Chrissy. Prim, put together, and unflappable. Not a hair or eyelash out of place. So the fact that she would entertain something as messy as cheating strikes me as antithetical.

"Wait," I interject, "your boyfriend is cheating on you, and you don't care?"

The girls both stare at me as though I haven't been paying attention.

"Two former presidents of the United States and the crown prince of Saudi Arabia were at his father's birthday party in the Seychelles last year," Chrissy says flatly. "You don't break up with guys like Sebastian over something as trifling as infidelity. He's the man you marry."

I frown at her. "You'd marry someone you know is cheating on you?"

She doesn't answer, just looks at me, blinking. Is an expectation of monogamy so banal and old-fashioned? I thought I was fairly open-minded, but apparently my beliefs about love and romance are scandalous.

"It's hardly even considered cheating," Melissa scoffs, waving a dismissive hand. "Seb hooked up with a scholarship chick? Who cares. Now, if it was a wifey, that's a whole other story. A real reason to worry."

"A wifey?" I echo.

Chrissy gives me a condescending look. "For men like Seb and Benji and Preston, there are two kinds of women. A wifey and a Marilyn. The ones you marry, and the ones you screw."

Can't you screw the one you marry? Or marry the one you screw? I swallow the questions. Because what's the point?

"Don't worry," Melissa says. She reaches across the table to put her hand on mine, in what she must think is a comforting gesture. "You're definitely wifey material. Preston knows that. All you need to worry about is locking that down and getting the ring. Everything else is . . ." She glances at Chrissy for the word. "Extracurricular."

That is the most depressing relationship advice I've ever heard. These women have their own family money and small empires—they don't need strategic marital alliances. So why do they sell themselves into loveless arrangements?

When I marry Preston one day, it won't be for money or family connections. Our vows won't include a caveat that cheating is tolerated as long as the stock price is up.

"I wouldn't want to live that way," I tell them. "If a relationship isn't built on love and mutual respect, what's the point?"

Melissa regards me with a patronizing tilt to her head and a faintly pouting lip. "Oh, sweetie, everyone thinks that way at first. But eventually, we have to start being more realistic."

Chrissy says nothing, but her cold, impassive expression strikes something inside me. It's fleeting and undefined, but it unsettles my stomach.

All I know is, I don't ever want to reach the point where I view infidelity as "extracurricular."

Later, when Preston's driving me back to Tally Hall, I broach the subject. Since Melissa and Chrissy didn't swear me to secrecy, I don't feel bad asking, "Did you know that Melissa and Chrissy think Seb's cheating on Chrissy?"

He doesn't flinch, changing gears as he takes us down the winding roads around the edge of campus. "I had a feeling."

I fight a frown. "Is it true?"

"I haven't asked," he says. Then, after a few seconds, "I wouldn't be surprised."

Whether Preston was at that boat party or knows of the particular incident is irrelevant. He wouldn't throw his friend under the bus if he didn't believe it was possible. Which tells me everything I need to know.

"She isn't even mad about it." I shake my head in disbelief. "Either of them, actually. Cost of doing business, as far as they're concerned."

"I figured." Pres pulls up to the parking lot outside my dorm. He takes off his sunglasses and looks me in the eyes. "There've been whispers for a few weeks. Seb and Chrissy have chosen to ignore it, best that I can tell. Honestly, it's not unusual."

"Cheating isn't unusual?" To me, cheating is so insulting. It says to your partner: I don't love you enough to be faithful, and I don't respect you enough to let you go. It's the worst kind of trap.

He shrugs. "For some people."

"Let's not be those people," I implore him.

"We're not." Preston leans over the center console. He cups the side of my face and kisses me softly. When he pulls back, his pale blue eyes shine with confidence. "I'd be a complete fool to jeopardize our relationship, babe. I know wife material when I see it."

I think he's saying it as a compliment, but the fact that he uses Melissa's exact phrasing brings a queasy feeling to my gut. If I'm the wifey, does that mean he has a Marilyn? Or multiple Marilyns?

Frustration rises in my throat. I hate that Melissa and Chrissy planted this nasty seed of suspicion in my head.

"I'm wife material, huh?" I tease, trying to tamp down my unease. "Why's that?"

"Hmmm, well . . ." His lips travel along my cheek toward my ear, where he gives the lobe a teasing nibble. "Because you're hot. And smart. Good head on your shoulders. Hot, of course. You're loyal. You're hot. Annoying how much you argue sometimes—"

"Hey," I protest.

"—but you don't fight back on the important stuff," he finishes. "We have similar goals about what we want out of life. Oh, and did I mention you're hot?"

His lips brush mine again. I kiss him back, albeit a bit distracted. The list he'd recited was really sweet. So sweet that guilt is prickling at my throat now, because I guess that makes *me* the asshole with this whole Cooper thing.

Friendship isn't cheating, even if the other party is attractive, but maybe it's cheating adjacent?

No. Of course not. Text messages aren't adultery. It's not like we're sending each other nudes and describing our sexual fantasies. And after last night, Cooper and I both have a clear idea where the line is. More than ever, I know better than to cross it.

I'm walking to my dorm when a text pops up from the devil himself. It's accompanied by a picture of Evan and the puppy playing fetch on the beach.

Cooper: *Change of plans. She's moving in.*

CHAPTER ELEVEN

COOPER

"Who's the prettiest girl in the world? Is it you? Because I think it's you! Look at you, you beautiful little angel. I could eat you up, that's how perfect you are, you pretty girl."

The litany of baby talk escaping the mouth of my grown-ass twin brother is shameful.

And the object of his adoration is shame*less*. The newest member of the Hartley household struts around the kitchen like she was just named supreme leader of the pack. Which she basically is. She's got Evan wrapped around her little paw. Me, I'm not going to fall in love with the first cute face I see.

"Dude," I warn. "Dial it down a notch. You're embarrassing yourself."

"Nah. Look how pretty she is now." He scoops the puppy off the floor and thrusts her toward me. "Pet her. Feel how soft and silky."

I dutifully pet her golden fur, which, for the fifty bucks it cost to groom her yesterday, better be soft. Then I swipe the dog from his hands and set her back on the floor.

On which she promptly pees.

"Motherfucker," I grumble.

Evan instantly becomes a mother hen, grabbing paper towels and cooing at his new girlfriend as he sops up her pee puddle. "It's okay, pretty girl. We all have accidents."

We're still working out this whole dog-training thing, learning as we go from vet blogs and pet websites. All I know is, in the past seven days I've cleaned up more piss and dog shit than I ever intended in my life. That thing's lucky she's so cute. Last week, after the vet at the shelter confirmed the dog wasn't chipped and had probably been abandoned for some time, I didn't have the heart to stick her in a cage or abandon her again. I might be a bastard, but I'm not without mercy. So the vet gave us some special food to fatten her up, sent us on our way, and now we have a dog.

And a busy day of manual labor, if Evan would quit fawning over his pretty girl.

This morning, I woke up with a fire under my ass to get stuff done. Evan and I have the day off, so I decided, what the hell, there's never going to be a right time to start getting this house in better shape. It's the only lousy legacy our family has left. So I shook Evan out of bed early, and we headed to the hardware store to figure out what we would need.

First job on the home renovation list: replacing the roof. It's not going to be cheap. Digs into my savings quite a bit, but Evan kicked in half with some convincing. At least doing the work ourselves will save us a few grand.

"Come on, we should get started," I tell my brother. We plan to spend the rest of the day pulling the old roof off, and then tomorrow we'll lay down the new materials. Shouldn't take us more than a couple of days if we work fast.

"Let's go for a quick walk first. It'll tire her out so she'll sleep while we work."

Without awaiting my response, he scoops up the puppy and heads for the back door, where her leash is hanging on a hook.

"Swear to God, if you're not back in ten minutes, I'm returning her to the shelter."

"Fuck off. She's here to stay."

Sighing, I watch him and the dog scamper down the deck steps toward the sand. Our delivery from the hardware store hasn't arrived yet, but we could at least be making ourselves useful by prepping the current roof. Unfortunately, Evan's work ethic isn't as solid as mine. My brother will find any opportunity to procrastinate.

On the deck, I rest my forearms against the railing and grin when I see the golden retriever make a beeline for the water. There goes her newfound softness. Serves Evan right.

As I wait, I pull out my phone and text Mac.

Me: *How about Potato?*

Her response is almost instantaneous. Makes my ego swell a bit, knowing I've got priority in her texting queue.

Mackenzie: *Absolutely not.*
Me: *Mary Pawpins?*
Mackenzie: *Better. I'm saying Daisy.*
Me: *Can you get any more generic?*
Mackenzie: *You're generic.*
Me: *Nah babe, I'm one of a kind.*
Mackenzie: *Not your babe.*
Me: *Whatcha doing right now?*
Mackenzie: *In class.*

She follows that up with a gun emoji next to a girl's head emoji. I snicker at my phone.

Me: *That bad?*

Mackenzie: *Worse. I stupidly chose biology for my required science. Why are all the species names in Latin!!! And I forgot how much I hate cell theory! Did you know the cell is the most basic building block of life?*

Me: *I thought that was sex.*

Mackenzie sends an eye roll emoji, then says she has to go because her professor is starting to call on students to answer questions. I don't envy her.

Even though Garnet has decent scholarship opportunities for locals, I've never had any desire to attend college. I don't see the point. Everything I need to know about construction or woodworking, I can learn from my uncle, online, or in library books. Last year, I took some bookkeeping classes at the community center in town so I could learn to better manage our finances (as meager as they are), but that only cost me a hundred bucks. Why the hell would I ever pay twenty-five grand per *semester* to be told cells are important and that we evolved from apes?

A honk from the front of the house catches my attention. Our order's here.

Out front, I greet Billy and Jay West with fist bumps and good-natured back slaps. They're some of the old crew, grew up in the Bay. Though we don't see much of them these days.

"This ought to be everything you need," Billy says, opening the tailgate of the pickup truck. We had to buy and borrow some specific tools, get an air compressor and whatnot. On the trailer, he's got the new shingles on pallets.

"Looks good," I say, helping him haul things off the truck.

"Dad said there's no charge on the compressor if you can get it back to him by Monday. And he's giving you the underlayment and valley flashing at cost."

"Appreciate it, B," I say, shaking his hand.

Around the Bay, we watch out for each other. We have our own bartering system—*do me a favor today, I help you out tomorrow*. It's the only way most of us have survived the storms over the past couple years. You need to be able to rely on your neighbors to come together, support one another; otherwise, this whole town goes to shit.

Billy, Jay, and I unload the trailer in the blistering heat, all three of us drenched in sweat by the time we lift the last pallet. We're setting it on the ground when Billy's phone rings, and he wanders off to take the call.

"Hey, Coop." Jay wipes his brow with the short sleeve of his shirt. "Got a sec?"

"Sure. Let's grab some water." We walk over to the cooler on the front porch to pull out a couple bottles of water. It's blazing out here. Summer refusing to die. "What's up?"

Jay awkwardly shifts his huge feet. He's the biggest of the five West boys—six five, over two hundred pounds of solid muscle. Steph calls him the "gentle giant," which is an apt description. Jay's a sweet guy, the first person to help someone in need. He doesn't possess a mean bone in his body.

"Wanted to ask you something." His cheeks are slowly reddening, and it's not because of the heat. "You and Heidi . . ."

I wrinkle my forehead. Definitely not what I expected him to say.

"I heard some rumors about you guys this summer, and uh . . ." He shrugs. "Wasn't sure if it's a thing or not."

"It's not."

"Oh. Okay. Cool." He chugs half the bottle before speaking again. "I ran into her at Joe's the other night."

I try not to chuckle at his shy expression. I know where he's going with this now, but he's taking the long way to get there.

"And how'd that go?" I ask. I haven't seen Heidi or the girls in several days.

"Fun. It was fun." He gulps down some more water. "You don't mind if I ask her out, do ya? Since you two aren't a thing?"

Jay West is the epitome of the boy next door, and Heidi will eat him alive. If she even gives him a shot to begin with, which I doubt, since I'm fairly sure I'm the only guy in town she's slept with. She dated some dude for a year in high school, but he didn't live in the Bay. Heidi's always had one foot out the door anyway. I'm honestly surprised she hasn't skipped town yet.

I don't have the heart to tell Jay she'll probably turn him down, so I simply clap him on the shoulder and say, "'Course I don't mind. She's a great girl—make sure you treat her right."

"Scout's honor," he promises, holding up one hand in the Boy Scout gesture. Of course he was a Scout. Probably earned all his badges too. Meanwhile, Evan and I got kicked out of our troop when we were eight because we tried setting our scout leader's gear on fire.

"Hey, didn't realize you boys were here." Evan comes up with the puppy on a leash, ruefully glancing at all the supplies we've unloaded—no thanks to him. "Otherwise I would've given you a hand."

I snort. Yeah right.

"When'd you get a dog?" a delighted Jay asks. He promptly kneels and starts playing with the puppy, who tries to nip his stroking fingers. "What's his name?"

"Her," I correct. "And we don't know yet."

"My vote is for Kitty, but Coop doesn't appreciate irony," Evan pipes up.

"We're still deciding," I say.

Billy wraps up his call and approaches us. He nods at Evan, who nods back and says, "Billy. How's things?"

"Yeah, good."

The two share an uneasy look, while I stand there in discomfort. Gentle giant Jay is oblivious to the tension, thoroughly occupied by the puppy. This is why we don't see Billy and his brothers anymore. It's too damn awkward.

But Evan can't help himself. Always takes it to the next level of awkwardness. "How's Gen?"

Billy grunts a curt "Fine," and can't get his trailer closed up fast enough before he and Jay are practically peeling out of our front yard.

"The hell was that about?" I say to Evan.

"What's what?" He says this as if I don't know exactly what goes on in his damn head.

"Thought you weren't hung up on Genevieve."

"I'm not." He brushes me off and goes to the porch, grabbing some water.

"She blew town with barely a heads up," I remind him. "Trust me, that chick isn't sitting around worrying about you."

"I said it's whatever," Evan insists. "I was just making conversation."

"With her brothers? I wouldn't be surprised if Billy blames you for her running all the way to Charleston. For all I know, he's been waiting to kick your ass."

Evan's ex was the real hellion of our group. We've all experimented with the occasional illicit substance, broken a few laws, but Gen was on another level. If it was stupid and stood a chance to kill her, she wanted seconds. And Evan was right there next to her. Allegedly, she left to get her shit together. New place, new life. Who knows if it's true? If any of the girls still talk to her, they don't bring it up. Which is all the proof Evan should need that Genevieve West doesn't give a crap that she tore his fucking heart out.

"You still in love with her?" I ask him.

He takes off his shirt to wipe the sweat from his face. Then he meets my eyes. "I don't even think about her."

Yeah right. I know that expression. I wore that same expression every day our dad wasn't around. Every time our mom walked out on us for weeks or months at a time. Sometimes he forgets I'm the one person in the world he can't lie to.

My phone vibrates, momentarily distracting me from my brother's bullshit. I check the screen to find a text from Mac.

Mackenzie: *My bio prof just shared with the class that he's got a dog named Mrs. Puddles. I say we steal the name and never look back.*

I can't stop a chuckle, causing Evan to eye me sharply over the lip of his water bottle.

"What about you?" A bite creeps into his voice.

"What about me?"

"Every time I look over, you're texting the clone. You two are getting awfully cute."

"Thought that was the idea, genius. She's not dumping her boyfriend for some asshole she doesn't like."

"What do you text about?" he demands.

"Nothing important." It's not a lie. Mostly we argue about names and how to train *our* dog. Mac has granted herself partial custody and visitation rights. I tell her she's welcome to chip in for puppy pads and dog food. She demands more photos.

"Uh-huh." He reads me with narrow eyes. "You're not catching feelings for the rich bitch, are you?"

"Hey." Evan can throw all the shit he wants at me, but his anger has nothing to do with Mac. "She didn't do anything to you. In fact, she's been perfectly nice. So how about you watch your mouth."

"Since when do you care?" He steps up to me, getting in my face. "She's one of them, remember? A clone. Her entitled shithead boyfriend got you fired. Don't get it twisted which side you're on."

"I'm on our side," I remind him. "Always."

There's nothing stronger than my bond with my brother. Period. A girl doesn't change that. Evan's just got a thorn in his paw about everyone who goes to Garnet. Far as he's concerned, they're the enemy. It's an attitude most kids who've grown up around here share, and I don't blame them. I don't remember the last time a clone did anything but use and abuse us.

When it comes down to it, Mac's a product of where she comes from, the same as me. That doesn't mean if we weren't different people—if we came from similar backgrounds, lived similar lives—I couldn't see myself liking her. She's smart, funny, sexy as hell. I'd be an idiot not to admit that.

But we aren't different people and this isn't some other life.

In the Bay, we play the cards we're dealt.

CHAPTER TWELVE

MACKENZIE

I'm twenty minutes into my Wednesday biology class before I realize it's Friday and I'm actually sitting in my media culture lecture. Now those *Real Housewives* clips on the projection screen make way more sense. I thought maybe they were nervous hallucinations.

Truth is, I haven't been quite right the past few days. School bores me, and my dissatisfaction over my business is growing. It's frustrating how little work there is to do on the apps, now that I've delegated most of my duties to other people. I need a new project, something big and challenging to sink my teeth into.

To make matters worse, I'm battling this constant feeling that someone is looking over my shoulder. Toeing a knife's edge. Every time my phone buzzes, it's a shot of endorphins followed by a rush of adrenaline, guilt, and a pit of nausea in my stomach. I'm an addict, jonesing for the hit despite knowing it's killing me.

Cooper: *How bout Moxie Crimefighter?*
Me: *I like Jimmy Chew.*
Cooper: *She's a girl!*
Me: *I still think she's a Daisy.*
Cooper: *Muttley Crue.*

It's some kind of twisted foreplay. Bickering about puppy names as a form of flirting, every escalation another piece of clothing we're daring the other to remove in a metaphorical game of strip poker. It's gotten to be too much. I can't stop myself, though. Every time he texts me, I say this will be the last time, then I hold my breath, type a reply, hit send, and wait for my next fix.

Why do I do this to myself?

Cooper: *What are you up to now?*
Me: *Class.*
Cooper: *Come over after? We'll take Moon Zappa for a walk on the beach.*

Why do I do it? Because Cooper turns my insides out, gets my head messed up. I wake in cold sweats from unbidden dreams of his sculpted body and his soulful eyes. As much as I want to deny it, I'm starting to like him. Which makes me a terrible person. A rotten, horrible girlfriend. Still, I haven't acted on anything. I'm capable of exerting self-control. Mind over matter and all that.

Me: *Be there in an hour.*

For our dog, I tell myself. *To make sure he's taking good care of her.*
Uh-huh.
Self-control, my butt.

An hour later, I'm at his front door and shit is awkward. I don't know if it's me or him or both, but luckily our puppy serves as a much-needed distraction. She jumps at my knees, and I spend the next few minutes entirely focused on petting her, scratching behind her ear and kissing her cute little nose.

It isn't until we're some ways down the beach from his house that Cooper nudges my arm.

I glance over. "Huh, what?"

"Something up?" he asks. The beach is empty, so Cooper lets the dog off the leash and tosses a small piece of driftwood for her to fetch.

It isn't fair. He has just removed his shirt, and now I'm forced to watch him stroll around bare-chested, a pair of worn jeans hanging off his hips. No matter where else I try to divert my eyes, they return to the yummy V that disappears into his waistband. My mouth actually waters like one of Pavlov's stupid dogs.

"Sorry," I say. I take the stick from the dog when she brings it to me, then toss it for her again. "Distracted with school stuff."

It doesn't take long for us to wear the puppy out and head back to Cooper's house. He puts his shirt on, a faded Billabong tee so thin it molds to each muscle of his perfect chest. It's getting harder and harder not to think very un-friend-like thoughts. Which means it's definitely time for me to go.

Yet when he asks if I want a ride back to my dorm, I find a way to refuse without quite saying no. Instead we end up in his studio, a detached garage on the side of the property that contains table saws, machines, and an array of other tools. There are racks of raw wood on the walls. The floor is covered in sawdust. At the far end of the space, I glimpse several pieces of finished wooden furniture.

"You made these?" I run my hands over a coffee table, a chair, a skinny bookshelf. There's also a chest of drawers and a pair of end tables. Everything is done in varying finishes, but they all have a modern coastal aesthetic. Clean and simple. Elegant.

"Sort of my side hustle," he says with obvious pride. "It's all reclaimed wood. Stuff I find. I break it down to its basic forms, then repurpose it, bring out what it was meant to be."

"I'm impressed."

He shrugs, brushing off the compliment as though I'm merely being polite.

"No, I mean it. Cooper, you have real talent. You could make serious money off this. I know a dozen of my mom's friends who would tear through this place like it was a Saks trunk sale, throwing money at you."

"Yeah, well." He hides his face while putting away tools and rearranging his workbench, as if he needs to keep his hands busy. "Without the capital to quit my day job, I don't have time to churn out the kind of volume I'd need to turn it into any kind of sustainable business. I sell a few things here and there. Make a little extra cash we can use to fix up the house. It's just a hobby."

I plant one hand on my hip. "You have to let me buy something."

Before I can blink, he walks over and throws a drop cloth over the pieces. He won't meet my eyes as he warns, "Don't."

"Don't what?" I say blankly.

"Don't do that. The second you start looking at me as a project, this"—he gestures between us—"stops working. I don't need your help. I didn't show you this to get money out of you."

"I know." I grab his arm, forcing him to look at me. "This isn't charity. You're not a pity case, Cooper. I consider it an investment in an undiscovered talent."

He snorts softly.

"Seriously. When you blow up, I'm going to tell everyone I got there first. Rich girls love being trendsetters."

He studies me, his dark eyes searching. He has an intensity about him, a natural aura that's both magnetic and dangerous. The more I tell myself to keep my distance, the closer I'm drawn in.

Finally, a reluctant smile surfaces. "Fucking clones."

"Good. You think about a fair price for the coffee table and chairs. The furniture we have in the dorm is hideous, anyway. Bonnie and I were going to shop for something but got sidetracked with school."

I hop up to sit on a nearby worktable, swinging my legs beneath me. I know I should go, but I enjoy this guy's company far too much.

It's becoming a real problem.

Cooper's still watching me, his expression indecipherable. His gaze jerks away from mine when he gets a text. He pulls out his phone, and whatever he reads makes him laugh to himself.

"What's so funny?"

"Nothing. My friend Steph just sent a funny post to our group chat. Here, look." He joins me on the table. It takes absolutely no effort for him to haul his big body up and plant his butt beside me.

I lean toward him to look at his phone, trying valiantly not to notice how good he smells. A combination of spice, sawdust, and the ocean—which isn't a scent that springs to mind when you think of aphrodisiacs and pheromones, and yet it makes me light-headed and tingly.

Oddly enough, his open chat thread shows a screenshot of none other than my website. This particular post is from *GirlfriendFails*, an anecdote about a girl who goes home with a guy late one night after meeting at a bar. They sleep together, but after he's fallen asleep, she realizes she's started her period and doesn't have a tampon or pad. So she goes rummaging through his apartment to see if there are any in one of the bathrooms. The first bathroom is devoid of menstrual products, so she has no choice but to creep into the second bedroom and sneak into the en suite bathroom. She finds a box of tampons under the sink just as someone walks in on her. It's the guy's mom, wielding a lamp as a weapon because she thinks she's being robbed. She's screaming like a banshee, demanding to know why this nearly naked girl in a T-shirt and underwear is rifling through her bathroom at four in the morning.

"Can you even imagine?" Cooper grins. "Kinda makes me glad my mom isn't around."

I should probably tell him that I'm the brains behind the site he's laughing over. But I don't have the heart to say, *Yeah, I own this website. Launched it and made my first million while I was still in high school. But tell me more about your struggling furniture business.* What a jerk that would make me.

I don't brag about my success in general, but it feels extra wrong to say something now. So I address his mom comment, asking, "Where is she?"

"No idea." There's a sting in his voice. Hurt and anger.

I'm realizing I've touched a nerve and am scurrying to think of how to change the subject when he releases a ragged breath and keeps talking.

"She was barely around when Evan and I were kids. Coming and going with a different guy every couple of months. She'd take off one day, then show up unexpected looking for money." He shrugs. "Shelley Hartley was never any kind of mother."

The burden he's carried—still carries—is obvious in the drop of his broad shoulders, the crease of his forehead as he picks at frays on his jeans.

"I'm sorry," I say earnestly. "What about your dad?"

"Dead. Died in a drunk driving accident when we were twelve, though not before racking up a mountain of credit card debt that somehow became our problem." Cooper picks up a chisel, handles it a moment, then absently scratches at the plywood surface of the table. "The only things either of our parents ever gave us were liabilities." Then with a sudden ferocity, he stabs the chisel straight into the wood. "But I'll be damned if I end up like them. Rather throw myself off a bridge."

I swallow. He's a bit scary sometimes. Not threatening, exactly. Unpredictable, wired with the kinetic potential of the demons that torment his mind. Cooper Hartley has depths that are dark and treacherous, and that reckless part of me—the impulses I keep buried deep—wants nothing more than to dive in and explore.

It's just one more reason I'm finding myself in over my head.

I wrap my hand over his. "For what it's worth," I tell him, because right now he needs a friend to say they hear him, they understand, "I don't think you're anything like them. You're hardworking, talented, smart. You have ambition. Trust me, that's more than most people have going for them. A guy with a little bit of luck and a lot of initiative can make his life anything he wants."

"Easy for you to say. How many ponies did your parents buy for your birthdays?" He lobs a sarcastic jab my way, and I know it's because I'm the only target in the room.

I offer a rueful smile. "I'm lucky if I can get past my own mother's assistant when I call. My birthday cards are issued by their personal staffs. My report cards and permission slips were signed by employees."

"Fair tradeoff for getting everything you've ever wanted by snapping your fingers."

"Is that really what you think?" I shake my head at him. "Yes, I'm extremely fortunate to have been born into a wealthy family. But money becomes an excuse for everything. It becomes a wall between all of us. Because you've gotten one thing right—we *are* clones. From the day I was born, my parents have groomed me to be like them. They don't think of me as an individual with my own thoughts and opinions. I'm a prop. I swear, sometimes I wonder if I was only born to help my father's political aspirations."

Cooper gives me a questioning look.

"My father is a US Congressman," I explain. "And everyone knows voters prefer candidates with families. At least that's what the pollsters say. So, *poof*, here I am. Born and bred for campaign photo ops. Built to smile pretty for the camera and say nice things about

Daddy at fundraisers. And I did it, all of it, without question or complaint. Because I hoped one day it would make them love me." A bitter laugh pops out. "Honestly, though, I don't think they'd notice if I were replaced with a totally different daughter. Recast in my own life. They're not all that interested in me as a person."

It's the first time I've vented all this out loud. The first time I've let anyone into this part of me. I mean, yeah, I've confided in Preston plenty of times, but not so unfiltered. The two of us come from the same sphere. It's normal to him, and he has no complaints about his lot in life. And why would he? He's a man. He gets to run the family empire someday. Me? I have to keep my aspirations on the down-low so my parents don't realize I have no intention of being a quiet housewife when I finally grow out of "my teenage trifles."

They think my websites are a complete waste of time. "A passing folly," as my mother kept referring to it during the gap year I had to fight tooth and nail for. When I'd proudly told my dad that my bank account had officially reached seven figures, he'd scoffed. Said a million bucks was a drop in the bucket. Compared to the hundreds of millions his company nets every quarter, I suppose my earnings seem pitiful. But he could've at least pretended to be proud of me.

Cooper regards me in silence for several long beats. Then, as if a daydream evaporates in his mind, his intense eyes refocus on me. "Alright. I'll grant you that having emotionally absent parents isn't much better than physically absent ones."

I laugh. "So where does that leave the scorecard in the tournament of childhood trauma?"

"Yeah, I've still got you beat by a mile, but you're on the board."

"Fair."

We exchange knowing grins at the futility of such arguments. It wasn't my intention to turn the discussion into a competition—I'd never make light of the pain Cooper has suffered—but I guess I was holding in a bit more frustration than I'd realized. It all sort of spilled out.

"Hey, you got any plans tonight?" he asks as he gets to his feet.

I hesitate. I should check with Preston, see if he's doing anything with the guys tonight.

Instead, I say, "No."

Because where Cooper's concerned, my better judgment has gone to hell.

His gaze rakes over me in a way that elicits a hot shiver. "Good. I'm taking you out."

CHAPTER THIRTEEN

COOPER

"I've always wanted to do one of these," Mac says, grabbing my arm and tugging me toward some spinning monstrosity a hundred feet in the air.

Is this chick serious? I roll my eyes at her. "If I wanted to get dizzy and choke on my own vomit, I could do that on the ground."

She spins on me, eyes wide and shining in the multicolored lights. "You're not chicken, are you, Hartley?"

"Never," I say, because the inability to back down from a challenge is one of my personality defects.

"Then put your money where your mouth is, chicken man."

"You're gonna regret that." I warn, gesturing for her to lead the way.

The annual boardwalk festival is a highlight of the fall season in Avalon Bay. It's supposed to commemorate the founding of the town or something, but really, it's become an excuse to throw a party. Local restaurants bring out their food trucks and vendor stands, bars sling signature cocktails from carts, and midway games and carnival rides cram the boardwalk.

Evan and I used to smoke a bowl with our friends, get smashed, and jump from one ride to the next to see who lost their lunch first. Last couple of years, though, I guess we've gotten tired of it.

For some reason, I feel compelled to be the one to introduce Mac to the festival.

The boardwalk is crowded. Carnival jingles compete with live bands playing at three stages spread out through Old Town. The aromas of corn dogs and cotton candy, funnel cakes and turkey legs, waft on the breeze. After the Wave Flinger and Moon Shot, we go down the fifty-foot Avalanche slide and tackle the Gravity Well. All the way, Mac is skipping around with a huge grin on her face. Not an ounce of trepidation. She's an adventurer, this one. I dig it.

"What next?" she asks as we're recovering from her latest ride selection. I wouldn't call myself a wimp, but the daredevil beside me is definitely giving me a run for my money.

"Can we do something chill?" I grumble. "Like, give me five seconds to readjust to gravity."

She grins. "Something chill? Gee, Grandpa, like what? Should we sit quietly on the Ferris wheel or board that slow little train that goes through the Tunnel of Love?"

"If you're going into the Tunnel of Love with your grandpa, then you've got a whole new set of problems we need to talk about."

She flips up her middle finger. "How about a cotton candy break, then?"

"Sure." As we amble toward one of the concession stands, I speak in a conversational tone. "I got a BJ in that tunnel once, you know."

Rather than look disgusted, her green eyes twinkle with delight. "Really? Tell me everything."

We stand in line behind a woman who's trying to wrangle three kids under the age of five. They're like a litter of puppies, unable to stay still, bouncing around from the sugar highs they're undoubtedly on.

I drag my tongue over my bottom lip and wink at Mac. "I'll tell you later. In private."

"Tease."

We reach the counter, where I buy us two bags of cotton candy. Mac eagerly snatches one, peels off a huge, fluffy piece, and shoves the pink floss into her mouth.

"Soooo good." Her words are garbled thanks to her completely full mouth.

X-rated images burn a hole in my brain as I watch her suck and slurp on the sugary treat.

My dick thickens against my zipper, making it difficult to concentrate on what she's babbling about.

"Did you know that cotton candy was invented by a dentist?"

I blink back to reality. "Seriously? Talk about a proactive way to ensure a customer base."

"Genius," she agrees.

I reach into the bag and pinch off a piece. The cotton candy melts the moment it touches my tongue, the sweet flavor injecting a rush of nostalgia directly into my blood. I feel like a little kid again. Back when my parents were both around and still somewhat in love. They'd bring me and Evan to the boardwalk, stuff us full of junk food and sugar, and let us go wild. We'd drive home laughing and giddy and feeling like a real family.

By the time Evan and I turned six, their relationship turned combative. Dad started drinking more. Mom looked for attention and validation from other men. They separated, and Evan and I became afterthoughts to booze and sex.

"No," Mac orders.

I blink again. "No what?"

"You have that look on your face. You're brooding."

"I'm not brooding."

"Yes, you are. Your face is totally saying, *I'm lost in my broody thoughts because I'm SUCH a tortured bad boy.*" She gives me a stern look. "Snap out of it, Hartley. We were discussing some pretty insightful stuff."

"We were talking about cotton candy." My tone is dry.

"So? That can be insightful." She raises one eyebrow, smug. "Did you know scientists are trying to use cotton candy to create artificial blood vessels?"

"That sounds like pure and total horseshit," I say cheerfully.

"It's not. I read about it once," she insists. "Cotton candy fibers are, like, super small. They're the same size as our blood vessels. I don't remember the exact process, but the basic premise is—cotton candy equals medical breakthrough."

"Junk science."

"I swear."

"Cite your sources."

"Some magazine."

"Ohhhh, of course! Some magazine—the most reputable of publications."

She glares at me. "Why can't you just accept I'm right?"

"Why can't you accept you might be wrong?"

"I'm never wrong."

I start laughing, which causes her to glower harder at me. "I'm convinced you argue just for the sake of arguing," I inform her.

"I do not."

I laugh harder. "See! You're so damn stubborn."

"Lies!"

A tall blonde holding hands with a small boy frowns as she passes by. Mac's exclamation has brought a flicker of concern to the woman's eyes.

"It's okay," Mac assures her. "We're best friends."

"We're bitter rivals," I correct. "She's always yelling at me, ma'am. Please, help me out of this toxic relationship."

The woman gives us one of those *you're incorrigible* looks anyone over forty sports when they're dealing with immature children. Joke's on her. We're both in our twenties.

We continue down the boardwalk, stopping to watch some sucker boyfriend hurl darts at a wall of balloons to try to win a massive stuffed animal for his girl. Forty bucks later, he still hasn't secured the prized panda, and the girlfriend is now spending more time checking me out than cheering him on.

"Can you believe that chick?" Mac says when we walk off. "I swear she was picturing you naked in her mind while her poor boyfriend was bleeding money for her."

"Jealous?" I flash a grin.

"Nope. Just impressed. You're hot stuff, Hartley. I don't think we've passed a single girl tonight who hasn't stopped to drool over you."

"What can I say? Women like me." I'm not trying to be arrogant. It's just a fact. My twin and I are good-looking, and good-looking guys are popular with the ladies. Anyone who says otherwise is damn naïve. When it comes to our basic animal instincts, who we're sexually drawn to, appearance matters.

"Why don't you have a girlfriend?" Mac asks.

"Don't want one."

"Ah, I get it. Commitmentphobe."

"Nah." I shrug. "I'm just not in the market for one right now. My priorities are elsewhere."

"Interesting."

Our eyes lock for a fleeting, heated moment. I'm seconds away from reexamining the aforementioned priorities when Mac visibly swallows and changes the subject.

"Alright, time for another ride," she announces. "We've been dilly-dallying long enough."

"Please go easy on me," I beg.

She simply snorts in response and dashes off in search of our next death-defying adventure.

I stare after her in amusement. And a touch of bewilderment. This girl is something else. Not at all like the other bored clones at Garnet. She doesn't care how she looks—hair wild, makeup sweating off. She's spontaneous and free, which makes it that much more confounding why she stays with that jackass Kincaid. What the hell does that guy have that makes him so damn great?

"Explain something to me," I say, as we approach some enormous bungee thing that slingshots a small, two-person basket of screaming victims nearly two hundred feet in the air.

"If this is you trying to stall, it won't work." She marches right up to the ride attendant and hands him our tickets.

"Your boyfriend," I start, stepping around her to get into the basket first.

The attendant straps me in and starts his spiel that amounts to: *Keep your hands and feet inside the vehicle, and if this kills you, we're not liable.*

For the first time tonight, Mac looks nervous as she slides in beside me. "What about him?"

I choose my words carefully. "I mean, I hear things. None of them good. And for a girl who insists she doesn't want to be her mommy and daddy's little princess protégé, I'm wondering why you would do the expected thing and settle for another Garnet clone."

The thick bundle of cords, which will in a moment launch us into the night sky, rises up the ride's arms that form an obtuse angle above us.

"That's not really any of your business." Her expression turns flat, her tone adversarial. I'm touching a nerve.

"Come on, if you two have crazy-good sex or something, just say so. That I understand. Get yours, you know? I'd respect it."

She looks straight ahead, as if there's any chance of her ignoring me in this four-foot-wide tin can. "I'm not having this conversation with you."

"I know it's not for the money," I say. "And the fact that you never talk about him tells me your heart's not in it."

"You're way off." Mac snaps her gaze to me, lifting a defiant chin. There's all sorts of fight in her now. "Honestly, I'm embarrassed for you."

"Oh, is that right, princess?" I can't help myself. Getting a rise out of her kind of makes me horny. "When's the last time you touched yourself thinking about him?"

"Fuck off." Her cheeks turn red. I can see her biting the inside of her cheek as she rolls her eyes.

"Tell me I'm wrong. Tell me he gets you hot and bothered just walking into a room."

Her pulse is visibly thrumming in her neck. Mac adjusts in her seat, crossing her ankles. As her gaze flicks to mine, she licks her lips and I know she's thinking the same thing I am.

"There are more important things than chemistry," she says, and I hear the uncertainty in her voice.

"I bet you've been telling yourself that for a long time." I slant my head. "But maybe you're not as sure of that as you used to be."

"And why's that?"

"Okay," the attendant announces, "hang on. Counting down from ten. Ready?"

Oh, fuck it.

"I'm calling in your marker," I tell her.

"My what?"

"*Eight. Seven.*" The attendant counts down.

"The bet we made, remember? The night we met? Well, I won, and I know what I want as repayment."

"*Six. Five.*"

"Cooper . . ."

"*Four. Three.*"

"Kiss me," I say roughly. "Or tell me you still don't want me."

"*Two.*"

"What's it gonna be, Mackenzie?"

"*One.*"

CHAPTER FOURTEEN

COOPER

We're propelled into the air, and for several heart-stopping, stomach-twisting moments, we're sort of frozen in time. Pinned by the force of the ride as the ground disappears beneath us. A brief, spectacular moment of weightlessness lifts us from our seats and then the tension of the cords releases slightly and we bounce, once, twice, past the highest point. I turn my head and that's when Mac's lips find mine.

It's like an electric shock, a sizzle of heat from her lips straight down to my groin.

She grabs me, finding fistfuls of my hair, kissing me wildly. She tastes like sugar and endless summer nights. I'm hungry for both as my tongue slicks over hers and we soar so high it feels like we might never come down.

Her gasp heats my lips.

I drive the kiss deeper, swallowing her soft moan.

The basket bounces again, slowly descending on our return to earth. We part only to suck in a startled breath, and I have to remember where we are to stop myself from tearing her clothes off. I'm hard and hungry.

"We shouldn't have done that." Mac adjusts the straps of her tank top and wipes the smeared lipstick from her lips.

"I'm not sorry," I tell her. Because I'm not. I've wanted to do that for weeks. And it's all on the table now. We set fire to the pretense, and there's nowhere to go but forward.

She's silent when we leave the ride. Maybe I came on too strong. Scared her away.

When I realize she's leading us toward the exit, I swallow a sigh. Yeah.

She's definitely running scared.

"I'll take you home, if you want," I offer, following her toward where we parked the truck.

"I want to say goodnight to Daisy first."

I don't bother to correct her this time. Guess she won that battle.

"I'll catch a cab from your place," she adds.

The entire ride to my house, I'm convinced I'm never going to see her again and I've screwed this whole plan. My head is reeling, trying to think of something to say, some way to mitigate the fallout. All I come up with is a dozen ways I want to screw her brains out. Which isn't helping.

"He grounds me."

Her quiet statement has me glancing over in surprise. "What?"

"Preston. There are many reasons I'm with him, but that's a big one. He keeps me grounded." From the corner of my eye, I see she's wringing her hands. "Reminds me to be more restrained."

"Why do you need to be?" My voice is gruff.

"For one, because my dad is in the public eye."

"So? Your father made that choice. You don't have to turn yourself into a plastic person because of his life decisions." I frown at her. "And you don't have to put up with a boyfriend who keeps you on a leash."

Her eyes flash. "I'm not on a leash."

"What do you think 'restrained' means?" I say sarcastically.

"I said he reminds me to restrain *myself*. He's not the one doing the restraining. Whatever. You don't get it." Lips flattening, she fixes her gaze out the passenger window.

"You're right, I don't get it. I just spent the past couple hours watching you seek out every wild ride at that festival. You get off on the thrill. You get off on life. There's fire in you, Mac."

"Fire," she echoes dubiously.

"Hell yes. Fire. And you choose to be with someone who puts out the fire? Screw that. You need a man to stoke it."

"And, what, that man is you?" A sharp edge to her question.

"Didn't say that. Just saying your current pick is seriously lacking."

The house is dark when we pull up. Evan said he was getting together with our friends, but maybe they hit up the festival after all. Another silence falls over us as Mac and I walk inside.

I flick the light switch. "Look," I start. "I don't regret the kiss—we both wanted it, and you know that. But if this friendship thing is gonna be weird for you now . . ."

I glance back to see her pressed against the door, looking insanely edible. She doesn't speak, just tugs the front of my shirt to draw me to her. Before I can blink, she rises on her toes to kiss me.

"Fuck," I gasp against her greedy mouth.

In response, she lifts her leg around my hip and bites my lip.

My brain stutters for a second before I wake up and go with it. I grab her thigh, pressing myself between her legs as I kiss her deeper. Her fingers find their way under my shirt.

"God, all these muscles. I can't even." Her palms travel to my chest, stroking, then around to my back, nails gently scratching down my spine.

Her eager touch sends all the blood in my body rushing to my groin. I'm gone. Hard. Panting. I want her so badly I can hardly breathe.

A detailed fantasy of bending her over my bed plays behind my clenched eyelids. I'm about to pick her up and throw her over my shoulder when I hear the sliding glass door shut loudly in the kitchen.

Our mouths break apart.

"Oh, sorry, didn't mean to interrupt." Heidi stands in the kitchen doorway, watching us with a sarcastic smile. "Didn't know you were back."

I'm still breathing hard, trying to find my voice.

She walks to the fridge for two handfuls of beers. "Please, as you were. Don't let me interrupt."

Heidi winks at me before leaving the way she came.

Great.

"I should go." Immediately Mac is disentangling herself from me, putting distance between us. The dog hasn't come running, which means Evan has her down at the beach, with Heidi and the rest of the gang.

"That's my friend Heidi," I hurry to explain, not wanting Mac to leave. "I'm sorry about that. I didn't know anyone was here."

"It's all good. I have to go."

"Stay. They're probably all down at the beach. I'll get Daisy for you."

"No, it's fine. I'm going to call a cab."

"I'll drive you," I counter.

She's out the door, slinking away before I can stop her.

Damn it. "At least let me wait with you."

She acquiesces to that much, but the moment's passed. Once again there's a massive crater between us as we wait in silence, and I get nothing more than a wave goodnight as she's pulling away.

I drag a hand through my hair and trudge into the house. Fucking hell. One step forward, two steps back.

Story of my life.

In the kitchen, I grab a beer for myself, twist off the cap, and take a long swig before stepping out onto the deck. Where Heidi is standing. Her arms are free of bottles, so she must have delivered them to the beach and come back to wait for me.

"Hey," I say roughly.

"Hey." She leans against the railing, one hand playing with the frayed ends of her denim skirt. "So. You've got the clone on the hook."

"I guess." I swallow a hasty sip of beer. Truth be told, the plan, the bet, the rules . . . they were the last thing on my mind back there. My entire world had been reduced to Mackenzie and how good she felt pressed up against me.

"You guess? The chick was looking at you with stars in her eyes. She's into you."

Rather than comment, I pivot by saying, "Speaking of people being into other people—Jay West was asking about you."

She narrows her eyes. "When?"

"A few days ago. Said he hung out with you at a bar or something."

"Oh, yeah. We ran into him and Kellan at Joe's."

I flick up one eyebrow. "He's gonna ask you out."

She doesn't say anything. Just watches me warily.

"Will you turn him down?"

"Should I?"

A sigh lodges itself in my throat. I know she wants me to stake my claim, throw myself at her feet, and beg her not to go out with anyone but me. But I'm not going to do that. I told her I didn't want a relationship when we first hooked up. I hoped it would only be a one-night thing, each of us scratching an itch, and then we'd go back to being friends. But I was naïve. One night led to a few more, and now our friendship is more strained than ever.

"Do whatever you want, Heidi," I finally say.

"Got it. Thanks for the advice, Coop." Sarcasm drips from every word. Then, with a frustrated shake of her head, she stomps down the steps.

I release the breath trapped in my lungs. Chug the rest of my beer. The taste of Mackenzie still lingers on my tongue. Sugar and sex, an addictive combo. I step inside to grab another bottle, hoping the alcohol might help erase the flavor of the woman I'm aching to kiss again.

I join everyone on the beach. I'm relieved—and then ashamed of my relief—when I spot Heidi about ten yards away at the water's edge, texting on her phone. Maybe reaching out to Jay? But I doubt it. She's never been attracted to the nice ones. Just the jerks like me.

Around the fire, Steph and Alana are ragging Evan about some girl he hooked up with yesterday, after getting into a fight with her boyfriend. First I'm hearing of either, but Evan's not particularly forthcoming when it comes to his transgressions. From what I gather, he threw down with some Garnet clones who refused to pay up after he schooled them at the pool hall.

"She came in tonight all moon-eyed, asking where she could track you down," Alana is telling him.

He pales. "You didn't give her my number, did you?"

Alana lets him sweat for a few seconds before she and Steph break out in grins. "'Course not. That would go against the friend code."

"Speaking of the friend code, does it say anything about subjecting your friends to a front-row seat to your slobbery make-out session?" Steph pipes up, gesturing to the culprit in question.

At the far edge of the fire pit, our friend Tate is sprawled on one of our old lounge chairs with a curvy dark-haired chick draped over him like a blanket. He's got a hand thrust in her hair and his tongue in her mouth, while she rubs herself against him like a cat in heat. They're oblivious to our presence.

"Shameless," Evan shouts at the couple with feigned outrage. Then he grins, because my brother's an exhibitionist himself.

Tate gives his girl's bottom a playful smack and they stumble to their feet, cheeks flushed and lips swollen. "Coop," he drawls. "Mind if we head inside and watch some TV?"

I roll my eyes. "Sure. But there's no TV in my room, so I'd better not find you in there." I love my friends, but I don't need them banging on my bed. I just changed the sheets this morning too.

After Tate and the brunette disappear, Alana and Steph bend their heads close and start whispering to each other.

"Share with the group," Evan mocks, wagging a finger at the girls.

With a look of evil glee, Steph jerks her thumb toward Alana and says, "This bad girl slept with Tate last weekend."

I lift a brow. "Yeah?"

An unimpressed Evan shrugs. "You finally took a ride on the Tatemobile, huh? Surprised it took you so long."

My brother makes a good point. From the moment Tate's family moved to the Bay when we were in junior high, all the local girls went crazy for him. One cocky smile from Tate and they're hooked.

Alana's expression reveals not an ounce of shame or regret as she offers her own shrug. "Sort of wish I had done it sooner. Man gives good dick. Great kisser too."

"He's not bad," Evan agrees, and I can't help myself—I burst out laughing.

"Shit," I wheeze. "I always forget about that night you guys made out."

He rolls his eyes. "It was just a kiss."

"Dude, it lasted like three full minutes." My mind is now flooded with the vivid images of Evan and Tate sucking each other's faces off at one of Alana's house parties when we were sixteen. The girls cheering them on, the guys catcalling. That was a weird night.

"In Ev's defense, making out with Tate was the only way they were gonna see me and Genevieve take our tops off—" Alana stops abruptly.

Well, hell. She actually did it. Uttered Genevieve's name, the Voldemort of our group. I have to assume the girls are still in touch. Steph, Alana, Heidi, and Gen were the fierce foursome.

Evan and I have a habit of reading each other's minds, but whereas I possess at least some self-restraint, he doesn't know the meaning of it. So he says, "You guys still talk to her?"

Alana hesitates.

Steph opens her mouth, only to be interrupted by Heidi's reappearance.

"What's going on?" she asks, carefully glancing around the group. Then she nods. "Oh. Cooper told you."

Genevieve is all but forgotten as everyone's gazes swivel to me. "Told us what?" Steph demands.

I shrug. So, naturally, Heidi doesn't waste a second filling them in on finding me and Mackenzie wrapped up at the front door.

"Gotta admit, Coop, I didn't think you'd get this far," Alana says, lifting a beer in salute. "I'm impressed."

"I've changed my mind, by the way." Heidi eyes me through the flames. "I'm totally on board with this plan. I cannot wait to see the look on that girl's face when she realizes what you've done."

"How are you gonna do it?" Steph asks excitedly.

This is the most fun these girls have had since they went ham on some clone's car after he ran off with Alana's bikini top while she was sunbathing on the beach.

"Yeah, we have to talk endgame," Evan says. "It'd be a shame to waste an opportunity."

"Yes," Heidi agrees. "You have to get her and Kincaid in the same place, let him see you two together, and then dump her in public. Make it dramatic." Heidi is in a mood tonight. I know I'm to blame for it, but I'm not sure how to fix things between us. "Maybe we can throw a party."

Steph splashes beer on the fire in her eagerness. "Nah, too tame. Has to be on their turf. It's no fun unless Kincaid is humiliated in front of his own kind."

"I know where we can get a couple buckets of pig's blood," Alana says, which gets the rest of them doubled over laughing.

I laugh with them, playing along. Because a few weeks ago, I wouldn't have given a damn what happened to the random clone girlfriend of a rich punk who crossed me.

But now I've gotten to know Mac and . . . I genuinely like her. She doesn't deserve their scorn just because she's connected to a jack-ass like Kincaid. And after that kiss, I know there's something real between us, even if she's afraid of it. I can't tell these guys I'm having second thoughts, though. They'd tear my ass a new one.

Now that they've gotten a whiff of blood in the water, they won't be satisfied until they've tasted flesh.

CHAPTER FIFTEEN

MACKENZIE

"Three days in a row, this boy lets the door slam in my face at the smoothie place. Not once does he apologize. I'm startin' to think he's doin' it on purpose. I'm old-fashioned, okay? I value manners. Open a door for a lady, will ya? So the fourth day, I see him comin'. I'm ready for him. I'm inside and grab the door before he can open it. I flick the lock. This whole smoothie joint is held captive because I ain't letting this guy in. Over my dead body."

It's Monday morning, and Bonnie and I are both dragging ass. She shouts from the bathroom, putting on makeup, as I make us coffee in the kitchenette. I'm only half paying attention and manage to spill milk on my shirt.

"How long did that go on?" I call from my room while I change shirts. I'm supposed to meet Preston for lunch at his house later, so I have to make sure my outfit is appropriate. Not for him, but for his mother. She likes me fine—I think?—but she's very . . . particular. A tank top and jeans are not going to cut it with Coraline Kincaid.

"Long enough that the manager jumps in demandin' I let people out. And I'm all, I'd love to—as soon as this guy apologizes or leaves. Well, eventually he must realize I'm not playin' around, so he takes off. Next day, he locks me out of the sandwich shop until I agree to go on a date with him. So he's pickin' me up Friday night."

"That's great," I shout, only to turn and realize Bonnie is standing right behind me with our coffee in two travel mugs. "Sorry."

"You seem edgy." She stares at me. "You have a secret."

"No, I don't."

Her eyes burst into wide, blue saucers. "You kissed a boy."

Witch.

"Who is he?" she demands.

There's no use denying it. I'm entirely convinced of Bonnie's otherworldly powers. She'll berate me until I give her what she wants.

"Some townie," I say. Technically, it's true. She doesn't need to know the townie in question is Cooper.

Ugh. Just the thought of his name quickens my heart rate.

What in the *world* have I done? The kiss at the festival? I can blame that one on the sugar high. But the full-on make-out grope session at his house afterward?

There's no excuse.

I'm a horrible person. A horrible, selfish, awful girlfriend who doesn't deserve a stand-up guy like Preston.

There is absolutely no coming back from what I did on Friday night. I know this. And yet despite the whirlpool of guilt currently foaming in my stomach, one stupid little butterfly continues to flutter inside me, flapping around and churning up memories of Cooper's hungry lips and heated gaze.

His tongue in my mouth.

My fingers skimming the defined muscles of his unbelievably ripped chest.

And it's not only the physical stuff that lingers in my mind. It's everything that came before it. Talking about our families in his workshop, running around the boardwalk like a pair of rowdy kids. When I'm with him, I don't need to put on a front. I don't have to pretend to be the proper, well-behaved lady I'm expected to be. I feel like I'm my true self when I'm around Cooper. And that . . . scares me.

"That's it?" Bonnie's voice jerks me from my unsettling thoughts. "Nuh-uh, I don't think so. I require more details."

I shrug awkwardly. "There's not much else to say. It just sort of happened."

"Is it going to just sort of happen again?" Her expression tells me she's hoping the answer might be yes.

"No. Definitely not. I feel terrible. Preston—"

"Doesn't need to know," Bonnie finishes for me. "Nothin' good will come of telling him. If it was a mistake, and even if it wasn't—a girl has a right to her secrets. Trust me."

I know she means well, but I've already kept too much from him. This whole thing with Cooper has gone too far. I'm not a liar, and I never, ever thought myself capable of kissing someone other than my boyfriend. It's a humbling experience, discovering you're not as morally virtuous as you once thought.

Bonnie's wrong. Preston needs to know what I've done to us.

The right thing to do now is tell the truth and accept the consequences.

Later that afternoon, Pres picks me up from class for lunch. All day, I practiced what I would say. How I would tell him. But when he kisses my cheek and wraps his arm around my waist, I lose my nerve and keep my mouth shut.

"You look great," he says, nodding in approval.

Relief flutters through me. Thank God. I went through three outfits before I decided on a silk blouse and navy pixie chinos. My own mother doesn't give me this much anxiety.

"Freddy is preparing lamb shank," Preston adds. "Hope you're hungry."

"Famished," I lie.

He steers his Porsche into the parking lot of Garnet's football facility and pulls into a spot. Like the gentleman he is, he hops out of the convertible and runs over to open my door. Then he extends a hand, I take it, and we walk toward Preston's helicopter.

Yup. His helicopter.

Most days, it's how he commutes to school. His family had the helipad installed behind the football stadium his freshman year. It's a bit ridiculous, even for our circle of society, and the sight of the gleaming, white aircraft makes me wonder what Cooper would say if he saw—

No. Nope. Not going there. Today, I come clean.

It isn't long before we're flying in over the Kincaid estate, a massive piece of gated property on the coast. Endless lawns and oak trees stretch out for acres, the property divided from the ocean by an expansive white mansion. There's a pool, tennis courts, basketball court, and flower garden. All maintained by at least a dozen employees at any given time.

On the back patio, his mother greets us. As always, she's impeccably dressed. Head-to-toe Prada. I'm not sure why she bothers, seeing as how most days she has little reason to leave the house. Like my mom, Coraline doesn't work and employs a personal staff that handles every aspect of the home and her affairs.

"Hey, Mom." Preston leans in to kiss his mother's cheek.

"Hi, darling." Smiling, she shifts her gaze to me. "Mackenzie, honey." She hugs me, but with the light touch of someone who might shatter if you squeezed too hard. She's a slight woman. Fragile, not frail. Just don't make her angry. "You look lovely."

"Thank you, Mrs. Kincaid. Your new roses around the gazebo are gorgeous."

I learned long ago that the easiest way to keep her happy is to find something new on the estate to compliment on every visit. Otherwise, she spends the entire time commenting on my split ends or the size of my pores.

"Oh, thank you, honey. Raúl planted them just this week. He really is an artist."

"Are you joining us for lunch?" I inquire. *Please say no, please say no—*

"I'm afraid not. I'm meeting with my architect soon. He'll be here any minute. Did Preston tell you we're building a new pool house?"

"No, he didn't. How exciting." Really, the only exciting thing about any of this is that she's not having lunch with us.

And it's a good thing she doesn't, because lunch ends up being hella awkward. Not that Preston notices. In the formal dining room among the lamb shank and fine china, he goes on about some professor he insists has it out for him, while I pick at my food and work up the nerve to confess my sins.

"Of course, I could go to the dean and have the whole matter sorted out. He'd be out of a job. Then I thought, well, where's the fun in that, right? I'll come up with something more creative. That's the thing with those people. You give them a little respect, and suddenly they forget their place. It's our job to remind them. Another refill, Martha," he says to the maid. "Thank you."

Finally, I can't stand the pit in my stomach any longer.

"I have something to tell you," I blurt out.

He sets down his fork and pushes his plate away for Martha. "You okay?"

No. Not even a little. It isn't until right now that I realize I do care about Preston. Not only because we've been together so long. Not because of some sense of loyalty.

Cooper might draw out my "true self," whatever the hell that even means, but Preston does exactly what I told Cooper the other night: He keeps me grounded. He's a stable presence in my life. He knows this world, knows how to handle our parents, which is important in maintaining our sanity. Around him, I'm not a ball of anxiety and dread.

And what I've done to him isn't fair.

I wait until Martha leaves the dining room before releasing a shaky breath.

Now or never.

"I kissed someone. A guy."

He waits, watching me, as if I might say more.

I should. I will. This seemed the most expedient way to begin. Except now I'm regretting not waiting until we were somewhere more private. If his mother decides to walk in right now, I might not make it off the estate alive.

"Is that all?" Preston prompts.

"No. I mean, yeah. We only kissed, if that's what you mean." I bite my lip. Hard. "But I cheated on you."

He gets up from his seat at the far end of the table and comes to sit beside me. "Do I know him?"

"No. Some local I met at a bar when I was out with Bonnie. It was a stupid thing to do. We were drinking and I wasn't thinking and . . ." And I can't help myself from softening the blow with another lie. I was going to tell him. Everything. Now, looking in his eyes, I can't hurt him that way. He is taking it better than I expected, though. "I'm so sorry, Pres. You don't deserve this. I was wrong and I have no excuse."

"Babe," he says, squeezing my hand. He smiles, almost amused. "I'm not mad."

I blink. "You're not?"

"Of course not. So you had too much to drink and kissed a townie. Welcome to your freshman year of college. Guess you learned a lesson about handling your liquor."

Chuckling, he kisses the top of my head, then offers his hand to help me up from the table.

"How are you taking this so well?" I'm absolutely dumbfounded. Of all the ways I thought he might react, this wasn't one of them.

He leads me out to the back veranda to sit on the porch swing, where the maid has already put out two glasses of iced tea. "Simple. I can see the big picture. You and I have a future together, Mackenzie. I'm not interested in throwing that away over some minor indiscretion. Are you?"

"Definitely not." But I thought there'd be some groveling involved, at the very least.

"I'm glad you told me the truth. I'm not thrilled about what happened, but I understand, and I forgive you. Water under the bridge." He hands me an iced tea. "Not too much sugar, just the way you like it."

Okay, then.

For the rest of the afternoon, I expect Preston to pull away. To be cold, unhappy, even though he insisted he was fine.

But that isn't the case at all. If anything, he's more affectionate. This whole ordeal has only brought us closer together, which in a way makes me feel worse. I can't say precisely how I would've handled it if the situations were reversed, but I'm fairly sure I wouldn't have shrugged and said, "Water under the bridge." I guess Preston is a better person than I am.

I need to follow his lead. Be better. Focus harder on our relationship. The big picture, as he'd phrased it.

So that night, when Cooper texts me, I'm ready for it. I'd been waiting all day, all evening, for him to reach out. I knew he would, and I know what I have to do.

Cooper: *We should talk.*
Me: *There's nothing to say.*
Cooper: *Let me come get you.*
Me: *I can't. I told Preston about the kiss.*

Cooper: *And?*

Me: *He forgave me. I can't see you anymore.*

There's a very long delay, nearly five minutes, before Cooper sends another message. By then, I'm on pins and needles, practically jumping out of my skin.

Cooper: *Is that really what you want?*

I stare miserably at the screen, a lump rising in my throat. Then I force myself to type.

Me: *Yes. Goodbye, Cooper.*

Part of me hates cutting him off so abruptly. It isn't his fault that I messed up. But I can't trust myself around him, and this is the decision I should have made weeks ago. I was stupid. I thought I could have him as a friend. I thought I could play both sides. Now, I'm choosing.

I'm choosing Preston.

CHAPTER SIXTEEN

COOPER

On Sunday afternoon, I'm in the garage when my uncle calls to say he's stopping by. Every time my phone buzzes in my pocket, there's a second or two where I think it might be Mackenzie. Then I look at the screen and remember that I blew it. Read her all wrong.

Goodbye, Cooper.

Yeah. It must've been fun for her to slum it with some townie trash, make believe she was living dangerously. And then, the second it got real, she split. I was stupid to think it would end any other way.

But goddamn it, I can't get the taste of her off my tongue. For the past week, I've woken up every morning with a hard-on from imagining her legs wrapped around me. I can't even jerk off without pictures of Mac forcing themselves into my mind. This chick is slow-acting poison. And all I can think about is getting more.

Today, thanks to Evan, I have to build a new coffee table. The one I "sold" to Mackenzie is still sitting under a drop cloth, because it doesn't seem right to take it in case she decides to come back for it. I tell myself it's for the money and leave it at that. Anyway, this one's going to be a quick and dirty piece. Fucking Evan. Last night during a sudden party that broke out at our place, he got into it with some guy we went to high school with. I don't know how it started, only that it ended with one of them slamming the other through the table and leaving a bloody trail out my back door. Evan insists he's fine, but I'm starting to worry about him. Lately, he's been finding more excuses to start fights. Always in a pissy mood. Drinking more. This shit's getting old.

When Levi shows up, he hands me a cup of fresh coffee he picked up on the way and I dust off a couple stools for us.

Levi is our father's brother. Tall, rugged, with a short brown beard and square face. Although he bears a resemblance to my dad, the two of them couldn't be more different. Where Dad never missed a chance to fuck himself up and pass it on to us, Levi actually has his life together.

"Your brother around?" he asks.

"Left a little while ago." Probably picking up a greasy hangover cure from the diner. "So. What's up?"

"Nothing." He shrugs. "Just wanted to stop by and say a quick hello. I haven't been to the house in a few months, so I wanted to check in." Levi eyes the table in progress. "Working on something new?"

"Nothing important."

"When are you going to get serious about that, Coop? I remember you talking about trying to make a go of it sometime back."

"Yeah, I guess that's kind of on the back burner."

"It shouldn't be. You're good enough. Much as I like having you on the jobsite, you could be doing more for yourself."

Levi gave us our first full-time jobs out of high school. He's done well at it too. Not rolling in dough by any means, but he stays busy. Like a lot of people, the storms gave him more work than he knew what to do with.

Shrugging, I take a sip of coffee. "I got a few pieces in some coastal furniture shops in the tri-county area. Maybe about ten grand saved up, but that's still nowhere near enough for all the overhead I'd need to start a real business."

"I'd give ya the money if I had it," he says, and I know he's being entirely sincere. He's always been there for us since our dad died. When our mom was strung out or missing, when the fridge was empty, when our homework was due. "Everything I've got is tied up in the business. I love having the work, but it's expensive to keep up with demand."

"It's no sweat. I can't take your money, anyway. You've done more than enough for Evan and me." I've never in my life asked for a handout, and I'm not about to start now. I make fine money working for Levi. If I keep at it and save up, I'll make my own way. Eventually.

"What about a bank loan?" he suggests.

I've always resisted the idea. Not the least of which because I dealt with the banks after our dad's death—and every one of them are filled with nothing but bloodsucking suits who would sooner grind us into food pellets than help us succeed.

"I don't know," I finally answer. "I don't like the idea of going into more debt. Or having to leverage the house." I know I sound like a whiny bitch. At some point, I'm gonna have to make up my mind. Either get serious about getting my business off the ground or stop moaning about it.

"Well, that's true. It costs money to make money. But give it some thought. If this is really something you want to build a business out of, I can help. Co-sign the loan for you."

It's a generous offer, and one I don't take lightly. Even if I'm not thrilled about the idea now, I'm not about to throw his graciousness in his face, so I nod slowly. "Thanks, Levi. I'll think about it."

Levi doesn't stay more than a few minutes. After we finish our coffee, he's off to meet with a client about another job, and I'm back to measuring a plank of cedar. My head's not in it, though. It's never a good idea to operate power tools when your concentration is shot, so I call it quits and leave my workshop. Whatever. Evan can eat his dinner off the floor tonight like his precious girlfriend Daisy.

Speaking of Daisy, she's nipping at my heels when I stride back in the house. For the next ten minutes, we practice her sit-stays, but my head's not feeling that either.

Goodbye, Cooper.

I feel . . . heavy. Like I'm being dragged under the surface by a hundred-pound steel anchor wrapped around my neck. It's not a foreign feeling for me. My whole life, I've felt weighed down. By my parents' debts, my brother's bullshit, that sense I get sometimes that I'm trapped in my own head.

"Sorry, girl, I gotta get out of here," I tell the dog, reaching down to scratch beneath her silky ear. "I'll be back in a minute. Promise."

That's a lie. It'll take more than a minute to do what I'm itching to do. Daisy'll be fine, though. Evan will shower her with love and attention when he gets home. Same way Mackenzie did every time she is the dog. I wonder if she'll come back to visit Daisy sometimes.

Doubt it. She's probably already forgotten about the both of us.

Gotta admit, I didn't expect her to be so cold. I guess in the end she is just like all the other Garnet clones. Cold-blooded to the core.

Honestly, it serves me right. I went into this with bad intentions, treated her as a means for revenge against Kincaid.

Karma's a bitch.

I forcibly shove her out of my mind. Ten minutes later, I'm parking my truck near the boardwalk. The tattoo parlor is empty when I enter, save for a frazzled-looking Wyatt sitting at the counter with a sketchpad in front of him.

"Yo," he greets me, his expression brightening.

"Yo. Got time for a walk-in?"

Wyatt's been tattooing me since I was a sixteen-year-old punk requesting a tombstone on my left biceps. 'Course, he was only a year older at the time, with a tattoo gun he picked up from the pawnshop, so my first ink wasn't exactly a masterpiece. If I have kids, first thing I'm telling them is to never let their dumbass teenage friends poke needles into their flesh. Fortunately, it turned out all right in the end. Wyatt honed his craft and now co-runs this joint with another artist, and my shitty tombstone was skillfully camouflaged within a full sleeve featuring a watery graveyard among the crashing waves of Avalon Bay.

"Depends," Wyatt says. "What's the piece?"

"Simple, small. I want an anchor." I rub my fingertips over the back of my neck. "Right here."

"What kind of anchor? Stockless? Admiralty?"

I'm not a boat guy, so I roll my eyes. "How the fuck do I know? A fisherman anchor—you know the one I mean."

He snickers. "Admiralty, then. Come to the back. It'll take less than an hour."

In no time at all, I'm straddling a chair while Wyatt preps his workstation. That's how it works in the Bay. If you're good to your friends, they're good to you. Wyatt probably won't even charge me for this new ink, no matter how much I insist. Instead, he'll show up at my place in a few months or a year from now asking for some random favor, and I'll happily oblige.

"So what were you looking all bothered about when I got here?" I ask.

He releases a frustrated groan. "Ah. Yeah. I was trying to design a piece so fucking sexy that Ren'll have no choice but to take me back."

I smother a laugh. "She dump you again?"

"What else is new, right?"

He's not wrong. Wyatt and Lauren aka Ren break up at least every other month, usually on account of the most random nonsense you can imagine. They're a great source of entertainment, though.

"What happened this time?"

"Lean forward," he orders, nudging me so that I'm bent over the chair, the back of my head at his mercy.

A second later, I feel a cool spray at my nape. Wyatt cleans the area with a soft cloth before reaching for a razor.

"Okay," he says as he starts shaving the short hairs on my neck. "I need you to imagine something. Ready?"

My snicker is muffled against my forearm. "Sure. Ready."

"You're on an island."

"Deserted or, like, a resort island?"

"Deserted. You were in a plane crash. Or your boat capsized. Not important."

"How is it not important?" I object. "If I was on a boat, I'd probably be more familiar with islands and tides and shit, which means I'd have a better shot at survival."

"Oh my God. That's not the point," he grumbles. "Why you gotta complicate it, Hartley? You're on a deserted island. The end."

"Cool story, bro."

"You realize I'm holding a razor near your neck right now?"

I swallow another laugh. "Okay. I'm on a deserted island. Now what?"

"Want me to stencil this out or freehand it?"

"Freehand. I trust you." Besides, if the tat is trash, at least it's somewhere I can't see it.

Wyatt keeps jabbering as he preps the ink. Black only. I'm not fancy. "So you're stuck there. This is your life now, this island. But! Good news. You're about to get some company. Two boats appear—"

"Sweet, so I'm rescued?"

"No!" He sounds aggravated. "I just said you're stuck there forever."

"But there are boats."

"The boats explode in five minutes, okay? There are no boats. Jesus."

It occurs to me that maybe I shouldn't be antagonizing the guy with the needles. But damn, it's fun to annoy Wyatt.

"On the first boat, there's your girlfriend, or partner, or whatever. But just them. Nothing else. The second boat has nobody on it. But it's got all the supplies you need to survive on the island. Fire kits, building materials, food, weapons, I'm talking *everything*."

My lips twitch. "Did Ren pose this thought experiment to you?"

"Yes," he says glumly.

I twist my head to peer at him. "You stupid bastard. Did you pick the supplies boat instead of her?"

"Like you wouldn't," he accuses.

Laughter rumbles out of my chest.

"It's a matter of life and death, Coop. I need food and shelter! Sure, it'd be great to have Ren there, but we'll die in five seconds flat if we don't have the tools to live. And anyway, with all the stuff at my disposal, I can build a raft and make my way home to her. It's common sense."

"Ren really dumped you because of this?"

"What? No. That's insane. She dumped me because I was an hour late to her sister's birthday dinner. I was out with Tate telling him about her dumb thought experiment and lost track of time."

I stare at him. How are these my friends?

On the other hand, I'm getting a free tattoo out of him, and his nonsense did succeed in helping me forget about Mackenzie.

Goodbye, Cooper.

Or not.

CHAPTER SEVENTEEN

MACKENZIE

I've been on my best behavior. I haven't spoken to Cooper in a couple weeks. Kept my distance from the boardwalk. I figured if I were to accidentally bump into him, it'd be there, so best to remove all temptation. My restraint hasn't stopped the dreams, though. Or the forbidden memories that flood my mind whenever I'm in class.

I catch myself reliving our first kiss during English Lit.

Remembering the way his hands held me firm against his front door during Biology.

In European History, I'm thinking about his hard chest beneath my palms, and suddenly I'm flushed and breathing heavy, wondering if everyone notices.

On the bright side, Preston and I are rock solid, and I finally made a Garnet friend who isn't Bonnie. Her name is Kate, and although she happens to be Melissa's younger sister, the two are not at all alike. Kate's hilarious, sarcastic, and hates sailing—all pluses in my book. We met at a Kappa Nu dinner that Preston urged me to attend because he thinks I should be making more of an effort to connect with Melissa and Chrissy and their sorority friends. Instead, I spent half the night in the corner with Kate debating the artistic merit of *The Bachelor*.

So when she texts on a Thursday night asking if I want to grab drinks with her and some friends in town, I'm totally down. It means risking running into Cooper, but I can't decline my first invite from someone other than Bonnie.

"You wanna come with us?" I ask my roommate as I braid my hair in our shared bathroom.

Bonnie's head appears in the mirror behind me. "I would, but I'm seein' Todd tonight."

I grin at her reflection. "Again? Looks like things are getting serious between you two . . ." I swear she's gone out with the sandwich shop guy a lot lately. So much for her bad boy fetish. I met Todd once and there was neither a piercing nor tattoo in sight.

"Serious? Pfft!" She waves her hand. "He's one of three on my rotation, Mac. Tomorrow night I'm seein' Harry, and Saturday it's dinner with that boy I was telling you about—Jason? The one who looks like Edward?"

"Edward?" I echo blankly.

"From *Twilight*?" She shivers happily. "Oooh, he is *sooo* handsome I wouldn't even care if he ended up being an actual vampire. How wild is that? And blood totally makes me squeamish."

I snort. "I'm pretty sure he's not a vampire." Though I still haven't ruled out the possibility of Bonnie being a witch.

I wish her luck on her date, then leave the dorm and head for the parking lot, where my Uber awaits me. I'm meeting Kate and her friends at the Rip Tide. As the car approaches the beachfront venue, my mind flashes back to the last time I came here, and my heartbeat accelerates. That was the night I met Cooper. The night Bonnie hooked up with his twin while Cooper and I stayed up all night, talking about everything and nothing.

Enough, a stern voice orders. *Forget about him.*

I really need to do that. I'm with Preston. Thinking about Cooper isn't good for my relationship.

I thank the driver and slide out of the car. As I rearrange my side braid, my gaze flicks toward the crumbling hotel I'd first seen over a month ago. It's still standing. Still vacant, from the looks of it. A weird sensation flutters in my belly as I stare at the sprawling hotel, its weathered, white façade gleaming from the glow of a lone streetlight.

It takes surprising effort to tear my gaze away. Great. First my brain gets hung up on Cooper, now it's obsessing over an abandoned hotel? I've got issues.

Inside the bar, I find Kate at a table at the side of the stage. She's with three other girls, two of whom I don't recognize. The third is Melissa. I stifle a sigh, because I hadn't realized Melissa was coming too. I don't have anything against her, but her gossipy nature puts me on guard.

"Hey girl," Kate greets me.

Like her sister, she has pale hair and big, gray eyes, but their styles are completely different. Kate's wearing a tiny blue dress that barely covers her thighs, flip-flops, and chunky bangles on both wrists. Meanwhile, Melissa's knee-length pink dress is buttoned all the way up to the neck, and there are two massive diamonds sparkling in her earlobes.

"Hey." I direct an awkward smile across the table. "Hey, Melissa."

Kate introduces me to her two friends, Alisha and Sutton. We decide to order daiquiris at Melissa's insistence, although when Kate and I head to the bar to place our order, she winks and gets us two vodka shots as well.

"Don't tell my sister," she says, and we sling them back with conspiratorial grins.

Back at the table, the first round of daiquiris is gone in the blink of an eye, so we quickly order more. By the third round, our conversation topics devolve from our classes and future plans to embarrassing stories and men. Kate tells us about the TA who has a massive crush on her and shows his love by stapling a dried flower on the last page of every paper she submits.

I burst out laughing. "No! He doesn't."

"Oh, he does. And if you think the eternal love flame he keeps burning earns me better grades, you're wrong. He gave me a C minus on my last essay." She looks outraged. "Screw your perfectly pressed petunia petals, Christopher. Give me the A."

Alisha beats Kate's story with one about a professor who accidentally emailed her an impassioned love letter that was supposed to go to his estranged wife.

"Her name was Alice so I guess he auto-filled the email with 'Al' and clicked my name instead." She twirls her daiquiri straw as she giggles. "The email was a list of all the reasons she shouldn't go through with their divorce. Basically stating his case of why he's amazing."

Melissa's jaw drops. "Oh my God. What were the reasons?"

"I don't remember them all, but the first one was . . . wait for it . . ." Alisha pauses for dramatic effect. "'Adequate lover.'"

Our entire table hoots with laughter.

"Adequate?" Kate says through giggles. "Oh, that poor wife."

I slurp down the rest of my drink. It occurs to me I haven't had a proper girls' night since high school, triggering the realization that I've been terrible at keeping in touch with my Spencer Hill friends. Granted, they haven't reached out either, so I guess that says a lot about our friendship. I vow to do a better job at nurturing these college friendships.

Our conversation devolves even further, as Sutton suggests we play a game. Well, not so much a game as "let's rate the hotness of every single guy who walks past our table."

"Oooh, how about him?" Alisha asks in a loud whisper.

We all examine a long-haired surfer dude in a red tank top and orange board shorts. "Two out of ten for fashion sense," Melissa says, lifting her nose. "Red and orange? Come on. Have some respect for yourself, sir."

I can't help but snicker. Drunk Melissa is still snooty, but she's also cattier, which I'm loving.

"Butt? Nine out of ten," Kate decides. "It's a great butt."

"I bet I could bounce a quarter off that thing," Alisha agrees.

Yes, we're objectifying these boys. Intoxicated girls have neither shame nor scruples.

"Seven overall," Sutton says.

"Three," Melissa corrects, jutting her chin. "I can't get past the red/orange combo. I just can't."

"Um, guys?" hisses Alisha, who leans forward eagerly. "Six o'clock, far end of the bar—I just found a ten across the board."

We all turn toward the bar. I nearly choke on my tongue.

Alisha's perfect ten is Cooper Hartley.

Kate whistles softly. "Oh yeah. I like."

"I *love*," Alisha corrects, her face taking on a dreamy glow.

I don't blame her. Cooper looks damn good tonight. He's wearing that threadbare T-shirt I like, the one with the Billabong logo that stretches across his broad shoulders and emphasizes his defined chest. Add to that the messy dark hair, the two full-sleeve tattoos, the cargo pants hugging an ass even tauter than the surfer's, and you've got one fine specimen of a man.

As if sensing the female attention, Cooper's head jerks sharply. A second later, he's looking at our table. Heat floods my cheeks when my gaze locks with his. Shit. Am I blushing? I hope I'm not blushing.

His eyes narrow at the sight of me. Lips flatten for a second before twisting in a slight smirk.

Beside me, Alisha gasps. "He's staring at you," she accuses me. "Do you know him?"

"I . . . uh . . ." My mind races in an attempt to come up with a suitable reason why a hot townie might be making prolonged eye contact with me.

"Mackenzie?" Melissa's shrewd gaze burns a hole in the side of my face. "Do you know that guy?"

My throat is completely dry. I wrestle my eyes off Cooper and reach for my drink. Taking a sip provides me with a few extra seconds to panic-think of an excuse. Melissa isn't only nosy—she's smart. If I admit to knowing Cooper, even in a just-friends capacity, it'll absolutely trigger her gossip setting. She'll ask more questions, and if even one of my answers doesn't ring true for her, she might tell Benji, who'll in turn tell Preston, who literally just forgave me for kissing another guy.

So, no. There's no way I can fess up to knowing Cooper in any capacity.

"Evan," I blurt out.

Melissa frowns. "What?"

I set down my plastic daiquiri cup. Relief and satisfaction course through me at my stroke of genius. "That's Evan Hartley. My roommate hooked up with him at the beginning of the semester."

She relaxes slightly, her manicured fingers toying with the diamond in her ear. "Really? Little Bonnie tapped that?"

"Oh yeah." I muster up a laugh and hope nobody hears the tension in it. "She totally abandoned me for a moonlight beach hookup with the guy."

Perfect. Now if Melissa tries to fact-check me, Bonnie can easily corroborate. As long as Cooper stays across the room and doesn't—

Walk over to us.

Son of a bitch, he's walking over here.

My heart beats faster than the canned dance music pouring from the speakers. What is he doing? I told him I couldn't see him anymore. I made it clear, damn it. He can't just come up to my table like nothing happened and—

"Evan!" I exclaim in a too-loud voice with a too-bright smile.

Cooper's gait stutters for a second. Then his long legs resume their easy stride until he's standing in front of me. He shoves his hands in his pockets, donning a lazy pose as he drawls, "Mackenzie."

"Evan, hey. How's it going?" I ask, all friendly and laidback as if we hadn't made out, as if I'd never felt the prominent ridge of his erection pulsing against my belly. "I haven't seen you since that night you stole my roommate away and seduced her."

Kate snickers.

I remain focused on Cooper, hoping my eyes are conveying everything I can't say out loud. *Play along. Please. I can't have these girls gossiping about us and risk it getting back to Pres. Please play along.*

The fact that I'm not acknowledging his true identity sparks guilt in me, but it doesn't compare to how awful I felt about cheating on Preston. Kissing Cooper had been a mistake. But I came clean to my boyfriend, my conscience is clear, and now I just want to move on. Which won't be possible if Melissa decides there's gossip potential here. So I silently implore Cooper, who isn't giving me an inch.

His smirk deepens, dark eyes glittering with something I can't decipher.

By the time he finally speaks, I'm a bundle of nerves and sweating through my tank top.

"I didn't hear Bonnie complaining that night," he says with a wink.

I almost faint with relief. Hopefully no one notices my hand shaking as I reach for my drink. "Well, she's not the one who had to Uber back to campus all alone at two in the morning." I take a hasty sip before making the introductions. "Alisha, Sutton, Kate, Melissa. Guys, this is Evan."

It's funny, I never realized how different Cooper and his twin are until this very moment, when Cooper transforms into Evan. His normally intense, brooding eyes gleam mischievously. His tongue gives his bottom lip a teasing swipe before he flashes a cocky grin at my friends.

"So." Even his voice sounds different now. Lighter, flirtier. "Which one of Mackenzie's friends will I be seducing tonight?"

You'd think a line that sleazy would evoke groans. Instead, the girls all but swoon over it. Even Melissa is affected. Her face turns pink, lips parting slightly.

I don't blame them. This guy is sex personified. Doesn't matter if he's being his broody self or pretending to be his manwhore brother, the sexual energy pours off him in waves.

"Keep it in your pants, *Evan*." My tone is meant to be teasing but sounds like a warning.

His grin widens.

"Alright." Sutton releases an exaggerated sigh and hops off her stool. "I guess I'll take one for the team." Her hazy expression tells me she's already having sex with Cooper in her mind. "How 'bout a dance first, and then we can discuss that seduction offer?"

There's not a single muscle in my body that isn't coiled tight. My fingers curl around my cup, squeezing hard. I'm worried I might crush it. It's a damn good thing it's made of plastic, otherwise there'd be glass shards everywhere.

Cooper's mocking eyes don't miss my response. He's watching me even as he answers Sutton. "A dance sounds great. Lead the way, babe."

Three seconds later, he's wrapped up with Sutton on the dance floor in front of the stage. Her arms loop around his neck, her slender frame pressed against his strong one. Cooper's hands skim the back of her lacy camisole, one palm trailing lower, resting right above the curve of her ass. His other hand glides up her spine and tangles in her dark ponytail before cupping the back of her neck.

Bitter rage coats my throat. I reach for my daiquiri hoping to get rid of the vile taste, only to find my cup is empty.

"Ugh, I can't believe her," Alisha is griping.

Her? I can't believe *him*. What is he doing, dirty dancing with a complete stranger?

Beside me, Kate pats Alisha's arm. "I'm sorry, hon. Next time you gotta be quicker."

"Lord, he is *hot*," Melissa remarks, her attention glued to Cooper and Sutton. "If I wasn't with Benji, I would totally consider slumming it with a townie for the night."

I lift a brow. "I thought extracurricular activities were perfectly acceptable?"

She laughs. "Um, no. Not for us, sweetie. At least not until we've got the *I Do*s locked down. Then you can screw the pool boys and gardeners to your heart's content."

Kate rolls her eyes at her older sister. "You're one classy bitch, Mel."

Melissa shrugs. "What? That's the way it's done."

I tune them out, distracted by the vertical sex display happening ten feet from our table. Sutton is now on her tiptoes, whispering in Cooper's ear.

He chuckles, and I stiffen. What are they giggling about over there?

And he *really* needs to remove his hands from her ass. Like, right now. He's laying it on thick for my expense, and I am not having it. I bite the inside of my cheek. Hard.

"I totally should've staked my claim the second he walked up to us," Alisha moans. She's also obsessively watching the dance floor.

"Early bird gets the dick," Kate says solemnly.

"Ugh. Whatever." Alisha slams her cup on the table and pouts. "She's all talk anyway. Sutton doesn't do casual sex. She's not going to fall into bed with some guy she doesn't even—" Alisha stops abruptly, her jaw dropping.

I follow her gaze just in time to see Cooper and Sutton leaving the bar together.

CHAPTER EIGHTEEN

MACKENZIE

The next morning, my media culture class is canceled. The professor sends a mass email that defies the laws of oversharing, informing us that his bowels had revolted against the meatloaf his wife prepared for dinner last night.

I feel your pain, bud. My stomach's been in knots since I saw Cooper leave the Rip Tide with his arm slung around Sutton.

Did they have sex? I feel queasy at the thought. And a little angry. How could he fall into bed with some chick he'd known for 2.5 seconds? Or maybe they didn't sleep together. Maybe she just blew him.

A red mist overtakes my field of vision at the thought of Sutton going down on Cooper. I want to rip his dick off for letting her touch it.

Hmm. Okay.

Maybe I'm more than a "little" angry.

But I'm not allowed to feel that way. Cooper is not my boyfriend. Preston is. I'm not allowed to have an opinion about who Cooper hooks up with, and I certainly shouldn't be reaching for my phone right now and pulling up our chat thread and—

Me: *You didn't have to do that on my account. And by "do that," I mean Sutton.*

Damn it. What is wrong with me? I regret sending the text the moment it appears on the screen. I frantically tap at the screen in search of an unsend option, but that's not how text messages work.

And now Cooper is typing a response.

Heart beating wildly, I sit up in bed and inwardly curse myself for my lack of self-control.

Cooper: *Oh we're talking again?*
Me: *No. We're not.*
Cooper: *Cool. Later.*

I stare at my phone in frustration. I'm more frustrated with myself than with him, though. I told him we couldn't be friends. I literally said, "Goodbye, Cooper." Last night I called him Evan and all but threw him at my single friends so that Melissa wouldn't suspect anything and tell Benji. This is on me. Of course Cooper doesn't want to talk to me.

And yet my stupid fingers have a mind of their own.

Me: *I'm just saying. Thanks for playing along when I called you Evan, but you didn't have to go full-on method acting.*
Cooper: *Hey princess? How about you worry more about your boyfriend's dick and less about mine?*

I want to scream. I wish I'd never met Cooper Hartley. Then I wouldn't be feeling this way. All twisted up inside. Not to mention the jealousy eating at my throat like battery acid thanks to his reply. Is he saying his dick *was* a factor last night, then?

I'm three seconds away from asking Kate for Sutton's number so I can confirm *exactly* what happened last night, when common sense settles in. If my goal last night was to ensure Melissa wouldn't get suspicious, going batshit crazy on Sutton won't help the cause.

Utilizing every iota of willpower I possess, I shove my phone aside and grab my laptop. No class means more time for work, which is always a great distraction.

I check my email, but there's nothing pressing that needs to be addressed. The matter with Tad and his micropenis has blown over, thank God. And my mods and ad managers are reporting that September was our best month yet in term of revenue. It's the kind of news any business owner should be thrilled to hear, and don't get me wrong, I *am* thrilled. But as I spend the next couple hours doing basic business housekeeping, the frustration returns, rising in my throat. I have the sudden urge to get off campus for a walk. Sick of the same old scenery. Sick of my obsessive thoughts about Cooper.

Ten minutes later, I'm in a cab heading for Avalon Bay. I need the fresh air, the sunshine. The car drops me off near the pier, and I walk toward the boardwalk, shoving my hands in the pockets of my cutoff shorts. I can't believe how balmy the temperature is for October, but I'm not complaining. The hot breeze feels like heaven against my face.

When my feet carry me all the way to the hotel, I suddenly realize what motivated me to come here today. The same thrill of possibility surges through my blood upon finding the hotel still sitting empty. Waiting.

It's crazy, but as I stare at the derelict building, my body starts humming. Even my fingers are itching, like a metaphorical need to get my hands moving. Is this the challenge I'd been looking for? This condemned hotel I can't quit fantasizing about?

It's not even for sale, I remind myself. And yet that doesn't seem to matter. The humming refuses to subside.

An idea forms in my mind as I make my way back through town, where I stop at a café for a drink. When the woman behind the counter hands me my juice spritzer, I hesitate for a moment. Avalon Bay is a small town. If we're going by the small towns I've seen on

TV shows like *Gilmore Girls*, that means everyone knows everything about everyone and everything.

So I take a wild guess and ask, "What do you know about the old abandoned hotel on the boardwalk? The Beacon? Any idea why the owner hasn't done anything with it?"

"Ask her yourself."

I blink. "Sorry, what?"

She nods toward a table by the window. "That's the owner."

I follow her gaze and spot an elderly woman wearing a wide-brim hat and huge black sunglasses that obscure most of her face. She's dressed more like a beachcomber than a hotelier.

What are the odds? The humming intensifies, until my entire body feels wired with a live current. This has to mean something.

Carrying my drink, I slowly approach the table by the window. "Excuse me, I'm sorry to bother you. I wondered if I might talk to you about your hotel. May I sit down?"

The woman doesn't look up from her coffee cake and cup of tea. "We're closed."

"Yes, I know." I take a breath. "I hoped I might change that."

She picks at her cake with brittle fingers. Pulls tiny crumbs, placing them slowly, gently, in her mouth.

"Ma'am? Your hotel. Can I ask you a few questions?"

"We're closed."

I can't tell if she's putting me on, or not all there. I don't want to be rude or upset her, so I try one last time.

"I want to buy your hotel. Is that something that would interest you?"

Finally, she lifts her head to look at me. I can't see her eyes because of the sunglasses, but the thoughtful purse of her lips confirms I've captured her interest. She takes a long sip of her tea. Then, setting down the cup, she pushes out a chair for me with her foot.

I sit, hoping I don't appear too eager. "My name is Mackenzie.

Cabot. I'm a student at Garnet College, but I'm sort of an entrepreneur too. I'm really interested in discussing your hotel."

"Lydia Tanner." After a long beat, she removes her sunglasses and places them on the tabletop. A pair of surprisingly shrewd eyes laser into mine. "What do you want to know?"

"Everything," I answer with a smile.

For more than an hour, we discuss the hotel's history. How she built it with her husband after the war. How it was practically demolished and rebuilt three times since then, before her husband died two years ago. Then after the last storm, she was too old and too tired to rebuild again. Her heart wasn't in it, and her kids weren't interested in salvaging the property.

"I've had offers," she tells me, her voice sure and steady. Not at all the timid old lady she might appear. "Some generous. Some not. Developers who want to tear it down and build some hideous high-rise in its place. People have been trying to tear down the boardwalk for years, turn this place into Miami or something. All concrete and shiny glass."

Her derisive sniff reveals exactly how she feels about all this. "This town will never be like Miami. It has too much charm," I assure her.

"The developers don't care about charm. They only see dollar signs." Lydia picks up her teacup. "My only terms are that whoever buys my hotel has to preserve the intent. Maintain the character. I want to move closer to my grandkids, spend whatever time I have left with my family." She sighs. "But I simply can't bear to leave without knowing The Beacon is well cared for."

"I can make you that promise," I say honestly. "It's the charm of the place that made me fall in love with it. I can commit to restoring everything as close to original as possible. Update the wiring and plumbing. Reinforce the bones. Make sure it survives another fifty years."

Lydia examines me, as if gauging whether to take me seriously or write me off as a silly college girl who's wasting her time.

Several seconds tick by before she gives a slow nod. "Well, then, young lady, write down a number."

A number? I know nothing about the hotel real estate market, so I'm completely flying by the seat of my pants as I type a figure into the Notes app on my phone. It's my best estimation of how much a property like this might cost, but also not enough to clean out my entire business account.

I slide the phone over. Lydia studies the screen, one eyebrow jerking up as if she's surprised I have real money to offer.

For the next ten minutes, we go back and forth. It takes some haggling on my part. And I might have been suckered into overpaying by pictures of her grandkids, but eventually we come to a deal.

Just like that, I'm about to be the proud owner of my very own boardwalk hotel.

I feel high after closing my first successful business deal, giddy excitement coursing through my veins. *Such* a rush. At the same time, it's insane. I'm twenty years old and I just bought a *hotel*. Despite how crazy it sounds, it feels so right. My mind immediately races with next steps. In an instant I see my future, my empire growing. I promised my parents I would focus on school, and I still plan to— I'll just be focusing on my new role as hotel owner at the same time. I can juggle both.

Maybe.

Hopefully.

Even after Lydia and I shake on it and I call my lawyer to start the paperwork, it doesn't feel real until I coax Preston to see the property the next day.

Rather than share in my excitement, however, he sticks a knife straight through my enthusiasm.

"What's this?" He scowls at the gutted hotel with its crumbling walls and water-damaged furnishings spilling out.

"My new hotel."

Eyes narrowed, Preston slants his head at me. As if to say, *Explain yourself.*

"I know it isn't much now. You have to imagine it after a complete renovation." I almost cringe at the note of desperation I hear in my voice. "I'm going to restore it entirely. Totally vintage. Postwar luxury all the way. Turn this place into a five-star resort."

"You're not serious." His expression falls flat. Mouth presses into a hard line. Not exactly the reception I'd hoped for.

"Okay, I get that I don't know anything about owning a hotel, but I'll learn. I didn't know anything about building a website or running a business either. But that didn't stop me before, right? Maybe I'll change majors to hospitality or something."

He doesn't answer.

Each second of silence slowly sucks away more of my joy.

"Preston. What's wrong?" I ask weakly.

He shakes his head, tosses up his hands. "I'm really at a loss here, Mackenzie. This has got to be the most irresponsible, immature thing you've ever done."

"What?"

"You heard me."

He sounds like my dad, which I don't appreciate in the least. Granted, I didn't put a lot of thought into this venture before pulling the trigger—I tend to act more on gut instinct. Still, I thought he'd be a little happy for me.

"I'm very disappointed in you, frankly. I thought after our talk—after your little mistake—we were on the same page. About the plan. Our future."

"Preston, that's not fair." Throwing the kiss back in my face is a low blow. One has nothing to do with the other.

He ignores me, finishing with, "That plan doesn't include a hotel." His lips twist into a disapproving frown.

"You don't see the potential here? At all?" I ask unhappily.

"Potential? Look at this place. It's a dump. A teardown at best. Maybe you can get something out of the land, but a renovation? You're out of your mind. You don't know the first thing about any of this. Did you even think for two seconds before leveraging your trust fund for this stupid distraction?"

Indignation shoots through me. "I'm more capable than you think. And I didn't use my trust fund. I have the cash on hand, if you must know."

"How?" he demands.

I jut my chin. "From my websites."

Pres looks startled. "Your silly little tech thing?"

Now I'm pissed. I can feel the heat pouring out of my face as my nails dig into my palms. "Yes, my silly little tech thing," I echo bitterly.

I've never elaborated on how much money my sites have generated, and he has never seemed particularly interested beyond poking fun at them. I thought it was a guy thing. Harmless teasing. Sometimes he'd come over when I was working on *BoyfriendFails* and tell me how cute I looked with my face all furrowed in concentration. He'd grin and call me his "sexy tycoon." I thought he was proud of me, proud of all the work I was putting into the venture.

It isn't until this very moment that I realize he wasn't smiling out of pride. He wasn't seeing me as a "tycoon."

He was laughing at me.

"That was supposed to be a hobby," he says flatly. "If I'd known you were earning an income from it, I would have—"

"You would have what?" I challenge. "Forced me to stop?"

"Guided you in the right direction," he corrects, and his patronizing tone makes my blood boil. "We've spoken about this before. Many times. We'd go to college together. You'd have whatever hobbies you wanted during school. I'd graduate first, take over at my dad's bank. You'd graduate, join the boards of your mom's foundations." Preston shakes his head at me. "You agreed I'd be the breadwinner in the relationship, while you focused on charity work and raising our family."

My jaw falls open. Oh my God. Whenever he'd said stuff like that, he'd used a teasing voice. Made it sound like a joke.

He was actually being *serious*?

"You're going to back out of the deal." The finality with which he issues the order shakes something loose inside me. "You're lucky I'm here to stop you before your parents find out. I don't know what's gotten into you lately, Mackenzie, but you need to get ahold of yourself."

I stare at him. Stunned. I never imagined he would hate this idea with such ferocity. At the very, *very* least, I thought he would be supportive of my decision. The fact that he isn't leaves me shaken.

If I could misjudge him on this to such an extent, what else have I been wrong about?

CHAPTER NINETEEN

COOPER

"We're out of booze."

I roll my eyes at Evan, who's sprawled on the living room couch with one arm flung over the edge. The coffee table I built last weekend is already stained with beer and covered with cigarette butts. Someone must've knocked over the overflowing ashtray last night, during another one of Evan's impromptu parties.

"It's noon on Sunday," I tell my brother. "You don't need booze. Chug some water, for fuck's sake."

"I'm not saying I want a drink right now. But someone needs to make a beer run. We're hosting poker night tomorrow."

By "someone," he clearly means me, because he promptly closes his eyes and says, "Take Daisy with you. She likes riding in the truck."

I leave Evan to his beauty sleep and whistle for the dog. I don't normally let my brother order me around, but truth is, I'm feeling stir crazy.

I didn't join in on last night's drunken festivities. Instead, I spent most of the night in my workshop, went to sleep before midnight, and was abruptly awakened at seven a.m. by a disturbing, X-rated dream about Mackenzie. I was in bed with her, on top of her, thrusting deep while she moaned against my lips. Then I lifted my head and Mac's face transformed into that chick Sutton's face, which jolted me right out of slumber.

Swear to God, this girl has wreaked havoc on my brain. Doesn't matter if I'm asleep or awake—thoughts of Mackenzie Cabot poison my consciousness and drum up a whole slew of emotions I'd rather not feel.

Anger, because she'd chosen Kincaid over me.

Frustration, because I know there was something real between us.

Guilt, because my original intentions had been shadier than shady.

And for the past couple days? Disgust. Because, in order to divert her friends' suspicions that we might know each other, she forced me to pretend to be my twin brother—and then had the nerve to bitch about me hooking up with another girl. Not that Sutton and I even hooked up. We went for a walk and then I put her in a cab. But still. Mackenzie had no right to be pissed. She's the one who kissed the hell outta me and then bid me fucking adieu.

"Come on," I mutter to Daisy. "Let's go buy some beer for your boyfriend."

When she sees me reaching for her leash, the golden retriever dances happily at my feet. We head out to my truck, and I open the passenger side door so Daisy can jump up. She only recently learned how to do that. Before, she'd been too little, but now her legs are in that gangly teenager stage, giving her enough leverage to leap higher. She's growing so damn fast.

"Too bad Mac can't see you," I muse to the dog, whose curious, excited gaze is glued out the window. Each time the wind tickles her nose, she releases a high-pitched yip. She derives joy from the simplest pleasures.

In town, I grab a few cases of beer, along with a bottle of tequila and some snacks. As I stow my purchases in the cab, someone calls my name.

I turn to see Tate striding down the sidewalk toward me. He's holding aviator sunglasses in one hand, and his keys and phone in the other.

"Hey," I greet him. "How's it going?"

"Good. I'm meeting Wyatt at Sharkey's for lunch if you want to tag along."

"Yeah, I'm in." The last thing I feel like doing right now is going home and cleaning up the mess Evan left. "Lemme grab Daisy."

"Oh, hell yes," Tate says when he notices the dog's head poking out the passenger window. "Bring the chick magnet."

Most of the bars and restaurants in the Bay are dog friendly—particularly Sharkey's, where the staff brings out water bowls and treats for canine guests. Once Tate and I climb the rickety wood staircase up to the second floor of the bar, Daisy is treated like the queen she thinks she is.

"Oh my goodness!" the waitress up front exclaims, pure delight in her eyes. "Look at this cutie! What's her name?"

"Daisy," Tate answers for me, then takes the leash from my hand as if to claim ownership of the puppy. "And you are?"

"Jessica," chirps the waitress. Now she's all starry-eyed, because she notices Tate's golden-boy looks. Dude has the infallible ability to dazzle every woman he meets.

This isn't to say I don't attract my fair share of attention. It's just a different kind of attention.

When women look at Tate, they're struck with romantic notions of weddings and babies.

With me, they see raw, dirty sex. Joke's on them, though. Tate is the biggest slut in the Bay. Jessica must be new in town, otherwise she'd be well aware of this fact.

"Let me show you to your table," Jessica says, and then she, Tate, and my dog saunter off.

With a grin, I trail after them, silently betting that Tate will have secured her number before we even pick up our menus.

I lose. He doesn't get it until she delivers our waters.

"Good job, partner," Tate tells Daisy, who's sitting at his feet and gazing up at him adoringly.

Wyatt arrives about ten minutes later. Since Ren isn't with him, I assume they're still broken up.

"No Ren?" Tate wrinkles his forehead. "She hasn't taken you back yet?"

"Nope." After greeting Daisy with a pat on the head, Wyatt plops himself on the stool across from me and grabs a menu. Then he sets it down without reading it. "Who am I kidding? We all know I'm getting the fish sandwich."

"What's taking Ren so long to forgive you?" Tate asks, grinning. "Your epic reunions usually happen fairly fast."

"She's dragging it out this time," Wyatt complains. "She went out with some meathead from her gym last night and sent me a selfie of them watching *The Bachelorette* together because she knew it'd piss me off."

I raise an eyebrow. "Why would that piss you off?"

"Because it's our favorite show, dickhead. She's goddamn TV-cheating on me with a guy who wears mesh tank tops."

Tate snickers. "Are you more upset about the fact that Ren's watching a dumb reality show without you, or that she might be banging a gym bro?"

Wyatt waves his hand. "She's not banging him. It's just revenge dating. Like when I went out with that chick who works at the surf school after Ren threw out all my band shirts without asking."

"Didn't you end up screwing the surf school chick?" Tate says in confusion.

Wyatt stares at him. "That was you, dumbass."

After a few seconds of pensive recollection, Tate nods decisively. "Oh yeah. You're right." He grins. "That chick was wild. She convinced me to try Viagra for the first time. Long night."

Laughter sputters from my throat.

"You took Viagra without me, bro?" Wyatt accuses.

I laugh even harder. "Since when is it a team activity?" I howl at Wyatt.

Jessica returns to take our food orders and proceeds to flirt shamelessly with Tate. "Does this cutie like walks?"

He winks. "This cutie *loves* walks."

"I meant the dog."

"So did I," he says innocently.

"I'm off in about an hour. Why don't you and Daisy meet me on the beach once you're done eating and I clock out?"

Before I can remind Tate that Daisy isn't his dog, he flashes his dimples at the waitress and says, "It's a date."

As Jessica saunters off, I roll my eyes. "Are you seriously using my puppy to get laid?"

"Of course. I told you, puppies are chick magnets." He shoves a strand of hair off his forehead. "Just let me borrow her for a few hours, dude. You know I'm good with dogs. I've got three at home."

"Fine. But I'm not hanging around town on your account. Drop her off at my place later. Her dinnertime's at five. Don't be late, asshole."

Tate grins. "Yes, Dad."

"You think if I had Daisy with me when I go to see Ren, I'd have a better shot at winning her back?" Wyatt asks thoughtfully.

"Definitely," Tate says.

Wyatt's head swivels toward me. "Can I borrow her tomorrow?"

My friends are idiots.

Then again, so am I. Because when my phone buzzes and Mac's name flashes on the screen, I don't do the smart thing and ignore the call.

I answer it.

CHAPTER TWENTY

MACKENZIE

The summer after I graduated high school, I traveled alone in Europe. A present from my parents. I had just walked back to the Colosseum from Vatican City when, in a sort of burst of manic impulsiveness, I marched right past my hotel to the train station. I didn't know where I was headed. I simply bought a first-class ticket on the next train, which happened to be going to Florence. From there, Bologna. Milan. Then, through Switzerland, France, and Spain. Two days after leaving Italy, I called my hotel to have them send my luggage to Barcelona.

To this day, I don't know what possessed me. A sudden, urgent need to break free, to get lost. To disrupt the order of my life and prove to myself I was alive and in control of my own destiny. Which is to say I don't remember deciding to call Cooper, only that one day after Preston shot down my hotel fantasy, two weeks since I'd kissed Cooper and told him never to contact me again, and fifteen minutes after we hang up, he's standing beside me on the boardwalk staring at the dilapidated exterior of The Beacon Hotel.

"You just . . . bought it?" Bemused, Cooper rakes a hand through his dark hair.

I'm momentarily distracted by his tanned forearm, his defined biceps. He's wearing a black T-shirt. Jeans that hang low on his hips.

It feels like I'm seeing him for the first time all over again. I hadn't forgotten what the sight of him does to me, but it's more potent now that my tolerance has waned. My heart beats faster than usual, my palms are damper, my mouth drier.

"Well, there's paperwork and due diligence. But if that goes well . . ."

I'm more nervous now than when I made the offer to Lydia. Than when I showed Preston. For some reason, I need Cooper to be happy for me, and I didn't realize how much until this moment.

"Can we look around?"

He gives nothing away. Not boredom or disapproval. Not excitement either. We barely said hello and didn't mention a word about our kisses or our fight. Just *Hey, so, um, I'm buying a hotel. What do you think?* I have no idea why he even showed up to meet me here.

"Sure," I say. "The inspector said the ground level is stable. We shouldn't go upstairs, though."

Together we tour the property, stepping over storm-tossed furniture and moldy carpets. Some interior rooms are in nearly perfect condition, while beach-view rooms are little more than empty carcasses exposed to the elements, where the walls have collapsed and storm surges long ago sucked everything out to sea. The kitchen looks like it could be up and running tomorrow. The ballroom, more like a setting of a ghost ship horror movie. Outside, the front of the hotel facing the street belies the damage inside, still perfectly intact except for missing roof shingles and overgrown foliage.

"What are your plans for it?" he asks as we peek behind the front desk. An old-fashioned guest book, with the words *The Beacon Hotel* embossed on its cover with gold lettering, is still tucked on a shelf with the wall of room keys. Some scattered, others still on their hooks.

"The previous owner had one demand: Don't tear it down and put up an ugly high-rise."

"I came here all the time as a kid. Evan and I would use the pool, hang out in the beach cabanas until we were chased out. Steph worked here a few summers during high school. I remember all the old hardwood, the brass fixtures."

"I want to entirely restore it," I tell him. "Salvage as much as possible. Source vintage antiques for the rest of it."

He lets out a low whistle. "It'd be expensive. We're talking about cherry furniture that'll have to be custom replicated. Handmade light fixtures. There are stone floor tiles and countertops in here they don't even make anymore except in small batches."

I nod. "And I already know the electrical is out of code. All the drywall has to come out."

"But I see it." He wanders through the lobby toward the grand staircase, where he runs his hand over the intricately carved bannister. "With the right touch, and enough money, it's got potential."

"Really?"

"Oh yeah. Teeming with potential."

"I know this sounds dumb," I say, taking a seat at the foot of the stairs, "but when I first set eyes on this place, I had this image in my head. Guests sitting on the veranda in rocking chairs, sipping wine, and watching the tide roll in. I saw it so clearly."

"It's not dumb." Cooper sits beside me.

I feel no animosity from him, as if we're almost friends again. Except for the same magnetic tug begging me to run my fingers through his hair.

"When I put a salvaged piece of wood on my bench, I don't have a plan for what it'll be. I just sit with it. Wait for it to express itself. Then it practically builds itself in my mind, and I'm following along."

I bite my lip. "My parents aren't going to be happy about this."

Lately it doesn't take much to set my father off. Most of it is work stress, but it seems as if he's engaged in constant battle about one thing or another. Probably where I get my combative side. Thing is, when the battles end badly, his frustration tends to manifest in being loudly disappointed in me.

"Who the hell cares?" Cooper scoffs.

"Yeah, easy for you to say."

"I mean it. Since when do you care about what anyone else has to say?"

"You don't understand how hard it is to get out from under their thumb. They run practically every part of my life."

"Because you let them."

"No, but—"

"Look. In the time I've known you, you've mostly been a stubborn, opinionated pain in the ass."

I laugh, admitting to myself that most of our conversations have devolved into stalemate arguments. "It's not my fault you're always wrong."

"Watch it, Cabot," he says with a playfully threatening glare. "Seriously, though. You've got your shit together better than most people I know. To hell with your parents approving. Be your own person."

"You don't know them."

"I don't have to know them. I know you." He turns to face me fully, leveling me with serious eyes. "Mac, you are a force to be reckoned with. You don't take shit, you take names. Don't forget that."

Damn it. Fucking damn it.

"Why do you have to do that?" I mutter, getting to my feet. I can't control my muscles. I have to move, find some air.

"Do what?" He gets up, following me as I pace the room.

"Be so . . ." I gesture incoherently in his direction. "Like that."

"You've lost me."

It's easier when he's being a dick. Flirting, coming on strong. Arguing with me and calling me princess. It's easier to dismiss him as just another hot guy with too much attitude, someone not to be taken seriously. Then he's all sweet and kind and gets my head messed up. Drags my heart into it, kicking and screaming.

"Don't be nice to me," I blurt out in frustration. "It's confusing."

"Yeah, well, I was a little confused when you were scraping your nails down my back, but hey, I went with it."

"Good," I say, spinning to point at him. "Do that. That I can work with. I handle you better when you're a prick."

"So that's what it is? You're afraid to give a damn because then you can't keep lying to yourself about us?"

"There is no us," I shoot back. "We kissed. Big deal."

"Twice, princess."

"And it went so well we didn't talk for two weeks."

"Hey, you called me." Defiant, he stares me down. A dare.

"And I see now it was a mistake."

Gritting my teeth, I stalk forward, my sights set on the arched doorway leading to the exit. But that requires walking past Cooper, who reaches for my waist before I can sidestep him.

In the blink of an eye I'm in his arms, pressed tight against his chest. I feel every warm, solid inch of him against my body. Silence descends as he tips his head to look down at me. My breath catches. I forget who I was before I met him. In this bubble, in this quiet place where no one will find us, we can be entirely ourselves.

"Well . . ." I whisper, waiting for him to say something, do something. Anything. The anticipation is killing me, and I think he knows it.

"You can leave anytime you want," he says roughly.

"I know." Still, my feet don't move. My heart beats a barrage against my rib cage. I'm suffocating, but all I want to do is sink deeper into his arms.

I shiver when his thumb lightly caresses my side over the thin fabric of my loose white shirt. Then the light touch becomes strong fingers curling over my hip, and my knees wobble. I'm smoke in his arms. I don't feel solid.

"What are we doing, Mac?" His deep, dark eyes penetrate me.

"I thought you knew."

Urgently, his lips cover mine. His fingers bite into my hip as mine snake into his hair and pull him toward me. The kiss is hungry, desperate. When his tongue prods at the seam of my lips, seeking entry, I whimper quietly and give him what he wants. Our tongues meet and I nearly keel over again.

"It's okay, I got you," Cooper whispers, and before I know what's happening, I'm off my feet, legs wrapped around him.

He walks us backward until I'm pressed into the exposed concrete of a cracked wall. He's hard against me. I can't fight the wave of insistent arousal that compels me to grind myself against him, seeking the friction that will unleash this knot of repressed longing that's sat taut inside me for weeks. This isn't me. I'm not the girl who loses her mind over a guy, who gets tangled up in midafternoon interludes of semi-public, semi-sexual exploits. And yet here we are, mouths fused, bodies straining to get closer.

"Fuck," he groans. His hands find their way under my shirt, callused fingers dipping beneath the cups of my bra.

The moment he teases my nipples, it's like someone's opened the curtains in a pitch-black room. Startling as blinding sunlight pouring through.

"I can't," I whisper against his lips.

Right away Cooper pulls back and sets me on my feet. "What's wrong?"

His lips are wet, swollen. His hair wild. A dozen fantasies rush through my mind as I struggle to slow my breathing. The wall at my back is the only thing keeping me upright.

"I still have a boyfriend," I say as an apology. Because although I might not be happy with Preston at the moment, we haven't officially broken up.

"Are you serious?" Cooper storms away before turning to stare at me with exasperation. "Wake up, Mackenzie." He throws his hands up. "You're a smart girl. How are you this blind?"

My eyebrows crash together in confusion. "What is that supposed to mean?"

"Your boyfriend is cheating on you," he spits out.

"What?"

"I asked around. For two years, everyone in the Bay has seen that asshole screwing everything that moves."

An angry scowl twists my mouth. "You're lying."

He's picked the wrong girl if he thinks I'm falling for such an obvious ploy. He's only saying this because he wants to get in my pants, to make me furious enough at Preston that I'll give in to the undeniable attraction between us. Well, Cooper doesn't even know Preston. If he did, he'd understand that Pres is the last one who'd be running around with random hookups.

"You'd love it if I was." Cooper approaches me, visibly seething. I'm not sure which one of us is more pissed off at this point. "Face it, princess. Your Prince Charming pulls more ass than a barstool."

Something comes over me.

Blind, hot rage.

I slap him. Hard. So hard my hand stings.

The crack echoes through the empty hotel.

At first he just stares at me. Shocked. Angry.

Then a low, mocking laugh slides out of his throat. "You know what, Mac? Believe me or don't believe me." He chuckles again. A raspy, dark warning. "Either way, I'll be the one watching smugly from the sidelines when you're finally hit with a dose of reality."

CHAPTER TWENTY-ONE

MACKENZIE

Cooper's accusation against Preston torments me for the next twenty-four hours. It clouds my mind, poisons my thoughts. I don't pay a lick of attention during my Monday classes. Instead, I run Cooper's words over and over again in my head, alternating between anger, uneasiness, and doubt.

For two years everyone in the Bay has seen that asshole screwing everything that moves.

Face it, princess. Your Prince Charming pulls more ass than a bar-stool.

Was he telling the truth? I have no reason to trust him. He could have made the allegation merely to get under my skin. It's what he's good at.

Then again, what reason does he have to lie? Even if I dumped Preston, that doesn't mean I'd run straight into Cooper's arms.

Does it?

When I got back to the dorm yesterday after our fight, I had to force myself not to call Preston and lay everything on the line. Ask questions and demand answers. I'm still pissed at him for how he reacted to my hotel. Pissed at the realization that he doesn't take me seriously as a businesswoman, and at the way he flatly laid out a future that robs me of all agency.

I already had plenty of reasons to question my relationship with Preston before Cooper lobbed those accusations. Now, I'm even more of a mess. My mind is mush, my insides twisted into knots.

I leave the lecture hall with my head down, not stopping to make small talk with any of my classmates. Outside, I inhale the fresh air, now crisp and a bit cooler, as fall begins to make its appearance after an extended summer.

My phone buzzes in my canvas shoulder bag. I reach for it, finding a text from Bonnie asking if I want to meet for lunch. My roommate has the uncanny ability to read my mind, so I tell her I have to study, then find an empty bench in the quad and pull out my laptop.

I need a distraction, an escape from my chaotic thoughts. Making plans for the hotel provides that respite.

For the next few hours, I scour the internet for the resources I need to get started on this project. I make a list of contractors, contacting each one to request a site visit, so they can give me hard estimates about how much it'll cost to get the building up to code. I research county ordinances and permit regulations. Watch a couple videos about commercial plumbing and electrical installations. Read up on the latest in hurricane-proof construction and pricing insurance policies.

It's . . . a lot.

My mother calls as I'm sliding the laptop back in my bag and getting up to stretch my legs. Sitting on a wrought iron bench for three hours did a number on my muscles.

"Mom, hey," I greet her.

Skipping the pleasantries, she gets right to the point. "Mackenzie, your father and I would like to take you and Preston to dinner this evening—how is seven o'clock?"

I clench my teeth. Their sense of entitlement is grating as hell. She's acting as if I have a choice in the matter, when we both know that's not the case.

"I don't know if Preston is free," I say tightly. I've been avoiding him for two days, ever since he shot down my dreams and told me I was irresponsible and immature.

The memory of his harsh, condescending words reignites my anger at him. No. No way am I bringing him to dinner tonight and risking a huge fight in front of my parents. I've already slapped one guy. Best to not make it two.

But my mother throws a wrench in that. "Your father already spoke to Preston. He said he's happy to join us."

My mouth falls open in shock. Seriously? They made arrangements with my boyfriend before calling *me*, their own daughter?

Mom gives me no time to object. "We'll see you at seven, sweetheart."

The moment she disconnects, I scramble to call Preston. He answers on the first ring.

"Hey, babe."

Hey, babe? Is he for real right now? I've been ignoring his calls and texts since Saturday afternoon. On Sunday morning, when he threatened to show up at my dorm, I texted that I needed some space and would call him when I was ready.

And now he's *hey, babe*ing me?

Does he not realize how mad I am?

"I'm glad you finally called." His audible remorse confirms he does recognize my unhappiness. "I know you're still sore over our little spat, so I was trying to give you some space like you asked."

"Really?" I say bitterly. "Is that why you agreed to have dinner with my parents without even consulting me?"

"Would you have picked up the phone if I called?" he counters.

Good point.

"Besides, I literally just hung up with your dad. You called before I had a chance to call you first."

"Fine. Whatever. But I don't want to go tonight, Preston. After what happened Saturday at the hotel, I really do need that space."

"I know." The note of regret in his voice sounds sincere. "I reacted poorly, I can't deny that. But you have to understand—you threw me for a total loop. The last thing I expected was being told you'd gone and bought a *hotel*. It was a lot to take in, Mac."

"I get that. But you spoke to me like I was a disobedient child. Do you even realize how humiliating—" I stop, drawing a calming breath. "No. I don't want to rehash this right now. We do need to talk, but not now. And I can't do dinner. I just can't."

There's a brief pause.

"Mackenzie. We both know you're not going to tell your parents you can't go."

Yeah.

He's got me there.

"Pick me up at quarter to seven," I mutter.

Back at Tally Hall, I steam a suitable dress my mom won't side-eye and make myself presentable. I decide on a navy boatneck that's just on the slutty side of modest. My silent protest against having my evening hijacked. As soon as Preston picks me up from my dorm, he suggests I put on a cardigan.

I sit in silence on the drive over to the fancy new steakhouse near campus. Preston is smart enough not to push me to talk.

At the restaurant, we're given a private room, thanks to my dad's assistant calling ahead. On the way in, Dad does his usual grip-and-grin with voters, then poses for a picture with the manager that'll end up framed on the wall and run in the local paper tomorrow. Even dinner becomes a major affair when my father shows up, all because his ego isn't content to anonymously eat out with his family.

Meanwhile, my mother stands to the side, hands clasped politely in front of her, a plastic smile on her face. I can't tell if she still loves this stuff or if the Botox means she feels nothing anymore.

Beside me, Preston has stars in his eyes.

Through cocktails and appetizers, my father goes on about some new spending bill. I can't find it in me to even feign interest as I push my beet salad around my plate. Preston engages him with an eagerness that, for some reason tonight, is getting on my last nerve. I'd always appreciated Preston's ability to chat up my parents, take some of the burden off me at these things. They love him, so bringing him along keeps them in a good mood. But right now, I'm finding him incredibly annoying.

For a fleeting moment I consider plucking up the courage to break the news to my parents—*Guess what! I bought a hotel!* But as Mom starts on how she can't wait until I get more involved with her charities, I'm convinced they won't react any better than Preston did.

"I was hoping you'd let me take Mackenzie along to Europe this summer," Preston says as the entrées arrive. "My father's finally bowed to the pressure and agreed to take my mother shopping for a new vacation home. We're sailing the yacht along the coast from Spain to Greece."

This is news to me. I'm pretty sure there's been no recent discussion of my summer plans, and even if there has been, that was before I had a hotel to restore. Preston knows damn well I can't leave Avalon Bay this summer.

Or maybe he's confident he can talk his immature, irresponsible, wife-material girlfriend into not going through with the purchase.

Bitterness coats my throat. I gulp it down with a bite of my lemon and garlic infused sole.

"Doesn't that sound marvelous," my mom says, with the slightest edge to her voice.

One of her greatest resentments over her husband's career—

not that she hasn't enjoyed the privilege of being a congressman's wife—is her enforced poverty of only two domestic vacation homes when all her friends are always skipping off to their private chalets in Zermatt or villas in Mallorca. Dad says it isn't a good look for them to flaunt their wealth while on the taxpayers' dime—even if the vast majority of the family money comes from inheritance and the corporation my father stepped down from to run for office, though he still sits on the board. But attention invites questions, and Dad hates those.

"She does put up with a lot from him," Preston jokes, grinning at my mother. "So does this one." He nods at me and finds my hand under the table to squeeze.

I shrug his hand off and reach for my water glass instead.

My patience is at an all-time low. I used to be so good at tuning out these conversations. Blowing them off as harmless banter to keep my parents happy. As long as Preston kept them entertained and everyone got along, my life was infinitely easier. Now, it seems the status quo isn't doing it for me anymore.

"What are your plans after graduation next year?" my dad asks Preston. He's barely said two words to me all night. As if I'm an excuse to see their real child.

"My father wants me at his bank's headquarters in Atlanta."

"That'll be quite the change of pace," Dad says, cutting into his bloody steak.

"I'm looking forward to the challenge. I intend to learn everything about the family business from the bottom up. How the mail gets processed to acquisitions and mergers."

"To how the regulations get passed," my father adds. "We should set something up for next term. Have you at the Capitol. There are some important pieces of legislation up for committee—it'd be an invaluable learning experience to sit in on those hearings. See how the sausage gets made, as it were."

"Sounds great," Preston says, beaming. "I'd appreciate that, sir."

Never once has my father offered to have me out to Washington for a take-your-daughter-to-work day. The only time I ever stepped foot inside the Capitol building was for a photo op. When Dad was sworn in, I was ushered into a room with the other freshman families, posed, and was promptly shoved out the door. The other ne'er-do-well congressional kids and I ended up running amok through the bars and clubs of DC, until some senator's kid started roughing up a diplomat brat and it turned into a showdown between Secret Service and foreign security forces.

"It's a shame you and Mackenzie only have one year together at Garnet before you'll be separated again. But I know you'll make it work," Mom chimes in.

"Actually," Preston says, "Mackenzie will be joining me in Atlanta."

I will?

"Garnet offers a full online curriculum to finish her degree so she won't have to transfer schools," he continues. "It's only a short flight from Atlanta if she should need to visit campus for any reason."

What the fuck?

I gawk at Preston, but he either doesn't notice or doesn't care. My parents, too, are oblivious to my rising distress.

"That is an excellent solution," Dad tells Preston.

Mom nods in complete agreement.

Why am I even here if my participation in the conversation, in my life, is entirely superfluous? I'm little more than an ornament, a piece of furniture they move from room to room. These are my parents. My boyfriend. The people who, ostensibly, care the most about me in the world.

Yet I feel completely invisible. And not for the first time.

As they chatter through the main course, oblivious to my existential crisis, I suddenly see the next five, ten, twenty years of my life closing in on me.

Less a future than a threat.

More a sentence than an opportunity.

But then it occurs to me. I'm not a child anymore. I don't have to be here. In fact, there's absolutely nothing holding me in this seat. My mind wanders back to that lunch with Preston's friends, how the girls were so accepting of Seb's apparent forays into extracurricular fellatio. And then later, the way Preston so easily forgave me for my own indiscretion. The clues align themselves and the picture becomes clear.

So fucking clear.

Pushing my plate away, I toss my napkin on the table and scrape my chair back.

My mother looks up, frowning slightly.

"I'm sorry," I announce to the table. "I have to go."

Without a second of hesitation, I bolt for the door before anyone has a chance to protest. Outside the restaurant, I try to camouflage in the shrubbery near the valet stand as I hurriedly call for a cab, but my hiding spot sucks and Preston spots me the moment he stalks outside.

"What the hell was that?" he demands.

I draw a slow breath. "I don't want to argue with you. Go back inside, Pres. I'm done here."

"Keep your voice down." Shushing me, he grabs my elbow and drags me around the corner, out of earshot, like I'm a child getting scolded. "What the *hell* has gotten into you?"

I yank my arm from his grasp. "I can't do this anymore. You, them—all of it. I'm so over it I'm bursting with apathy. That, in there, was me spending my very last fuck."

"Have you completely lost your mind?" Preston stares at me, incensed. "That's what this is—this tantrum, the hotel nonsense. It's stress. The stress of freshman year is getting to you. You're cracking under the pressure." He starts nodding. "I understand. We can get you help, send you to a spa or something. I'm sure we can make arrangements with the dean to finish your semester—"

"A spa?" I can't help it. I erupt, laughing in his face. In this moment, I don't think he's ever known me less.

He narrows his eyes at my mocking laughter.

"This isn't stress. It's clarity." My humor fading, I meet his gaze. "You're cheating on me, Preston."

He frowns. "And who told you that?"

That's his response? If I'd doubted it before, I'm not doubting it now. He can't even be bothered to muster up a denial?

"Are you saying it's not true?" I challenge. "That you aren't just like your buddy Sebastian, sleeping around with girls that aren't 'wife material' while pledging his undying love to Chrissy? Chrissy, who doesn't even care that he's sleeping around." I shake my head incredulously. "Look me in the eye and tell me you're not like that."

"I'm not like that."

But he doesn't look me in the eye.

I bark out a harsh laugh. "That's why you weren't at all disturbed by Seb's actions, right, Preston? Because you're exactly like him. And you know what's funny? I'm not even mad. I should be," I tell him, because there's plenty of anger from all the ways he's disrespected me tonight. "I should be pissed. But I realized tonight that I don't care anymore."

"You can't break up with me," he says sternly, as if he's telling me I can't have candy because it'll rot my teeth.

"I am. I did."

"Forget whatever it is you think I've done. That's just extracurricular bullshit—"

There's that word again.

"It has nothing to do with our relationship. I love you, Mackenzie. And you love me too."

For years, I've confused what we had for love. I do love Preston. Or at least I did, at some point. It started that way. I'm sure of it. But we were never *in love*. I mistook boredom for comfort and comfort for romance. Because I didn't know what true passion was. I didn't know what I was missing, how it's supposed to feel when you can't contain yourself, when desire for another person consumes you so completely, when your appreciation and affection for them is total and unconditional.

"Stop it, Mackenzie." Oops. Now he's pissed. I might be sent to my room with no dessert. "You're throwing a temper tantrum and it isn't cute. Come back inside. Apologize to your parents. We'll forget this whole thing ever happened."

"You don't get it. I've made up my mind. I'm done."

"No, you're not."

I didn't want to resort to the nuclear option, but he's given me no choice. "There's someone else."

"What the fuck? Who?" he snaps, anger reddening his face.

My cab pulls up to the curb. Thank God.

"You don't get to know," I say coolly. "And now I'm leaving. Don't follow me."

For the first time tonight, he listens.

CHAPTER TWENTY-TWO

MACKENZIE

Fifteen minutes later, I'm standing at Cooper's front door. I think I knew when I left the dinner table where I was going to end up. I knew—when I walked away from Cooper yesterday, when I spent hours spinning his words over in my head, remembering our hungry kisses—that if I found my way back here again, it would be with a purpose.

When he opens the door, I almost lose my nerve. He's wearing a T-shirt and ripped jeans. Hair damp as if he just showered. His looks, his body, his tattoos are pure temptation. I hate that he doesn't have to do anything, say anything, to get me all sideways and messed up. It isn't fair.

"Hey." I swallow against the sudden onset of dry mouth.

He stares me down hard without a word. I expected anger. Maybe to be chased off with a warning not to show my face in these parts again.

This is worse.

"Look, I came to apologize."

"That right?" Cooper takes up the whole doorway, strong arms braced on either side.

"I was out of line," I say remorsefully. "I never should have insinuated you have herpes. Perpetuating the stigma of STDs and slut-shaming is wrong, and I'm sorry."

Though he tries his best to hide it, Cooper can't entirely smother the smirk that pulls at the corner of his mouth. He drops his arms.

"Fine, come in."

He leads me through the empty house to the lit back deck that looks out onto the bay. Neither of us is quite sure how to start, so we both lean against the railing, pretending to watch the waves through the darkness.

"I've never slapped anyone before," I confess, because it's my responsibility to break the ice, and for some reason this is harder than I expected.

"You're pretty good at it," he says dryly. "Fucking hurt."

"If it makes you feel any better, my hand was still sore when I woke up today. You have a hard face."

"It does make me feel better," he says with a smile in his voice. "A little."

"I am sorry. I way overreacted and totally lost it. I felt terrible about it. I still feel terrible."

Cooper shrugs. "Don't sweat it. I've had worse."

Part of me wants him to lash out. Tell me I'm a brat and a spoiled bitch. But he's so cool and calm. Unreadable, giving nothing away, which makes all of this nearly impossible. Because for everything I learn about Cooper, I don't know him at all. Sometimes I think we have a connection, then I get to thinking about it until I convince myself I've concocted the entire thing in my head. As if every time we meet, I'm waking up from a dream and I don't remember what's real.

"Want to ask me where I was tonight?" I don't know why I say it except that I want him to know and coming right out with it seems . . . presumptuous?

He cocks an eyebrow.

"Well, first off, I walked out on my parents."

"Is the building still standing?" he asks, not even trying to hide his amusement.

"Uncertain. I sort of ran off in the middle of dinner." I pause. "Know what else I did?"

"What's that?"

"I broke up with my boyfriend."

This gets his attention. He turns to put his back against the railing and folds his arms, attentive.

Cooper chuckles, shaking his head. "There, now it makes sense. You're on the lam and you figured, where better to hide out? No chance anyone will come looking for you here. Am I right?"

"Something like that," I answer sheepishly. That wasn't the explicit thought in mind when I gave the cab driver Cooper's address, but it was certainly an unconscious instinct.

"So how long do you plan on lying low? Not to be a dick about it, but I'm not running a hotel here, princess."

"Touché."

Silence engulfs us, louder than the crashing of the waves against the shore.

This morning, I woke up sweating. As I blinked against the sun, the final frames of Cooper holding me against the wall—my legs wrapped around his hips, his hands burning across my skin— evaporated with the morning dew on my windowsill. What do I do with that? These are new feelings for me. I've never been this wound up over a guy. And yeah, okay, he's shown some interest too, but if he doesn't make the next move, I don't know what any of this means.

"Part of me wishes we never met," he finally says, shadows playing across his face from the deck lights.

"Why's that?" I mean, besides the obvious, I guess. I have been a major pain in the ass to him and probably way more trouble than it's worth.

"Because this is gonna get messy." Arms at his sides, he closes the small space between us until he's got me pinned against the railing with only his eyes.

Something in his expression shifts, and like a subliminal signal to my system, I'm suddenly alert.

"What's going—"

Before I can finish the thought, his lips are on mine.

Caging me against the rail, Cooper kisses me deeply. Urgently. This whole time, for weeks, we've held our breath until this moment. Relief. As his hands find my hips and press me into the splintered wood, I forget myself, consumed by lust. I kiss him back like a starved woman, moaning when he parts my legs with his and I feel his erection.

"Tell me now," he mutters, running his mouth down my neck. "Are you going to tell me to stop?"

I should consider the question. The future implications. All the ways I'm completely unprepared for what happens when I wake up tomorrow and survey the damage of tonight.

But I don't.

"No," I answer. "Don't stop."

Unleashed, Cooper doesn't hesitate. He yanks down the front of my dress just enough to expose my breasts. When he wraps his lips around one budded nipple, the rush of excitement, the adrenaline syringe through my chest, is overwhelming. I'm a different person with him. Unbridled. I grab his hand and push it down until he finds his way under my dress. Then his fingers are pulling away my bikini underwear, sliding across my clit, entering me.

"Ah fuck," he whispers against the feverish skin of my neck. "So wet."

Two fingers move inside me, while his thumb tends to the bundle of nerves that's pulsing with excitement. I hold on to his broad shoulders, biting my lip so hard I taste blood, until my legs are shaking through an orgasm.

"Mmm, that's my girl." A grin appears as he bends to kiss my lips, swallowing my gasped breaths.

His words send a thrill shooting through me. His girl. I know he doesn't mean it that way, just a turn of phrase, but the idea of being his, being entirely owned by him tonight, triggers a fresh wave of desire.

I hurry to undo the front of his jeans and pull him out, stroking. His answering groan is music to my ears. His hands slide down to squeeze my ass, dark eyes glittering with heat.

"Let's go inside," I urge.

"I've got a condom in my pocket." His voice is hoarse as I hold him throbbing in my hand.

"Really, why?"

"Let's not ask those questions."

Fair. Until an hour ago I had a boyfriend. Whatever Cooper was getting up to, or about to get up to, is none of my business.

He tears open the condom and slips it on, then hoists one of my legs up around his hip. Suddenly I'm sitting on the ledge of the railing, clinging to him as he slowly, achingly enters me. If he let me go right now, I'd topple over the rail. But I trust him. I submit completely, trusting his steady grip, welcoming the thick, hard length of him inside me.

"You feel so good, Mac." He's kissing me again. Thrusting deep, making me mindless with need.

A warm breeze sweeps through my hair. I don't care that at any moment we could be caught. That I don't even know if his brother is home. That someone might be watching us from among the silhouettes that circle the house. I don't care about anything but the foreign sensations coursing through my body, this feeling of fullness, rightness. When Cooper's fingers tangle in my hair and tug my head back to kiss my throat, nothing distracts me from his long, deep thrusts and the wild, carnal need that drives us both.

"You gonna come again?" he whispers in my ear.

"Maybe."

"Try."

He withdraws until only his tip remains in me, then plunges back in. Hard, purposeful. Keeping one strong arm wrapped around me, he brings his other hand between my legs and swipes his fingers over my clit. I gasp with pleasure.

"Oh, keep doing that," I plead.

His husky chuckle tickles my mouth as he bends his head to kiss me. His hips continue moving, but slower now, teasing, coaxing me back to the edge. Under his deliberate worshiping of my body, it doesn't take long for the pleasure to rise again, to tighten and knot and then burst in a blinding rush.

"Yes," he hisses, and his tempo speeds up. He thrusts into me with abandon until he's groaning from his own release, shuddering, panting out unsteady breaths.

I swallow, inhaling deeply to try to regulate my erratic heartbeat. "That was . . ." I have no words.

He grunts unintelligibly, also at a loss. "It was . . . yeah."

Laughing weakly, we disentangle from each other. I clumsily slide off the railing. Fix my dress. Cooper takes my hand, leading me inside.

After a shower, I borrow some clothes from him, and we take Daisy out on a walk along the moonlit beach. My fingers are still a little numb, my legs heavy. He was everything I expected and better. Raw, zealous.

Now, I'm struck by how not awkward it is. I'd never been with anyone except Preston, so I didn't know what to expect after a . . .

I don't know what this is. A hookup? A tryst? Something we won't really talk about in the morning? Somehow, I don't care. For now, we're good.

Walking back toward the house, Cooper teases Daisy with a long reed.

"So you wanna spend the night?" he asks me.

"Yeah, okay."

Starting now, I'm not overthinking it. Clean slate. Starting from scratch.

It's time I get to enjoy myself.

CHAPTER TWENTY-THREE

COOPER

My head is wrecked. Waking up with Mac in my bed, my first thought is to make some bad decisions all over again. Then I remember that I'm in deep trouble. I was all about it last night when she practically jumped on my dick. But afterward, something really messed up happened. I didn't want her to leave. I started thinking, well shit, what happens if she goes home and I get another goddamn text like, *Sorry, my bad, I made a mistake and I'm getting back together with my dipshit boyfriend*?

Which is about the point I realized that I'm fully screwed.

"Morning," she mumbles, eyes closed.

When she rolls over and drapes her thigh over my leg, teasing my hard-on, I don't stop myself from grabbing a handful of her ass.

"Morning," I answer.

She responds by kissing my left pec before giving it a little bite.

This chick is something else. It's always the good girls, right? All sweater sets and manners until you get them alone. Then they're shoving your face between their legs and leaving with blood under their fingernails.

We cuddle there for a few minutes, warm and lazy in my bed. Then Mac lifts her head to peek at me. "Can I ask you something?" She's apprehensive.

"Sure."

"It's kind of a nosy question."

"Alright."

"Like, totally none of my business."

"You gonna ask it or should we keep discussing the question-asking process itself?"

She bites me again, a teasing nip at my shoulder. "Fine. Did you have sex with Sutton?"

"No. We took a walk on the pier and then she puked over the railing, so I put her in a cab."

Mackenzie keeps prying. "If she hadn't thrown up, would you have done anything? Kissed? Brought her back here?"

"Maybe. Probably." When I feel her body stiffen beside me, I thread my fingers through her long hair. Other guys might have held back, but I'm not other guys. She asked. I answered. "You wanted to know."

"Yeah, I did. And I'm the one who threw her at you. I guess I'm not allowed to be jealous." Mac growls softly. "But I fucking am."

"Welcome to the club," I growl back. "The thought of anyone but me putting their hands on you makes me homicidal."

She laughs. "Anyone ever tell you you're a bit intense?"

I shrug. "Got a problem with that?"

"Not at all."

I twist a chunk of her hair around my finger. "You know," I say pensively, "as pissed as I was at you that night, I'd forgotten how fun it is to be Evan. It'd been ages since we pulled a twin switch."

She tilts her head curiously. "You two would switch places a lot?"

"All the time. He used to take all my geography tests for me in high school—swear to God, that kid has a weirdly good memory when it comes to state capitals. Sometimes we'd break up with each other's girlfriends."

Mackenzie gasps. "That's awful."

"Not our finest moments," I agree. "We also switched places to mess with our friends, although most of them can tell us apart, even when we make ourselves identical from head to toe. But yeah, sometimes it's nice to take a break from myself and be Evan. Live life with zero regard for consequences. Do what you want, screw who you want, no regrets."

"I don't know . . . I like you just fine." Her palm slowly trails down my bare chest. "More than fine, actually."

"Wait. I want to make you breakfast," I say, stopping her when her hand reaches into my boxers.

"Can't we do this first?" Mac looks up and licks her lips.

Goddamn. Yes, princess, by all means I'd love to see how you look with my cock in your mouth, but I'm trying out this new being-a-gentleman thing, if you'll let me.

Like I said, my head's wrecked.

"You start that," I warn, "and we aren't leaving this bed."

"I don't mind."

Groaning, I push her off me and slide out of bed. "Tempting. And trust me, I'd absolutely smash that, but Evan and I are getting a delivery today for the house renovations. We've gotta get an early start."

Mac pouts, my T-shirt hanging off one tanned shoulder. Her bare legs are begging me to come back to bed. Fucking death of me, right there.

"Fine. I guess breakfast will do. Got any scones?"

"Fuck off," I laugh, heading to the bathroom.

After I grab a spare toothbrush from the cabinet, Mac tears open the packaging. We brush our teeth side by side, but draw the line there. She shoos me out so she can pee, and I go and answer a text from Billy West about today's lumber order. I'm still texting when Mac wanders out of my room toward the kitchen.

By the time I'm done, the aroma of freshly brewed coffee is wafting through the house.

"Sure, honey, help yourself," I hear Evan drawl.

I round the corner to see Mac standing by the coffeemaker with a mug in her hand.

"I thought I'd get a pot going for whoever wants some," she says, noting as I do the sarcasm in his voice. "I hope that's alright."

"Of course it is," I say pointedly at Evan. Because I don't get his sudden attitude. "Have a seat. I'm gonna get some eggs going. You want bacon?"

"Shall I have the maid fetch the good china, or would her majesty prefer to be hand fed?" Evan inquires, grabbing a box of cereal.

"Hey." I shove him as he tries blocking me from the fridge. Fucking child. "Give it a rest, man."

Mac is visibly uncomfortable. "Yeah, you know, I've actually got to get back to the dorm, so I'm going to head out."

"Come on, stay," I urge. "I'll drive you back after breakfast."

But it's too late. Whatever bug's crawled up Evan's ass this morning, he's already scared her off. Mac can't get away from us fast enough, hurrying off to my bedroom, where she calls a cab while changing back into her dress from last night.

"I'm sorry about him," I tell her, catching her around the waist before she walks out the front door. "He's not much of a morning person."

"It's fine. Really."

I study her face. Her makeup's been washed off and her hair's in a loose knot on top of her head. It's the most beautiful she's ever looked. And now I'm thinking we should have gone with her plan of staying in bed all day.

"I'm sure if I had siblings, they'd be a pain in the butt too." Mac lifts up on her toes to kiss me. I take that to mean we're still gonna be on speaking terms.

After she's gone, I find Evan in the garage.

"Hey, what was all that about?" I ask tersely.

"Better ask yourself that question," he retorts, brushing by me with his tool belt over his shoulder. "Since when are you playing butler to the princess? The plan was to get her to break up with Kincaid, not play house."

"Yeah, and it worked." I follow him across the yard and back toward the house, choosing to ignore the way the inflection of hatred in his voice pricks my nerves. "She dumped him last night."

"Great," he says, cracking open a beer from the cooler on the front porch—at seven in the morning. "Then it's time to cut her loose. We get both of them in the same place, let him see you two together, then be done with the clones. End of."

I snatch the beer from his hand and pour it out. "Would you quit it with this shit? I don't want you wasted and shooting a nail gun at me."

"Sure, Dad," he says, flicking me off.

"Hey." I point a stiff finger at his chest because he fucking knows what he just did. "You say that again, we're gonna have problems."

He smacks my hand away. "Yeah, whatever."

Evan's on one today, and I'm about sick of this crap. But I can't worry about what's got him all twisted up, because I need to figure out how the hell I'm going to handle this thing with Mackenzie. There's no way my brother and our friends are going to let me off the hook. All four of them have been circling, waiting for the feeding frenzy. They want blood.

I stew about it all day, but no solutions come to me. By the time we all hit up Joe's later while Steph's there on her shift, I haven't come up with anything better than stalling and hoping they don't mention the plan.

We're on good terms again, Joe and me. I'm still disappointed in how easily he caved in firing me, but I get why he did it. Hard to hold a grudge against a guy who has a mortgage and his kid's college loans to worry about. It wasn't fair to expect him to go to the mat for me when he's got his own family to protect.

We grab a booth near the bar, with Evan sliding next to me, and Heidi and Alana across from us. Steph wanders over with drink menus none of us need or glance at. The chicks order shots. Evan and I stick with beer. We took today off to rebuild our front porch, which means we're pulling a double shift for Levi tomorrow. We've got to wake up at dawn, and I'd rather not do that with a hangover. Evan, I'm sure, doesn't give a shit.

Of course, he wastes no time updating the girls on the latest Mackenzie developments.

"I'm so turned on right now," Alana says, with an evil grin that is honestly disturbing. Chick is scary sometimes. "Look at me." She holds out her arm to us. "I've got goose bumps."

With her phone out, Heidi is scrolling through Kincaid's Instagram. "All we have to do is keep an eye out for where he's going to be one night. Somewhere public. Then you bring his ex, and we humiliate the hell out of him. Shit, we could probably sell tickets."

"Make it soon." Steph groans. "If he doesn't stop coming around here, I'm going to poison his drink with laxatives. I want him afraid to show his face in public."

"Why not this weekend?" Evan suggests, elbowing me as I concentrate on my beer, trying to ignore the rest of them. "Tomorrow. You ask the princess out on a date. Steph, you get Maddy or somebody to invite him out, and we corner him then."

I finally contribute to the conversation. "No."

Evan frowns. "What?"

Hearing him taking shots at Mac again does me in. I'm sick of this whole stupid plot, and I'm sick to death of pretending I'm still on board. I jumped off this train the moment I realized how cool Mac was. How smart and sexy and intriguing. She's unlike any woman I've ever been with.

"It's over," I tell my friends, eyeing them over the rim of my bottle. "Forget about it."

"What do you mean forget about it?" Evan snatches the beer from my hand.

My shoulders stiffen. He'd better be real careful how he comes at me next.

"We had a deal," he snaps.

"No, you have a vendetta, and I want no part of it anymore. I'm the one who got fired, not you. Which means I get the final say about this. And I'm calling it off."

He shakes his head incredulously. "I knew it. She got to you, didn't she? Fucking clone got you wrapped around her prissy little finger."

"Enough." I smack my hand down on the table, rattling our drinks. "That goes for all of you," I tell the girls. "She's off-limits. As far as you're all concerned, she's not to be messed with."

"When did this happen?" Steph looks at me in confusion. I don't blame her. Until this second, I've kept everyone out of the loop.

"This is why we can't have nice things," Alana says.

"I'm serious. Look, I like Mac." I let out a breath. "Didn't expect to, but here we are. I'm into her."

Across the booth, Heidi's lips twist into a scowl. "Men," she mutters under her breath.

I ignore the jab. "I don't know where this is going with us, but I expect you all to be nice to her. Forget we ever hatched this stupid plot. It's not happening anymore. No more rude comments," I say to my brother. To the girls, "And no scheming behind her back. For better or worse, you assholes are my family. I'm asking you to do this for me."

In the silence that follows, each of them gives a curt nod.

Then Evan storms off, because of course he does. Steph shrugs as she goes to check on her tables. Heidi and Alana just stare at me like I'm the biggest dumbass they've ever met. It's not the enthusiastic confirmation I want, but it's honestly better than I hoped for. Still, I'm under no illusions that this'll be painless for any of us.

Heidi shoves a hand through her short hair and continues to eye me. In her expression, I see a flicker of anger. A hint of pity. And a gleam of something else. Something vindictive, alarming.

"No one breathes a word of this to Mac," I warn Heidi. "Ever."

CHAPTER TWENTY-FOUR

MACKENZIE

I spend the next week dodging Preston with such skill it's a shame avoidance isn't an Olympic sport. If it were, Bonnie would also make a worthy competitor. She covers for me at our dorm one night, answering the door topless to scare him off. For whatever lewdness Pres gets up to in his free time, he remains terrified of public embarrassment. So when Bonnie starts shouting at the top of her lungs, and our hallway neighbors poke their heads out their doors to see what all the commotion is about, Preston is quick to retreat.

Ignoring his texts and phone calls is easy. Hiding from him on campus has been trickier. I've taken to ducking out the back entrance of every class a few minutes early or several minutes late to make sure he isn't waiting for me. Getting classmates I've befriended to text me a heads-up when he's spotted nearby. It's a lot of effort, but a hell of a lot less messy than getting cornered.

Seems like everything in my life has been reduced to the act of sneaking around. Avoiding Pres. Going behind my parents' backs to work on the hotel. Slipping around town to meet up with Cooper. I can't risk anyone on campus recognizing him and ratting me out to Preston, and I think Cooper's hiding me from Evan, so our rendezvous have become increasingly creative.

And while we still haven't had The Talk about our dating situation, we can't keep our hands off each other. I'm addicted. Utterly addicted to him. Bonnie calls me dick crazed. I'd argue with her if she hadn't been right about absolutely everything since the moment we met.

On Saturday night, I meet Cooper at one of our usual spots down the beach from his house. This end of the Bay was the hardest hit from the last couple hurricanes and has been pretty much abandoned for years. It's nothing but empty houses and decaying waterfront restaurants. An old fishing pier broken and mostly overtaken by the ocean. We let Daisy off her leash to run around a bit, and she wastes no time terrorizing the tiny sand crabs and chasing birds.

After stopping to sit on a piece of driftwood, Cooper pulls me to straddle his lap, facing him. Both hands cradle my ass as I scratch my fingertips lightly up and down the back of his neck, in the way I know gets him a little hard.

"You keep doing that," he warns, "I'm gonna bang you right here in front of the seagulls."

"Animal," I say, biting his lip.

"Tease." He kisses me. Strong hands slide up my ribs to give my breasts a teasing squeeze before settling around my waist. He eases his mouth away, his gaze finding mine. "I was thinking. There's a party tonight. Come with me."

I lift a brow. "I don't know. We'd be going public. Sure you're ready for that?"

"Why wouldn't I be?"

Our sneaking around hasn't been an explicit topic of conversation, but more an unspoken agreement. Altering that agreement, while inevitable, comes with a whole new net of consequences. That isn't to say I'm unhappy at making this official. Surprised, maybe.

"So . . ." I run my palms down his chest, feeling every hard muscle until my hands meet his waistband. "Like a date."

"*Like* a date, sure." Cooper does this thing where he licks his lips when he thinks he's being charming. It's annoyingly hot.

"Which would mean we're *like* dating."

"Let's put it this way." Cooper brushes my hair off my shoulder. He wraps the length around his fist and tugs. Only a little. It's a subtle, evocative gesture that has become our shorthand for *I want to rip your clothes off.* Like when I bite his lip or tug the front of his jeans, or look at him or breathe. "I'm not fucking anyone else. I don't want you fucking anyone else. If anyone looks at you funny, I'm breaking their face. How's that work?"

It isn't exactly poetry, but that might be the most romantic thing a guy's ever said to me. Cooper might be a bit uncouth and rough around the edges, but I'm kind of into it.

"Works for me."

Grinning, he nudges me off his lap. "Come on, let's take the little monster home. And I want to take a quick shower before we head out. I swear there's always a layer of sawdust on me."

"I like it. It's manly."

He rolls his eyes.

We walk to his house, entering through the back deck. I fill Daisy's water bowl while Cooper goes to his room to shower. I'd join him, but I blow-dried my hair before coming over and I don't want to mess it up, especially now that we're going to a party.

"Hey," grunts Evan, his tall, broad frame appearing in the kitchen doorway. He's barefoot, wearing threadbare jeans and a red T-shirt. "Didn't know you were over."

I slide onto a stool at the counter and watch as Daisy laps noisily at her water. "Yup. Here I am. Cooper's in the shower."

Evan opens a cupboard and grabs a bag of potato chips. He tears it open and shoves some chips in his mouth. As he chews, he watches me suspiciously. "What're you two up to tonight?"

"Cooper says there's a party? I guess we're going to that."

He raises his eyebrows. "He's bringing you to Chase's?"

"Yeah." I pause. "Got a problem with that?"

"Not at all, princess."

"Oh, really."

"It's about time you came out with us," Evan adds, shrugging. "If you're with my brother, you'll need to meet the gang sooner or later. Win 'em over."

Well, hell. Now I'm nervous. Why'd he have to phrase it that way? What if Cooper's friends hate me?

My distress is momentarily forgotten at the sound of Daisy's urgent barking. I glance over at the puppy, only to find she's standing there barking at the wall.

"Daisy," I chide.

"Don't worry," Evan says. "It's probably just the ghost."

I roll my eyes at him.

"Coop didn't tell you about our ghost?" He tips his head. "For real? That's usually the first thing I tell guests. It's like a badge of honor, living in a haunted house."

"Your house is haunted," I say skeptically. Because, come on. I'm not that gullible.

"Sort of? She doesn't really bother us," Evan explains. "So it's not exactly a haunting. But she definitely hangs around."

"She. She who?"

"Patricia something or other. Little girl who drowned out back like a hundred years ago. She was six, seven? I can't remember her age. But when it storms you can hear her screaming, and every now and then, the lights in the house flicker, usually when she's feeling playful—"

He halts abruptly as the light fixture over the kitchen island honest-to-God flickers.

Oh *hell* no.

Evan catches my alarm and grins. "See? She's just teasing us.

Don't worry, princess. Patricia's a nice ghost. Like Casper. If you want more details, I think the town library has some old newspaper articles about it." He walks over to pat Daisy, who's quieted down. "Good dog. You tell that little ghost girl."

I make a mental note to visit the Avalon Bay library. I don't really believe in ghosts, but I do like history, and now that I own a hotel here, I'm even more curious to learn about the history of this town.

"I'm gonna ride with you guys, if that's cool?" Evan says, then wanders out of the kitchen before I can answer. I guess it was a rhetorical question.

Sighing, I stare at the empty doorway. I think there's only one person I really need to "win over" at the moment, and that person is Cooper's twin brother.

Cooper's friend Chase has a split-level house in town with a massive yard backing onto a wooded area. The moment we get there, I'm slightly overwhelmed by the number of people. There's a ton of them here. Inside playing beer pong. Outside around a fire pit. Music blasting. Raucous laughter. We make the rounds as Cooper makes the introductions. It'd be fun if I didn't notice everyone staring at me. Meanwhile, an oblivious Cooper keeps one arm around my waist as he talks with his friends. Everywhere I look are side-eyes, over-the-shoulder glances, and conspicuous whispers. I don't usually get self-conscious in social situations, but it's hard not to when everyone is making it clear with their eyes that they think I don't belong. It's nerve-wracking. Suffocating.

I need more booze if I'm going to survive tonight.

"I'm going to get another drink," I tell Cooper. He'd been chatting with a tattooed guy named Wyatt, who's complaining about how his girlfriend won't take him back. Nearby, a small crowd is watching a game of bikini-and-briefs Twister in the backyard.

"I'll get it for you," he offers. "What do you want?"

"No, it's okay. Stay and chat. I'll be right back."

With that, I slip away before he can argue with me. I wind my way through the house and end up in the kitchen, where I find a lone, unopened bottle of red wine and decide it's the least likely to give me a raging hangover in the morning.

"You're Mackenzie, right?" asks a gorgeous girl with long hair and a dark complexion. She's in a bikini halter top and high-waisted shorts, mixing a drink at the counter. "Cooper's Mackenzie."

"Yep, that's me. Cooper's Mackenzie." It sounds like a '70s cop drama or something.

"Sorry," she says with a friendly smile. She puts a lid on the cocktail shaker and vigorously shakes it over her shoulder. "I just meant I've heard a lot about you from Coop. I'm Steph."

"Oh! The goat girl?"

Her lips twitch. "I'm sorry—what?"

I laugh awkwardly. "Sorry, that was random. Cooper and Evan told me this story about rescuing a goat when they were preteens at the behest of their friend Steph. That was you?"

She bursts out laughing. "Oh my God. Yes. The Great Goat Robbery. Totally my idea." She suddenly shakes her head. "Except did they tell you the part about abandoning the goat in the woods? Like, what the hell!"

"Right?" I exclaim. "That's what I said! That poor thing totally got eaten by mountain lions or something."

She snickers. "Well, we live in a seaside town, so maybe not mountain lions. Definitely got mauled by some predator, though."

I set the wine bottle on the counter and open a drawer in search of a corkscrew.

Steph pours her concoction into two red cups then offers me one. "Leave the wine. That stuff's terrible. Try this." She pushes the drink at me. "Trust me. It's good. Not too strong."

No sense in offending the only person to speak to me all night. I take a sip and am pleasantly surprised by the slightly sweet taste of orange and botanicals.

"This is good. Really good. Thanks."

"No problem. Don't tell anyone where you got it," she says, tapping the side of her nose. As if to say, if the cops raid the party and catch you underage drinking, don't snitch on me. "I was hoping Cooper would decide to share you soon. We've all been anxious to meet you."

"We?"

"Just, you know, the gang."

"Right."

Evan had also used that phrase. I wonder who else comprises this "gang." Cooper and I haven't done much in the getting-to-know-you realm this week. I mean, beyond anatomy.

Speaking of anatomy, an insanely attractive, anatomically perfect guy strides into the kitchen. Tall, fair, and armed with a pair of dimples, he flashes a smile at Steph. "Who's your friend?" he asks, curious blue eyes landing on me.

"Mackenzie," I say, holding out my hand.

"Tate." He shakes my outstretched hand, his fingers lingering.

Steph snorts. "Keep it in your pants, babe. She's with Coop."

"Yeah?" Tate sounds impressed. His gaze rakes over me in slow, deliberate perusal. "Lucky Coop." He grabs a few longnecks from the fridge. "You girls coming outside to the fire?"

"In a bit," Steph answers.

"Cool." He nods and leaves the kitchen.

Once he's gone, Steph is quick to give me the skinny on Tate. Apparently he sleeps around, but his dimples and easygoing charm make it hard to view him as a douchebag. "He's just so darn likeable, you know?" She sighs. "I hate people like that."

"Those likeable pricks," I agree, solemn.

We continue chatting as we drink our cocktails. The more we talk, the more I like her. Turns out we both have a thing for amusement parks and the one-hit wonders of early 2000s pop music.

"I saw them last year in Myrtle Beach. They were opening for . . ." Steph thinks about it then laughs to herself. "Yeah, I can't remember. They're in their fifties now."

"Oh God, I can't believe they're still together."

"It was weird," she says, pouring us another couple of mixed cocktails.

"What was weird?" A girl with platinum hair and dressed in a black cropped T-shirt with the sleeves cut off slides in next to Steph.

"Nothing," Steph says. She's smiling until she clocks the hard glare on the blonde's face. Then all the humor falls. "Heidi, this is Mackenzie."

There's too much emphasis on my name. I can't help wondering what Cooper's told them. It leaves me at a significant disadvantage.

"Nice to meet you," I offer to cut the tension. I'm assuming Heidi is yet another member of this "gang."

"Great," she says, bored the minute she looked at me. "Can we talk, Steph?"

Beside her, a redhead is sporting a smirk that signals I'm not in on the joke, whatever it is.

I get the distinct impression I'm no longer welcome here.

"You know, I should go find Cooper," I tell Steph. "Nice meeting you all."

I don't wait for a reply before shuffling off, leaving my drink behind.

Cooper's still in the backyard, only now he's standing around the bonfire next to a very cute brunette whose ass is trying to climb out of her shorts. When her hand touches Cooper's chest I want to charge her like a bull. Instead, I keep my cool and saunter up to him, grabbing him by his belt loops. That gets his attention. The corner of his mouth lifts wryly.

"Come on," I say, ignoring the irritated look from the brunette. "I want to grope you in the dark."

Cooper doesn't miss a beat. He sets his bottle on the cement blocks lining the bonfire pit. "Yeah, okay."

Together we round the side of the house to the street out front, where Cooper's truck is parked. He lifts me up to sit on the open tailgate. With a dirty grin, he steps between my legs.

"Came to piss on my leg, huh?" He runs his callused fingertips up and down the tops of my exposed thighs. My teeny yellow dress has ridden up almost to my waist, but Cooper's big body shields me from view.

"In not so many words, yeah, I guess so."

"I'm into it," he says, smirking. "You were gone awhile. Everything cool?"

"All good. Just mingling. I met your friend Tate." I wink. "He's cute."

Dark eyes narrow at me. "Did he hit on you?"

"For about a second. Backed off when he learned I came here with you."

"Good. I don't have to kill him. Meet anyone else?"

"A few others," I say vaguely, because I don't want to talk about it.

Truth is, tonight has been a bust and I'm feeling anxious about the prospects of how Cooper and I are going to fit into each other's lives. The longer I'm left to think on the subject, the more the doubt digs its roots into my brain. I don't want to think. I want Cooper to make it all go away. So I tangle my hands in his hair and pull him toward me, kissing him with purpose until I feel the slightest groan from his chest, and he wraps his arms around me, deepening the kiss.

"What's the matter, you two?" I jump when Evan sneaks up behind us, shining the flashlight from his phone in our eyes. "Party run out of Dom Pérignon already?"

"Fuck off," Cooper grumbles, swatting the phone away. "Can't you find someone else to entertain you?"

"I'm good. Came to check on you crazy kids."

Evan flashes a grin and waves at me with a bottle of beer in his hand. The first night we met on the beach, I thought Evan was all right. Since then, I've found him rude and pointedly unfriendly. It isn't enough to be a dick to me; he wants me to know he's *trying* to be a dick. It's the commitment to effort that's been getting to me.

"Now you have." Cooper levels his brother with a look. A whole silent conversation is happening that I can't translate. "Bye."

"Tell me something, Mac."

"Give it a rest, dude." Cooper backs away from me, trying to escort his obviously drunk brother toward the house.

Evan eyes me over the top of his beer. He takes another gulp while pushing his brother away. "I've been dying to ask. Do rich chicks do anal?"

"That's enough, asshole. Leave her alone."

"Or do you pay someone else to do it for you?"

It happens in a blink.

One second Evan is laughing at his own unfunny joke.

Then he's flat on the ground, blood pouring from his mouth.

CHAPTER TWENTY-FIVE

COOPER

I put him on the ground with one punch. Evan was already well on his way to wasted, or else he might have taken the hit better. I feel a small pang of regret when I see the blood leaking onto the asphalt, but all remorse fades when Evan lumbers to his feet and charges at me.

He drives his shoulder into my gut, grabbing me around the waist as we stumble backward against my truck. Somewhere I hear Mac screaming at us, but it's no use. Evan is on one now. And when he lands a couple of hard jabs to my ribs, I don't give a shit who he is anymore. Something in me snaps and my entire world reduces to the sole task of kicking my brother's ass. We trade blows until we're rolling around in the middle of the street, picking up road rash. Suddenly my arms are locked up and people are pulling Evan and me apart.

"Fuck you, man," Evan shouts at me.

"You came asking for it," I growl.

He lunges again.

My fists swing up.

Bodies crowd the space between us as we're forcibly separated.

"What is *wrong* with you two?" Heidi shouts. She and Jay West cage Evan, stepping between us as I shove away the hands of at least three other guys from the party.

"I'm fine," Evan grumbles. "Back off." He wrestles out of their grips and storms down the street on foot.

"I'll get him," Steph offers, sighing softly.

Seeing the fight's over, everyone but my closest friends drifts back to the house.

"Nah, let him cool off," Alana advises.

Heidi side-eyes me before stalking away, Jay trailing after her like a lovesick puppy. I wonder if they came together. I hope so. Maybe then she'll stop hating on me so much.

Steph and Alana wear matching frowns as they study me. Whatever. I don't give a flying fuck what they think right now. Evan deserved every last blow.

Mac grabs my face, inspecting the damage. "You okay?"

I wince when her fingers skim over the rapidly swelling spot beneath my left eye. "I'm fine." I search her face just as intently. "Are we okay?" I don't regret slugging Evan over what he said—nobody gets to talk to Mac like that—but I am sorry she had to see it.

Fuck, if this is the thing that drives her way . . .

She kisses my cheek. "You should go after him."

I hesitate.

"I'll be here when you get back," she promises, as if reading my mind.

I don't have any choice but to believe her. Besides, Evan loaded up on anger and alcohol roaming the streets at night alone is begging for disaster. So I head down the road to find him. I glance over my shoulder once, twice. Sure enough, Mackenzie is still there, standing by my pickup.

Eventually I catch up to Evan, finding him on a bench in a small playground lit only by a couple of dim streetlights.

"Still got all your teeth?" I ask, taking a seat beside him.

"Yeah." He rubs his jaw. "You hit like a ten-year-old."

"Still kicked your ass."

"I had you."

"You had shit," I say, eyeing him with a smirk.

We sit quietly for some time, watching the swings waving in the breeze. It's been years since Evan and I fought this bad. Really going to blows. I'd be lying if I said I hadn't felt it coming. Shit's been building up with him for a long time now. Maybe I'm the asshole for not talking to him about it sooner. Then again, taking his own issues out on Mac is weak, and I'm not about to let him keep that up.

"You were out of line back there."

"Ah, come on. It was a little funny." He slouches on the bench, spreading his legs like he might slip right off the thing in a pool of liquid.

"I'm serious. She hasn't done a goddamn thing to you. You got a problem with me, grow up and say so. The snide comments and passive-aggressive bullshit, it stops now."

"Kind of sounds like you're giving me an ultimatum." Evan tips his head toward me. "That what it's come to?"

"Damn it, dude. You're my brother. We're blood. Nothing changes that." I shake my head, frustrated. "So why are you getting so bent outta shape about her?"

"It's the principle of the thing. She's a clone, Coop. Those people, they've been standing on our necks since we were kids. Or don't you remember? Assholes rolling up in their stupid golf carts, throwing drinks on us, running our bikes off the road."

Evan ended up with a broken arm once. Flipped over his handlebars into a ditch when one of them bumped his tire. We went back a week later and slashed all four of theirs. There are years of that shit. Getting into fights. Tit for tat.

"People," I remind him. "Not her. You can't punish Mac for everything one of them's ever done to you. That's exactly what I was about to do to her if I'd stuck to the plan. And I would've been a bastard for it too." I groan quietly. "Why can't you let me have this?"

His shoulders stiffen.

I mean, hell, all of us lived through the daily soap opera that was the Evan and Genevieve show. Constantly bickering in front of everyone. Making us choose sides in arguments we wanted no part of. Breaking up. Screwing around. Getting back together like nothing happened. I never threw a tantrum about it, and I certainly didn't treat her like crap hoping she'd go away. If Evan was in love with her, that was his own damn problem.

So why now, when I find someone I care about, does he have to be such a jackass about it?

Evan sighs. Scratches his hands through his hair. "I can't help it, man. It gnaws at me. Why'd it have to be one of them? You could point in any direction and land on ten chicks who would fall to their knees for you."

"I don't know what to tell you. She's different. If you gave her even half a chance, you'd see that."

There's no good reason Mac and I should work. I can't give him one. And hell, maybe we won't work. She's a stubborn, opinionated pain in my ass. She's also gorgeous, funny, spontaneous, and ambitious. Turns out, that's my type. She makes me crazy. I've never met a girl that stays on my mind days and weeks after I've seen her. She's under my skin. And for all the ways we're completely different, she gets me in a way few others do.

If I'm kidding myself, if this whole thing's bound to blow up in my face, so be it. At least I tried.

"No talking you outta this, then?" he says, his resolve slowly crumbling.

"I'm asking you, as my brother, to accept it."

He thinks on it. Too long for my taste. For the first time in our lives, we're on opposite sides, and I have to wonder if there's too much bad blood there—too much rage toward the clones—to get him back on mine.

Then he sighs again and rises from the bench. "Yeah, fine. Guess there's no saving you from yourself. I'll back off."

I take what I can get from Evan and we call it squashed. Back at the party, I send him home in Alana's car to make sure he gets there safe while I drive Mac to her dorm.

"I'm sorry about that," I tell her when she hasn't spoken in several minutes. She's staring out the passenger window looking deep in thought, which gets me worried. "It had nothing to do with you. Evan's got a lot of misplaced anger."

"Brothers shouldn't fight."

I wait, uncertain if there's more to that statement. My concern deepens when more doesn't come.

"Talk to me, Mackenzie." My voice comes out a bit husky.

"What if this is a bad idea?"

"It isn't."

"Seriously." Out of the corner of my eye, I find her watching me. "I don't want to be the reason you fall out with him. It's good for no one. You can't be happy because he's upset, and I can't be happy because you're upset. We all lose."

This is exactly why Evan needs to get over his bullshit and let us be. She's not the person he imagines in his head, and if he understood her at all, he'd realize how unfair he's been.

"Evan will get over it."

"But what if he doesn't? These things can fester."

"Don't worry about it, Mac. Seriously." I don't care if my brother wants to be a cranky little brat about it, as long as he's on his best behavior around Mac and keeps his comments to himself. My whole life I've lived for the two of us. Evan and me. This one thing, though, I get to have for myself.

Clearly I'm not doing a good job at easing her unhappiness,

because she lets out a miserable-sounding moan. "I don't want to come between you and your twin, Cooper."

I glance over. Sternly. "I've made my choice. I want us to be together. Evan can deal."

Distress flickers through her eyes. "What does that even mean, being together? I know earlier we said we're dating, and I thought I was cool with that—"

"You *thought*?" I growl.

"But then we went to the party and did you see how everyone was looking at us? No, looking at *me*—like I didn't belong there at all. That one girl? Heidi? Completely froze me out with her gaze. And I overheard a couple chicks calling me a rich snob and saying my dress is ridiculous."

"Why is your dress ridiculous?" From where I'm sitting, her short yellow dress looks ridiculously sexy.

"Because it's Givenchy and I guess nobody wears a thousand-dollar dress to a house party?" Mac's cheeks redden with embarrassment. "My mom's assistant buys most of my clothes. In case you haven't noticed, I don't care about fashion. I live in jeans and T-shirts." She sounds more and more anguished. "I only wore this stupid dress because it's cute and summery and short enough that I knew it'd drive you crazy."

I fight a laugh. I also force myself not to comment on the fact that the scrap of yellow fabric barely covering her delectable body cost a *grand*.

"But maybe it did come off like I was flaunting? I don't know. I wasn't trying to. All I know is that nobody wanted me there tonight."

"I wanted you there."

"You don't count," she grumbles.

I reach over the center console and grab her hand. Forcibly lacing our fingers together. "I'm the only one who counts," I correct.

"They count too," she argues. "You've got an entire group of friends, and you've all known each other forever. I have like two friends, one of whom is my roommate so she's kind of forced to like me."

The laugh slips out.

"I wish I had a huge friend group like yours. I'm jealous," she says frankly. "And I really wanted everyone to like me tonight."

I release her hand and steer the truck to the shoulder of the road. I put it in park and turn to her with a firm stare. "Babe. *I* like you. Okay? And my friends, they'll come around and grow to like you too. I promise you that."

She frowns. "Don't make promises you can't keep."

"I mean it. Give it a little more time," I say gruffly. "Don't bail on me, on this, just because the reception tonight wasn't the warmest, and some girls got all judgmental about your dress—which, just so you know, is the hottest thing ever and I want to rip that thousand-dollar fabric off your body with my teeth."

Mac laughs, albeit weakly.

"Please." I almost cringe at the pleading note I hear in my voice. "Don't bail on me, princess."

The shadows in the truck dance over her pretty face as she sits in silence for a moment. It feels like an eternity before she finally responds.

Green eyes gleaming from the headlights of a passing vehicle, she leans toward me and kisses me. Hard. With a lot of tongue. Then she pulls back breathlessly and whispers, "I won't bail on you."

CHAPTER TWENTY-SIX

MACKENZIE

Give it time, he said.

They'll come around, he said.

Well, I'm calling bullshit on Cooper's bullshit. Since the disaster at the party, I've been on a hearts-and-minds campaign, doing my damnedest to try to win over Cooper's "gang." Though he'd never admit it, I know he's bothered by the fissures where his friends and I are concerned, and I don't want to be the reason he drifts away from the people he cares about. They've been in his life a lot longer than I have. The way I see it, there's no reason we can't all get along.

So I'm trying. I'm really, really trying. Whether it's out at the sports bar playing darts or hanging on the beach at a bonfire, I've been working to make inroads in recent weeks. Most of Cooper's guy friends—Tate, Chase, Wyatt—seem to have completely warmed up to me. We even went out for dinner one night with Chase and his boyfriend, a cute guy named Alec who also goes to Garnet. Except they don't count, because they're not the ones I need to win over. That would be the gang, the inner circle.

Aside from Steph, who continues to be an ally, I can't seem to crack the iron curtain that is the Alana and Heidi blockade. And while Evan hasn't been overtly hostile lately, it seems he's opted for the silent approach where I'm concerned. *If you can't say anything nice*, and all that.

Which is why I thought tonight would be the perfect opportunity for a more intimate get-together. Just *the gang*. S'mores, scary movies, maybe a little Truth or Dare and Never Have I Ever. Bonding stuff and all that jazz.

So of course, by midafternoon the scattered showers predicted for this evening turn into severe thunderstorm and tornado warnings throughout the Carolinas.

Awesome. Even the weather is against me.

An hour ago, Cooper and Evan left to help Levi batten down the hatches at one of his construction sites. So now I'm sitting here at their house with ten pounds of cold buffalo wings and cheesy garlic bread, and beyond the sliding glass doors, the sky grows gray and foreboding over the bay. Without much else to do, and because I happen to love storms—there's something about the fierce, electric anticipation of chaos—I open the back door to let the cool air in and then curl up on the couch with some homework. The TV is on quietly in the background, turned to the local news, where the weather people are standing in front of a radar image awash in red and orange, tossing around words like *hunker down*.

I get my anthropology reading done and am watching some clips on my laptop for my media culture class when a huge crack of lightning flashes outside and the resulting thunder shakes the house. The startling barrage knocks the wind right out of me. Daisy, who was curled up under a blanket at my feet, bolts out of the room for her favorite hiding place under Cooper's bed. Rain begins to pour outside in a sudden deluge that swallows the horizon behind a silver curtain. I jump off the couch and quickly shut the sliding door, then wipe up the water that snuck inside with a dishrag.

It's then I hear it, a faint wailing in the distance.

"Daisy?" I shout, glancing around. Had she run outside when I wasn't looking?

Nope. A quick peek into Cooper's room reveals her lying under the bed, front paws flat on the hardwood, with her little face squished between them.

"Was that you crying, little one?" I ask, only to jump when I hear it again. It's more of a scream than a wail, and it's definitely coming from outside.

When it storms you can hear her screaming . . .

My pulse accelerates as Evan's words buzz around in my head. Was he serious about this place being haunted? What the hell had he called her again—

"Patricia?" I say feebly, my cautious gaze darting around the room. "Is that you?"

The light fixture above my head flickers.

A startled yelp rips out of my throat, causing Daisy to crawl backward and disappear deeper under the bed.

I leave Cooper's room, heart pounding. Candles. I should probably find some candles in case the power goes out. Because nothing sounds less appealing to me than sitting in the dark listening to the shrieks of a century-old dead child.

As if on cue, the shrill noises start up again, a cacophony of sound mingling with the crashes of thunder outside the old beach house.

"Patricia," I call out. Steady voice now. Hands, not so much. "Look, let's be cool, okay? I know it's probably not fun being dead, but that doesn't mean you have to scream your lungs out. If you use your indoor voice, I'm happy to sit down and listen to whatever you—"

Another scream pierces the air.

"Or not," I backpedal. "Fine. You win, Patricia. Just keep scaring the crap out of me, then."

In the kitchen, I start opening lower cabinets in search of candles or flashlights. I find a pack of tea lights and breathe in relief. Good. Now I just need to grab one of the gazillion lighters on the coffee table and I'm all set.

On my way back to the living room, a buzzing noise catches my attention. I think it might be my phone, until I realize it's still in my pocket. I follow the sound to the kitchen counter where Cooper's phone has now stopped vibrating. Shit. He'd forgotten his phone. With the screen still lit, I see he has several missed calls and text messages. I don't look long enough to read them, not wanting to invade Cooper's privacy, but I do note Steph's and Alana's names.

Given the number of calls and texts, it could be urgent. I'd get in touch with Evan to give him the heads-up, but I don't have his number and can't unlock Cooper's phone to get it. If it's important, the girls will try Evan eventually, I reason. So I mind my business and go back to my homework.

But the buzzing continues. For another half hour, about every five minutes, Cooper's phone rattles on the kitchen counter. Fuck it. I grab the phone the next time a call comes in and this time I answer it.

"Hello, Steph?" I say, reading her name on the screen.

"Who's this?"

"Mackenzie. Cooper's out with Evan and Levi. He left his phone at home."

"Damn," she says with a frustrated huff. "I've been trying to get ahold of Evan, but he's not answering either."

"What's going on?"

"There's water coming in through the ceiling of the bathroom. We heard something that sounded like a tree falling on the roof, and then suddenly water's running down the wall."

"You okay?"

"We're fine, but we need to fix this before the entire house is flooded. We've got towels down, but there's too much water and we don't have any way to stop it."

Shit. If they can't reach Evan, it probably means the twins are still wrapped up helping their uncle. The storm is really wailing now, thunder and lightning coming every few minutes and the wind and rain battering the windows. And according to the radar on TV, this thing isn't passing quickly. Which means Steph and Alana are going to need a raft soon.

Pausing for a moment to think, it occurs to me Cooper's truck is still here, and his keys are sitting on the coffee table. I bet he's got all kinds of stuff in the garage—a ladder and tarps.

A plan forms in my head.

"Okay. Write down my phone number and text me your address," I tell Steph. "I'm coming over."

"Uh . . ." There's muted chattering in the background that I assume is Alana. "I'm not sure if that's—"

"I'm going to grab some supplies from Cooper's garage and head over there. Trust me, this'll work."

"Alright," she finally relents. There might even be a hint of relief in her voice.

After we get off the phone, I borrow a rain jacket from Cooper's closet then grab his keys and dash through the rain and mud to his garage. Inside, against the wall, he's got all sorts of building materials stacked up from the renovations he and Evan have been doing on the house. Among them, some black vinyl-type material and rope. Thankfully, Cooper keeps his tools well organized and I find a hammer, nails, and a heavy-duty staple gun with little effort. Good enough.

Ten minutes after hanging up with Steph, I back Cooper's truck up to the door of the garage, get everything loaded into the bed, wrestle with the twelve-foot ladder, and then head to Steph and Alana's house.

Everything looks normal when I pull up to the little blue house. No obvious signs of damage from the front. As soon as I ring the doorbell, Steph flings the door open and pulls me inside with the rain trailing after me and a puddle around my feet.

"It's this way," she says after brief hellos. She takes me to the screened-in rear porch. From there, I see the branches of a tree hanging off the back corner of the house. "We were lucky to make it through the last hurricane with those branches overhanging the house. It was only a matter of time."

"Evan kept saying he'd come trim them back." Alana steps onto the porch with an armful of wet towels. "But of course he forgot."

Steph glances at her. "Maybe toss those in the dryer so we can have something to put down when the others soak through?"

Alana sighs. "Hope no one wanted a shower tonight."

"Give me a hand outside," I say to them. "First thing, we've got to get on the roof and pull those branches off. With the wind and everything, leaving them up there could make it worse."

"What?" Steph looks at me, aghast. "You're not going out there?"

"What'd you expect?" I give a wry laugh. "You weren't calling Cooper for more towels."

"But it's dangerous. There's lightning."

Steph has a point, of course. The alternative is flooding their whole house and ending up with a massive hole in their roof. Anyway, I spent three years of high school on the stagecraft crew with the drama department. I can be pretty handy when I need to be.

"I'm going to get up on the roof and tie a rope around the branches to lower them down to you two. Then I've got some stuff to cover the hole. It'll be quick." I'm lying. It won't be quick. But it's got to be done, and the more Steph keeps us standing around worrying, the worse it'll get.

"Just tell us what to do," Alana says, nodding. This might be the most words she's said to me that weren't accompanied by a sarcastic smirk. That's progress, I suppose.

Together the three of us trudge through the downpour to get all the supplies positioned in the backyard and stand the ladder against the side of the house. RIP their living room carpet. I know I'm taking my life into my own hands climbing a metal ladder in the middle of a thunderstorm, but it's been several minutes since the last flash of lightning, so I take my chances and climb up with the rope over my shoulder.

Wearing a borrowed pair of Steph's hiking boots, I walk across the slanted roof. Every step is like being on ice skates for the first time, except here I can't hug the railing for support. Careful not to make any sudden movements, I manage to tie the rope around the huge, forked branch of the tree, then ball up the slack and make my best Hail Mary pass at throwing it over an exposed limb of the tree to act as a pulley. I succeed on the first attempt. Hell yeah.

On the ground, Steph and Alana take up the weight as best they can as I gingerly help push the branch off the side of the house. As they lower it to the ground, I immediately see where some shingles are missing and a foot-wide dent has been punched through the roof, water pouring inside.

I gingerly make my way down to the ground, where the girls have untied the rope.

"How bad is it?" Steph asks, wiping in vain at the water pouring down her face. We're standing in about four inches of mud at this point. The yard has pretty much turned to liquid and my feet squish inside Steph's boots.

"It's not big, but there's definitely a hole," I report.

We're practically shouting through the deafening wind and rain beating down on the metal porch roof and pelting the trees.

I shove my wet hair off my forehead. "Best we can do is cover it up and hope the rain stops soon."

"What do you need?" Alana eyes me anxiously from under the rim of a baseball cap. Her bright red hair is plastered to her neck.

"I'll take the staple gun, hammer, and nails with me. Then you and Steph tie the tarp to the rope so I can pull it up once I'm up there."

"Be careful," Steph reminds me for the fifth time.

I appreciate the concern, but really, I want to get this done and get dry. My fingers are already turning pruney, I've got a water-logged wedgie riding up my ass, and the chill has soaked into my bones. After they raise the tarp to me and I cut a large-enough piece off with Alana's pocketknife, I tack it down with the staple gun to hold it in place while I put in some sturdier nails. I'm shivering so violently, my teeth chattering, it takes forever to get the nails in.

"You okay?" Steph shouts from the ground.

I get a nail about halfway in, then miss it when the hammer slips, and bend the damn thing. Oh, to hell with it. Good enough.

"Coming down," I shout back.

I scurry my ass down the ladder and we all bolt inside, leaving the rope and tarp in the yard, right as a massive crack of lighting seems to strike right on top of us.

In the laundry room, we strip down to our underwear and toss our wet, muddy clothes in the washing machine.

"That was close." Alana gives me a wide, exhilarated smile that I wholeheartedly return, both of us seemingly aware that we escaped by the skin of our teeth.

"Too close," Steph says with a frazzled look. "What would I tell Cooper if you got electrocuted up there?"

"Yeah, no." From the linen closet, Alana pulls out three blankets for us to warm up in. "We would've had to hide the body and tell Cooper you skipped town." When I raise an eyebrow at her, she shrugs, grinning blithely. "What? You haven't seen Cooper's temper. It's self-preservation at that point."

Alana and I go into the living room. Steph puts on a pot of cof-fee. I'm shivering, wrapped up in my blanket cocoon on the couch, when Alana gets a phone call.

"Hey," she answers. "Yeah, we figured it out. She's here, actually. Sure. See ya." She sets the phone down and takes a seat beside me. "They're on their way over."

"Think I could borrow some clothes to go home in?" I ask. With my stuff in the wash, I'd rather not leave here in nothing but my underwear and Cooper's rain jacket.

"No problem."

Steph comes back with the coffee. I normally take cream and a mound of sugar, but I'm not picky at the moment, and scalding hot black coffee is exactly the thing to chase the frigid out of my blood.

"Okay, so that was legit badass," Steph admits, squeezing on the couch between Alana and me. "I wouldn't have taken you for the manual labor type." She regards me with a regretful smile when it dawns on her that I might take it as an insult.

"Sophomore year of high school, I had this chemistry teacher whose fetish was dragging down his students' GPAs with impossible pop quizzes. The only way to get extra credit was through volunteer hours, so I helped build sets and stuff for the school plays. It was fun, actually. Except for the time I almost lost a finger when Robbie Fenlowe ran a drill over it." I show Steph the scar on my index finger. "Mangled flesh and everything."

"Eww, that's disgusting."

"For real, though," Alana says, her cheeks turning a shade of crimson not far off from her hair. "Thanks for coming over. We would have been shit out of luck."

"Yeah," Steph laughs, "Alana's a total wuss. She's terrified of heights."

Alana glowers at Steph, flashing her middle finger. "Thanks, bitch."

"What?" Steph shrugs. "It's true."

"I'm being nice, okay? Give me a break."

I don't know Alana well, but I'd call this a breakthrough. All it took was a death-defying act of heroism to break some ground with her. That's two-thirds. Now if I can figure out how to crack Heidi, I'll be golden.

For the next fifteen minutes, the girls and I keep chatting. When I tell them about the hotel I purchased, Steph offers a ton of details about the place, gathered from the three summers she worked there. Realizing her knowledge is invaluable, I make a mental note to invite her to the site once I take possession. Her familiarity with the hotel could be a real asset.

"Help has arrived, ladies!" Evan bursts through the door not long after, shirtless and dripping. "Where's the fire?"

Somewhere, someone has fantasized about exactly this. Which is weird, because even as I'm sleeping with his identical twin, a half-naked Evan does nothing for me.

"You're about two hours too late," Alana says flatly, unimpressed with his grand entrance.

"Oh, I'm sorry." Evan shakes the water from his hair with all the grace of a stray dog and shoots Alana a sarcastic glare. "I guess I didn't get your retainer fee this month to be at your beck and call."

Cooper has to practically push his brother through the door to get inside and out of the storm. He appears a bit perplexed to see me on his friends' couch, wrapped up in a blanket like a soggy corn dog.

"Couldn't help noticing my truck outside," he says with a raised eyebrow. "Went and helped yourself, huh?"

I shrug, meeting his crooked grin. "Stole a bunch of stuff too. I think you're a bad influence on me."

He huffs out a laugh. "That right?"

Something about the gleam in his eyes starts to feel like foreplay. That's how quick it happens when he's around. From zero to *fuck me* in ten seconds flat. I can't help feeling like everyone else can see it, and yet I don't care. Cooper Hartley walks into a room and I lose my whole damn mind. I hate it. I love it.

"We're lucky she came," Steph says as the guys pour themselves a couple cups of coffee in the kitchen.

"This crazy bitch got up on the roof and patched the hole all by herself." Alana holds out her coffee mug for Evan to refill, which he does, rolling his eyes at the sight of the three of us bundled up in our cocoons. "On a related note," she adds, "no one use the guest bathroom. It's an aquarium now."

"I've always hated the wallpaper in there anyway," Steph remarks, and for some reason that gives Alana and me the giggles.

"Hold on." Cooper comes up short, standing in the middle of the living room. His distrustful gaze singles me out. "You got up on the roof?"

"I might have found a new calling," I tell him, sipping my coffee. "I should do the hotel renovation myself like the people on TV."

"Ooh." Steph smacks my arm. "I call dibs on hosting the reality series."

"I still can't believe you bought The Beacon," Alana marvels. "That's so frickin' random."

Cooper slams his coffee cup down on the TV console, liquid splashing out and startling the room silent. "Neither of you even tried to stop her?"

"Coop, it was fine." Steph disregards his outburst. "It was only a little rain."

"It wasn't your ass up there."

The venom in his voice is striking in its severity. I'm not sure where all this sudden anger is coming from. Was it a particularly responsible thing to do? No. But nobody got hurt. Except Cooper's butt, apparently.

I fix a small frown in his direction. "Hey, it's fine. I'm fine. They needed help so I offered to come over. It was my decision."

"I don't give a shit whose dumbass idea it was. You shoulda

known better," he tells me with a condescending tone, not unlike the one I heard from Preston when I showed him the hotel.

And now I'm kind of pissed. Why does every guy I date think he needs to be my dad? I didn't break up with Preston to start letting another guy treat me like a child.

"And you two," he glowers at the girls, "shoulda stopped her."

"Dude, chill." Alana throws her head back with a bored sigh. "She's a big girl. And we're glad she's here." I sense that's about as sincere an apology one gets out of Alana. Our efforts tonight have thawed the cold shoulder she's been giving me, and I think we're on good footing now.

"Shove it, Alana. She only pulled this stunt so you and Heidi would stop freezing her out."

"I don't remember asking you to speak for me," I snap at him, because thanks, asshole. I was making progress here and this isn't helping.

Cooper stalks toward the couch, looming over us. "You could've been killed," he snaps back. "In case you hadn't noticed, we're practically in the middle of a hurricane."

My jaw drops. "Are you kidding me right now? *In case I hadn't noticed?* And *now* you're suddenly worried about my safety? You're the one who left me at your house in the middle of a hurricane. I was all alone there! Just me and Patricia screaming like a banshee!"

He blinks at me as if I'm insane. "Her name is Daisy."

I stumble to my feet, clutching the blanket against myself like a toga. "I'm not talking about the dog! I'm talking about Patricia!"

"I don't know who Patricia is, you lunatic!"

"The little dead girl who drowned outside your house a hundred years ago and—"

I stop, my outraged gaze swinging toward Evan, whose lips are twitching wildly.

"You asshole!" I snarl. "Seriously?"

Evan crosses his arms over his chest. "Mackenzie. Sweetheart. I'm not gonna apologize for you being gullible. This one's on you."

On the couch, Alana and Steph are in hysterics. Steph has tears running down her cheeks as she wheezes out *little dead girl* between giggles.

In front of me, Cooper is clearly trying not to laugh too.

"Don't you dare," I warn, jabbing a finger in the air between us.

"I mean," Cooper trembles as he battles his laughter, "he's not wrong. That one's on you."

I glare at him. "He's a sadist! And you're a jerk."

"I'm a jerk? Remind me, who went out on the roof and almost got struck by lightning?"

"Oh my God, I did not almost get struck by lightning. You're being ridiculous right now." Indignant, I plant my hands on my hips, forgetting about the blanket wrapped around me.

It falls to the wet carpet, leaving me in nothing but a black sports bra and neon-pink bikini panties.

Evan licks his bottom lip. "That's what I'm talkin' about."

Despite the flicker of heat in his expression, Cooper's tone remains cool. "Get your clothes, Mac. We're leaving."

"No," I say stubbornly.

His eyes narrow. "Let's go."

"No. I live here now."

Alana snickers.

"Mackenzie." He takes a menacing step forward. "Let's go."

"No." My throat is suddenly dry. Tension thickens the air. I don't know if Cooper is angry or turned on, but his blazing eyes are sucking up all the oxygen in the room.

Cooper glances at his brother. "Evan, gimme your keys. You can take my truck home."

With a knowing grin, Evan reaches into his pocket then tosses a set of keys at his twin.

I jut my chin. "I don't know what you think is happening right now, but I am *not* going—"

Before I can blink, I'm being flung over Cooper's shoulder. Staring at his wet boots as he marches us to the door.

"Put me down!" I yell, but the downpour that hits us the moment we leave the house drowns out my furious request.

Cooper unceremoniously shoves me into the passenger seat of Evan's Jeep before running to the driver's side. When he starts the engine and turns to look at me, I have the answer to the *angry* versus *turned on* question.

His gaze has turned molten. "I'm going to be inside you the moment we get home." A threat. A promise.

Turned on.

Most definitely turned on.

CHAPTER TWENTY-SEVEN

MACKENZIE

"Shower. Now."

Cooper's growly order sends a shiver skittering through me. We'd just run from the Jeep to his house, getting soaked in the process. I'm still in nothing but my underwear, and my teeth are chattering again. Luckily, I'm not cold for much longer. In his bathroom, Cooper cranks the hot water, and soon there's steam rolling out of the tiled shower stall.

I strip out of the sports bra and panties and step into the shower, moaning happily as the heat suffuses my body. A moment later the temperature spikes another hundred degrees, because a naked Cooper is coming up behind me.

Strong arms encircle me, holding me against him. My back is flush against his broad chest. I can feel the long ridge of his erection pressing against my ass.

"You make me crazy." His hoarse words are muffled in the spray of the shower.

"Really? Seems to me like you're the one making *me* crazy." I shiver in pleasure when his big palms slide up my ribcage to cup my breasts. My nipples pucker.

"You could've gotten hurt up on that roof."

"But I didn't."

"Were you really scared here alone?" He sounds guilty.

"Kind of? I was hearing this shrieking from outside and the lights kept flickering."

He chuckles. "The wind gets pretty loud here. And we need to rewire most of the house. The electrical sucks."

"Stupid Evan," I mutter, pissed that he'd managed to make me question my former disbelief in the existence of ghosts.

"How about we don't talk about my brother when we're both naked?" Cooper suggests.

"Good point." I turn, reaching between us and taking him in my hand.

He shudders. "Yeah. Keep doing that."

"What? This?" I curl my fingers around his shaft and give it a teasing stroke.

"Mmmm."

"Or . . ." I give another pump, another slow glide, before sinking to my knees. "I could do *this*?"

Before he can respond, I wrap my lips around him and suck gently.

Cooper groans, and his hips thrust forward.

A rush of pure power surges through my blood. I could get used to this feeling. The satisfaction of knowing I'm the one who put that needy, desperate look on his rugged face. That right now, in this moment, I have him in the palm of my hand. Or rather, on the tip of my tongue. I give a little lick, and he makes a husky noise that brings a smile to my lips.

"You're teasing," he mutters.

"Uh-huh." I lick him again, a long, wet swipe along the length of him. "It's fun."

His hand comes down, long fingers tangling in my soaked hair. The water beats down on us. Droplets cling to his chest before dripping downward, traveling over muscle and sinew.

I brace one hand on his firm thigh, wrap the other around his erection, and suck him deep. He guides me wordlessly, encouraging me by cupping the back of my head. My entire body is scorching, taut with desire. When I peer up at Cooper, see those tattooed arms, the stubble shadowing his jaw, and feel him throbbing on my tongue, I don't regret a single thing that brought me to this point.

There's fire in you, Mac. He'd told me that the night of the carnival. Said I get off on the thrill, on *life*. He wasn't wrong. Since I broke up with Preston and started dating Cooper, I'd never felt more alive.

"I don't want to come this way," he mumbles, and then he's pulling me to my feet and kissing me hard enough to rob me of breath.

His hands hungrily roam my body as his tongue toys with mine. I'm hot and achy and more than ready for him. But for all my thrill-seeking, unprotected sex isn't on my thrill list, and Cooper and I only just got together.

"Condom." I whisper the reminder against his eager lips.

Without argument, he shuts off the shower and we sprint into his bedroom, dripping water everywhere and laughing at our own urgency.

"On the bed," he orders, devouring my naked body with his eyes.

My wet hair soaks the pillow the moment I lie down, but I'm too turned on to feel bad and Cooper doesn't seem to mind. He's wearing a condom and on top of me before I can blink. He kisses me again, hot, greedy, his tongue sliding into my mouth at the same time he thrusts deep.

I gasp, shaking from the jolt of pleasure that sizzles up my spine. I scrape my nails down his damp back and wrap my legs around him to draw him in deeper.

"You feel so good," he croaks against my lips.

"So do you." I lift my hips to meet his hurried thrusts, rocking against him. Mindless with need. "Faster," I beg.

He moves faster, and it isn't long before I'm seeing stars and trembling with release. He doesn't last much longer than me. Soon he's slamming into me harder, still kissing me, biting my lip as he comes.

Afterward, we lie on our backs and catch our breath. A feeling of pure contentment washes over me. I can't remember the last time I felt so sated after sex. Sated in general.

"I'm still pissed you went up on the roof."

I twist my head to look at him. "Seriously?"

"It was a dumbass move."

"I stand by it," I say haughtily.

"Of course you do." It sounds like he's trying not to laugh. Or maybe he's trying not to strangle me.

Apparently we both suck at backing down from an argument. It isn't in our natures, I suppose. But I can live with that. I wouldn't respect him otherwise. The last thing I want is a doormat.

On the other hand, all that bickering can't be good, can it?

I sigh. "We argue a lot. I feel like that's a second strike against us."

"What's the first strike?" he asks curiously.

"We're total opposites. And yeah, they say opposites attract and fighting can be a healthy release of passion and all that, but our backgrounds are so different." I hesitate, then confess, "Sometimes I have no idea how we're supposed to fit in each other's lives. And then add in the fact that you're an argumentative jackass and I want to punch you half the time, and . . ." Another sigh slips out. "Like I said, two strikes."

"Mac." The mattress shifts as he sits up. Dark eyes peer down at me. Intense, with a hint of amusement. "First of all, *they say*? Who's *they* and who cares? Every relationship is different. Some people fight, some people don't. Some want calm, some want passion. We define our own relationship. And second, I hate to break it to you, but we're *both* argumentative jackasses."

I grin at him.

"The only opposite thing about us is our bank accounts. We're a lot more alike than you and your uptight ex."

"Is that so?"

"Oh, it's fucking so. You know what I think?"

"Please, do tell," I say graciously.

"I think you were with that prick because he was safe. You said it yourself—he helped you stay restrained. And you needed that, because in your world, you can't act out or be yourself or do anything that might bring negative attention to your family, right? Well, you don't need to do that with me. Those two strikes you listed might be strikes in your other world, but here, you and me, we're exactly who and what we need to be."

My heart squeezes. Oh hell. When he says stuff like that, he makes it pretty damn hard to not catch feelings.

* * *

Bonnie: *Won't be home tonight! Try not to miss me too much, k? I know it'll be tough but I have faith in you!*

I grin at the text. Bonnie is the best. Sitting up in bed, I type a quick response.

Me: *Oooh, staying out on a school night, you bad girl. Let me guess, you're having a slumber party with . . . Edward?*
Bonnie: *You mean Jason. He just looks like Edward. And nope.*
Me: *Todd?*
Bonnie: *Out of rotation.*

I scan my brain trying to remember who else she'd been seeing these past few weeks. But I've kind of been distracted by all the wild sex I'm having with Cooper.

Bonnie: *Tell ya what, hun. Gimme the name of your townie, and I'll spill all the beans about my new beau.*

She's like a dog with a bone, this one. Bonnie's been on my case day and night about who I'm dating. I feel bad hiding Cooper from her—she was there when it started, after all—but I also know that knowledge in the wrong hands is a weapon. I'm not sure I'm ready to arm that cannon yet.

Me: *My townie is still my dirty little secret.*
Bonnie: *FINE! Then mine's a secret too.*

Two seconds later, she texts again.

Bonnie: *Who are we kiddin'? We both know I can't hide anything from you. His name is Ben and he is beautiful!*

She follows it up with a screenshot of an Instagram picture featuring a tall boy with the face of a Norse god.

Me: *Niiiiice. Have fun.*
Bonnie: *Oh I will. See you tomorrow!*

I set the phone on the nightstand and pick up my anthropology textbook. It's Monday night, and while I'd rather be naked in Cooper's bed right now, we spent all weekend together. So I'm forcing myself to stay in the dorm tonight. Not just to keep on top of my course work, but because too much time together could lead to burnout and the last thing I want is for Cooper to get sick of me. God knows I'm nowhere close to being sick of *him*. I spend, conservatively, three full hours a day fantasizing about him.

So, like a good girl, I finish all my readings for anthropology and bio, write an outline for my English Lit paper, and go to bed at the very reasonable time of ten forty-five.

Alas, the good night's sleep I'd hoped for doesn't come.

Around two in the morning, I'm rudely awakened by three consecutive phone calls from Evan.

Followed by a text message that reads: *Forget it. Not an emergency.*

If anyone else had been serial calling me in the middle of the night while maintaining it wasn't an emergency, I would've told them to fuck right off. But the fact that it's Evan gives me pause. We only recently exchanged numbers, after the night of the storm when I had no way to reach him. So I'm pretty sure he wouldn't be abusing phone privileges unless it was, indeed, an emergency. Or at least somewhat dire.

I shove my hair out of my eyes and call him back. "You okay?" I demand when he answers.

"Not really." There's a heaviness weighing down those two words.

"Where are you?"

"Outside Sharkey's. Can you come get me?" he mumbles. "I know it's late and I didn't want to call but—"

"Evan," I interrupt. "It's fine. Just stay put. I'm on my way."

CHAPTER TWENTY-EIGHT

MACKENZIE

Fifteen minutes later, I jump out of an Uber and scan the sidewalk in front of Sharkey's Sports Bar. It doesn't take long to spot him. Evan's sitting on the curb, looking like a month's worth of sludge at the bottom of a trash can that's been left in the rain.

"What happened to you?" I ask, noting the blood smeared on the side of his face, his shirt torn at the shoulder, and hands scraped and swollen. I can smell the alcohol on him from two feet away.

With his arms propped up on his bent knees, he looks exhausted. Defeated, even. He barely raises his head to acknowledge me. When he speaks, his voice is strained and weak. "Can you get me out of here?"

It's then I realize I'm his last resort. That turning to me for help is more painful than whatever he's endured tonight and what he needs the most now is grace.

"Yeah." I bend down to gather one of his arms over my shoulder to help bear his weight. "I've got you."

As we're getting up, a trio of guys rounds the corner. Wearing their Greek letters on their shirts, they shout something slurred and incoherent as they approach.

"Oh, hey, baby," one says when his bleary eyes land on me. A slimy grin appears. "What you got there? Find yourself a gutter stray?"

"Piss off, asshole." Evan grumbles a half-hearted insult. He can barely stand up straight, leaning on me for balance, but that isn't enough to deter him from picking a fight apparently. Got to admire his fortitude.

"It's this fucker again?" The tallest of the frat boys staggers closer, peering at Evan before turning to his buddies. "Look who's back, boys."

I level the three guys with a deadly glare. "Leave us alone."

"Haven't you had enough, my man?" The third guy comes closer, ducking to meet Evan's eyes as Evan fights to lift his head. "Thought you were fucking hilarious when you were trying to scam us, huh? Not laughing now, are you? Townie piece of trash."

My eyes become murderous. I'm tired, cranky, and I've got my hands full with Evan. There's not an ounce of patience left for these idiots.

"Hey, I know you," the tall one suddenly says, squinting at me.

"I doubt that," I snap.

"No, I do. I know you. You're Preston Kincaid's girlfriend." He laughs gleefully. "Yeah, you're Kincaid's girl. I'm in his frat. I saw you two at some sorority party a while back."

Strands of unease climb up my throat. Wonderful. The last thing I need is tonight's activities getting back to Preston. I tighten my grip on Evan and say, "I have no idea who you are, dude. Now, please, get out of our way."

"Does Kincaid know you're messing around on him?" His laughter turns maniacal. "And with this piece of shit, no less? Jesus. Women are such trash."

"Trash," one of the other guys echoes drunkenly.

When both of them try advancing closer, I've officially had enough.

"Back off, motherfuckers." My voice cracks like a whip off the brick wall of the bar.

"Or what?" mocks the tall one.

With an angry, impatient growl, I shove my hand in my purse and whip out a can of pepper spray, aiming it at the frat bros until they stagger back. "I promise you, I'm crazier than I look. Please test me."

Somewhere in the distance, a siren blares. It's enough to spook them. "Man, forget this bitch, let's get out of there."

They hurry to pile in a car across the street and flee, tires squealing as they pull a hard U-turn.

"Where the hell did that come from?" Evan manages a faint laugh, still clinging to me with one arm over my shoulder.

"All women are wolverines."

"Clearly."

"I've also done a fair bit of solo traveling, which if nothing else has taught me to be prepared for what lurks in the shadows." With that, I all but drag him to his Jeep and fish his keys out of his pocket. He manages to climb into the passenger seat while I slide behind the wheel.

"I can't go home," he says. Eyes closed, his head lulls against the window. Too heavy for his neck.

I adjust the driver's seat to accommodate my shorter legs. "Okay . . . Steph and Alana's house?"

"No. Please." He speaks in gusts of breath. "Coop can't find out."

I'm not sure why or which part he's referring to, but I understand his desperation. Which leaves me no choice but to bring him back to Tally Hall.

Getting him up to my dorm room on the fourth floor is a challenge, but we make it there in one piece. Once inside, I sit him on the edge of the bathtub to clean him up. A sense of déjà vu hits me. What is it about these Hartley boys, huh?

As I'm wiping the blood from his face with a wet washcloth, I can't ignore his gaze following my every move. He has some bruising and small cuts, but nothing serious. Just need to dab a little ointment and apply a couple bandages.

"Sore losers," he says.

"Huh?"

"Those guys. I beat them at pool, and they didn't take it well. Shouldn't play with money they aren't prepared to lose."

"Do you always shark people outnumbered?"

He breathes out a laugh then winces, holding his side. "I thought I had the home field advantage. Turned out there were a few more people holding a grudge than I figured."

I cock a brow at him. "Don't you townies have a saying about shitting where you eat?"

"Yeah, I might have heard that one."

"You've got to diversify."

"Adapt or die, is that it?"

"Something like that." Once I've got him fixed up, I get him a glass of water and some aspirin and bring him an ice pack. "You can sleep it off in Bonnie's room," I offer. "She's out tonight and I know she won't mind."

"She'd better not. I made her come three times that night."

I choke out a laugh. "How kind of you." Man, it seems like ages ago that Evan and Bonnie had wandered down the beach together. A day later, she was already chasing after her next conquest. No muss, no fuss between those two.

I prop him on the edge of Bonnie's bed and proceed to undress him in the most clinical of manners. I try not to stare at his body and compare it to Cooper's, but it's difficult. His chest is right there, and yes, it's as muscular as his brother's. No tattoos, though. At least until I help him roll over and realize he has a huge one on his back. It's too dark to make out the ink.

"Thank you," he says once he's lying down.

Though he doesn't offer more than that, I know it's sincere. Whatever is going on between him and Cooper, it's enough that turning to me for help was the more attractive option. I take it as a step in the right direction that Evan trusts me this much. Baby steps.

I pat him gently on the head, as if he's a child with a slight fever. "You're welcome."

The next morning, I'm getting ready for class when Evan bursts out of Bonnie's room with his phone to his ear.

"Yeah, I know, I know. I'm on my way. I said I heard you, fuck." He's stumbling around trying to pull his jeans up while rummaging through Bonnie's room for something. "Ten minutes."

When I question him with a look, he holds up his fingers to mime dangling keys. Keys! I still have his Jeep keys in my room. I dash off and grab them, then toss them at him. He snatches them easily from the air.

"No," he says into the phone. "Dude, I'm leaving right now, chill the fuck out."

Cooper? I mouth at him, to which Evan nods his head. I hold my hand out for the phone. He's skeptical at first, then relents.

"Here, the princess wants to talk to you." This time, instead of a sarcastic sneer, there's a smile in his eyes. Maybe a plea.

"Hey," I say, not giving Cooper a chance to cut me off. "I invited Evan out for breakfast but the place was slammed and I lost track of time. I just had to order the soufflé, you know."

"Breakfast, huh?" He's wary, of course. As he should be.

But I stick to the story. "Yeah, I thought it'd be a chance for us to chat, you know? A little family time."

I can practically feel Cooper's eyes rolling through the phone.

"Whatever. Tell him to get his ass to work."

"K, smooches, bye," I sing sweetly, because the more I throw Cooper off balance, the more he'll accept this completely preposterous premise. Ending the call, I hand the phone back to Evan. "I think he bought it."

He gives me a look of confused amusement. "You're a lifesaver."

"I know. Now can I ask why I'm lying to your brother?"

Running his hands through his hair, Evan sighs. He's the type who hates explaining himself. I get that. But fair's fair.

"Coop's already on my case," he says reluctantly. "If he finds out about last night, he'll force an intervention on me or some dumb shit."

"Do you need one?" I know Cooper's been concerned that Evan is spiraling, but he hasn't told me any specifics. Judging by last night, I suspect booze and fighting are possible culprits.

"Definitely not," Evan assures me.

I'm not sure who he's trying to convince, but it doesn't work on either of us.

I let out a breath. "Make me a promise."

He rolls his eyes. It's these times I forget he and Cooper are two different people.

"I'll cover for you as long as you're honest with me. If you won't talk to Cooper, I'll feel better if you at least let me keep an eye on you."

"I don't need a babysitter." He punctuates that with a dark scowl.

Yup. I get why they fight so much. Cooper's overbearing and Evan is an obstinate ass. Together they create a perfect storm.

"I don't want to be one," I tell him. "So how about we settle for friends. Deal?"

He licks his lips to smother a grin. It's almost charming. "Alright, princess. Deal."

We shake hands. I give it about a fifty-fifty chance that he holds up his end of the bargain. Still, it's miles from where we started, and I'm smart enough to take what I can get.

CHAPTER TWENTY-NINE

COOPER

Mac's got yet another inspection at the hotel today, so I take the afternoon off to go there with her. She says it's so I can translate for her, but I think she's nervous about what she's gotten herself into. Can't blame her. Even if I had boatloads of family money, jumping into something as complex as renovating a hotel—not to mention running the damn thing—would make me a whole lot of anxious too. So as the inspector does his thing, Mac and I hang out on the boardwalk waiting for the verdict.

"I'm starting to think one does not simply buy a condemned hotel," she says glumly.

I can't help a smile. "That so?"

"Yup." She bends to pet Daisy, who's sitting at her feet. That dog doesn't leave me alone for a second when we're home, and then as soon as Mac comes around, she doesn't know me.

"You can walk away." From what I understand, the final sale of the property is still pending the completion of this last inspection. Crossing *t*'s and all that.

"No, I'm committed. It's just overwhelming, you know? Thinking about everything there is to do. How much I don't know."

"So you'll figure it out."

She bites her lip. "Right." Then she nods. Swiftly, decisively. "You're right. I will figure it out."

This is what I dig about her. Her confidence. The courage. She had an idea and some gumption and went for it. Most people spend their whole lives talking themselves out of their dreams. Point out all the reasons it's too hard or farfetched. Not Mac.

"When you look at this place, do you still feel the same way as you did when you put the offer in?" I ask.

She smiles, the gleam of ambition fresh in her eyes as she stares at the crumbling building. "Yes."

"Pull the trigger. Can't win if you don't play."

"That's the lottery," she says, nudging my shoulder.

"Same difference."

To be honest, I'm glad she asked me here. Even if only for moral support. There isn't much I can give a girl like Mackenzie Cabot. Nothing she doesn't already have or can't get on her own. We all want to feel useful, though. I don't know when it happened, but somewhere along the way, I started needing her to need me.

After a couple hours, the inspector comes out with his clipboard and runs down the list with Mac. Most of it we expected, some we didn't. All of it carries a price tag.

"What's the bottom line?" Mac asks him after he's gone over every bullet item line by line.

"It'll cost ya," the man says through his overgrown mustache. "That said, there's no reason this place can't be operational again. I wish you luck."

After a handshake, he gives her the paperwork and walks off to his car.

"So?" I prompt, taking Daisy's leash from her.

She hesitates. Only for a second. Then she smiles wryly. "Guess I better call the bank."

Gotta admit, it's kind of hot that she can just call up a few million like placing a bet on the Panthers. She wears it well.

After she gets off the phone, we take a walk on the beach and let Daisy run around a little.

"So listen." Mac sifts through the sand with her toes, picking out shells that catch her eye. She scoops one up, admires it, then drops it back in the sand. "I know I'm out of my depth here. I'm better at writing checks than rewiring a building."

"That's no sweat. I know everyone in ten square miles who does this kind of work."

"That's what I mean. You know the area, the people."

There's an ask coming, and I can't imagine what it could be that has her dancing around the subject.

"Spit it out, Cabot."

She rounds on me, arching an eyebrow. "I want to hire your uncle Levi to do the work."

I furrow my brow. "What part?"

"All of it. As much as he can handle. Whatever he can't, I want him to sub-contract out to people he trusts. The guys he'd get to do his mother's house. Keep it in the family, so to speak."

"Wow. Okay . . ." I mean, I'd expected her to pick his brain, maybe. Get some references. Maybe toss him a project or two.

This is . . . a lot.

"You seem unsure," Mac observes.

"No, no. I'm not. It's, uhh . . ."

"A big commitment?" She's smiling. Grinning, actually. I think this chick is laughing at me.

"I'm not afraid of commitment, if that's what you're suggesting."

"Uh-huh," she says.

"I'll commit the shit out of you."

"Good." Thinking she's already won, she spins on her toes and resumes walking. "Then we have a deal. You'll set up a meeting with Levi so we can discuss scope and an equitable price."

"Hang on, princess. He's got other jobs on the books already. I don't know what kind of time he has. Don't get ahead of yourself."

"Details." She waves her hand at me. "All can be negotiated. Where there's a will, there's a way."

"Okay, I'll put the offer to him if you keep the cheesy platitudes to yourself."

Mac picks up a piece of driftwood and tosses it for Daisy. "I make no promises."

I roll my eyes at her back. This woman is kind of insufferable, but I love it. Somehow, she got under my skin. Even when she's being obnoxious, I'm still into it.

"Be honest," I say before I can stop myself. "Does this whole thing even put a dent in the trust fund?"

I hesitate to even guess at a number. At a certain point, all the zeros start to run together. The difference between a hundred million and five hundred million is the difference between swimming to China and New Zealand to a drowning man.

She goes quiet for a second. Then another. An apparent unease steals the humor from her face. "Actually, I can't touch my trust fund until I'm twenty-five."

That gives me pause, because how did she buy a hotel, then? I know her parents aren't giving her the money. She's been vocal about their lack of approval for her ambitions.

"Unless you've been a drug kingpin this whole time—I'd be totally sympathetic if you were—where the hell does a twenty-year-old get that kind of cash?"

"You're going to think it's silly," she says, stopping to stare at the ground.

I'm getting a little nervous. Suddenly, I'm wondering if I'd be okay if she told me she was a camgirl or something. Or worse, if she asked me to join her essential oils pyramid scheme.

Fortunately, she works up the nerve to spit it out before my imagination really takes off.

"You remember that time you showed me the funny boyfriend story? The one where the girl was looking for tampons in her date's mom's bathroom?"

My eyebrows fly up. What does that have to do with anything?

"Yeah . . ."

"I built that website. *BoyfriendFails*. Which spun off to *GirlfriendFails*."

"Wait, for real?"

She shrugs. "Yeah."

Holy shit. "And you made all this money from that?"

Another embarrassed shrug. It confuses me, because what is she so shy about?

"Mackenzie, that's badass," I inform her.

"You don't think it's stupid?" She looks at me with these big, hopeful green eyes. I'm not sure if I should feel like a dick that she thought I'd judge her for this.

"Hell no. I'm impressed. When I was twenty, I was still burning mac and cheese." I mean, I'm *still* burning mac and cheese.

"My parents hate it." Her voice grows sour. As it does every time the subject comes up, but more so lately. "You'd think I got a tattoo on my forehead or something. They keep waiting for me to 'grow out of it.'" She makes angry air quotes, kicking sand. "They don't get it."

"What's not to get? Their daughter can't even rent a car yet but she's already a self-made millionaire."

"They're embarrassed. They think it's crass and silly high school nonsense. And, whatever, maybe it is. But what's so wrong with that if it makes people laugh, you know? Far as they're concerned, my business is a distraction. All they want for me is to frame a respectable degree and marry rich, so I can be like Mom and sit on charity boards. It's about appearances. It's all fashion to them."

"See, that sounds dumb as hell." I shake my head, because I truly don't get it. Rich people buying status symbols to impress other rich people who bought the same status symbols to impress them. A vicious cycle of waste and pretension. "Hundreds of thousands of dollars to a university just for looks? Fuck that noise."

"I didn't even want to go to Garnet—it was the only way they'd support my gap year so I could have the time to build my apps and expand the business. But since I got here, all I've been thinking about is tackling a new challenge, finding a new business venture that excites me as much as my websites did when I was first launching them."

"Well, you know what I think? Do you, and to hell what everyone else thinks."

"Easier said than done," she says with that familiar tone of trepidation.

Daisy brings us a small hermit crab hiding in its shell, which Mac takes and sets back in the sand before finding another stick to throw instead.

"Yeah, so what?" Where she's concerned, her parents have always been a daunting obstacle to realizing what she really wants out of life. For someone with every advantage, that's bullshit. She's stronger than that. "If you want it bad enough, fight for it. Take the bruises. What's the worst they can do, cut you off? If you're honest with them about how much this all means to you and they still don't support your dreams, how much are you really going to miss them?"

She lets out a soft sigh. "Honestly, sometimes I wonder if they love me at all. Most of the time, I'm a prop or a piece on a board in their larger game of strategy. I'm plastic to them."

"I could bore the hell out of you with crappy family stories," I tell her. "So I get that. It's not the same, but trust me, I get feeling alone and unloved. Always trying to fill that void with something, anything else. I can almost forgive my dad for being a mean bastard, you know? He had an addiction. It turned everything he touched to shit. Eventually killed him. I wasn't even that sad about it, except then all we had left was our mom. For a while, anyway, but then she split too. The two of them couldn't get away from us fast enough." My throat closes up. "I've spent so much time scared that I'll turn into one of them. Afraid no matter what I do, I'm fighting against the current and I'll end up dead or a deadbeat."

Fuck.

I've never said those words out loud before.

It's terrifying how much Mac brings out of me. How much I want her to know me. It's terrifying how I don't feel in control of my heart that's racing to catch her. To keep her. Worried that at any moment she might come to her senses and ditch my ass.

"Hey." Then she takes my hand, and all I can think is that I'd stand in traffic for this girl. "Let's make a pact: We won't let each other become our parents. The buddy system never fails."

"Deal." It's so corny I half manage a laugh. "Seriously, though. Don't waste this moment. If your heart's telling you to follow something—go for it. Don't let anyone hold you back, because life is too damn short. Build your empire. Slay dragons."

"You should put that on a T-shirt."

Daisy comes back, curling around Mac's feet. Guess she finally ran herself ragged. I put her on the leash as Mac and I sit in the sand. A comfortable silence falls between us. I don't understand how she manages to instill equal parts chaos and peace inside me. When we're arguing, sometimes I want to throttle her. She drives me mad. She does crazy shit like climbing metal ladders during lightning storms. And then suddenly we have moments like this, where we're sitting side by side, quiet, lost in our own thoughts yet completely in tune. Connected. I don't know what it means. Why we can yell at each other one second, and be totally at peace the next. Maybe it just means we're both nuts.

Or maybe it means I'm falling for her.

CHAPTER THIRTY

MACKENZIE

A few days after my hotel inspection, I meet up with Steph and Alana at a sandwich shop in town. Seems strange that a couple of weeks ago we were barely on speaking terms, and now we chat almost every day. It started when Steph looped me into a group text with Alana to share some pictures of Evan on their roof fixing the hole from the storm. His jeans had ridden down, revealing half his ass, and she'd captioned the pics with: *Someone's doing a half-ass job.* Then Alana shared a funny screenshot from *BoyfriendFails*, and—although I was worried it might sound like a brag or serve as another glaring allusion to the topic of money—I confessed to the girls that I'm the one who created those sites. Luckily, it only made them like me more.

"Settle something for us," Alana says, gesturing across the table with a pickle spear. "True or false—Cooper has his dick tattooed."

I almost cough up a french fry. "What?"

"A few years back, there was this story about some chick who got banged on the roof of the police station on Fourth of July weekend," Steph says beside me. "And there was a picture going around of a dude with a tattoo on his dick, but we never nailed down who it was."

"You didn't ask Heidi this question?"

The girls stare at me with apprehension.

"What, was I not supposed to know about that?" My tone is glib. I'd thought it was obvious those two had been hooking up at some point in the recent past.

Steph and Alana exchange a look, silently debating how to respond.

I offer a shrug. "It's fine. I get it, she's your best friend."

"They didn't date or anything," Steph says as a consolation. "It was, you know, friends with benefits."

For Cooper, maybe. But when it comes to those types of arrangements, I know that one person, without fail, is always more invested than the other.

"Heidi's still got a thing," Alana adds flatly, never one to mince words.

I'd already suspected that unrequited feelings or maybe a breakup was the source of Heidi's irrational hatred of me. My instincts are rarely wrong about these things, so Alana's confirmation is almost vindicating.

"I figured," I tell them. "But maybe she'll be ready to move on one of these days. Cooper said there's some guy interested in her? Jay something?"

That earns me two groans.

"Don't get me started on that one," Alana gripes. "Yeah, I want her to get over this Coop thing so life can go back to normal—but Genevieve's brother, of all people?"

"Who's Genevieve?"

"Evan's ex," Steph answers. "Gen lives in Charleston now."

"I miss her," Alana says, visibly glum.

Steph snorts. "So does Evan. Otherwise he wouldn't be trying to bang her out of his system. Or rather, bang everyone else." She flips her ponytail over one shoulder and turns to grin at me. "It's all super incestuous here in the Bay. Evan and Genevieve. Heidi and

Cooper—although thank God that's over. Friends shouldn't hook up, it's just asking for trouble." Her gaze pointedly shifts to Alana. "And then we've got this bitch here who keeps going back for seconds with Tate? Or are we on thirds now? Fourths?"

"Tate?" I echo with a grin. "Oh, he's hot."

Alana waves her hand. "Nah, that's done now. I don't like the friends with bennies thing either."

"I've never done it." I give a self-deprecating shrug. "My hookup history consists of Cooper, and a four-year relationship with a guy who was apparently sleeping with anything that moves."

Steph grimaces. "Honestly, I can't even believe you were dating that creep."

I feel a groove dig into my forehead. "Do you know Preston?" There'd been a troubling sense of familiarity in her statement.

"What? Oh, no, I don't. I mean, I know *of* him. Cooper told us he was cheating on you—I just assume all cheaters are creeps." Steph reaches for her coffee, sips it, turning her face away from me for a second before glancing over with a reassuring smile. "And look, don't worry about Heidi. Cooper's crazy about you."

"And Heidi's been sufficiently threatened to behave herself," Alana finishes, then reacts with a knitted brow when Steph gives her the facial equivalent of a kick under the table. They're about as subtle as a jackhammer.

It's not the first time I've caught a similar exchange between the two of them, as if they're having an entire unspoken conversation I'm not a part of. My relationship with Steph and Alana has warmed significantly—and I have no doubts about Cooper's sincerity where the two of us are concerned—but I get the distinct impression there's a lot more I don't know about this tight-knit group. Obviously, I can't expect to fully penetrate the circle of trust so quickly.

But why does it feel like their secrets are at my expense?

I don't get the chance to ponder that question, as my phone

vibrates in my pocket. It's my mother. Again. I woke up this morning to several missed text messages from her, picking up mid-rant from the several missed text messages from the night before. I've taken to periodically blocking her number just to get some peace from her blowing up my phone. It's one tirade after another over my breakup with Preston. There's nothing left to say on the subject. For me, anyway.

But it seems my mother is determined to force me to talk about it. I glance at my phone to find she's abandoned texting and is now calling me. I send the call to voicemail just as a 911 text from Bonnie pops up to alert me that judgment day has arrived.

"What's wrong?" Steph leans over my shoulder, apparently alarmed at the blood draining from my face.

"My parents are here."

Well, not here. At my dorm. Poor Bonnie's in lockdown mode awaiting further instructions.

Bonnie: *What do I do with them?*
Me: *Send them to the coffee shop. I'll meet them there.*

I knew this was coming. I've been dodging calls and texts, making myself scarce. But it was only a matter of time before they came for my reckoning.

No one walks out on my father.

I bail on lunch with an apology and haul ass back to campus with my blood pressure spiking. After a short phone call, the best I could do was lure them to a public venue. My parents wouldn't dare make a scene. Here, I have the strategic advantage—and an escape route.

Still, when I walk in the café to see them seated by the window, awaiting their rogue daughter, I struggle to put one foot in front of the other. No matter how old I get, I'm still six years old, standing in our living room as my father berates me for spilling fruit punch on my dress before the Christmas card photo shoot, after he specifically told me I could only have water, while my mother stands fraught in the corner by the bar cart.

"Hey," I greet them, draping my purse strap over the chair. "Sorry if I kept you waiting. I was having lunch with some friends in town—"

I halt when I read the expression of impatience on my father's face. He's dressed in a suit, one sleeve pushed up to expose his watch. I get the message. Loud and clear. He's missing meetings and who knows what other world-altering events to tend to his errant off-spring. How dare I make him deign to parent.

Then there's Mother Dearest, who's tapping her manicured nails on her leather Chanel clutch as if I'm also holding her up. Honestly, I couldn't say what the hell she does all day. I'm sure there's a call with a caterer somewhere in her schedule. Her weeks are an endless haze of decisions like chicken or fish.

For a split second, as the two of them glare at me with annoyance and disdain, I see the template of their lives superimposed on my future, and it stitches up my side. My throat closes. A full-blown panic explodes through my nervous system. I imagine this is how drowning must feel.

I can't live this way anymore.

"I'm glad you're here," I start, only for Dad to hold up his hand. *Kindly shut up*, the hand says. Okay then.

"I believe you owe us an apology, young lady." Sometimes I wonder if my father uses the term because, for a moment, he's forgotten my name.

"Really, you've gone too far this time," my mother agrees. "Have you any idea the embarrassment you've caused?"

"Here is what's going to happen." Dad doesn't look at me, instead scrolling through emails on his phone. All of this is a prepared speech that doesn't include my participation. "You will apologize to Preston and to his parents for this episode. After which they've agreed to the resumption of your relationship. Then you're coming home for the weekend while we evaluate how to proceed. I'm afraid we've allowed you too much latitude lately."

I stare at him.

When I realize he's being serious, I cough out an incredulous laugh. "Um, no. I can't do that."

"Excuse me." My mother adjusts her scarf, a sort of nervous tic she gets when she's acutely aware she can't snap at me in front of quite so many witnesses. "Your father isn't giving you a choice, Mackenzie."

Well, at least one of them knows my name. I try to imagine them picking out baby names. If ever there was a moment in time they looked forward to a child, it was then, right?

"I won't get back together with Preston." My tone invites no argument.

So, of course, I get one.

"Why not?" Mom wails in exasperation. "Don't be a fool, sweetheart. That boy will make a loyal, upstanding husband."

"Loyal?" I snort loud enough to draw gazes from a few neighboring tables.

Dad frowns at me. "Keep your voice down. You're attracting attention."

"Trust me when I say Preston is *not* loyal to anyone but himself. I'll spare you the details." Like how he was a cheating prick who was probably messing around since the moment we got together. How in some ways he saved us both, because I was no saint either. "But suffice it to say we don't have a connection anymore." I hesitate. Then I think, fuck it. "Besides, I'm seeing someone else."

"Who?" Mom asks blankly, as if Preston were the last man on earth.

"A townie," I reply, because I know it will drive her nuts.

"Enough."

I jump when my father smacks his phone down on the table. Ha. Who's attracting attention now?

Realizing what he did, Dad lowers his voice. He speaks through clenched teeth. "This disobedience stops now. I will not entertain your provocations any further. You will apologize. You will take the boy back. And you will fall in line. Or you can kiss your allowance and credit cards goodbye." His shoulders shake with restrained rage as I now have his complete attention. "So help me, I will cut you off and you can see exactly how cold and dark this path can get."

I don't doubt him for a second. I've always known he was ruthless where I'm concerned. No coddling. No special treatment. That used to scare me.

"Tell you what," I say, pulling my purse off the back of my chair, "here's my counteroffer: no."

His eyes, the same dark shade of green as my own, gleam with disapproval. "Mackenzie," he warns.

I reach into my bag. "Do what you must, but I'm tired of living in fear of disappointing you both. I'm sick of never living up to your ideal. I have had my absolute fill of killing myself to make you happy and constantly falling short. I'm not ever going to be the daughter you want, and I'm done trying."

I find what I'm looking for in my purse. For the first time my life, my parents are speechless as they watch me fill out a check.

I slide it across the table to my father. "Here. This ought to cover what you spent for the first semester. I've decided my interests lie elsewhere."

With nothing left to say—and certain this burst of madness and courage will not last—I hold my breath as I get up from the table and walk out, not sparing a glance behind me.

Just like that, I'm a college dropout.

CHAPTER THIRTY-ONE

MACKENZIE

I'm waiting on Cooper's doorstep when he gets home from work that evening.

After leaving my parents, I had all this pent-up energy and nowhere to release it, so I walked the boardwalk for a while, then strolled down the beach until I wound up at his place. A while later, I'm still sitting on the porch when Cooper's truck parks in their driveway and both brothers get out.

"What's up, princess?" Sauntering up to the front door, Evan gives me a wink as he lets himself inside. We're old pals now, me and the Bad Twin.

"How long have you been out here?" Cooper looks surprised to see me as he comes up the steps.

I momentarily forget what he asks, because I'm too busy gawking. He puts me on my ass every time I see him. His dark eyes and windswept hair. The suggestion of his body under his T-shirt and faded jeans flirts with my memory. There's something wildly masculine about him. He's spent all day on the jobsite, dusty remnants still coating his skin, his clothes. The smell of sawdust. It gets me positively reckless. Reduces my entire being to *want want want*.

"Mac?" he prompts. A knowing smile curves his lips.

"Oh. Sorry. An hour, maybe?"

"Something wrong?"

"Not at all." I take the hand he extends and let him help me to my feet. We go inside. Once we kick off our shoes, I lead him straight to his bedroom.

"I have news," I announce.

"Yeah?"

I close his door and lock it. Because more than once lately, Evan has gotten his kicks by jiggling the handle when he knows we're getting up to something, just to scare the shit out of me. Guy needs a hobby.

"I dropped out of school." I can barely contain my excitement. And maybe there's some fear too. It all feels the same, bubbling inside.

"Holy shit, that's big. How'd that happen?"

"My parents ambushed me on campus and kind of forced my hand."

Cooper peels out of his shirt and tosses it in his hamper. When he starts to unbuckle his belt, I cross the room and pull his hands away, taking over. As I undo his zipper, I feel him watching the top of my head and his abdomen clenches.

"How'd that go?" He sounds a bit distracted now.

Leaving his jeans on, I reach inside his boxers and begin to stroke him. He's already half hard when I do. Quickly, he's fully erect and his breathing is shallow.

"I told them to get bent." I swipe my thumb over the drop of moisture at his tip. He hisses in a sharp breath. "Not in so many words."

"Feeling pretty fucking full of yourself, huh?" His hands comb through my hair and tighten at my scalp.

I lean closer and kiss him under the corner of his jaw. "Just a bit."

Then I walk us backward until his legs hit the bed and he sits on the edge.

Hunger darkens his gaze. "What brought this on?"

"Mostly me." From his nightstand I grab a condom and toss it to him. Then I pull my dress over my head. "A little you."

My bra and underwear drop to the floor.

"Independence looks good on you," he says roughly, running his fist up and down his shaft as he watches my every move.

Slowly, I climb onto his lap. He curses in my ear, grabbing my ass with both hands. With my palms flat against his chest, I ride him. Gently at first, as a flurry of shivers race through me. It's always a shock to my system, being with Cooper. Everything about him feels right, and yet I'm still not used to this. I don't think I want to be. I'm still finding surprises. Still shaken every time his lips travel along my skin.

I rock back and forth. Shamelessly. I can't get him deep enough, close enough. My head falls to his shoulder and I bite down to keep from making a sound as I grind on him.

"Oh hell, I'm not gonna last," he mumbles.

"Good," I breathe.

He groans and gives an upward thrust, his arms tightening around me.

I smile as I watch the haze of bliss fill his expression, as I listen to the husky noises he makes when he comes. After he tosses the condom, he lays me on the bed and kisses his way from my breasts to my stomach, and then lower, until he settles between my legs and opens me to his tongue. Cooper licks me until I'm tugging at his hair and moaning with pleasure. He's too good with his mouth. It's addictive.

Later, after a shower and another round of orgasms, we sit on the front porch with Daisy while a frozen pizza bakes in the oven.

"I don't know if I would've gone through with it if I hadn't met you," I tell Cooper, as our puppy sleeps in his lap. "Dropping out, I mean."

"Yeah, you would have. Eventually. I'm the excuse that gave you a nudge."

"Maybe," I admit. "But you inspired me."

He rolls his eyes.

"Shut up. I mean it." Something I've learned about Cooper: He's terrible at taking compliments. It's one of his more endearing qualities. "You're not afraid of anything or anyone. You make your own rules. Everyone else be damned."

"It comes easy when you don't have shit to start with."

"You believed in me," I say. "You're the only one who ever has. That means a lot. I won't forget that."

But even as I bask in my newfound independence, I'm not naïve enough to believe my parents will take my decision lying down. They'll figure out a way to make it hurt. No one crosses my father and gets away with it. So there will definitely be fallout from this sudden outburst of disobedience. It's only a question of *how bad*.

It doesn't take long for the consequences of my actions to make themselves known. Exactly six days after dropping out, I receive an email from the dean of students. It's short and concise. A polite *Get your ass in here.*

I'm a few minutes late for the meeting, and I'm ushered into a cherry wood–trimmed office by the secretary. The dean is otherwise engaged and will be with me in a moment. Would I care for some water?

I guess my parents made a few calls hoping a neutral third party can lobby me on their behalf to not drop out of school. Though as far as I'm concerned, all that's left are the formalities of paperwork. Admittedly, I've made little progress on finalizing my withdrawal from Garnet. Between the hotel and my websites occupying most of my attention, I've enjoyed what counts for me as slacking off.

"So sorry about that." Dean Freitag, a petite woman whose leather skin clings in brittle ripples to her bones, enters the room. She comes around her desk, breathless, fluffing the humidity out of her shoulder-length helmet of blonde hair. She adjusts the jacket of her cranberry suit ensemble and pulls the silk scarf from her neck. "Hotter than the devil's bathtub out there."

The dean flicks on a small desk fan and aims it at herself, basking for a moment in the breeze before turning her attention back to me.

"Now, Ms. Cabot." Her demeanor shifts. "I understand you've not attended a single class in the last week."

"No, ma'am. I've come to the decision to withdraw from the semester."

"Oh? If I recall, you've already delayed your freshman year by twelve months." One pencil-thin eyebrow props up. "What's so pressing that your education must wait?"

Something about her friendly ignorance unnerves me. As if I'm walking into a trap.

"Actually, I'm withdrawing from Garnet entirely. I won't be back next semester."

She regards me, impassive, for several seconds. So long that I'm almost moved to elaborate to get her going again. When she finally speaks, I can't help but interpret some vengeance in her voice.

"And I suppose you've given this a fair bit of thought?"

"I have. Yes, ma'am."

A brief *suit yourself* smile crosses her lips before she rattles her computer mouse to wake the screen. She trains her attention on it as she speaks.

"Well, then we can certainly help you with that. I'll have my secretary pull the necessary forms." She glances at me with a look that falls short of reassurance. "Don't worry, it's just a signature or two." Clicking her mouse around. "Of course you'll need to vacate your dorm at Tally Hall within twenty-four hours of submitting notice to the Office of Student Housing." She hits me with the Miss Melon Pageant smile. "Which—here we are!—I've just submitted it for you."

And there it is. Total setup.

A big *screw you* from Daddy.

She's right, of course. I have no business squatting in a dorm room if I'm not a student here. A minor detail that seemed to slip my mind. No doubt my parents spent the last week waiting for me to come crawling back home for a place to stay.

"Will there be anything else?" The dean grins at me as if I've done this to her. A personal slight.

I don't waste a second agonizing over it, however. For better or worse, we're broken up.

"No, ma'am." I offer a saccharine smile and rise to my feet. "I'll just be on my way."

An hour later, I'm in my dorm, boxing up my belongings. A little over three months. That's how long my college career lasted, and yet . . . I'm not sad to see it end.

I'm pulling clothes off hangers when I hear the buzz of an incoming text. I grab the phone from my desk. It's a message from Kate, who I haven't seen in weeks. I asked her to hang out a couple times—I didn't want to be one of those girls who ditches her friends the moment she starts dating a new guy—but she's been busy rehearsing with some band she joined last month. She plays the bass guitar, apparently.

Kate: *Hey girl! Sooo, heads up—I spoke to my sister on the phone earlier and your name came up. Mel said your ex is asking around, trying to find out who you're dating. I guess someone saw you in town with some local?*

I curse out loud. Damn Evan. I knew that night would come back to haunt us.

Me: *Ugh. Awesome.*
Kate: *Yeah. Preston's on a mission now. You've been warned.*
Me: *Thanks for letting me know.*
Kate: *Np. Btw—our first gig is next Friday, open mic thing at the Rip Tide in town. Come!*
Me: *Text me the deets!*

Before I can get back to packing, the phone vibrates again in my hand. Speak of the devil. This time it's Preston, and he's not happy.

Preston: *You dropped out of Garnet? WTF is wrong with you, Mackenzie. Why are you throwing your life away?*

My jaw tightens. I'm so sick of his high and mighty bullshit. The judgmental, patronizing way he treats me, acting as if I'm incapable of living my own life.

Me: *Out of curiosity, are you spying on me personally or are you paying other people to keep tabs on me?*
Preston: *Your father called me. He thinks you've gone off the rails.*
Me: *I don't give a shit what he thinks.*
Me: *I also don't give a shit what you think.*
Me: *Stop texting me.*

When I see him typing, I switch on Do Not Disturb mode. I can't bring myself to block his number yet. A concession to our history, I guess. But I have a feeling I'll need to, sooner or later.

When Bonnie returns to the dorm following her afternoon class,

I'm completely done packing. The little blonde stops short in our common area and stares at the half dozen boxes lined up against the wall.

"You goin' on the run?" She tosses down her backpack and grabs a water from the mini fridge, then stands there with the door open, cooling her legs.

"Got kicked out," I answer with a shrug. "It was bound to happen."

"Well, shit." She pushes the fridge closed with her foot. "You think I'll get to keep the place to myself now?"

I smile at her. Bonnie isn't an especially sentimental girl, but I know she cares. "I'll miss you too."

"What are you going to do with all your stuff?" She nods toward the boxes. Then she gives a catty smile. "I suppose we can ask our cheatin' ex to borrow his Porsche?"

I snicker. "I'm sure that would go over well." Walking toward my former bedroom, I fish my phone from my pocket. "It's fine, I know someone with a truck. Let me see if he can come get me."

"Oooh, is it the townie with the magic dick?"

"Maybe." Laughing, I duck into the bedroom to make my call.

"Hey babe. What's up?" Cooper's rough voice tickles my ear and sends a shiver up my spine. He even sounds sexy.

"Hey. So. I have a big ask."

"Shoot." The banging of hammers and whir of saws fade in the background, like he's stepping away from his jobsite.

"I have to vacate my dorm. Was tossed out, basically. I guess I'm not allowed to live in student housing when I'm not a student."

"You realize that's a completely reasonable decision on the school's part, right?"

"They gave me twenty-four hours' notice," I argue. "How reasonable is that?"

He chuckles. "Need help packing?"

"Nope, but I'm hoping you can pick me up after you're done working so I can load some boxes in your truck? I'll put most of it in a storage unit in town until I find an apartment." I hesitate. "And, um, I could use a place to crash until I find something more permanent. If it's not too much to ask."

I mean, it is a lot to ask. We've barely started dating. Moving in, even on a temporary basis, is no small favor. Yes, Evan and I are on good terms now, which eases the possible tension, but they didn't exactly sign up for a third roommate.

"No, you know what," I interject when he starts to answer, "I'll get a hotel. That'd make way more sense."

Because seriously, what was I thinking? This was a stupid idea. How did I think my first option should be to force my way into Cooper's house, as if I've known him for longer than a few months? That's insane.

"There's that motel at the north side of the beach. I bet they rent rooms weekly—"

"Mac?"

"Yeah?"

"Shut up."

I bite back a laugh. "Rude."

"You're not staying at a shithole motel on the north side. You're staying with me. The end."

"You're sure? I didn't really think this through before I called, I just—"

"I'm done at six. I'll come grab you from campus afterward."

A lump of emotion rises in my throat. "Thanks. I, uh . . . damn it, Cooper, I really appreciate it."

"I got you, princess." Then he hangs up with a harried goodbye, leaving me to smile at the phone. Not that I expected Cooper to be a dick about it, but he's taking the whole thing remarkably well.

"I'm sorry, do my ears deceive me?" a highly excited voice bubbles from my open doorway. "Or did I just hear you refer to our mysterious caller as *Cooper*?"

I meet her wide eyes. Sheepish.

"As in Cooper Hartley?"

I nod.

Bonnie gasps loud enough startle me, even though she's right in front of me. "Oh sweet little baby Jesus! *That's* who you been hidin' from me?" She barrels into the room, blonde curls flying around her shoulders. "You are not leavin' this dormitory till you provide me with every last detail. I need *everything*."

CHAPTER THIRTY-TWO

COOPER

This chick is out of her mind.

"What is the peanut butter doing in the refrigerator?" I shout from the kitchen.

I swear to God, having three people in this house has turned the place into a circus. I used to know where Evan was by the creaks and groans the house made around him. Now there's two of them and it's like this old place is haunted—constant noises coming from every direction at once. Hell, at this point, you could probably convince *me* that Patricia exists.

"Hey!" I shout again into the void. "The hell did you go?"

"Right here, dipshit." Evan appears beside me, shouldering me out of the way as he grabs the two six-packs of beers from the fridge and throws them in the cooler.

"Not you. The other one."

He shrugs in response and leaves the kitchen with the cooler.

"What's up?" Mac pops in from fuck knows where in a tiny bikini. Her tits are pouring out of the top, and the little strip of fabric between her legs is begging me to rip it off with my teeth. Damn.

"Did you do this?" I hold up the jar of some peanut butter brand I've never heard of. It was sitting in the door of the fridge the whole time I was emptying every cabinet in the kitchen looking for a jar of Jif.

She scrunches her face at me. "Do what?"

"Who puts peanut butter in the fridge?"

"Uh . . ." She comes over and takes the jar from me, turns it around in her hand. "It says so right on the label."

"But then it gets all hard. It's gross." I open the jar to see an inch-thick layer of oil on top of the solid butter. "What's all this shit?"

"It's organic," she tells me like I'm stupid for asking. "It separates. You have to stir it up a little."

"Why on earth would anyone want to *stir* their peanut butter? You actually eat this?"

"Yes. It's delicious. And you know what? You could do with laying off the added sugar. You seem a little wound up."

Am I having a stroke? I feel like I'm losing my mind. "What does that have to do with anything?"

Mac rolls her eyes and kisses my cheek. "There's regular peanut butter in the pantry." Then she walks out onto the deck after Evan, shaking her ass at me.

"What pantry?" I yell after her.

When she ignores me, I turn to examine my surroundings until my gaze finally lands on the broom closet. A sinking feeling settles in my gut.

I open the closet door to discover she's moved out the tools, emergency hurricane supplies, and other shit I'd neatly organized in there. It's been replaced by all the real food that had mysteriously gone missing after she moved in and started filling our cabinets with non-GMO certified fair-trade flax seed crackers and whatever the fuck.

"Let's go." Evan pokes his head inside.

"You see this?" I ask him, pointing at the "pantry."

"Yeah, it's better, right?" Then he slips outside again, calling over his shoulder, "Meet you out front."

Traitor.

It's only been a week since Mac moved in, and already she's turned the dynamic of the house upside down. Evan's in a weirdly good mood lately, which I don't trust in the slightest. All the counter space in my bathroom has been annexed. The food's weird. The toilet paper's different. And every time I turn around, Mac's moving stuff around the house.

But then something like this happens. I lock the front door and step onto the porch to find Mac and Evan laughing their asses off about who knows what as they wait for me. They seem happy. Carrying on as if they've known each other forever.

I still don't know how or when things changed. One day, Evan stopped leaving the room when she walked in and muttering under his breath. She'd been inducted into the brotherhood. One of us. Practically family. A scary thought, if only because I hadn't dared hope for as much. I figured to some extent we'd be fighting the blood feud, townies versus clones, till we were all sick of each other. I'm happy to be wrong. Though some part of me doesn't trust it, because nothing comes this easy for long.

Evan and I carry the cooler to the truck, setting it in the bed of the pickup. My brother hops up too, using his backpack for a pillow as he stretches out like a lazy asshole.

"Wake me when we get there," he says smugly, and I vow to hit as many potholes as possible on the drive to the boardwalk, where we're meeting some friends. Earlier, Wyatt called everyone to organize a volleyball tournament. Nearly all of us were down, wanting to make the most of the good weather while it lasts.

"Hey," Mac says as I slide into the driver's seat. "I grabbed a book off your shelf in case you wanted something to read between games."

She's rummaging through the oversized beach bag at her feet. To my disappointment, she's slipped a tank top and a pair of shorts on, covering up that insanely hot bikini.

"Thanks. Which one?"

She holds up the paperback—*Rags to Riches: 10 Billionaires That Came from Nothing and Made Everything*. The title is corny as hell, but the content is pure gold.

"Nice." I nod. "That's a good one."

"Your bookshelf is fascinating," she says matter-of-factly. "I don't think I've ever met anyone who reads so many biographies."

I shrug. "I like them."

I steer the truck down the dusty, sand-covered drive to the stop sign at the end of the road. I signal left and when I twist my body to ensure the way is clear, I suddenly feel Mac's fingertips graze the nape of my neck.

Heat instantly travels to the southern region of my body. A common reaction to her touch.

"I just noticed this," she says in surprise. Her fingers trace my most recent tattoo. "Did you always have this anchor?"

"Nah. Got it done a couple months ago."

When she removes her hand, I feel a sense of loss. If it were up to me, this girl's hands would be on me twenty-four seven.

"I like it. It's simple, clean." She smiles at me. "You're really into all the nautical stuff, huh?"

I grin. "I mean, I do live on the beach. Although, to be honest, it's just a coincidence that a lot of my ink involves water. And the anchor was a spur of the moment tat when I was in a bad mood." I give her the side-eye. "It was after you told me you were picking your ex over me."

"Dumbest mistake I ever made."

"Damn right." I wink at her.

"Luckily, I rectified it." She smirks and plants her palm over my thigh. "So the anchor represents what? You being pissed at me?"

"Feeling weighed down. I'd just been rejected by the coolest, smartest, funniest girl I've ever known. And she didn't want me."

I shrug. "I felt like I've been dragged down my entire life. By this town. The memory of my parents. Dad was a loser. Mom is a loser." Another shrug, this one accompanied by a dry smile. "I have a bad habit of getting very straightforward, un-metaphorical tattoos. No subtext at all on this body."

That gets me a laugh. "I happen to like this body very much." She squeezes my thigh, not at all subtly. "And you're not a loser."

"Certainly trying not to be." I gesture to the book in her lap. "I read stuff like that—biographies, memoirs by these men and women who crawled out of poverty or bad circumstances and made something of themselves—because they inspire me. One of the dudes in that book? Mother was widowed, left with five kids she couldn't take care of, so she sends him to an orphanage. He's poor, alone, goes to work at a factory when he's still young, making auto part molds, eyeglass frames. When he's twenty-three, he opens up his own molding shop." I tip my head toward Mac. "And that shop ends up creating the Ray-Ban brand."

Mackenzie's hand travels to my knee, giving it a squeeze, before seeking out my hand on the gearshift. She laces our fingers.

"You inspire me," she says simply. "And I have no doubt, by the way, that your name will end up in a book like this someday."

"Maybe."

At the beach, Wyatt and the rest of the crew have already claimed one of the volleyball nets. Nearby, the girls are set up on the sand with an umbrella. Steph reads a book, Heidi tans on her stomach, and Alana looks characteristically bored with all of it while she sips a concealed cocktail from a water bottle.

Evan and I greet the guys with fist bumps. We've barely finished saying our hellos before Wyatt starts shouting at everyone to break up into teams.

"Getting dumped turned him into a real dictator, eh?" Tate mutters as we watch our buddy order us around like a drill sergeant.

I chuckle. "She still hasn't taken him back?"

"Nope. I think it might actually be over this time—" Tate stops, narrowing his eyes.

I look over to see Wyatt tugging Alana out of her beach chair. She sighs and takes his hand. I guess she's on his team. Although what's up with the way he's whispering in her ear?

"What's that about?" I ask Tate.

"No clue." His jaw is tight.

Okay, then.

The volleyball tournament gets under way. And since we're all a competitive bunch here in the Bay, it turns intense fast. Mac's on my team, and I'm pleasantly surprised to discover she has a killer serve. Thanks to her, we take an early lead that has us winning the first game. Wyatt's crew wins the second. For the tiebreaker, Mac tags Steph in and walks down to the water.

"I'll sub back in," she calls to me. "Just cooling off for a bit."

I nod and return to the task of crushing Wyatt and Evan's team into the sand. It isn't until an hour passes that I realize Steph's still playing in Mackenzie's place.

"Dude!" Tate grouses when I miss a spike.

But my focus is now on finding Mac. My gaze roams up and down the beach until finally I spot her. She's at the water's edge talking to someone.

Despite the sun beating down on my head and bare chest, my entire body runs cold when I recognize who she's with.

Kincaid.

CHAPTER THIRTY-THREE

COOPER

"Coop, it's your serve," Steph says expectantly.

"I'm out," I tell the group, throwing up my hands. I seek out my brother's eyes on the other side of the net.

"Evan" is all I have to say for him to jog to my side. When I nod in Mac's direction, his expression darkens.

"Fuck," he curses.

"I know."

Trying to look like we're not in too much of a hurry, we make our way over there to protests from our teams for walking off the game. Screw the game. My ass is about to be in deep shit if this goes sideways.

"How are we playing this?" Evan murmurs.

"Not sure. Follow my lead." As we approach the water's edge, it occurs to me that it might've been better if I'd pretended not to notice Kincaid and kept my distance, camouflaged myself in the group of volleyball players. But there's no way in hell I'm leaving Mac hanging with that asshole around.

"There a problem here?" Putting my arm around Mac's shoulder, I square up to Kincaid, who is conspicuously alone.

A moment of confusion crosses his face as he recognizes me. It was probably too much to hope he had forgotten all about me.

His eyes narrow as he does the math in his head.

"Hang on, this is the guy?" he demands, his head swiveling back to Mackenzie.

Mac shoots me a frustrated glare. She notices Evan lingering nearby and lets out a sigh. "Yes, this is the guy. And now we're leaving. Enjoy the rest of your afternoon, Pres."

"Hang on a minute." He sounds incensed as we start to walk away. "This is goddamn convenient. I *know* this loser."

I feel Mac stiffen slightly. She stops, turning toward her ex. "What are you talking about?"

Kincaid meets my eyes with a pompous smirk. "She has no idea, does she?"

I have a split second to decide. Deep down, though, I know there's no choice, at least not with Kincaid here providing an audience.

So I say, "Am I supposed to know you?"

No one plays dumb better than a kid who pulled the twin swap on damn near every algebra test in school.

"Yeah, nice try, bro." He returns his attention to Mac. "Let me guess, this guy showed up right after you got to town? Some friendly townie you happened to run into on a night out with the girls. Stop me if this sounds familiar."

A frown touches her lips. "Cooper, what is he talking about?"

The second she fixes her concerned green eyes at me, my mouth turns to sand. Acid rises in my stomach.

"No idea," I lie.

I scare myself with how easily I can lie to her. How convincingly the words slide out of my mouth. Not the slightest flinch.

"Mackenzie, babe, listen to me." Kincaid reaches out to touch her, and it takes a hell of an effort to not break his hand as I step between them. Mouth flattening, he drops his arm. "The weekend before school started, this guy picked a fight with me in a bar and

I got him fired on the spot. Remember? I had a black eye when I helped you move into the dorm?"

"You told me you got it playing basketball," she accuses with no small amount of venom in her voice.

"Yeah, okay, I lied." He concedes the point grudgingly, hurrying to make his case as Mac's crossed arms and lack of eye contact say he's losing her interest quickly. "But I'm not lying now."

"How am I supposed to tell the difference?" Nobody matches up to Mac in a battle of attrition. She'd argue all day about the number of clouds in the sky just to be right.

"Isn't it obvious?" He's losing his patience, tossing his hands in the air. "He's only fucking you to get back at me."

"Alright, that's enough." If I can't put his face in the sand and end this here, I'm not sticking around to let him blow up my life. "You need to get outta here, man. Leave her alone."

"Mackenzie, come on," he pleads. "You're not seriously falling for his BS, right? I know you're young, but you can't be this stupid."

That does it. The thick accents of condescension trigger Mac's last nerve, and her expression grows stormy.

"The dumbest thing I ever did was dating you for so long," she retorts. "Fortunately, that's not a decision I have to live with."

She tears off toward our group, brushing past Evan. As the two of us fall in line behind her, I have a vivid flashback to the many times we got marched to the principal's office by our teachers. I feel rather than see Evan asking me if we're good, but I don't have an answer until we reach our patch of sand and Mac spins on me.

"Out with it," she orders.

"With what?"

Even as I stonewall her, I wonder if this is the moment I should come clean. Admit I had less than honorable intentions at first, but that things changed after we met.

She'd understand. Maybe even get a kick out of it. We'd have a good laugh and it'd become a funny story we tell at parties.

Or she'd never talk to me again, until I come home one day to my house on fire and a sign stuck in the ground with *We should see other people* written on it in ash.

"Don't mess with me." Mac sticks a finger in my chest. "What was he talking about? You two know each other?"

Once again, we have an audience, and once again, feeling our friends' eyes on us, my courage abandons me. If I tell her the truth in private, there's a chance I'll lose her. If I tell her the truth in front of a dozen other people, losing her is a guarantee. She'd be humiliated in front of everyone. She'd never forgive me.

This time, the lies burn my tongue. "Everything I know about him I heard around town, or from you. Couldn't have picked that guy out of a lineup."

She becomes eerily still, barely breathing as she stares at me.

Panic churns in my gut, but on the outside I maintain a neutral expression. I stick to my story. I learned a long time ago, those who get caught are the ones who break. The key to a successful lie is to believe it. Then deny, deny, deny.

"Was there a fight?" Mac cocks her head as if she's trapped me.

"Mac, they could fill football stadiums with the number of idiots who get drunk and start shit. If he was one of them, I honestly wouldn't remember."

Visibly frustrated, she turns to Evan. "Did Cooper really get fired?"

For a split second, I worry their new platonic romance might end me.

"He had a summer job at Steph's bar." With a shrug, Evan even has me convinced. Guess we're still on the same side when it counts. "It was temporary."

She looks past Evan to where Steph has resettled in her chair and picked up her book. "Steph?" Mac says. "Is that true?"

Without looking up from her book, Steph nods behind her thick black sunglasses. "It was a summer gig."

Relief trickles into me, then dissolves when I notice Heidi edging closer to the group. There's indecision in her expression.

Fuck.

I know that look. Mischief for mischief's sake. Heidi's the girl who's never missed an opportunity to set a fire just to hear the screams. Add to this the fact that she's been mad at me more often than not lately, and that she's not a fan of this arrangement or Mac. But when our gazes briefly meet, I silently plead with her to give me this one thing.

"Seriously, guys, I'm starved," she says with a bored whine. "Can we get the hell out of here already?"

By the skin of my teeth, I make it out alive.

Every day after that, I'm holding my breath, waiting for the other shoe to drop. Looking over my shoulder for Kincaid to sneak up on us again. Mac seems to let the matter go, and Evan and I have been avoiding the subject by miles. But it was a close call. Too close. A reminder how fragile our relationship is and how easily it can all be ripped from my hands. That realization hits me harder than I thought possible. She's under my skin and getting deeper.

The night of our run-in with Kincaid, after Mac had gone to bed, I ended up in my workshop sucking on a cigarette like a madman, hoping the nicotine would ease the guilt, the stress, the fear. Usually, I only smoke when I'm drinking, and even that isn't a hard and fast rule. But lying to Mackenzie had wrecked me.

Evan found me there at one in the morning, nearly half a pack's worth of cigarette butts in the ashtray on my worktable.

"I need to tell her the truth," I'd said miserably.

He'd balked. "Are you fucked? What's that gonna achieve, man? The plan was aborted. You're with her because you like her."

"But it started as a way to get back at Kincaid. Me and her, this whole relationship, was founded on bad intentions."

In the end, Evan convinced me to stay quiet. Though who am I kidding, it didn't take much convincing. The thought of losing Mackenzie rips my insides to shreds. I can't lose her. And Evan was wrong—I'm not with her because I like her.

I'm in love with her.

And so I banish the guilt to the furthest recesses of my mind. I work hard to be the kind of man Mac needs, deserves. And then, one morning, we're lying in bed and I take my first deep breath in almost a month. She's barely awake when she rolls over and drapes her leg over my hip. An overwhelming sense of calm I've never known before envelopes me as she cuddles into my chest.

"Morning," she whispers. "What time is it?"

"Dunno. Ten, maybe?"

"Ten?" She sits abruptly. "Shoot. Your uncle will be here soon. We gotta clean this place up."

It's cute she thinks Levi gives a shit.

She leaves me alone in bed to take a shower, reappearing ten minutes later with wet hair and a flushed face.

"Ugh. I can't find my blue dress," she grumbles from the closet, half of which now contains her clothes.

It's been weeks since she came to stay with us, and yet nobody's brought up the prospect of her moving out. I'm happy to ignore the subject. Sure, having another person in the house has been an adjustment. And maybe we're still learning how to respect each other's quirks. But she makes the place feel warm again, like a home rather than a house. She gives the place some life after years of bad memories and empty rooms.

She just fits.

"So wear something else. Or don't and come back to bed."

"It's my *take me seriously* dress," she calls from under what sounds like a mountain of hangers.

She's got no reason to be nervous about meeting with Levi. He might look intimidating, but he's the friendliest guy you'd ever meet. And yes, there's a lot to be said for not mixing business with pleasure, but I'm choosing to look at this possible endeavor of them working on the hotel together from an optimistic perspective.

"How about this one?" She comes out modeling a green top that matches her eyes and a pair of navy pants that hug her ass in a way that is not helping my semi.

"You look great."

Her answering smile. The way her head tilts and eyes shine. Those looks that are only for me. They get me right in the fucking chest.

I've absolutely lost my head over this chick.

"What?" she asks, lingering at the foot of the bed and wrapping her hair in a knot atop her head.

"Nothing." All I can do is smile at her and hope I don't screw this up. "I think I'm happy, is all."

Mac comes over and plants a kiss on my cheek. "Me too."

"Yeah? Even with, you know, your parents basically disowning you?"

Shrugging, she walks into the bathroom. I get dressed and watch her in the mirror as she puts on her makeup.

"I don't love not being on speaking terms with them," she admits. "But they're the ones being stubborn. Choosing to live my own life is hardly grounds for excommunication."

I've been worried that the longer this dispute with her parents rages on in silent conflict, the more she'll come to regret her decision to leave school. To buy the hotel. To be with me. But so far, there's been no sign of remorse on her part.

"They're going to have to get over it eventually," she says, turning to look at me. "I'm not stressing over it, you know? Rather not give them the satisfaction."

I search her face for any traces of dishonesty and find none. As far as I can tell, she *is* happy. I'm trying not to let myself sink into that paranoid place. I have a way of spiraling with anticipation of catastrophe. But that's always been the rhythm of my life. Things start looking too good and a house falls out of the sky.

This time, I'm hoping she's broken the curse.

CHAPTER THIRTY-FOUR

MACKENZIE

Well, it's not winter in Jackson Hole or Aspen—the weather's been in the seventies all weekend like Carolina's stuck in autumn—but shopping for a Christmas tree with Cooper and Evan has thus far been an adventure. Already we've been chased out of three tree lots because these ruffians are incapable of behaving themselves in public. Between challenging each other to see who can bench press the biggest tree and holding a jousting contest in the middle of a grocery store parking lot, we're running out of options to find a tree without crossing state lines.

"What about this one?" Evan says from somewhere in the artificial forest.

To be fair, one of the lots we got kicked out of was for Cooper and I getting caught making out behind the Douglas firs. Proving he hasn't learned his lesson, Cooper sneaks up on me and smacks my ass while I try to navigate my way toward his brother.

"Looks like your eighth-grade girlfriend," Cooper remarks when we find Evan standing next to a round spruce that's big on the top and bottom but noticeably naked in the middle.

Evan smirks. "Jealous."

"This one's nice." I point to another tree. It's full and fluffy, with plenty of evenly spaced branches for ornaments. No gaping holes or apparent brown spots.

Cooper sizes up the tree. "Think we can get it through the door?"

"Can bring it in through the back," Evan answers. "Pretty tall, though. We might have to poke a hole in the ceiling."

I grin. "Worth it."

I've always been a big-tree girl, though I was never allowed to pick out my own. My parents had people for that. Every December a box truck would show up and unload a mall's worth of decorations. A huge, perfect tree for the living room, and smaller ones for nearly every other living area in the house. Garlands, lights, candles, and the whole lot. Then an interior decorator and a small army of help would transform the house. Not once did my family get together to decorate the trees; we never looked for the perfect branch for each keepsake ornament like other families seemed to do. All we had was a bunch of expensive, rented junk to accomplish whatever motif my mother was interested in that year. Another set dressing for their life of parties and entertaining influential people or campaign donors. A completely sterile holiday season.

And yet despite that, I find myself a bit emotional at the idea of not seeing my parents for the holidays. We're still barely speaking, although my father did courier over a stack of Christmas cards and order me to sign my name under his and my mother's. Apparently the cards are being delivered to hospitals and charities in my father's congressional district, courtesy of the perfect Cabot family who cares so much about humanity.

That evening after dinner, the three of us scrounge for decorations and lights in the attic, buried under years of dust.

"I don't think we've decorated for Christmas in, what?" Cooper questions his brother as we carry the boxes to the living room. "Three, four years?"

"Seriously?" I set my box on the hardwood floor and sit in front of the tree.

Evan opens a box of tangled lights. "Something like that. Not since high school, at least."

"That's so sad." Even a plastic Christmas is better than nothing.

"We've never been big on holidays in this family." Cooper shrugs. "Sometimes we do stuff at Levi's house. Usually Thanksgivings, because every other year for Christmas they go see Tim's family in Maine."

"Tim?" I ask blankly.

"Levi's husband," Evan supplies.

"Partner," Cooper corrects. "I don't think they're actually married."

"Levi's gay? How come this is the first I'm hearing of it?"

The twins give identical shrugs, and for a second I understand why their teachers had a tough time telling them apart. "It's not really something he talks about," Cooper says. "They've been together for, like, twenty years or something, but they don't flaunt their relationship. They're both really private people."

"Most folks in town know," Evan adds. "Or suspect. Everyone else just assumes they're roommates."

"We should've had a dinner here and invited them." I feel glum at the lost opportunity. If I'm going to be living in Avalon Bay and staying with the twins, it might be nice to form deeper connections.

It's strange. Although we grew up in two opposite worlds, Cooper and I aren't that different. In many ways, we've had parallel experiences. The more I come to understand him, the more I realize that our shared language is deeply influenced by the ways we've felt neglected.

"Dude, I think some of these ornaments are from Grandma and Grandpop." Evan drags a box closer to the tree. The guys dig into it, pulling out little, handmade ornaments with photos inside. Dates from '53, '61. Souvenirs from trips all over the country. Evan holds up a little cradle that must have belonged to a manger set at one point. "What the ever-loving fuck is this?"

He shows us a swaddled baby Jesus that more closely resembles a little baked potato in tinfoil with two black dots for eyes and a pink line for a mouth.

I blanch. "That's disturbing."

"Didn't even know these were here." Cooper admires a picture I can only guess is his dad as a boy. Then he tucks it back in the bottom of the box.

Once again, a lump of emotion clogs my throat. "I wish I had boxes like these at home, full of old pictures and knickknacks, with interesting stories behind them that my parents could tell me about."

Cooper gets up to heave one of the larger boxes back to the hall-way. "I don't know . . . Having a bunch of servants to do the heavy lifting can't have been all that bad," he calls over his shoulder.

"Not to mention waking up to a ton of presents," Evan pipes up.

"Sure," I say, picking out the ornaments that are still in good shape and appear the least emotionally detrimental. "It *sounds* great. It was like waking up in Santa's workshop. Until you get old enough to realize all the cards on your presents aren't written in your parents' handwriting. And instead of elves, they're actually people your parents pay to keep as much distance as possible between them and anything approaching sentimentality."

"Bet they were sick presents, though," Evan says with a wink. We've moved well past the *how many ponies did you get for your birthday* jokes, but he can't always resist getting in a jab.

I shrug sadly. "I'd give them all back if it meant my parents would want to spend time together, even just once. To act like we were a family rather than a business venture. My dad was always working, and Mom was more worried about her charity functions—

which, yeah, I know, she wasn't boiling puppies or something. There are worse things than raising money for a children's hospital. But I was a child too. Couldn't I have gotten some of that holiday spirit?"

"Aww, come here, you little shit." Evan throws his arm around my neck and kisses the top of my head. "I'm messing with you. Parents fucking blow. Even rich ones. We're all screwed up, one way or another."

"All I mean is, doing this, the three of us, means a lot to me," I tell them, surprised at myself when my eyes start stinging. If I cried in front of these guys, I'd never hear the end of it. "It's my first real Christmas."

Cooper pulls me on his lap and wraps his arms around me. "We're glad you're here."

Evan disappears for second, then returns with a small box. "Okay. So I was going to sneak this in your stocking later, but I think you should have it now."

I stare at the box. He's done an absolutely awful job of wrapping it, the corners all uneven and held down with way more tape than anything the size of my palm should require.

"Don't worry," he says, "it's not stolen."

I crack a smile as I tear into the present with all the grace of a petulant preschooler. Inside, I find a plastic figure of a girl in a pink dress. Her hair is colored black with a permanent marker and a tiny, yellow crown cut from paper is glued to her head.

"I swear I looked in six different stores for a princess ornament. You have no idea how fucking hard it is to find one." He grins. "So I made my own."

My eyes water. Another lump lodges in my throat.

"I wanted to get you something. To celebrate."

My hands shake.

"I mean, it's supposed to be funny. I promise I wasn't trying to be a dick or anything."

Doubling over, I start laughing hysterically. So hard my ribs hurt. Cooper can't hold me, and I tumble to the floor.

"Is she laughing or crying?" Evan asks his twin.

It's honestly the sweetest thing anyone's ever done for me. All the more meaningful that Evan put so much effort into the perfect gift. His brother's going to have to step up his game if he wants to compete.

Once I've collected myself, I get up and hug Evan, who seems relieved that I'm not kicking his ass. I guess there was always the chance the gift would backfire, but I think Evan and I have reached an understanding.

"If you two are done, can we get this damn tree finished?" Apparently feeling left out, Cooper pouts behind us.

"Keep that attitude up and you're not getting your present tonight," I warn him.

"Please," Evan says, hushing us with his finger over his mouth. "Baby Potato Jesus can hear you."

A few days later, after the most low-key—and best—holiday I've ever had, I'm with Cooper in his workshop, helping him dust, polish, and wrap some furniture. I think watching me manage the hotel renovation gave him a kick in the butt to push himself harder with his own business venture. He's been pounding the pavement and making inquiries, and this week, he received a couple calls from boutique stores that want to sell a few of his pieces. This morning, we sent off new photographs for their websites, and now we're getting everything ready for transport.

"You're not selling my set, right?" I ask anxiously.

"The one you never paid for?" He winks, coming up to me covered in the sawdust that clings to everything in here.

"Things got a little hectic. But you're right, I owe you a check."

"Forget it. I can't take your money." He shrugs adorably. "Those pieces were always yours whether you bought them or not. Once you laid hands on them, it would have felt wrong to let them go anywhere else."

My heart somersaults in my chest. "First of all, that's one of the sweetest things you've ever said. And second of all, you can totally take my money. That's the thing about money. It works everywhere."

"Spoken like a true clone."

For that, I smack him with my polishing rag.

"Hands, Cabot."

"Yeah, I'll show you hands, Hartley."

"Oh yeah?" With a smirk, he tugs me toward him, his mouth covering mine in a possessive kiss.

His tongue is just slicking over mine when an unfamiliar female voice chirps from the open garage door.

"Knock, knock!"

CHAPTER THIRTY-FIVE

COOPER

I freeze at the sound of that voice behind me. My blood stings ice cold. I hope as I grudgingly turn around that the sound was a vivid hallucination.

No such luck.

At the entrance, Shelley Hartley stands waving at me.

Goddamn it.

I don't how long it's been since the last time she blew into town. Months. A year, maybe. The image of her in my mind is distorted and constantly shifting. She looks the same, I guess. Bad blonde dye job. Too much makeup. Dressed like a woman half her age who wandered into a Jimmy Buffet concert and never left. It's the smile, though, as she waltzes into the workshop, that gets my back up. She hasn't earned it.

My brain is reeling. Someone's pulled the pin and handed me a live grenade, and I've got seconds to figure out how not to let it blow up in my face.

"Hey, baby," she says, throwing her arms around me. The stench of gin, cigarettes, and lilac-scented perfume brings hot bile rising to the back of my throat. Few smells send me so violently back to childhood. "Momma missed you."

Yeah, I bet.

It takes her about six seconds to catch her eyes on Mac and the diamond bracelet she wears that belonged to her great-grandmother. Shelley all but shoves me out of the way to grab Mac's wrist under the pretense of a handshake.

"Who's this pretty girl?" she asks me, beaming.

"Mackenzie. My girlfriend," I tell her flatly. Mac flicks her eyes to me in confusion. "Mac, this is Shelley. My mom."

"Oh." Mac blinks, recovering quickly. "It's, ah, nice to meet you."

"Well, come on and help me inside," Shelley says, still holding onto Mac. "I've got groceries for dinner. Hope everyone's hungry."

There's no car in the driveway. Just a bunch of paper bags sitting on the front porch steps. No telling how she got here or what dreadful wind blew her back into town. She was probably kicked out by another pathetic sap who she drained for every last dime. Or she ran out on him in the middle of the night before he discovered she'd robbed him blind. I know this for certain: It won't end well. Shelley is a walking catastrophe. She leaves only ruin in her wake, most of it laid at the feet of her sons. I learned a long time ago that nothing with her is ever as it seems. If she's breathing, she's lying. If she's smiling at you, guard your wallet.

"Evan, baby, Momma's home," she calls when we get inside.

He comes out of the kitchen at the sound of her voice. His face blanches at realizing, as I did, it isn't a trick of his imagination. He stands dead still, almost as if expecting her to evaporate. Indecision plays behind his eyes, wondering if it's safe, or if he'll get bitten.

Story of our lives.

"Come here." Shelley coaxes him with open arms. "Gimme a hug."

Tentative at first, keeping one eye on me for an explanation I don't have, he embraces her. Unlike me, he actually returns the hug.

Disapproval flares inside me. Evan's got an endless supply of for-giveness for this woman that I will never understand. He's never wanted to see the truth. He expects that every time our mom walks back through our door, she's here to stay, that this time we'll be a family, despite the years of disappointment and hurt she's put us through.

"What's going on?" he asks.

"Dinner." She picks up a couple of the grocery bags and hands them off to him. "Lasagna. Your favorite."

Mac offers to help because she's too polite for her own damn good. I want to tell her not to bother. She doesn't have to impress anyone. Instead, I bite my tongue and stick close by, because there's no way I'm leaving Mac alone with that woman. Shelley'd probably shave Mac's head for the price her hair would fetch with a black-market wig maker.

Later, when Shelley and Evan are in the kitchen, I take the op-portunity to pull Mac aside under the pretense of setting the table.

"Do me a favor," I say. "Don't talk about your family when she asks."

Her forehead wrinkles. "What do you mean? Why not?"

"Please." My voice is low. Urgent. "Don't mention money or what your dad does. Anything that suggests they're well off. Or you, for that matter."

"I'd never try to make your mom uncomfortable, if that's what you mean."

Mac's good about not rubbing her fortune in everyone's face, but that's not what I'm getting at.

"It's not that, babe. I don't care what you have to say. Lie. Trust me on this." Then, remembering her bracelet, I hold her wrist and undo the latch, sticking it in the pocket of her jeans.

"What are you doing?" She looks alarmed.

"Please. Until she's gone. Don't wear it in front of her."

I have no idea how long Shelley's planning to stick around or where she intends to stay. Her room is exactly how she left it. We don't go in there. If past experience is any indication, however, she'll be out trawling for a new man before midnight.

We're all painfully well-behaved during dinner. Evan, poor guy, even seems happy to have Shelley home. They chat about what she's been up to. Turns out she's living in Atlanta with some guy she met at a casino.

"We fought over a slot machine," she gushes with a giggle, "and ended up falling right in love!"

Uh-huh. I'm sure they'll live happily ever after. Given that she's here, they've probably already broken up.

"How long are you staying?" I interrupt her love story, my brusque tone causing Mac to find my hand under the table. She gives it a comforting squeeze.

Shelley looks offended that I would dare ask her that question.

Evan shoots me a dark look. "Dude. Chill. She just got here."

Yes, and I want to know when she's leaving, I want to snap. It takes superhuman effort to keep my mouth shut.

"So, Mackenzie," Shelley says after the strained, prolonged silence that falls over the dinner table. "How did you end up dating my son? How did you two meet? Tell me everything."

For the next fifteen minutes, Mac dodges dozens of prying questions where she can and spits some Grade-A bullshit for the rest.

I get a surreptitious *what the fuck* glance from Evan, who manages to keep his damn mouth shut and go with it. My brother might be a pushover where Shelley's concerned, but he's not an idiot. For my part, I speak as little as possible. Afraid at any moment my filter will malfunction, and I'll be unable to stop the tirade that will inevitably follow. Few people get me worked up like Shelley Hartley.

After dinner, I'm at the sink rinsing plates when she corners me alone.

"You were awfully quiet," she says, taking a plate from me to put in the dishwasher.

"Tired," I grunt.

"Oh, my sweet boy. You work too hard. You need to get more rest."

I make a noncommittal noise. My skin crawls every time she tries playing the maternal role. It doesn't suit her.

"Mackenzie seems sweet." There are all sorts of euphemisms in that statement, none of them nice.

I do my best to ignore her as I rinse and pass, keeping my head down. "Yeah. She's cool."

"Noticed that bracelet. And the purse in the living room."

My shoulders tense.

"Very pricey. Nice job, baby."

I taste blood from the inside of my cheek when she flashes a knowing smile. It's blatantly obvious what she thinks—that I've found myself a meal ticket. She's been running the same con so long, I'm not sure she remembers any other way to live.

"So, listen, baby . . ."

Here it comes. Of fucking course. There's always an ask. An angle.

"You know, I almost didn't make it here in one piece," she continues, oblivious to the anger bubbling up in my gut. "That old car of mine started spewing smoke on the highway. Had to get it towed from a truck stop. Turns out some little plastic box in the engine went and blew up." She laughs sheepishly. "Now I talked the guy down, but I'm gonna come up a little short on the repair cost."

"What's up?" Evan enters the kitchen in time to overhear the end of her bullshit story. Fucking perfect. "Your car broke down?"

"It's always something with that piece of junk, wouldn't you know?" she says, playing the damsel because Evan can never resist a chance to be a hero. "Anyway, I was working this job, but I got laid off after the holidays. It's been tough finding something new. This'll wipe out everything I had saved up."

"We're tapped out," I inform her, glancing at Evan. "We've been putting everything into fixing the house."

"And the place looks great." She won't meet my eyes. Not when she's got such an easy target with Evan. "I need a couple hundred to get the car back. Then I can get around to look for a new job around here. I'll pay you back."

"You're staying?" Evan says.

Poor, dumb bastard. The hopefulness in his voice is pitiful. I want to slap him upside the head.

Shelley goes to him, hugging his side as she buries her head under his chin. "If you'll let me. I miss my boys."

Evan reaches right into his pocket and pulls out several twenties. Probably everything that was left from his last paycheck. "Here's one-fifty." He shrugs. "I'll hit up the ATM for the rest." Meaning his savings account.

"Thanks, baby." She kisses his cheek and immediately extricates herself from his arms. "Who wants milkshakes? Like we used to get from the boardwalk? I'm gonna run out real quick for smokes and I'll bring some milkshakes back for us."

I'll be shocked if she's back before sunrise.

Later in bed, I can't sleep. I'm racked with tension, still stewing about Shelley. I didn't bother waiting around to see if she'd materialize with the milkshakes. As soon as she left, Mac and I went to hide in my room. Or rather, I did, and she came to keep me company. Now, she rolls over, and flicks on the bedside lamp.

"I can feel you thinking," she murmurs, finding me staring at the ceiling fan.

"Yeah. I just . . . I'm sorry I asked you to do that earlier. My mother took one look at you, your bracelet, your purse, and figured you were loaded." Resentment tightens my throat. "Shelley never met anyone she couldn't use. I didn't want her to know your family has money because, sure as shit, she'd find a way to help herself to some of it."

"Okay, but that has nothing to do with us." Mac runs her hand over my chest and rests her head on my arm. "I wouldn't want you to judge me by my parents, either."

"She thinks I'm only with you because you're rich."

"Yeah? Well, she's wrong. I know that isn't true. I mean, hell, you should probably be referring me to collections for that furniture I keep forgetting to pay you for."

"I'll put the interest on your bill." I kiss the top of her head and pull her closer. Having her in my arms does take the edge off. "Seriously, though. I'd never use you that way. I'm nothing like that woman."

"Cooper." Her voice is gentle, reassuring. "You don't have to convince me."

Maybe. Seems I've never stopped having to convince myself.

Mac snuggles closer to me. "How long do you think she'll stick around for?"

"I give it twenty-four hours. Maybe forty-eight."

"That's really sad."

I chuckle softly. "It's really not. Maybe it was sad, once upon a time, but these days I wish she'd just stay away for good. Every time she comes back, she toys with Evan's emotions. She stresses me out, and I end up snapping at everyone around me. I spend the entire time holding my breath, waiting for her to leave, praying that this time it'll be forever."

"But she keeps coming back. That has to mean something, right?" Mac, bless her heart, is clearly trying to equate Shelley's visits with some sort of loving, maternal need to reunite with her sons.

"It means her latest relationship blew up in her face, or she's broke, or both," I say simply. "Trust me, princess. We've done this same old song and dance since I was fourteen years old. Shelley isn't here for us. She's here for herself."

I feel Mac's warm breath on my collarbone as she rises on her elbow to kiss the side of my jaw. "I'm sorry, Cooper. You don't deserve that."

"It is what it is."

"Stop," she chides. "Just accept my sorry and now let me help you forget for a little while." She kisses her way down my body, reaching inside my boxers.

I close my eyes, moan quietly, and let myself forget.

Forty-eight hours.

I would've wagered on twenty-four, but hey, I still called it. Exactly two days after her sudden arrival, I catch Shelley making for the back door with a duffel bag over her shoulder.

It's barely seven a.m. and I'm the first one up. I'd just put on a pot of coffee after letting Daisy out when Shelley came creeping into the kitchen.

"Sneaking off already?" I inquire from the counter.

She turns around, startled, but covers it with a laugh. "Baby. You scared me. I was trying not to wake anybody."

"Weren't even going to say goodbye?" Personally, I don't give a damn. But taking off on Evan is a heartbreak he doesn't deserve.

"Why don't I throw on some pancakes?" She drops her bag by the door and prances over with her typical misdirecting smile. "We can enjoy a nice breakfast together."

Fine. Guess we're doing one last song and dance. I can play along if it means her departure is the end result.

Mac and Evan are up shortly after, entering the kitchen in time for Shelley to serve them breakfast. I shove some pancake in my mouth and chew slowly, then lean back in my chair, waiting for the bullshit to start spewing. But Shelley is studiously avoiding my expectant gaze, regaling Mackenzie with some dumb story about our childhood. We're almost done eating when it becomes clear that Shelley won't get on with it without a little prodding.

"So where you off to now?" I ask dead-faced, interrupting yet another story of Evan and me growing up, which I'm sure is entirely fabricated to make her out to be less of a bad mom.

Shelley pulls up short and barely covers the glare of annoyance. She wipes her mouth then drains the last of her orange juice. "It's been so good seeing you boys," she says to Evan, putting on a sad voice. "I really wish I could stay longer, but I'm afraid I'm heading out this morning."

A frown mars his lips. "Why?"

"Thing is, you know, there ain't any jobs around here for me right now. I know this fella, though. Met him back in Baton Rouge. He's got some work. I mean he practically begged me to come back and run the place." Her bottom lip sticks out. "You know I don't want to leave my boys, but I gotta make some money. I want to help you two fix this place up."

She goes on like that for a bit longer. Blowing smoke. Convincing herself there's some noble end to her perpetual abandonment and broken promises. She's full of shit—yesterday I saw at least five HELP WANTED signs around the Bay. And I'm pretty sure this *fella* is her ex, who she probably sweet-talked into a second chance. Or maybe it's just been long enough that she could hit him up for round two. Doesn't matter. If it wasn't one excuse, it'd be another. She'd leave us for a bologna sandwich as long as it was away from here.

"Once I get settled in, you should come visit me," Shelley says fifteen minutes later when she's hugging Evan goodbye. "I'm gonna have to get a new phone. Last one got shut off. I'll call you soon as I have it."

She won't. There won't be any calls or texts. No family vacations. It's routine at this point, the bullshit farewells and insincere placations. It doesn't faze me anymore, but fuck her for putting Evan through this again.

"Yeah, make sure you give us the new number when you get it," Evan says, nodding seriously. "We need to have a way to contact you."

Why? I almost ask, but tamp down the urge. If Evan wants to live in some delusional world where his mother loves him, who am I to judge?

"Bye, baby." Shelley pulls me in for a hug despite my visible reluctance. She even plants a kiss on my cheek. Someone give her a *Mom of the Year* award, quick. "See you soon, I promise."

And then, as quickly as she blew in, Shelley's gone. Inflicting minimum damage, fortunately.

Or so I think.

It isn't until about a week later, one evening after work, when I discover the true extent of the damage done by my mother's visit. Mac's birthday is coming up—turns out it's the day before mine— and although she told me not to get her anything, I'm determined to buy her something awesome. Mac gives me so few chances to spoil her, I made the executive decision to ignore her and do whatever the hell I want instead.

In my room, beneath a loose floorboard under my dresser, I pull out the old toffee tin where I've kept my cash and contraband since I was eleven years old. I open the lid, expecting to find the money I've stashed there, all the under-the-table cash I'd earned from side gigs, kept hidden from the bank and tax authorities' grubby hands.

Twelve grand held together by two rubber bands. The *if all else fails* fund.

But the money's not there.

Every last dime.

Gone.

CHAPTER THIRTY-SIX

MACKENZIE

From the living room, I hear a commotion in Cooper's bedroom. A sharp snap off the wall and something clattering to the wooden floor. Suddenly, Cooper barrels down the hall.

Daisy, barking her head off because she gets rambunctious about an hour before it's time to feed her, chases after him as he tramples through the living room.

"Hey, you okay?" I jump up from the couch.

"Fine," he says, growling the words through gritted teeth. He doesn't pause to even look at me.

"What's wrong?"

Rather than get a reply, I watch him fling open the sliding glass door and stomp outside. He slams the door shut in Daisy's face, barely missing her, though she seems only disappointed that he's going outside without her.

To appease her, I put out her food, then grab my shoes to go hunting for Cooper. I find him a hundred yards down the beach throwing small pieces of driftwood at the waves. By the time I reach him, I'm regretting not grabbing a sweater first or at least putting on some long pants, rather than running out in shorts and a T-shirt. It's nearly dark and a steady breeze turns my skin bumpy in minutes.

"What happened?" I ask him.

"Go home." His voice is eerily flat, a stark contradiction of his angry, violent movements.

"Okay, no. So let's move on to the part where you just tell me."

"Damn it, Mac, not now, alright? Let it be." He kicks up sand, searching for something else to throw and growing more frustrated at the lack of options.

"I want to. I would, if I thought it would help. But I don't think it will, so . . ."

He drags his hands through his hair. He'd throw his own head at the tide if he could get it off his neck. "Why do you have to be so damn . . ." The rest comes out only as grunts.

"Born this way, I guess." Disregarding his frustration, I sit and invite him to join me.

Several seconds of silence eventually break his will and he plops down on the sand.

"What's up?" I ask quietly.

"She stole it."

"What?"

Cooper refuses to look at me, his gaze glued to the water. "My emergency fund. Every last dollar."

"Wait, your mom?" Dismay ripples through me. "You're sure?"

He huffs out a humorless laugh. "Positive. Not even Evan knows where I keep my stash."

Damn. That's harsh.

"I should have hidden it the second she showed up," he says, groaning. "She found my pot when I was thirteen and smoked it all when I was at school. I forgot about that until tonight, forgot she knew about the hiding spot. Or maybe I just gave her too much credit not to steal from her own kids."

"I'm sorry." It sounds inadequate under the circumstances. How do I apologize to someone for a lifetime of pain? "How much did she take?"

"Twelve grand," he mutters.

Jeez. Okay. My brain kicks into solution mode, because that's how I operate. Whenever there's a problem with one of my websites, an unwelcome snag in the hotel renos, I become analytical. I assess the problem and try to find a way to fix it.

"That sucks, it really does. I know you're pissed off and feel betrayed, and you have every right to feel that way." I link my arm through his and lean my head on his shoulder. For support. And because I'm freezing. Cooper always runs warm, a perpetual source of heat. "But at least it's only money, right? I can help you. I can replace it."

"Seriously?" He rips his arm from me. "Why would you—" Cooper can't finish the sentence. He jumps to his feet. "What the fuck, Mac? Why is that always where your head goes? Throw money at the problem."

"I thought money was the problem," I protest.

The thunderous look on his face pricks my nerves. Why is it every time I offer to do something nice for him, I get sand kicked in my eye?

"How many different ways do I have to say it?" he shouts at me. "I don't want your goddamn money. Do you even grasp how infantilizing it is to have your girlfriend constantly following you around with her purse open?"

"That's not what I do," I answer, my jaw tight. This guy is pushing the limits of my patience. He wants to be mad at his mom, fine. He wants to vent, good. But I'm not the bad guy here. "I'm only trying to help. You need money, I have more than enough. Why is that wrong? The money doesn't mean anything to me."

"We know." The words come out as a long, sullen sigh. "That's the whole fucking point. You clones throw it around like party favors and expect the rest of us to be grateful for the invitation. I'm not another servant groveling at your feet for tips, goddamn it."

So it's like that. I'm back to being a "clone." Fine.

"You know what, Coop? How about you deal with your own hang-ups instead of heaving all your insecurities on me? I'm getting real fucking sick of withstanding the worst of everyone's little townie microaggressions. Get over it. Because let me tell you something from experience: Rich or poor, bad parents are just bad parents. Your mom sucks. Welcome to the club. Having money wouldn't have made her stay."

I regret the words the second they fly out of my mouth.

Both of us stand there astonished at what we've witnessed. How quickly we went for blood. Every pent-up feeling I've had since my parents cut me off came rushing back to the surface, and I threw it all in Cooper's face as if it were his fault—exactly what I accused him of doing seconds ago.

Overwrought with remorse, I scramble to apologize. But he's already storming off, shouting over his shoulder not to follow him unless this is the last conversation we ever want to have. This time, I take his word for it.

Hours later, though, when he hasn't returned and Evan asks if I know why Cooper's phone is going straight to voicemail, I start to worry. If he were only mad at me, fine, I'd accept that. But the way he tore out of here . . . the rage in his eyes . . . There are a thousand ways a guy like Cooper can get himself into trouble.

It only takes one.

CHAPTER THIRTY-SEVEN

COOPER

There's a dive about an hour west of Avalon Bay. A shack, if you can even call it that, off a two-lane county road that cuts through nothing but empty swamps and small farms. You can usually hear the rumble of motorcycle engines idling in the dirt parking lot from half a mile away. I pull my truck in and cut the engine, then duck inside to find the place is dead, save for a few mean-looking bikers by the pool table and some old guys spread out at the bar. I take a seat on a stool and order a couple fingers of Jack. By the second glass, a guy a couple seats down starts jawing at no one in particular. He's going on about football, responding to everything the ESPN talking heads are saying on the lone television above us. I try to ignore him until he leans toward me, smacking the bar with his flat palm. I get flashbacks to being a bartender and have to restrain myself from snapping at him.

"Who ya got?" he demands to know with slurred urgency. When I ignore him, he repeats himself louder and slower. "The Super Bowl. Who ya got, kid?"

I spare him a look. "I'll buy you a drink to get lost."

"Ohhh." He laughs, mocking me. "Get a load of him, huh? Shhh . . ." He holds his finger over his mouth and shows it to everyone.

"Y'all quiet the hell down. The kid wants some damn peace and quiet, ya got that?"

I came here to get lost, to be left alone. There's no chance Mac would find me here, and this was the only place I could think of that Evan doesn't know about. While he was still clinging to Shelley after our dad's death, my uncle brought me here to blow off some steam at the dartboards. I want to be alone, but I'll embarrass the shit out of this asshole if he wants to make a thing of it. Hell, maybe I should channel Evan and start a bar fight, let off some steam. I mean, why the hell not, right?

Just as I'm talking myself into the idea, a hand slaps down on my shoulder from behind.

"Let me get two beers," a familiar voice tells the bartender.

I glance over to find my uncle taking the stool beside me. Fucking hell.

"Gary," he says to the drunk who was getting in my face. "Why don't you get on home to the missus?"

"Super Bowl's on," a belligerent Gary slurs, jerking a hand toward the TV. "Can't expect me to leave during the Super Bowl."

"That's a rerun of last year's game," Levi replies with the patience of a saint. "Super Bowl's next month, Gary. Now you better go home to Mimi, yeah? Sure she's about to send the dogs after you."

"That damn woman." Gary grumbles his way to opening his wallet and throwing down a few bills on the bar. He mutters something about *can't let a man drink* then teeters his way outside.

Despite wanting to knock his teeth in mere seconds ago, I can't help but stare with a bit of concern after the stumbling man.

"Don't worry. He'll get about a quarter mile on foot before she finds him passed out in the weeds," Levi says. "He's fine."

I look at my uncle in suspicion. "Mac send you?"

"Evan texted me. Said you left in a hurry."

Of course he did. Because Mac would've run right to her new

best friend so they could talk shit about me. I've had it up to my fucking eyeballs with those two ganging up.

"I don't want to talk about it," I mutter, leaving no room for argument.

"Good," he shrugs, "I came here to drink."

Levi tosses back his beer and trains his eyes on the TV, never once sliding a glance my way. It's a relief. At first. Then an hour goes by. And another. And soon, I'm as drunk as Gary was when he left, and my mind is torturing me with all the shit that went down tonight, from finding my life savings stolen to the fight with Mac on the beach. Replaying broken bits of the conversation in my head, I can't quite remember what I said to her, but I'm certain it wasn't good.

"Shelley came back," I finally say, the alcohol loosening my tongue. "For two days. Then made off with my life savings."

Levi makes a full quarter turn to stare at the side of my face.

"Twelve grand." I draw circles in the condensation ring on the bar with my cardboard coaster. "Poof. All gone. Right out from under my nose."

"Jesus. Got any idea where she ran off to?"

"Nope. Baton Rouge, maybe. But that was probably bullshit. A lot of difference it makes. She's not coming back this time. No way."

"I'm sorry, Coop, but that woman is no good." Levi drains his beer and plunks it down. "I got tired of apologizing for my brother a long time ago. I make no excuses for him. He left you boys in a bad way with all those debts. But that goddamn Shelley ain't lifted a finger to help in all these years." Bitterness colors his tone. "You and Evan have worked so hard to dig yourselves out. Now she struts in and rips all that out from under you? Hell no. Not on my watch." His hand comes down hard on the splintered wood bar, jarring my whiskey glass.

I've never seen my uncle this upset. He's a quiet guy. Steady.

For years, he bit his tongue while Shelley popped in and out as she pleased. After he eventually became our guardian, he never once made us feel like a burden for it. Hearing him talk this way is about as close to spitting mad as I've heard him get. For all the good it does us.

"What is there to do?" I feel as bitter as he looks. "There's no catching up to her now. If she doesn't want to be found, she won't be."

My gut still twists with anger. For the money, sure, but more so for the humiliation. The betrayal. For all the ways this woman has made a fool of us over the years. And we've taken it. How Evan still thinks, maybe—even when he knows better—maybe this time it's real. Goddamn Shelley.

"We ain't licked yet," Levi tells me. "And we're done enabling that woman's bad behavior, you hear me?"

Before I can answer, he signals someone at the opposite end of the bar. "Steve, hey, got a question for ya," Levi hollers.

Following my uncle's gaze, I spot the off-duty cop whose uniform shirt is open to expose a sweat-stained white undershirt.

"What do you need, Levi?" Steve hollers back, because in the Bay, everyone knows everyone.

"How might we go about pressing charges against someone who skipped town?"

What? My startled gaze flies to my uncle, but he's focused on the cop.

Shaking the glaze out of his eyes, Steve sits up straighter. "What we talking about?"

Levi's tone is grim. Deadly, even. "Grand larceny."

CHAPTER THIRTY-EIGHT

MACKENZIE

Even Daisy has given up on me. At first, she scampered around my feet as I paced the house, typing then deleting texts to Cooper. Next she sat with her chew rope beside the refrigerator when I compulsively cleaned the kitchen. Which is fucked up, because I've never been a stress cleaner. How could I? I grew up in a house full of maids. When the vacuum comes out, Daisy bolts. I don't blame her. I'm terrible company at the moment anyway. But when spotless floors fail to ease my anxious mind, I end up in Evan's room, where Daisy is curled up at his feet as he plays a video game.

"Hey," I say, knocking on his open door.

He pauses the game. "What's up?"

"Nothing."

Evan answers the unspoken question in the air. "He hasn't texted me back either."

"Yeah, I figured." Hugging the doorframe, I don't know what I came here for, but I was bored of stewing alone. I'm a doer, not a waiter. I hate sitting still. If Cooper wanted to punish me for our fight, this is doing the trick.

"Come here." Evan jerks his head and picks up the second controller for his console. It's several iterations old and running on a flat screen that looks like it was pawned after getting tossed out on someone's lawn. There are dead spots on the picture and a crack in the frame held together by black tape.

My first instinct is that Evan needs a new one. As if he senses the thought, he gives me a knowing smirk that says not to bother.

Right. Boundaries. I need to work on that. Not everyone wants my help.

"You're going to be this guy," he informs me, then provides a rapid explanation of the game as we sit on the edge of his bed. "Got it?"

"Yep." I grasp the gist of it, I think. I mean, my objective and how to move around. Basically. Sort of.

"Follow me," he instructs, leaning forward.

It does not go well. We're ambushed, and instead of shooting at the bad guys, I set off a grenade and kill us both.

Evan snorts loudly.

"I like the racing games better," I confess with an apologetic shrug. "I'm good at those."

"Yeah, princess. I've seen you drive."

"Bullshit. I'm a great driver. I just prefer to go with a sense of urgency."

"If that's what you want to call it."

I nudge him with my elbow as the level resets for another try. This time, I attempt to focus. We make it a little further before I get blown up again.

"This isn't helping, is it?"

I bite my lip. "Not really."

I don't know why I thought sitting next to the spitting image of Cooper would take my mind off him. It's weird, but I almost never see Evan and Cooper as remotely similar, their personalities diverging in so many ways. Yet if I'm being honest, there are times where I imagine how everything might have been different if not for the whimsy of Bonnie's indiscriminate libido.

Whatever he reads on my face, Evan exits out of the game

and sets our controllers aside. "Let's have it, then. What's on your mind?"

Though our rapport has evolved over the past couple months, Evan's hardly the first person I'd turn to for a heart-to-heart. Most of the time he displays the emotional depth of Daisy's water bowl. At this moment, though, he's the next best thing to his brother.

"What if he doesn't come back?" I ask in a small voice.

"He has to come back. He lives here."

I let out a breath. "I mean, to *me*. What if he doesn't come back to me?" My pulse quickens at that horrible notion. "I just . . . I can't shake the feeling that it's over this time. One fight too many and there's no getting past it. What if Cooper's fed up with me?"

"Okay." Evan seems to ponder that for a second. It's still eerie after all this time how his mannerisms exactly match Cooper's, yet they're like a recording where the audio doesn't quite sync with the video. Everything's a half second off. "So not to be a dick or anything, but that's dumb."

"Which part?"

"All of it. You remember my brother almost knocked my teeth out because I was an ass to you once, right?"

"Once?" I echo with a raised eyebrow.

Evan grins. "Yeah, well. Point is, it'll take a lot more than a few arguments to run him off you. There was one summer Coop and I were at each other's throats over I don't know what, and we were beating the tar out of each other about every other day." He shrugs. "Doesn't mean shit. Fighting is how we worked things out."

"But you're brothers," I remind him. "That's a huge difference."

"And what I'm saying is, Coop cares that much about you. You're not staying here for the rent money or because he likes your cooking."

He has a point. I don't cook. At all. Ever. Not once. As for rent, every month I've been here I've left what I thought was a fair market value of a rent check on Cooper's dresser, but he keeps refusing to cash them. So I always leave a backup with Evan.

"But . . ." My teeth worry my bottom lip again. "You didn't see the look on his face when he stormed off."

"Um. I've seen every look on his face." He mugs for me, seeking a laugh.

Fine. That was sort of funny.

"Look," he says, "at some point, Cooper's going to stumble in piss drunk and grovel for you to forgive him once he's come to his senses. He's got a process. You just gotta let him work through the steps."

I want to believe him. That despite all the ways we have absolutely nothing in common, Cooper and I somehow developed a connection stronger than what separates us, deeper than the scars that keep him up at night. The alternative is too painful. Because I can't change where I come from any more than he can. If this is the distance our relationship can't span, I'm not ready to consider what my new life would be without him.

Evan throws his arm around my shoulder. "I know Coop better than anyone. Trust me when I say he's crazy about you. And I've got no reason to lie."

Evan's pep talk digs my mood out of the gutter at least marginally. Enough that when a yawn slams into me, I'm motivated to get ready for bed.

"Promise you'll wake me up if he calls you?" I fret.

"I promise." Evan's voice is surprisingly gentle. "Don't stress too hard, Mac. He'll be home in no time, okay?"

I give a weak nod. "Okay."

"No time" ends up being a quarter past midnight, as I'm woken from a restless sleep when the bed dips beside me. I feel Cooper slide under the covers. He's still warm from a shower and smells of toothpaste and shampoo.

"You awake?" he asks in a whisper.

I roll over to lie on my back, rubbing my eyes. It's pitch black in the bedroom but for the pale glow of the floodlight on the side of the house, filtering in through the blinds.

"Yeah."

Cooper lets out a long breath through his nose. "I talked to Levi."

That's what he's leading with? I'm not sure what relevance it has to our situation or our fight, and part of me wants him to stop stalling and tell me if we're going to be all right. But I keep my impatience at bay. Evan said his brother has a process. Maybe this is part of it.

So I say, "Yeah?"

"Yeah." A long beat. "I'm going to press charges against Shelley. For stealing the money."

"Wow." It hadn't occurred to me that would even be an option. But it makes sense. Mother or not, she stole more than ten thousand dollars from him. "How do you feel about it?"

"Honestly? Fucked up. She's my mom, you know?" I'm startled to hear his voice crack. "I don't want to think about her getting thrown in jail. At the same time, what kind of person steals from their own kid? If I didn't need the money, I'd say whatever. To hell with it. But that was every cent I had saved up. Took me years."

He's talking to me. That's a good sign.

Except then, he falls silent, and the two of us lie there, not touching, both seemingly afraid to disturb the air too much. After several seconds tick by, I realize there's nothing stopping me from going first.

"I'm sorry," I tell him. "I was out of line earlier. I got defensive and lashed out. It was mean and you didn't deserve that."

"Well . . ." he says, and I think I detect a hint of a smile in his voice. "I had it coming a little. Shelley gets under my skin, you know? I just want to throw shit when she's around. And then she goes and steals my money . . ." I can feel the tension building up in him, the effort it's taking to stay calm. Then on a deep breath, he relaxes again. "A lot of what I said came out at you because I was mad at her. You were right. I've got some bullshit that was there way before you came along."

"I get it." Turning on my side, I find his silhouette in the dark. "I thought offering you the money was helpful, but I see now how in that moment it hit a nerve. I wasn't trying to throw money at the problem or emasculate you, I promise you that. It's just . . . that's how my brain works. I go into problem-solving mode—*Money stolen? Here's money.* You know? It wasn't meant to be a statement about our respective bank accounts." I swallow a rush of guilt. "In the future, when it comes to that kind of thing—family stuff, money stuff—I'm here if you need me. Otherwise, I'll butt out."

"I'm not saying I don't want you involved." He shifts, rolling over to face me too. "I don't want all these lines and rules and shit." Cooper finds my hand in the dark and brings it against his chest. He's shirtless, in only his boxers. His skin is warm to the touch. "The money thing is always going to be there, and I've gotta stop getting bent outta shape about it. I know you're not trying to make me feel any sort of way."

"I was afraid you weren't coming back." I swallow again. Harder. "As long as I was here, I mean."

"Gonna take more than that to get rid of me." He tangles his fingers in my hair, rubbing his thumb against the back of my neck. It's a sweet, soothing gesture, practically putting me right back to sleep. "I figured something out tonight."

"What's that?"

"I was sitting in this grimy little bar with Levi and a bunch of sad old bastards hiding from their wives or avoiding their sad old houses. Guys only twice my age but who've already done everything that's ever going to happen to them. And I thought, fuck me, man, I've got this crazy hot girl at home and our biggest problem is she's always trying to buy me shit."

I smile against my pillow. When he puts it that way, we sound like a couple of dumbasses.

"And this jolt kind of hit me suddenly. I thought, what if she isn't there when I get back? I was glaring into the bottom of a glass feeling sorry for myself. What if I'd run off the best thing that ever happened to me?"

"That's sweet, but I wouldn't go that far."

"I'm serious." His voice is soft yet insistent. "Mac, things around here were never good. Then my dad died, and it was confirmation that nothing would get any better. Shelley split. We made do. Never complained. And then you showed up and I started getting ideas. Maybe I didn't have to settle for slightly better than nothing. Maybe I could even be happy."

He breaks my heart. Living without joy, without anticipation that tomorrow can still be extraordinary, will suck the soul right out of a person. It's the cold, dark, strangling infinity of nothingness, of being swallowed up by despair. Nothing can grow in the empty places where we resign ourselves to the numbness. Never really alive. It's the same long tunnel into complacency that I saw closing in around me the harder I looked at the future Preston and my parents imagined for me.

Cooper saved me from that. Not because he whisked me away, but because meeting him finally revealed the possibilities I'd been missing. The exhilaration of uncertainty. Passion and curiosity.

I was half asleep until I met him.

"I thought I was happy," I tell him, gliding my fingers up and down his ribs. "For a long time. What was there to complain about, right? I'd been given everything I could ever ask for—except purpose. A choice. The potential to fail, to get hurt. To ever love something so much the thought of losing it tears me open. Tonight, when I thought you and I might really be over, all sorts of things ran through my head. I was making myself crazy."

Cooper tilts my chin toward him and presses his lips to mine with the lightest touch. Enough to make me seek him out for another taste.

His breath is a warm whisper against my lips. "I might just be falling in love with you, Cabot."

My heart jumps. "Uh-oh."

"You have no idea."

He drags his fingers down my spine, setting every nerve alight. I bite his bottom lip, tug a little, in our wordless language that says I need him. Now. Take this ache away. But he's methodically, frustratingly patient in removing my tank top before he palms one breast while licking at the other. He pushes his boxers down. I wiggle out of my underwear as he puts on a condom. A shiver of anticipation skitters through me when he drags the hot length of him over my core.

He holds me tight as he moves inside me. Unhurried. Slow, languid strokes. I cling to him, muffling my moans against his shoulder.

"I love you too," I say, shaking in his arms while I come.

CHAPTER THIRTY-NINE

COOPER

A few days after filing charges against Shelley, I receive a call to come to the police station. On the phone with the sheriff, I learn that the cops picked her up in Louisiana, where she must have forgotten about all the unpaid parking tickets she'd left behind after her "fella" kicked her to the curb. When the South Carolina warrant popped up, the sheriff in Baton Rouge had her transferred back up to the Bay.

Mac and my brother come to the station with me, but I make Evan wait outside while we go in to speak to Sheriff Nixon. Evan was equally furious to learn that Shelley robbed me blind, but I know my brother—he'll always have a soft spot for that woman. And right now I need to keep a clear head, not allow anything to cloud my judgment.

"Cooper, have a seat." Sheriff Nixon shakes my hand, then settles behind his desk and gets right down to business. "Your mother had about ten grand in cash on her when the Baton Rouge boys brought her in."

Relief slams into me like a gust of wind. Ten grand. It's a couple thousand short of what she stole, but it's better than nothing. Hell, it's more than I expected. She was gone four days. Shelley is more than capable of blowing twelve grand in that amount of time.

"However, it could be a while before you get the money back," Nixon adds.

I frown at him. "Why's that?"

He starts rambling on about evidence procedures and what not, as my brain tries to keep up with all the information he's spitting out. First things first, Shelley will be arraigned in front of a judge. Mac asks a lot of questions because I'm kind of in a stupor about the whole thing now. All I keep thinking about is Shelley in an orange jumpsuit, her wrists shackled. I despise everything that woman's ever done to us, but the thought of her behind bars doesn't sit right. What kind of son sends his own mother to jail?

"She's here now?" I ask Nixon.

"In holding, yes." He rubs a hand over his thick mustache, looking every inch the part of a small-town sheriff. He's new to town, so I doubt he knows much about me and my family. His predecessor, Sheriff Stone, hated our guts. Spent his afternoons tailing Evan and me around the Bay all summer, looking for a reason to glare at us from his unmarked cruiser.

"What would happen if I changed my mind?"

Beside me, Mac looks startled.

"You want to withdraw the charges?" he says, eyeing me closely.

I hesitate. "Will I get my money back today?"

"There'd be no reason to hold it in evidence. So, yes."

Which is all I wanted in the first place.

"What would happen to her after that?"

"It's your prerogative as the victim. If you're not interested in prosecuting, she'll be released. Mrs. Hartley was only held in Louisiana at the request of this department. Whatever fines she faces there are a separate matter. We aren't aware of another warrant for her at this time."

I glance at Mac, knowing it isn't a decision she would make for me one way or the other, but wanting the confirmation that I'm doing the right thing. I guess in this situation, it's all degrees of shitty either way.

She studies my face, then offers a slight nod. "Do what you feel is right," she murmurs.

I shift my gaze back to the sheriff. "Yeah, I want to drop the charges. Let's get this over with."

It still takes about an hour to sign the paperwork and wait around for an officer to appear with a plastic bag of my cash. He counts out every bill, then has me sign some more papers. Another huge wave of relief hits me when I hand Mac the cash to stuff in her purse. The very next thing I'm doing is sucking it up and depositing the money in the bank, the taxman be damned.

Outside, Evan's waiting for us by the truck. "All good?" he says.

I nod. "All good."

We're about to leave when Shelley walks out of the building rubbing her wrists.

Shit.

She lights up a cigarette. As she exhales, her gaze lands on us, catching our attempted escape.

"I'll get rid of her," Mac offers, squeezing my hand.

"It's fine," I say. "Wait in the truck."

In typical Shelley fashion, my mother strides over with a cheerful smile. "Well, what a day, huh? Someone sure screwed up, didn't they? I don't know where they got their wires crossed. I told them, I said, call my boys. They'll tell you I didn't take anything that didn't belong to me."

"Jesus, give it a rest, would you?" I snap.

She blinks. "Baby—"

"No, don't *baby* me." I can't take another second of her bullshit, her smiley evasions. I've been choking on them since I was five, and I'm fucking full. "You found my stash and stole from me, and *that's* why you skipped town. Hope it was worth it." I stare at her. "*Mom*."

"Baby, no." She reaches for my arm. I take a step back. "I was only borrowing a little to get set up. I was going to send it right back after I got on my feet. You know that. I didn't think you'd mind, right?"

Amazed laughter trickles out of my mouth. "Sure. Whatever. I don't want to hear it anymore. This is the last time we're gonna do this. I don't want to see you anymore. Far as I'm concerned, you don't ever need to come back here. You have no sons, Shelley."

She flinches. "Now, Cooper, I get you're upset, but I'm still your mother. You're still my boys. You don't turn your back on family." She looks at Evan, who has remained silent, lingering behind me. "Right, baby?"

"Not this time," he says, gazing off at the passing traffic. Emphatic. Stoic. "I'm with Coop. I think it's better if you didn't come around anymore."

I fight the urge to throw my arm around my brother. Not here. Not in front of her. But I know the pain he's feeling. The loneliness. Evan lost his mom today.

I lost mine a long time ago.

Shelley makes one last attempt to get us in line until she realizes we aren't budging. Then the act falls apart. Her smile recedes to flat indifference. Her eyes grow dull and mean. Voice bitter. In the end, she has little in the way of parting words. Barely a glance as she blows smoke in our faces and walks to a waiting cab that carries her off to be someone else's problem. We're all better for it.

Even if it doesn't feel that way right now.

Later, as Mac orders us a pizza for dinner, Evan and I take Daisy for a walk. We don't talk about Shelley. Hell, we don't talk much at all. We're in somber spirits. Each of us is lost in our own thoughts, and yet I know we're thinking the exact same things.

When we return to the house, we find Levi on the back deck, sipping a beer. "Hey," he calls at our approach. "I came by to see how it went at the police station."

Evan heads inside to grab two beers for us, while I stand at the railing and fill our uncle in. When I reach the part where Shelley disappeared in a taxi without so much as a goodbye, Levi nods in grim satisfaction.

"Think she got the message this time?" he asks.

"Maybe? She looked pretty defeated."

"Can't say I'm sorry for her." Levi never got along with Shelley, even when she was around. I don't blame him. The only redeeming quality about either of my parents was giving us a decent uncle.

"We're orphans now," Evan remarks, staring at the waves.

"Shit, guys, I know this ain't easy. But you're not alone in this. If you ever need anything . . ."

He trails off. But he doesn't need to finish the sentence. Levi's tried his damnedest to make us feel like a family despite all the missing pieces, and he's done a pretty good job considering what he had to work with.

"Hey, I know we don't say it enough," I tell our uncle, "but we're only standing here because you were there for us. You always are. If it weren't for you, we would've ended up in the system. Shipped off to foster care. Probably separated."

"We love you," Evan adds, his voice lined with emotion.

It gets Levi a little choked up. He coughs, his way of covering it up. "You're good boys," is his gruff response. He's not a man of sentiment or many words. Still, we know how he feels about us.

Maybe we never got the family we deserved, but we ended up with the one we needed.

CHAPTER FORTY

MACKENZIE

He's being utterly unreasonable.

"You said you were going to pick up ice on your way home," I shout from the backyard, where I'm standing with six coolers of warm beer and soda.

With February came a sudden ferocious winter, so while I'm freezing my butt off out here, the drinks are still hot to the touch because Evan left the cases sitting too close to the firepit. Now he's taking a load off, and I'm left to wrestle with a folding table that is refusing to budge as I try prying the legs open. These folding tables must've been designed by a sadist, because I cannot for the life of me get them open.

"The freezer at the liquor store was broken," Cooper responds from the deck. "Heidi said she's going to swing by Publix on the way here and get some."

"But the drinks won't have time to chill before everyone else arrives. That's the whole reason I sent you out early!" I'm about to rip my damn hair out. This is the third time I've tried explaining this to him, and still it's like arguing with an ornery sand crab.

"I would have stopped, but it was out of the way and I wanted to get home to help set up. You'd rather I left you here to do everything by yourself?" he shouts back, throwing his hands up.

"I was here to help her," Evan says from his chair. Where he's been sitting on his ass drinking the last cold beer, instead of helping me set up. "She's got a point, Coop," he adds, nodding graciously at me, as if to say *See, I'm on your side.*

"Stay out of it," Cooper tells him.

I glare at them both.

There have got to be few worse hells than sharing a birthday one day apart with a couple of barely housetrained twins. Last night, they had this brilliant idea to throw a massive last-minute party instead of the dinner I was planning, so now we're rushing to put something together, except Evan is lazy and Cooper has all the logistical abilities of a herring.

"Forget it." I didn't even want this stupid party, but they insisted that since it's my twenty-first, we had to go big. So, of course, I'm stuck doing most of the work. "I'll go get the food from one end of town, the cake from the other, then double back for ice and try to make it back before dark. Wish me luck."

Cooper lets out an exasperated groan. "I'll call Heidi and ask her to come sooner. Okay? Happy?"

I kick over the folding table, because fuck it, and rush up the steps toward the sliding door, which is currently being blocked by Cooper. "Don't bother. For my birthday, all I really want is one less minute of her snide comments and sneering looks. Is that too much to ask?"

"I've talked to her, okay? I can't control how she acts. Just give it time. She'll get over it."

"You know, I'm not even mad at Heidi. If I'd been led on for an entire summer, I'd be pretty cranky too."

"That's not what happened," he growls.

"It's what she thinks, and that's all that matters. Maybe that's the talk you should be having."

"Fuck, Mac. Could you get off my case for ten minutes?"

"Hey dumbass," Evan yells from the yard. "She's right."

Cooper flips his brother off and follows me into the house as I hurry to grab my purse and find his keys. Not seeing them in the kitchen or living room, I make my way to his bedroom. He trails after me, looking as frazzled as I feel.

"You know what?" I turn to look at him. "I don't think this is working anymore."

Our bickering is draining. And annoying, because it's usually about stupid stuff. We dig in and refuse to relent until we exhaust all our energy fighting and forget what started the argument in the first place.

"What the hell does that mean?" He snatches his keys from his dresser before I can reach for them.

I grit my teeth, then let out a harried breath. "Crashing here was supposed to be a temporary thing. And seeing as how we're constantly at each other's throats, I've clearly overstayed my welcome."

Like a gust of wind knocks him sideways, Cooper deflates. He places the keys in my upturned hand. When he speaks, his voice is gentle.

"That's not what I want. If you're ready to get your own place, I understand. But don't think you have to move out for me. I like having you here."

"You sure?" I've noticed complaints about my invasion of his space have grown exponentially since I shacked up here. "I'd rather you tell me the truth. Not what you think I want to hear."

"I swear."

His gaze locks with mine. I search his face, and he searches mine, and something passes between us. It's what always happens. When all our anger and frustration subsides, when the storm passes and I notice him again. The way his tattoos carve along the muscles of his arms. The broad plane of his chest. The way he always smells of shampoo and sawdust.

Cooper places his hands on my hips. Looking down at me with heavy-lidded eyes, he walks me backward and closes his bedroom door to press me against it.

"I like having you close," he says roughly. "Going to bed with you. Waking up to you. Making love to you."

His hands capture the hem of my dress and move upward, pulling the fabric up with him until I'm exposed from the waist down. My pulse thrums so fervently in my neck I can feel the frantic little thumps. I've been conditioned to him. He touches me and my body squirms in anticipation.

"I'm not cramping your style?" I tease. My palms splay against the door, fingers digging into the grooves.

His answer is a dismissive flicking of his eyes. He steps closer until only a sliver of air stands between us. Then, licking his lips, he says, "Tell me to kiss you."

My brain doesn't have a response for that, but everything clenches and my toes grab at the floor.

He presses his forehead to mine, gripping my ribs. "If we're done fighting, tell me to kiss you."

I hate fighting with him. But this. The making up. Well, it's the undiluted syrup at the bottom of the chocolate milk. My favorite part.

"Kiss me," I whisper.

His lips brush mine in a featherlight caress. Then he pulls back slightly. "This . . ." he mutters, his breath tickling my nose.

He doesn't finish that sentence. But he doesn't have to. I know exactly what he means. This.

Just . . . *this*.

As it turns out, I own at drinking games. In fact, the more I drink, the better I get. I'd never played flip cup before tonight, but after a couple rounds, I couldn't lose. One challenger after another left slayed at my feet. After that, I destroyed three beer pong opponents, then managed to embarrass the hell out of some dude with neck tattoos at the dartboard. Apparently, once I've consumed a bottle of wine, I can't *not* hit a bull's eye.

Now, I'm standing by the fire, listening to Tate lay out some thought experiment that's hurting my tipsy brain.

"Wait. I don't get it. If there are boats coming to the island, why can't I get on one and sail home to safety?"

"Because that's not the point!" Tate's blue eyes convey pure exasperation.

"But I've essentially been rescued," I argue. "So why can't I get on a boat? I'd way rather do that than pick between Cooper and a bunch of supplies without having access to either boat."

"But that's the actual dilemma! Not how you're going to get off the island. You have to choose."

"I choose the boats!"

Tate looks like he wants to murder me, which is confusing, because I think the answer to this deserted island thing is stupidly simple.

"You know what?" He lets out a breath, then grins, his dimples making an appearance. "You're lucky you're cute, Mac. Because you suck at thought experiments."

"Aww." I pat his arm. "You're cute too, Tater-Tot."

"I hate you," he sighs.

Nah, he doesn't. It's taken time, but I think I've finally settled into my place in Cooper's life. No longer the square peg. Not just his life—ours.

"I'm cold," I announce.

"Seriously?" Tate points to the raging bonfire in front of us.

"Just because there's a fire doesn't mean it's not February," I say stubbornly.

I leave him at the firepit and make my way toward the house to get a sweater. Just as I reach the back steps, I catch my name and turn to answer before realizing it's Heidi talking to someone on the upstairs deck. I tilt my head back. Through the gaps in the slats, I make out Heidi's blonde head and Alana's red one, along with the faces of a few other girls I don't know. I'm about to climb the first step when Heidi's next words stop me.

"I can forgive her for being dumb, but she's so painfully boring," Heidi says, laughing. "And Cooper's no fun at all anymore. All he wants to do is pretend they're married. He hardly ever comes out anymore."

Little waves of anger ripple through me. This shit. Every time. Not once have I stopped Cooper from hanging out with Heidi or asked him not to invite her somewhere, because I can at least tolerate her for his sake. Why she's so committed to not giving me the same courtesy, I don't understand. Instead, it's always dirty looks and passive-aggressive bullshit. And, apparently, trash-talking behind my back.

"I still don't know how she bought Cooper acting like he never met that guy." Heidi laughs again, smug now. "I mean, wake up and smell the conspiracy, right?"

Wait, what?

Is she talking about Preston?

"I'd feel sorry for her if she wasn't so gullible."

Screw Heidi. She doesn't know what she's talking about. Still, I'd rather know what other bile she's been spewing behind my back, so I hug the shadows as I creep up the steps, keeping bodies between myself and Heidi, hiding among the other people lingering on the stairs talking.

"Okay, but it's been long enough," another girl says. "He must be into her, don't you think?"

"What does it matter?" Heidi offers that dismissive shrug she does. "Eventually she's got to figure out he's been lying to her from the start. That he only got with her as a means for revenge."

"Leave them alone," Alana says. "You promised to let it go."

I stop dead. Did I hear her right? Because that sounded suspiciously like confirmation.

What else could it mean?

"What?" There's a coy note in Heidi's tone.

I'm barely three feet away now. So close I'm shaking.

"I didn't say I was going to tell her. Not on purpose, anyway."

My heart thumps erratically against my ribs. Alana is standing right there, mouth shut. Not disputing Heidi's version of events.

Which means, if I've read it right, Cooper has been lying to me since the moment we met.

Worse, he lied when I confronted him directly. He lied to my face. And he made all his friends—*our* friends, I thought—go along with the lies. Evan. Steph. Alana.

I feel small, like I could fall right through the space between the deck boards. Utterly humiliated. Who else knew about it? Have they all been laughing at me behind my back this entire time? Poor, dumb clone.

"Go on, then," I say, charging forward to confront the group. "Don't wait for word to get around, for something to slip—why don't you tell me to my face, Heidi?"

Alana has the decency to look contrite. Heidi, however, doesn't even pretend to hide her smirk.

Seriously, this girl makes me want to boob-punch her. I've tried with her. I really have. Make conversation. Be civil. Give her time. But no matter how much or how little I give, she's flatly refused to budge from her total contempt. Now I understand why—she and I weren't in an uneasy truce, but a cold war to which I was oblivious. That was my mistake.

"I get it, you hate my guts," I say testily. "Find a new hobby."

She narrows her eyes.

I dismiss her from my gaze, turning to Alana instead. "Is it true? This was some sort of revenge plan against my ex? Cooper lied?"

Saying it out loud makes me queasy. All the alcohol I consumed tonight churns dangerously in my belly as I replay the events of the last six months. My memory flips through a dozen early conversations with Cooper, wondering what obvious clues I ignored. How many times was the answer right in front of me, but I was too enamored of his fathomless eyes and crooked smile?

Ever enigmatic, Alana reveals no emotion. Only hesitation. I thought we'd grown close, gotten past the rough patches to actually become friends. Yet here she is, silent, her expression shuttered, while Heidi makes me the butt of her jokes. Guess I really am dumb. They all had me fooled.

"Alana," I press, almost cringing at the helplessness I hear in my voice.

After an interminably long pause, her aloof expression slips, just enough for me to glimpse a flicker of regret.

"Yes," she admits. "It's true. Cooper lied."

CHAPTER FORTY-ONE

COOPER

I catch a glimpse of Mac through the flames of the bonfire, a glowing fleeting glimpse, before a wave of beer smacks me in the face.

"Asshole."

Confusion jolts through me. Staggering backward from the firepit, I wipe my eyes with sandy fingers. I blink a few times, using my forearm to mop beer off my face. I blink again, and Mac is directly in front of me, holding an empty red cup in her hand. As our friends all stand there staring at us, I struggle to understand what the hell is happening.

"Lying asshole," she repeats with seething ferocity.

Evan tries to approach her. "Whoa, what was that for?"

"No. Fuck you too." She points a warning finger at him. "You lied to me. Both of you."

Beyond her slender shoulder, I spot Alana weaving her way through the crowd, trailed by Heidi. Alana looks guilty. Heidi's expression is one of pure apathy.

Mac's expression? Sheer betrayal.

And now I get it. Reading her face, I feel like I'm falling. It's like that second when our brains jerk inside our skulls and we experience a frozen moment of terror before the descent, because we know: *This is going to hurt.* There's nothing to grab on to now. She's got me dead to rights.

"Mac, let me explain," I start hoarsely.

"You *used* me," she shouts.

Her arm thrusts forward and the empty cup bounces off my chest. A stunned audience stands silent, retreating to the opposite side of the pit.

"It was all about revenge this whole time." She shakes her head repeatedly, the emotions in her eyes running the gamut from embarrassed to incensed to disappointed.

I think about the first night I approached her, how irritated I was at having to feign interest in some stuck-up clone. How she snuck up on me with her smile and wit.

What the hell did she ever see in me to make it this far?

"It started that way," I admit. I've got seconds, maybe, to get this out before she runs off and never speaks to me again, so I drop the bullshit and lay it all on the table. "Yes, I found you because I wanted to get back at him. I was stupid and pissed off. And then I met you and it blew up my whole life, Mac. I fell for you. It's been the best six months of my life."

Some of the hardest months too. All of which she's endured with me. Despite me. I've thrown more shit at this girl than she had any reason to withstand, and still she found her way to love me regardless. Of course I was gonna mess that up. How could I ever think otherwise?

But holy fucking shit, it hurts worse than I ever could've imagined, the thought of losing Mackenzie. My heart feels like it's being crushed in a vise.

"And, yeah, I should have come clean a long time ago. But goddamn it, okay, I was scared." My throat starts closing in on me, cutting off my airway. I suck in a ragged breath. "I was scared of this moment right here. I made a terrible mistake, and I thought if you didn't find out, it wouldn't hurt you. I wanted to protect you."

"You humiliated me," she spits out through tears and rage. I want to throw my arms around her and take her pain away, but I'm the one doing this to her, and every second she levels me with that look of devastation rips me apart. "You made me look like an idiot."

"Please, Mac. I'll do anything." I grab her hands, squeezing when she tries to turn away. Because I know the second she takes that first step, she's gonna keep walking forever. "I love you. Let me prove it. Give me a chance."

"You had a chance." Tears stream down her cheeks. "You could have told me the truth months ago. You had a million opportunities, including the day I asked you point-blank if you knew Preston, if he got you fired. But you didn't tell me the truth. Instead you let everyone laugh at me behind my back." Mac pulls her hands from mine to wipe her eyes. "I might have been able to forgive you for everything else if you hadn't lied right to my face. Got to hand it to you, Cooper. You did it so well. And then you got everyone I thought was my friend to lie too. Put me in this perfect little glass house of bullshit for your own amusement."

"Mackenzie." I'm grasping at a rope as it's sliding through my fingers. With every breath I take, she's slipping further away. "Let me fix it."

"There's nothing left to fix." Her expression flattens to an eerie dullness. "I'm going into the house and I'm packing up my stuff and I'm leaving. Because that's the only thing left for me to do. Don't try to stop me."

Then she turns her back and disappears beyond the glow of the fire.

There's silence in her wake.

"Forget what she said," Evan blurts out, shoving my shoulder. "Go after her."

I stare out at nothingness. "She doesn't want me to."

I know Mac well enough to see when she's made up her mind. Anything I do now will only chase her off faster, hardening the hatred. Because she's right. I was a shit person when I met her.

Nothing I've done since has proven different.

"Then I'll go," Evan growls, throwing off my attempt to stop him.

Whatever. He won't succeed in changing her mind. She's leaving.

She's gone.

Everyone else slowly wanders away until I'm left alone on the beach. I sink down to the sand. I sit there for I don't know how long—so long the bonfire is reduced to cold embers. Evan doesn't return. No point telling me what I already know. The sun peeks above the waves by the time I trudge back to the house through the remnants of the aborted party.

Daisy doesn't come running to be let out when I walk inside. Her water bowl isn't in the kitchen.

Half the closet is empty in my room.

I throw myself on the bed and stare up at the ceiling. I feel numb. Empty.

I wish I'd known then how hard it would be now to miss Mackenzie Cabot.

CHAPTER FORTY-TWO

MACKENZIE

I lived my whole life without Cooper Hartley. Then, six months together and I've forgotten what it was not to know him. Six months, and only minutes to shred it to hell.

One overheard conversation.

A single devastating admission.

Quick as blowing out a match, my heart went numb.

After leaving Cooper's house in a despondent haze, I sat in the back of a cab with Daisy and paid the guy to drive through town for nearly two hours. At some point, the cab dropped me off at Tally Hall. I showed up at Bonnie's door with my bag in one hand and Daisy's leash in the other, and with a sympathetic pout, she welcomed us home. Lucky for me, her new roommate sleeps out most nights. Less lucky, the moment people started getting up for class and trudging through the halls in the morning, Daisy began barking at the unfamiliar foot traffic. In an instant, the resident advisor was on us, demanding that we vacate.

For Bonnie's sake, I told him we'd only popped in for a few minutes to say hello, though I'm not sure he bought it. By the afternoon, Daisy and I were in the backseat of another cab, searching for a plan B. Turns out there isn't a hotel in the Bay that allows pets. Something about a dog show years back that went horribly awry.

So that's how I find myself at Steph and Alana's house. Daisy, the little traitor, hops right onto the couch and into Steph's lap. I'm a bit more reluctant as I sit down next to Steph, while Alana pleads their case. They'd sent a dozen or so text messages after I'd stormed out of the party. It wasn't so much the content but the persistence that convinced me of their sincerity.

"In our defense," Alana says, standing with her arms crossed, "we didn't know you'd end up being cool."

I have to hand it to her, she's unapologetically herself. Even in admitting that she had no small part in crafting the revenge plot, she doesn't have it in her to mince words.

"For real, though," she continues. "By the time Cooper told us you two were really a thing, it seemed meaner to tell you the truth."

"No," I say simply. "It was meaner to lie."

Because while the truth hurts you, the lie degrades you. When I realized Preston had slept around on me, I understood what it was to be That Girl. For years, our friends had smiled in my face, knowing all along I was his patsy, while I remained oblivious to his "extracurriculars"—his parade of Marilyns. It never occurred to me that Cooper would turn around and lie to me as well. Or that, yet again, the people I called friends would play accomplices to my ignorance. Some lessons we have to learn twice.

Nevertheless, I'm not entirely without mercy. The mathematics of loyalty are tricky, after all. They were Cooper's friends first. I can't not factor that into the equation. It would be well within my rights to hate them both for their part in this charade, but I also see where they got caught in the middle. They should have told me the truth, yes. It was Cooper, though, who swore them to secrecy. It was his ass they were covering.

If anyone deserves the brunt of the blame, it's him.

"We feel awful about it," Steph says. "It was a crappy thing to do to someone."

"Yep," I agree.

"We're sorry, Mac. *I'm* sorry." Tentative, she reaches over to squeeze my arm. "And if you need a place to crash, you're welcome to stay in our spare room, okay? Not just because we owe you, but because you really are cool, and I, we"—she glances at Alana— "consider you a good friend."

Despite the awkward implications, staying here is the most attractive option until I find a more permanent solution. Besides, Daisy already seems quite at home.

"And we won't discuss Cooper unless you want to," Alana promises. "Although for what it's worth, he's pretty torn up about everything. Evan says he sat on the beach all night in the cold, just staring at the bay."

"Am I supposed to feel sorry for him?" I ask with a raised brow.

Steph laughs awkwardly. "Well, no, and we're not saying you don't deserve to be pissed. I'd have complete sympathy if you wanted to torch his truck."

"The whole revenge plan was juvenile bullshit," adds Alana. "But he wasn't faking liking you. We told him he wasn't allowed to pretend to fall for you, so that part was completely real."

"And he is sorry," Steph says. "He knows he messed up."

I wait a few seconds, but it seems they've wrapped up their pitch. Good. Now we can set some boundaries.

"I get that you two are stuck in the middle of this and that sucks," I tell the girls. "So how about we set a house rule: I won't get weird every time someone mentions his name or bitch about him in front of you, and you guys agree not to campaign for him. Deal?"

Steph gives me a sad smile. "Deal."

That night, I allow myself to cry alone in the dark. To feel the pain and anger. Let it rip me open. And then I put it away, bury it deep. I wake up in the morning and I remind myself that there's a lot more to my life than Cooper Hartley. For the last year, I've complained about all the things keeping me from concentrating on my business. Well, there's nothing stopping me now. I've got time in the day and more than enough work between my websites and the hotel to fill it. Time to wipe up my smudged mascara and be a bad bitch.

Fuck love. Build the empire.

CHAPTER FORTY-THREE

COOPER

"Hey, Coop, you in here?"

"Back here."

Heidi finds me in my workshop, where I've been holed up for the past six hours. Orders keep pouring in for new furniture pieces via the website Mac had set up for me. She'd asked someone who worked on her apps to design it, and one of her marketing people created an advertising account for my Facebook business page too. Just another way she'd changed my life for the better. The orders are coming almost faster than I can fill them, so every second I'm not on one of Levi's jobsites, I'm in here busting my ass to push out new work. Can't say I mind the distraction. It's either keep myself occupied, or wallow in self-destructive misery.

My head jerks up in a quick nod of greeting. I have a raw piece of oak from a fallen tree that I'm chiseling into a chair leg. The repetitive motions—long, smooth strokes—are all that keep me sane these days.

"Why does your porch look like a funeral home?" Heidi says as she hops on my worktable.

"Mac. She keeps sending my gifts back."

For two weeks now, I've tried sending flowers, baskets. All kinds of shit. Every day, they end up on my front porch instead.

Initially, I was sending them to the hotel, knowing she was out there daily checking on the work Levi has one of his crews starting on. But then I wore Steph down and she told me Mac is staying with her and Alana. I thought for sure I'd at least get one of them to accept delivery. No such luck.

The intensity with which this chick refuses to let me apologize is fucking ridiculous. She even took our dog. I still wake up in the middle of the night thinking I hear Daisy barking. I'll roll over and ask Mac if she's taken her out, only to realize neither of them are there.

I miss my girls, damn it. I'm losing my mind.

"Guess that answers the question of where you two stand." Heidi draws a sad face in the fine yellow dust. "Not for nothing, but I told—"

"I swear to God, Heidi, you finish that sentence and I better never see your face here again."

"Whoa, what the hell, Coop?"

I put too much force behind the chisel and crack the wood. A huge gash opens down the middle of the chair leg. Dammit. The chisel flies out of my hand and pings off the floor somewhere across the garage.

"You got exactly what you wanted, right, Heidi? Mac won't talk to me. And now, what, you've come to gloat? Fucking spare me."

"You think I did this to you?"

"I know you did."

"God, Cooper, you are such an ass." Cheeks stained red with anger, Heidi throws a handful of sawdust in my face.

"Motherfucker," I curse. There's sawdust in my mouth and up my nose.

Muttering under my breath, I douse my head with a bottle of water and spit up tiny splinters on the concrete floor. My wary gaze tracks Heidi's pissed off movements as she starts pacing the garage.

"I warned you this was a bad idea," she fumes. "I said it was cruel to play with someone like that. But you didn't listen because *Oh that Heidi, she's just jealous*. Right? Isn't that what you thought?"

A sliver of guilt pricks my chest, because, yeah, it's precisely what I thought when she'd protested Evan's revenge scheme.

"Well, I'm sorry it blew up in your face exactly how I knew it would." She jabs her index finger in the air. "Don't put that on me."

I jab my finger right back. "No, you only made Mac miserable every second she was around until you finally got your chance to drive her away."

"She was eavesdropping. Play stupid games, win stupid prizes."

I'm so goddamn over Heidi and her attitude. For six months, I've made myself grin and bear it, but there's a limit.

"You made it pretty clear you hated her from the second we got together. I asked you, as a friend, to do me this one favor. Instead you stabbed me in the back. Honest to God, I thought we were tighter than that."

Heidi launches forward and chucks a sanding block at my head, which I manage to catch before it wallops me in the face. "Don't pull that loyalty card nonsense on me. All you've done since the summer is act like I'm the heartsick psycho who can't get off your dick, but it was you who showed up at my door drunk and horny one day, and the next you're treating me like a stalker."

"Where did this come from?"

"You, jackass." Heidi paces around the table. Too close to my chisels and mallets for my liking. "Yes, okay, sorry, I made the unforgiveable mistake of catching feelings for you. Fucking crucify me. I don't remember you telling me our shit was over. I don't recall a conversation where you said, *Hey, it's only sex and we're cool, right? One day I'm getting the brush-off and that's it.*"

I falter, forcing myself to look back to last summer. My memory is a bit fuzzy on the details. I'm not even sure how we ended up in bed the first time. Can't say I remember having a meeting about the particulars either. There'd been no *what are we* talk. No discussion where we laid out some ground rules. I just . . . assumed.

And that's when I realize, as I feel the color drain from my face and guilt twist up my insides, that maybe I was the asshole.

"I didn't realize that's how you felt," I admit, keeping my distance because another violent outburst is not out of the question. "I thought we were on the same page. And then, yeah, I guess I felt kind of cornered and took the easy way out. I didn't want to make it awkward."

Heidi stops. She sighs, slumping down on a stool. "You made me feel like some random hookup. Like, even as a friend, I didn't mean anything to you. That really hurt, Coop. Then I was so mad at you."

Fuck. Heidi's always had my back. I was so up my own ass I didn't think for a second how I did her wrong.

"Come here," I say gruffly, holding out my arms.

After a second, she comes forward and lets me hug her. Though she does slug me in the ribs before wrapping her arms behind my back.

"I'm sorry," I tell her. "I didn't mean to hurt you. If I'd seen someone else treat you that way, I'd have beaten him senseless. It wasn't cool at all."

She peers up at me, and there's moisture clinging to her lashes. She hastily wipes her eyes. "I guess I'm sorry too. I should have put on my big girl pants and cut your brake lines like an adult instead of taking it out on your girlfriend."

Ah, fucking Heidi. Never can tell with this one. I wouldn't for a second put it past her.

I give her another squeeze before releasing her. "Are we good?"

She shrugs. "Eh. We will be."

"If you need me to grovel some more, say the word." I flash a self-deprecating grin. "I've gotten damn good at groveling these past couple weeks."

Her lips twitch with humor. "The flowers on your porch say otherwise. But sure, I'll take some groveling. You can't act like a fuckboy and expect to get away with it."

I wince. "God. No. Definitely don't let me get away with it." A groan slips out. "I just realized something. I'm Evan. I fucking Evan'd you."

Heidi starts to laugh uncontrollably, bending over to clutch her side. "Oh my God, you did," she howls. When she regains her composure, her cheeks are flushed and stained with tears of laughter rather than pain. She grins at me and says, "I almost feel like that's punishment enough."

I know Heidi well enough to be sure we'll work our stuff out, and it's especially promising after our talk in the garage. The harder mission right now is Mac, whose determination to ignore me has surpassed even my most pessimistic estimations. Two weeks becomes three, and the stubborn woman continues to act as if I don't exist.

I've taken to texting her as I get off work, a reward to myself for making it all day without leaving her a dozen voicemails. Not that she ever replies, but I'm holding on to hope that one day she will.

I've just hit send on my latest *Please please call me* when Levi signals me and Evan as we're getting into my truck and asks us to meet him down at his lawyer's office on Main Street. He mentioned something recently about amending his will, so I figure it's about that. But when we get there, he drops a bomb on us.

After we're ushered into a small conference room and take our seats, Levi slides a small stack of documents across the table.

"For you boys," he says.

"What's this?" I ask.

"Have a quick read."

Confused, I scan the documents. My eyes widen when they land on the words *Hartley & Sons*. "Levi. What is this?" I repeat.

Evan pulls the papers toward him to take a better look.

"I'm restructuring the company," Levi explains, pushing two pens toward us. "And, if you're interested, Coop, bringing your furniture business under the new H & S umbrella."

"Wait." Evan pops his head up after a careful reading of the contract. "You want to make us owners?"

Levi nods with a reserved smile. "Equal partners."

"I . . ." Am lost for words. Dumbstruck. I didn't see this coming whatsoever. "I don't understand. What brought this on?"

Levi clears his throat and gives his lawyer a look that gets the older man peeling out of his big leather chair to give us some privacy. "The day Shelley left town for good, when I came by the house to check on you," he starts. Then stops, clearing his throat again. "What you boys said really got to me. About being all alone now. Feeling like orphans. And, well, if I'm being honest, I always thought of you two as my sons."

Levi's never been married or had kids of his own. It wasn't until we were in high school that Evan and I caught on that his friend and roommate Tim was his boyfriend. They've been together as long as I can remember, though they try not to be obvious about it. The Bay that Levi grew up in is of another time, so I get it. He prefers to keep his personal life private, and we've always tried to respect that.

"I figured, well, let's make it official." He gulps, shifting awkwardly in his chair. "If you're good with it, that is." Another gulp. "I want to make sure you boys have a legacy you're proud of in this town."

All I can do is stare at him. Because . . . wow. No one has ever invested anything in us before. Growing up, most people wrote us off as a lost cause. Bound to end up like our parents. Drunks.

Deadbeats. Drop-outs. All waiting for the day they could wag their fingers and say, *See, I knew it.* But not Levi. Maybe because he's family, but mostly because he's a decent guy. He saw us as worth protecting. He knew, if given a chance, an ounce of help, we'd turn out okay. A little frayed, maybe, but still in one piece.

"So, what do you say?" he prompts.

My brother wastes no time grabbing one of the pens. "Hell yes," he says, the crack in his voice revealing he's as affected by this as I am.

I always knew our uncle cared, that he'd never let us down, but this is more than I ever expected. It's a real future. Something to build on. It's the feeling that Evan and I finally have some firm footing in this world. One thing that isn't crumbling around our heads.

Evan scribbles his signature on the bottom of the page. He jumps to his feet, meeting Levi first with a handshake and then a back-slapping hug. "Thanks, Uncle Levi," he says in a very serious un-Evan-like tone. "We won't let you down. I promise."

My hand shakes slightly as I add my own signature to the page. I get up and embrace our new business partner. "I can't thank you enough," I tell our uncle. "This means so much to us."

"Don't thank me yet," he says with a smirk. "You're owners now. That means early mornings and late nights. I've got a lot to teach you."

"I look forward to it," I answer, and I mean every word.

"Good. I'm thinking first thing we do is get one of you boys to head up the demolition crew at Mackenzie's hotel. Frees me up to focus on the Sanderson restaurant."

I flinch. Just hearing someone say her name stirs up a world of pain. "Yeah. Maybe Evan'll handle that. I don't think Mac is ready to have me around on the site every day."

Levi's brow furrows. "You two are still on the outs?"

I nod miserably. "She won't answer my calls or accept my gifts."

"Gifts?" he echoes in amusement.

My brother speaks up, taking great delight in describing to our uncle the field's worth of flowers I'd sent, the numerous heart-shaped chocolate boxes, the overstuffed baskets. "So many baskets," Evan stresses. "It's disgusting."

"And futile," Levi says after a bout of gentle laughter. "Boy, you're not winning back a girl like that with candy and flowers."

"No?" Frustration jams in my throat. "Then what do I do? How do I get her to talk to me?"

My uncle claps a hand over my shoulder. "Easy. You need to think bigger."

CHAPTER FORTY-FOUR

MACKENZIE

On my way back to Steph and Alana's house from the hotel, I stop to grab takeout from their favorite Chinese food place. It's only been a few weeks since Levi's guys started work on ripping out all the old carpet and drywall, tossing the damaged furniture and fixtures and anything too far gone to salvage, yet the place is almost unrecognizable on the inside.

A blank canvas.

Already I'm rethinking much of the interior design aesthetic. I still intend to preserve the original look as much as possible, but with an eye toward editing. I want to open the place up more, bring the outside in. Brighten it with natural light and greenery. Reflect a sense of luxurious relaxation. My architect is about sick of me with all my phone calls and emails tweaking the plans. I'm sure I'll calm down once the new construction begins. I just want it to be perfect. This is my legacy I'm building, after all. With any luck, it'll be standing for another fifty years.

I pull into the driveway in the used SUV I purchased from the local dealership last week. I finally caved and got a car after realizing I can't spend the rest of my life in this town in the backseats of taxis and Ubers.

I'm killing the engine when I receive a text message from my mother.

Mom: *Mackenzie, I'm forwarding you the name of my designer, as promised. If you insist on continuing on with this little project, then you must do it right.*

My snicker echoes loudly in the vehicle. That's the closest thing to a stamp of approval my mother is currently capable of providing. After months of playing the silent treatment game with my parents, I ended up contacting them a week after I moved out of Cooper's. I blame it on my highly emotional state. But honestly, despite their overbearing, condescending personalities, they're still my parents. The only family I have. So I bit the bullet and extended the olive branch, and to my surprise, they accepted it.

A few days ago they even made it out to the hotel—for about ten minutes. Long enough for my dad to grimace a lot and my mom to give me an earful about linen patterns. I can't say they were entirely enthused about the project, but they made the effort anyway. A small step toward normalizing relations.

I send back a quick text.

Me: *Thanks, Mom. I'll give her a call tomorrow.*
Mom: *If you need another set of eyes once you enter the interior design phase, contact Stacey and she'll add you to my calendar if I have the time.*

I roll my eyes at the screen. Classic Annabeth Cabot. But nothing I can do about that.

I'm barely in the door of the house before my roommates pounce and tear the takeout bags from my hands. We set the table and start digging in while Steph turns on her nightly paranormal investigations marathon on TV. Six straight hours of grown men in night vision goggles, running through an abandoned mall and screaming about a rat kicking around an errant food court cup or something. But whatever. It's her thing.

"So what were you saying about some shit that happened at work?" Alana says, picking all the pork out of the lo mein before anyone else has gotten their hands on the carton.

"Oh, right." Steph talks with her chopsticks like she's conducting an orchestra. "So Caitlynn tells Manny that his ex blasted him on *BoyfriendFails*. Everyone's on it now at the bar," she tells me with a grin.

"How'd they know it was about him?" Alana demands.

"Oh, 'cause we were all there when the original incident happened. Long story short: Manny met some girl at a bar last month and took her home. Few days later, he sees her again and asks her out. They're dating for a few weeks when a group of us are out bowling, and he apparently calls her by the wrong name. I don't know how he'd managed to go all that time never calling her by name, but turns out he'd slept with her older sister that first night, then met the younger sister and confused the two."

"Ouch." Every time I think I've heard it all, there's a new twist on an old favorite.

"Anyway, fast forward to tonight. Caitlynn's showing Manny the *BoyfriendFails* post when this teenage kid walks in. He marches right up to the bar. And it's the middle of the lunch rush so we're pretty slammed. The kid shouts something at Manny in Spanish, then grabs some dude's drink, splashes it on the bar, and throws a match."

I gasp loudly. "Oh my God, is he okay?"

Steph waves away my concern. "Oh, yeah, he's fine. Joe's been watering down the wells for decades."

And this is why one of the first things I did after the money started coming in was get a lawyer to write up a liability disclaimer for the website.

"When the bar doesn't ignite, he's furious and jumps over it," Steph continues. "Kid isn't more than five-foot-nothing and can't be older than fifteen. Must not be the first time Manny's been chased because I'd never seen him move so fast."

Alana snickers.

"He ducks out from behind the bar and hauls ass. The kid's diving over tables. Takes a swing at him with a chair until Daryl picks him up and tosses him outside. Daryl has to barricade the doors until the kid finally gives up and leaves. Manny sneaks out the back." Steph starts cracking up. "Turns out it was those girls' little brother come to beat Manny's ass. It was adorable."

"You know," I say, trying not to choke on my food, "good for the kid."

"Right?"

I swallow my lemon chicken and reach for a can of Diet Coke. "Speaking of bitter exes, I ran into Preston today when I was having lunch with Bonnie on campus."

Steph lifts a brow. "How'd that go?"

"Not terrible," I admit. "He was with his new girlfriend. Cute, typical Garnet girl whose father is some hedge fund guy and mother is an heir to an electric fan fortune or something. They've been together for a couple months now."

Alana makes a face. "Poor girl."

I shrug. "I don't know, far as I can tell, she worships Preston. Which is all he really wants, I guess. Someone to smile and thank him for making the decisions." I pop another piece of chicken into my mouth, talking while chewing. "If it makes them both happy, then who am I to judge?"

"Oh, hey, did you see this?" Alana shoves the last bite of an eggroll in her mouth, then wipes duck sauce from her fingers before handing me her phone. "From today."

I glance at the screen to find a new post from *BoyfriendFails*. Except it starts with a caveat. This isn't from a disgruntled girlfriend anonymously blasting her ex—it's from the boyfriend confessing his misdeeds to the world.

I'm the #BoyfriendFail

You read the title right. I'm the boyfriend fail. As in, I failed. Big-time. I failed the woman I love, I failed our relationship, and I failed myself.

I raise my head to shoot a suspicious look at Alana. She pretends to be overly focused on her food.

I messed up the best thing that ever happened to me. Let my perfect girl slip through my fingers because I was a selfish asshole. The night I met her, I had revenge on the brain. I had a beef with her boyfriend. I wanted to punish him for getting me fired, for stirring up all my insecurities about being a loser townie, being stuck here without prospects for anything better. Anything more.

But then I got to know her, and something happened. She inspired me. She showed me there's more to me than this anchor around my neck weighing me down. She made me believe I'm capable of greatness.

She was right. But also wrong. Because I don't want greatness, I don't want a bright sunny future—if she's not by my side to enjoy it.

A pit grows in my stomach as I read on. It's sweet and sincere. My fingers go numb and my eyes sting.

> She doesn't owe me a second chance, I know that. She doesn't owe me anything. But I'm still going to ask.
> Give me a second chance, princess. And if you do, I promise you this—I will never lie to you again. I will never take you for granted. I will never, for the rest of my life, forget the goddamn treasure you are.

I almost can't see by the time I finish reading, my vision completely blurred by tears. The post closes with a plea to meet him at six o'clock this Saturday at the place where we rescued our dog.

"Damn it," I mumble when I put the phone down on the table. "I thought we had a deal."

Alana hands me a napkin to wipe my face. "We did. But he's a mess. You're miserable. Neither of you are coping. I'm sorry I resorted to a sneak attack, but come on. What's the harm in hearing him out?"

"I'm not miserable," I say in my defense. "I'm moving on."

Steph gives me a look that begs to differ.

"You're in denial," Alana corrects. "Spending ten hours a day at the hotel and another five holed up in your room on your websites is not the sign of someone who's moved on."

So it's been difficult. Fine. When everything else is spinning out of control, work is where I find my center. It's a distraction, and the most effective way I've found to keep my mind off Cooper.

Truth is, he's a hard man to get over. Hardly a day passes without me waking up and expecting to feel his arm around me in bed. Ten times a day I almost text him some funny joke or exciting update about the hotel—until I remember he isn't mine anymore. Daisy still searches for him. Picking up his scent here and there. Lying at the foot of his side of the bed. Waiting at the door for someone who never comes.

Nothing about being in this town feels right without him.

And none of that changes the fact that he lied to me. Repeatedly. He took away my power to make my own decisions. He tricked me, and I can't so easily disregard that. If I can't have respect for myself, no one will.

"Meet him," Alana urges. "Listen to what he has to say. Then go with your heart. What's the harm in doing that much?"

Irrevocable damage. A small crack in the levee that gives way to insurmountable anguish. When I left Cooper, I built my walls sturdy, made to last. I wasn't designed to open and shut at will. More than anything, I fear that if I let myself see him, I won't ever stop feeling this terrible ache. That if I forgive him, I'm setting myself up to be ruined again. Because I don't know how to walk away from Cooper Hartley twice.

I might not survive it again.

CHAPTER FORTY-FIVE

COOPER

It's seven o'clock.

I feel like a moron. I should have dressed better. Brought her some flowers. I was knocking around my house all afternoon trying to not get worked up about this that I drove myself fucking batshit. I walked out of the house in my cargo shorts and a T-shirt, looking like a goddamn bum asking this amazing woman to forgive him for being a complete bastard since the day she met him.

What the fuck am I doing here?

My eye twitches. It's been doing that for two days. Alana told me she'd shown Mac the post I'd written, but wouldn't elaborate much on her reaction, except to say she didn't chuck the phone into the street. It's been an hour since the time I'd asked to meet, though, and with each passing second my hope evaporates. Somehow, I'd gotten into my head this plan was foolproof. Mac would see my sincerity and thoughtfulness, and of course she'd forgive me.

This was a stupid plan. Why did I think pouring my heart out on a website she built to drag dumbasses like me would be romantic? I'm a joke. Maybe if I'd gone after her that night at the party, I wouldn't be standing here with the seagulls, which are circling as if they're mobilizing for an assault. I kick a mound of sand in the air to remind them of their place in the food chain.

Seven fifteen.

She's not coming.

Maybe I shouldn't have expected to win her over with one grand gesture, but I never thought she'd blow me off entirely. It knocks the wind out of me like a punch right to the center of my chest. The boardwalk lights flicker on as the sun dips behind the town.

She's really not coming.

Accepting my fate, I slowly turn back toward the way I came, and that's when I see a lone figure walking toward me.

I careen into a full-blown panic at the sight of Mac approaching. She's only ten yards away now. Five. She looks stunning, her tall, slender body wrapped up in an ankle-length blue dress with a low V neckline. I haven't forgotten a single freckle or the way her eyes have little flecks of blue in their green depths. The crease of her lips when she says my name. Seeing her again, though, it's wiping the dust off the window.

"I didn't think you were coming," I tell her, trying to keep my composure. I got her here. Last thing I want to do is scare her off, even if every ounce of me wants to hold her one more time.

"I almost didn't."

She comes to a stop, keeping a few feet of distance between us. Those three feet feel insurmountable. It's strange how I can read her less now than the first time we met. She's impenetrable. Not giving anything away.

Too much time passes where I'm lost, remembering what it was like to feel her hair between my fingers, and she gets impatient.

"So . . . what's up?" she asks.

For days, all I've done is rehearse how I'd do this. Now I'm here and everything I'd planned to say sounds like some corny bullshit. I'm dying here.

"Look, the truth is I'm gonna be bad at this no matter how I say it, so I'm just gonna say it." I take a deep breath. *Now or never, asshole*. "I've regretted every day I was too chickenshit to tell you the truth. I was selfish and stupid, and you have every right to hate me. I've had nothing but time to think about how to convince you I'm sorry and why you should take me back. Honestly, I don't have a good reason."

Mac looks away, and I know I'm losing her because this is all coming out wrong, but I can't seem to stop the words from tearing out of my mouth.

"What I mean to say is, I know what I did was wrong. I know I destroyed your trust in me. That I betrayed you. I was careless with something very precious. But, damn it, Mac, I'm so in love with you and it's killing me that you're still out here, out of reach, when I know in my soul I can make you happy again if you let me. I've been a bastard and want you to love me back anyway. It's not fair. I should have to suffer for how I hurt you. I fucking am suffering. But I'm begging you to put me out of my misery. I don't know how to be without you anymore."

I'm out of breath by the time my jaw snaps shut, the delayed message finally making its way to my brain, saying *Shut the hell up*. Mac wipes at her eyes and I have to lock myself down to stop from reaching for her. Seconds pass as I wait for her to respond. Then the cold, dead silence when she doesn't.

"I want to show you something," I blurt out when I sense she's ready to bail. "Will you take a walk with me?"

She doesn't budge. "What is it?"

"It's not far. Please. It'll only take a minute."

She ponders my offer for almost longer than my nerves can tolerate. Then her head jerks in agreement.

I hold my hand out for hers. Instead, she walks ahead of me.

We go a little ways down the beach, where I coax her up to the boardwalk in front of her hotel. It's still a gutted shell, though the debris has been hauled away. On what's left of the veranda, two matching rocking chairs sit looking out on the water. Flickering candles line the railing.

Mac's breath hitches. Slowly, she turns to meet my earnest gaze. "What's this?" she whispers.

"First time you brought me here, you told me that you pictured guests sitting out here in rocking chairs, sipping wine, watching the waves roll in."

She looks up at me with the thousands of tiny lights of the boardwalk shining in her eyes. "I can't believe you remembered."

"I remember every word you've ever said to me."

Her gaze returns to the veranda. I can feel her softening, the stiffness of her body melting away.

"Mac, when I picture my future, I see myself old and gray, sitting in a rocking chair on a porch. With you beside me. That's my dream."

Before her, I didn't bother looking ahead even five years. The image was never a pretty one. I figured I'd spend my days scraping by, getting the bare minimum out of life. I never considered the possibility that someone might be crazy enough to love me. But Mac *did* love me, and I'd gone and run her off.

"I can't say I won't ever mess up again," I choke out through the gravel lining my throat. "I don't have a great frame of reference for functioning relationships. Sometimes I get too far up my own ass, or too stuck in my own brooding thoughts. But I can promise to try to be a man you deserve. To be someone you're proud of. And I will never lie to you again." My voice grows hoarser by the second. "Please, Mac. Come home. I don't know what I am if I can't love you."

She stares down at her feet, twisting her hands together. I'm bracing for the worst the longer she doesn't speak, but finally she takes a breath.

"You broke my heart," she says, so softly a slight breeze could blow the words right out of the air. "I've never been so hurt by anyone in my life. That's not an easy thing to let go, Cooper."

"I understand." My heart is racing and I'm thinking I might drop to my knees if she doesn't say yes.

"You'd have to promise me something else."

"Name it." I'd freeze a kidney for her if she asked for it.

A slight smirk curves her lips. "You have to start cashing my rent checks."

My brain stutters to catch up. Then her smile widens and she grabs the front of my shirt, pulling my lips to hers. Overcome with relief, I hoist her up and wrap her legs around my hips, kissing her until we're both gasping for air. I've never kissed anyone with more conviction or intent. Never needed anything the way I've needed to feel her in my arms again.

"I love you," I mumble against her lips. It doesn't seem enough to say it, and yet I can't get the words out fast enough. "So much." As far as close calls go, this one was razor thin. I almost lost her, lost this.

She clings to me, kissing me back with urgency. And my chest fills to the brim with the kind of naked, honest love I never thought myself capable of feeling. Of finding. I've learned a lot about myself over the last several months. Not the least of which is learning to take better care of the people I love.

Mac pulls back slightly, her gorgeous eyes seeking mine. "I love you too," she breathes.

And in that moment I vow, even if it takes me the rest of my life, to show this girl she didn't waste her heart on me.

ACKNOWLEDGMENTS

As anyone who knows me can attest, I've been obsessed with quaint beach towns for ages. Avalon Bay might be a fictional town, but it's an amalgamation of all my favorite parts of various coastal towns I've visited over the years, and it was an absolute joy to lose myself in this world. Of course, I couldn't have done that without the support and general awesomeness of the following people: my agent, Kimberly Brower, and editor, Eileen Rothschild, for their contagious enthusiasm for this story; Lisa Bonvissuto, Christa Desir, and the rest of the terrific staff at SMP, and Jonathan Bush for the incredible cover!

Early readers and author friends who provided feedback and amazing blurbs; Natasha and Nicole for being the most efficient human beings on the planet; every single reviewer, blogger, Instagrammer, Booktokker, and reader who has shared, supported, and loved this book.

And as always, my family and friends for putting up with me whenever I'm in deadline mode. Love you all.

Bad Girl Reputation

Available Autumn 2022

GENEVIEVE

The guy's got some nerve walking in here looking like he does. Those haunting dark eyes that still lurk in the deepest parts of my memory. Brown, nearly black hair I still feel between my fingers. He's as heart-stabbingly gorgeous as the pictures that still flicker behind my eyes. It's been a year since I last saw him, yet my response to him is the same. He walks into a room and my body notices him before I do. It's a disturbance of static in the air that dances across my skin.

It's obnoxious, is what it is. And that my body has the audacity to react to him, *now*, at my mother's funeral, is even more disturbing.

Evan stands with his twin brother Cooper, scanning the room until he notices me. The guys are identical except for occasional variances in their haircuts, but most people tell them apart by their tattoos. Cooper's got two full sleeves, while most of Evan's ink is on his back. Me, I know it from his eyes. Whether they're gleaming with mischief or flickering with joy, need, frustration . . . I always know when it's Evan's eyes on me.

Our gazes meet. He nods. I nod back, my pulse quickening. Literally three seconds later, Evan and I convene down the hall where there are no witnesses.

It's strange how familiar we are with some people, no matter how much time has passed. Memories of the two of us wash over me like a balmy breeze. Walking through this house with him like we're back in high school. Sneaking in and out at all hours. Stumbling with hands against the wall to stay upright. Laughing in hysterical whispers to not wake up the whole house.

"Hey," he says, holding out his arms in a hesitant offer, which I accept because it feels more awkward not to.

He always did give good hugs.

I force myself not to linger in his arms, not to inhale his scent. His body is warm and muscular and as familiar to me as my own. I know every inch of that tall, delicious frame.

I take a hasty step backward.

"Yeah, so, I heard. Obviously. Wanted to pay my respects." Evan is bashful, almost coy, with his hands in his pockets and his head bowed to look at me under thick lashes. I can't imagine the pep talk it took to get him here.

"Thanks."

"And, well, yeah." From one pocket, he pulls out a blue Blow Pop. "I got you this."

I haven't cried once since finding out Mom was sick. Yet accepting this stupid token from Evan makes my throat tighten and my eyes sting.

I'm suddenly transported back to the first time a Blow Pop ever exchanged hands between us. Another funeral. Another dead parent. It was after Evan's dad, Walt, died in a car accident. Drunk driving, because that's the kind of reckless, self-destructive man Walt Hartley had been. Fortunately, nobody else had been hurt, but Walt's life ended on the dark road that night when he'd lost control and smashed into a tree.

I was twelve at the time and had no clue what to bring to a wake. My parents brought flowers, but Evan was a kid like me. What was he going to do with flowers? All I knew was that my best friend and the boy I'd always had a huge crush on was hurting badly, and all I had to my name was one measly dollar. The fanciest thing I could afford at the general store was a lollipop.

Evan had cried when I quietly sat beside him on the back deck of his house and clasped the Blow Pop in his shaking hand. He'd whispered, "Thanks, Gen," and then we sat there in silence for more than an hour, staring at the waves lapping at the shore.

"Shut up," I mutter to myself, clenching the lollipop in my palm. "You're so dumb." Despite my words, we both know I'm deeply affected.

Evan cracks a knowing smile and smooths one hand over his tie, straightening it. He cleans up nice, but not too nice. Something about a suit on this guy still feels dangerous.

"You're lucky I found you first," I tell him once I can speak again. "Not sure my brothers would be as friendly."

With an unconcerned smirk, he shrugs. "Kellan hits like a girl."

Typical. "I'll make sure to tell him you said so."

Some wandering cousins glimpse us around the corner and look as though they might find a reason to come talk to me, so I grab Evan by the lapel and shove him toward the laundry room. I press myself up against the door frame, then check to make sure the coast is clear.

"I can't get hijacked into another conversation about how much I remind people of my mom," I groan. "Like, dude, the last time you saw me, I still wasn't eating solid food."

Evan adjusts his tie again. "They think they're helping."

"Well, they're not."

Everyone wants to tell me what a great lady Mom was and how important family was to her. It's almost creepy, hearing people talk about a woman who bears no resemblance to the person I knew.

"How you holding up?" he asks roughly. "Like, really?"

I shrug in return. Because that's the question, isn't it? I've been asked it a dozen different ways over the past couple days, and I still don't have a proper answer. Or at least, not the one people want to hear.

"I'm not sure I feel anything. I don't know. Maybe I'm still in shock or something. You always expect these things to happen in a split second, or over months and months. This, though. It was like just the wrong amount of warning. I came home and a week later she was dead."

"I get that," he says. "Barely time to get your bearings before it's over."

"I haven't known which way is up for days." I bite my lip. "I'm starting to wonder if there's something wrong with me?"

He fixes me with a disbelieving scowl. "It's death, Fred. There's nothing wrong with you."

I snort a laugh at his nickname for me. Been so long since I've heard it, I'd almost forgotten what it sounded like. There was a time when I answered to it more than my own name.

"Seriously, though. I keep waiting for the grief to hit, but it doesn't come."

"It's hard to find a lot of emotion for a person who didn't have a lot for you. Even if it's your mom." He pauses. "Maybe especially moms."

"True."

Evan gets it. He always has. One of the things we have in common is an unorthodox relationship with our mothers. In that there isn't much relationship to speak of. While his mom is an impermanent idea in his life—absent except for the few times a year she breezes into town to sleep off a bender or ask for money—mine was absent in spirit if not in body. Mine was so cold and detached, even in my earliest memories, that she hardly seemed to exist at all. I grew up jealous of the flowerbeds she tended in the front yard.

"I'm almost relieved she's gone." A lump rises in my throat. "No, more than almost. That's terrible to say, I know that. But it's like . . . now I can stop trying, you know? Trying and then feeling like shit when it doesn't change."

My whole life I made efforts to connect with her. To figure out why my mother didn't seem to like me much. I'd never gotten an answer. Maybe now I can stop asking.

"It's not terrible," Evan says. "Some people make shit parents. It's not our fault they don't know how to love us."

Except for Craig—Mom certainly knew how to love him. After five failed attempts, she'd finally gotten the recipe right with him. Her one perfect son she could pour a lifetime of mothering into. We might as well have been raised by two different people. He's the only one of us walking around here with red, swollen eyes.

"Can I tell you something?" Evan says with a grin that makes me suspicious. "But you have to promise not to hit me."

"Yeah, I can't do that."

He laughs to himself and licks his lips. An involuntary habit that always drove me crazy, because I know what that mouth is capable of.

"I missed you," he confesses. "Am I an asshole if I'm sort of glad someone died?"

I punch him in the shoulder, to which he feigns injury. He doesn't mean it. Not really. But in a weird way I appreciate the sentiment, if only because it gives me permission to smile for a second or two. To breathe.

I toy with the thin silver bracelet circling my wrist. Not quite meeting his eyes. "I missed you, too. A little."

"A little?" He's mocking me.

"Just a little."

"Mm-hmm. So you thought about me, what, once, twice a day when you were gone?"

"More like once or twice *total*."

He chuckles.

Truthfully, after I left the Bay I spent months doing my best to push away the thoughts of him when they insisted their way forward. Refusing the images that came when I closed my eyes at night or went on a date. Eventually it got easier. I'd almost managed to forget him. Almost.